RENEGADE HEARTS

"Molly, don't tempt me."

Ignoring him, she rubbed her lips over his warm skin, pressed her nose against him, breathing in his scent.

"Molly, don't—"

"I . . . I just need to be close, Buck. Please," she begged softly. "Don't push me away."

His breathing was ragged as he turned toward her and pulled her into his arms. She let out a small cry as the wonder of his touch washed over her. She waited for him to move away. He didn't. She'd thought that just being near him would be enough. What a fool she was . . . Now that she had that, she wanted more.

She wanted it all.

"Patience, Molly," he whispered. He sat up, pulling her up with him. He looked down at her, his gaze hotter than the fire that glowed beyond them.

Slowly, he unbuttoned her shirt. Cool air touched her bare flesh.

"It's your last chance," he murmured. "If you want me to stop, tell me now."

She shook her head, unable to speak. It was too hard to breathe.

All those years, she thought, on the verge of tears. All those years of hiding their feelings.

Her body shivered with anticipation, every nerve inside her bouncing and throbbing, heavy with a desire she'd never known . . .

*St. Martin's Paperbacks Titles
by Jane Bonander*

SECRETS OF A MIDNIGHT MOON
HEAT OF A SAVAGE MOON
FORBIDDEN MOON

FORBIDDEN MOON

JANE BONANDER

ST. MARTIN'S PAPERBACKS

FORBIDDEN MOON

Copyright © 1993 by Jane Bonander.

ISBN: 0-312-95155-8

Printed in the United States of America

St. Martin's Paperbacks edition/April 1994

10 9 8 7 6 5 4 3 2 1

To my two favorite Olivias: Harper and Hall
Exemplary writers, tough critics and
stellar friends

Experience teaches us that love
does not consist of two people
looking at each other, but of
looking together in the same direction.
Antoine de Saint-Exupery

🟦 Prologue 🟦

Northern California, Autumn—1879

He could almost smell the whiskey. With a dark curse, he swallowed the saliva that pooled in the folds of his tongue and around his teeth. No time for that now. Later . . . maybe later. He swore again. This time it was aimed at the little bitch who was the cause of his present discomfort.

Buck Randall heard the raucous laughter and loud voices of the drunken youths half a mile away. Kicking his horse into a gallop, he sped to the vacant line shack where he suspected Molly Lindquist was drinking with her wild friends. Not that he gave a damn about the hellion, but he cared a great deal for her mother, June.

Arriving at the cabin, he flung himself off his mount, strode to the door and kicked it open. He was too angry to pay any mind to the sound of dried wood as it splintered beneath his boots. He stepped boldly inside, letting his gaze slide over the small group.

"Hey, Bucko, wanna swig?"

With difficulty, Buck pushed the bottle away with the back of his hand and studied the girl in the corner. She was pressed tightly against a drunken youth whose arm hung around her shoulders, his fingers dangerously close to her breast. Her wild tawny hair picked up the light from the lamp, making the white-gold highlights shimmer.

"Molly." His voice was harsh, deadly. She didn't respond. "Molly, dammit, I'm taking you home."

Turning away from her scrawny boyfriend, she gave Buck a lazy, slightly fuzzy look. "Whatsa matter, Bucky? Honey kick you out again, tonight?" She jabbed her elbow into her partner's ribs. "You know what they used to call ol' Buck here? Cub." She giggled. "Sweet little chubby cubby bubby." She stroked her partner's chest and tossed Buck a defiant grin.

Fury knotted his gut. She could rile him easier than anyone he'd ever known. Crossing the room in two strides, he grabbed her arm and yanked her out of the boy's embrace.

Molly struggled against him, no longer sweet-tempered from the drink. "Let me go, you bastard," she said on a hiss of breath.

"Shut up." He gripped her, pinning her arms against her body. "You're coming with me. *Now.*"

Molly continued to struggle. "You and what army is gonna make me?" She turned her head to the side and tried to bite the arm that held her.

"Oh, no, you don't." Buck's free hand came around and pinched her jaw. "You're making a spectacle of yourself."

She kicked at him with her heel, but he quickly wrapped one of his legs around hers, holding her off balance. "Everything was fine until *you* showed up."

"Say good-bye to your drunken friends, Molly." His voice dripped with sarcasm as he pulled her toward the door.

"Well, it takes one to know one," she retorted, squirming against him.

"What, a friend?" he baited.

"No, you fool, a *drunk.*"

"I know what I am." He squeezed her chest so tightly she gasped. He had to get her out of there. Having her end up a drunk was something he couldn't live with, in spite of how much he wanted to spank her senseless. "Your smart mouth only makes me want to break your neck rather than just your arm."

She grunted. "I wanna stay here. You can't make me go with you."

He dragged her outside. "Your mother is worried sick about you."

"So, what's that to you? You're not my father," she flung at him. "Why don't you just go home to your sweet little wife and leave me be? I don't need you sniffing around after me."

Another mention of his wife, Honey, only fueled his anger. Their marital problems had escalated over the past two months, and she was the *last* person he wanted to think about right now.

"Hell, someone has to, and no one else has the patience, you bi—" He caught himself before he spat out the word. Struggling with her defiant efforts to get free, he moved toward his mount.

Molly suddenly went limp in his arms.

Buck let out a humorless chuckle. "Oh, no. You don't expect me to fall for that one, do you?"

She didn't move. Her head hung to her chest; her arms were loose at her sides and her knees buckled.

He gave her a violent shake. Still nothing. "All right," he said, "we'll sling you over the horse."

As he hoisted her up, she jabbed her elbows into his chest, briefly making him lose his grip. She tore across the ground.

Buck swore and raced off after her. When he finally caught up with her, he nudged the backs of her knees, sending her sprawling.

"You sack of shit!" she howled, trying desperately to kick his hand as it gripped her ankle.

Buck fell on top of her, pinning her to the ground. "Someone ought to wash your mouth out with soap. When will you learn that ladies don't talk that way?"

"I'm . . . not a lady," she gasped beneath him.

As much as he wanted to take her over his knee, he was too angry. He'd hurt her, and he wouldn't care—at least not while he was doing it. But he'd regret it later, only because her mother had begged him to go easy on her. The brat didn't deserve such a sweet, loving parent.

"Youch! I . . . can't breathe, you . . . pig brained lummox!"

"Will you behave?"

"I'll . . . do what I damn well please!"

He allowed more of his weight to press on her. She squirmed beneath him, unaware that she was shoving her butt against his crotch. He swore under his breath and moved to the side, still maintaining a tight grip on her wrists.

She winced but didn't say anything.

"Will you behave?"

Sucking in a big breath, she nodded. Yet when he pulled her to her feet, she tried to run again.

He jerked her back toward the cabin. "Settle down, you selfish little hellcat, or I'll tie you up and throw you into the creek."

Squirming harder, she sputtered, "You wouldn't dare. You're just a big fat turd who doesn't want me to have any fun. A big fat turd, Buck. That's what you are."

His hold on her was so tight, he heard her inhale sharply. "We can do this my way, or the hard way." He squeezed her lungs again, forcing her to gasp for breath. "Which will it be?"

Suddenly she was calm. "All right. Your way."

Suspicious at the sudden change, he released her only slightly and helped her onto the back of his mount. By the time he'd joined her, she'd deftly turned around and was facing him.

"What in the hell are you doing?" As long as he didn't have to look at her, he was fine. But he couldn't handle that beautiful, wild face so close to his.

She smiled slyly, her full, pouty lips beckoning. Her

tawny mane curled recklessly around her face and down past her shoulders. Suddenly she threw her legs across his and slid closer. So close her crotch settled over the bulge in his jeans.

"Dammit, Molly." He came alive under the pressure of her body, desire pumping thickly through his veins. "Stop this right now!"

She slung her arms across his shoulders, locking her fingers behind his head. "Ummm, I feel so *good*, Bucky." She nestled closer, nuzzled his neck with her nose, and bit his earlobe.

He swore and pulled away, trying to avoid her. "For Christ's sake, Molly, you're drunk as a skunk. Behave yourself or I'll smack your butt black-and-blue."

She giggled and pressed her budding breasts against his shirt. "Promises, promises."

He cursed again. Suddenly her mouth was on his and she pulled him closer, kissing him deeply. Taken by surprise, he sat stiffly, not wanting to respond. But . . . *ah, dammit.* She tasted sweet even with the whiskey on her breath. Briefly he allowed himself to enjoy it. He even responded a little. Then reality hit him square in the gut. He pulled her away.

"Dammit, hellion!" He noticed the gravelly sound of his voice. Grabbing her waist, he lifted her and turned her around. "Now, don't move or I'll tie you to the saddle."

She sighed, giving him no fight. "I think you can kiss better than that, Bucky. We'll try it again before we get home."

"You're drunk, brat. It would serve you right if you remembered all of this in gritty detail in the morning."

He cursed himself a thousand times over. Hell, he'd let a mere girl kiss him on the mouth . . . *and a damned good kisser she is, too.* Scowling, he wondered who she'd been practicing on and tried to shake off the surprising bite of jealousy the thought invoked.

Suddenly she relaxed against him completely, and he

knew she was asleep. Or had passed out. Either way, he had
to hold her tightly, or she'd have fallen to the ground in a
heap.

Nudging his mount toward the ranch, he thought about
what Anna Gaspard had told him the day before. If Molly
didn't settle down, she'd be sent to the strict girls' school in
San Francisco the Gaspard daughters attended. No one
could handle Molly. Everyone had tried.

They passed Buck's mother and stepfather's house,
where he and Honey lived with Dusty, their little boy. A
grim smile cracked his mouth. Honey was probably waiting
for him, anxious to nag at him again. He'd rather sleep in
the barn than go through another night of her com-
plaining. At least the barn was quiet. Lately he'd slept
there more often than he'd slept in his own bed.

Molly's head lolled against his shoulder, and he pressed
his cheek into her hair. A shiver of pleasure shook him as
her fragrance invaded his senses. He allowed the scent to
coat his nostrils, then he dragged it into his lungs. The
heady sensation was followed by a wash of guilt. He jerked
his head away. An image of Honey's face exploded before
him. What in the hell was he thinking? He was a married
man. Not happily at the moment, but married just the
same.

Another wave of guilt smacked him. That he was married should have been his *first* thought when Molly had
kissed him. But it hadn't been. It had been that Molly,
bless her wild little heart, was only fourteen years old, and
her kiss had stirred him. Deeply.

God, he thought, running his hand over his face, he
needed a drink.

❦ One ❦

The strained melodies of Vivaldi floated valiantly through the reception area. The musicians, all girls ages fourteen and fifteen, often looked up from their music, longing stamped on their sweet faces as their more fortunate classmates mingled with their families.

Molly Lindquist caught the violinist's eye, smiled and winked. The girl grinned back, but there was pleading in the response.

"And just who is the recipient of that beautiful smile?"

Molly's smile widened. "Why, Charles Campion, would you believe you are?" She looked up at her handsome fiancé. *Fiancé.* How long she'd waited to hear that word, and how ecstatic she'd been when he'd proposed.

Charles took her arm and steered her toward the back of the room. "I'd believe that if you'd let me announce to the world that we're engaged."

She squeezed his arm, feeling a tiny bite of apprehension. "Oh, Charles, I . . . I just want to wait a little while. I don't want anything to go wrong."

Snorting softly, he answered, "What could possibly go wrong?"

"Just humor me for a while, please?" She looked up at him, letting her gaze slide over his tanned face. He had little crinkles in the corners of his brilliant blue eyes from squinting into the harsh Texas sun.

Putting his arm around her waist, he edged toward the punch bowl. "How long will you make me wait before I shout it to the world?"

"Perhaps after I've been to visit you and Nicolette in Texas. Perhaps then." He had a tense look about him, and she knew he was trying hard to keep the conversation light. Brushing her gloved fingers over the shoulder of his dove gray dress coat, she said, "Have I told you how handsome you look tonight?"

He relaxed, gave her a wicked smile and handed her a cup of deep red punch. "Don't think flattery will always work on me, Margaret."

"But it did this time, didn't it?" She accepted the drink, smiling at him over the rim of the cup.

His smile changed as he glanced around the room. "The staff will miss you when you leave."

" 'When you leave.' That sounds so final."

"It *is* final. You *will* marry me." It sounded like an order, but a soft smile played over his sensual lips.

"Yes, master," she teased. "But I won't be missed for long. There are many excellent music teachers in San Francisco. They'll have no trouble finding a replacement."

"You won't miss it?" He stared down at her intently.

Miss it? No, she didn't think so. She'd worked too long and too hard to find a man like Charles. A young, rich, handsome man who owned more land in Texas than she could even imagine. He adored her beyond measure. His sister, Nicolette, her pupil, had already told her she wanted her as a sister-in-law. He was everything she'd ever dreamed of having. And much, much more: He was white.

"You will, won't you?"

"What?" she asked, startled out of her reverie.

He waved an arm around the splendid surroundings. "Miss this."

The room was indeed splendid, enhanced by the glittering candlelit chandelier. Mirrors surrounded them, maximizing the size of the room. Jewels flashed on most of the women as they laughed and moved about, their arms linked with their husbands. It seemed a room without worries or regrets. Or grief. Or shame. Or need. This was how life should be. She'd worked so very hard to become part of it.

"Perhaps I'll miss San Francisco a little," she answered. But only because it had been her home for nearly the past seven years. And it had been here that she'd decided never to go back to that other life again.

He took the punch cup from her and put it on the table. "Come on," he urged. "Let's find Nicolette, say our good nights and get out of here."

"Really, Charles, we've hardly been here fifteen minutes," she scolded softly.

His heated gaze swept over her silvery gray and light green crepe gown. "We will have magnificent children, you know."

Her heart leaped, but not with yearning. "Charles, that's hardly proper," she said on a shaky breath. She knew he desired her; it had been blatant the moment they'd been introduced over a year ago. She hadn't felt the same burning urgency, but she knew why.

Long ago, when she'd been in the bloom of youth, her urges had nearly gotten her into trouble. So she'd carefully and methodically killed them. Buried them. They belonged with her past. They belonged with . . . with the man she would forever try to forget. But try as she might, now and then thoughts of him snaked into her finely tuned routine, stirring up old memories that brought her nothing but feelings of shame. And regret. And desire. Feelings that couldn't be trusted.

Charles squeezed her fingers. "But it's true," he whispered close to her ear.

Pulling her hands from his, she frantically searched the room for Nicolette. She found her by the door. The girl waved, and weaved through the crowd toward them.

"There you two are!" She kissed her brother's cheek,

then hugged Molly tightly. "So, are you coming to visit us?"

Molly looked at the blond teenager, who was as beautiful as her brother was handsome. They both adored her. She wondered if she deserved such happiness. After a brief inner struggle, she decided she did. It hadn't just fallen into her lap. She'd worked for it. "How can I say no?"

Cedarville, Texas
April

Six years. His miseries had started six years ago, but it had only been three years since he'd had a drink. Three years since he'd had the shakes so bad, he couldn't pull on his own boots. Three years since he'd awakened, his head lying in a puddle of his own vomit. And three years since he'd used whiskey to dull the pain of his wife's death. . . . Three damned, long years, and temptation had eaten at him every one of those one thousand ninety-odd days.

Buck Randall sat in a Cedarville whorehouse and stared at the whiskey. It caught the light, beckoning him like diamonds to a jewel thief. He circled the short, thick glass with his forefinger, then brought the glass to his nose. He closed his eyes and inhaled deeply. His mouth watered. Chilly bumps of anticipation raced over his skin. Hell, he still wanted the stuff; he knew he always would.

Uttering a ragged sigh, he set the glass down.

Tessa Black, the owner of the brothel, sashayed up to him from behind the bar. The neckline of her emerald green silk gown plunged low, revealing the shimmering tops of her large breasts. "Hey, Buck."

He shoved the full shot of whiskey toward her. "Hey, Tessa. How're you doing?"

She took the drink and dumped it back into the bottle. "I can still get it wet," she answered, giving him a brazen once-over.

Buck shook his head and grinned. "I'll bet you can, Tessa girl, I'll just bet you can."

Continuing to smile at him, she folded her arms in front of her and leaned against the bar, exposing more of her generous, white bosom. "Some day I'm gonna get you just a little bit drunk, Buck Randall. I bet you're one hell of a stud in bed."

Buck chuckled and ran one finger over her bare fleshy arm. Goose bumps erupted on her skin. "Now, how would you know that unless Nita told you?"

Tessa snorted and pulled her arm away. "I got eyes. That bulge in your jeans tells me somethin', and I've seen a lot of bulges in my time," she added with a smirk. "Nita may have been one of my best girls, but, sweetie," she added, pressing her breasts dangerously close to his hand, "I've always wanted to give you a try. You wouldn't be disappointed."

He glanced at her ample charms, then up at her face. Her eyes were thick with paint and mascara and her cheeks circles of rouge. Her hair, a brassy shade of gold, hung in lacquered curls to her shoulders. A woman ten years younger wouldn't dress the way Tessa did.

He gave her a slow, lusty smile. "Now, you know I could never satisfy you, Tess."

She answered his smile, her gaze peering over the bar at his crotch. "I'd sure as hell like to waste an afternoon tryin'." She walked away, the shelf of her wide hips swaying seductively.

Buck shook his head, turning as a gleeful whoop cut through the already noisy bar. Two men waited to be taken upstairs, passing the time playing an animated game of ringtoss. The object was to toss the ring over one of the enormous breasts of a painted wooden sculpture, a woman who looked suspiciously like Tessa.

"Hey, Bucko, *mi amigo!*"

Buck watched Che Ruiz and Hector Alejandro stroll toward him. The three of them were in town to escort their boss and his sister's houseguest back to the ranch. "Stage is in, Che?"

The shifty-eyed Mexican leered at him, flashing a smile that displayed gaping holes and ragged, rotting teeth. He jabbed his thumb toward the door. "*Si*, and the boss, he's comin' down the street with the little piece of ass now."

Buck tossed a coin on the bar and followed the other two toward the door. Their boss had ridden them hard to finish that damned front porch before his houseguest came for a visit. The last coat of paint had been slapped on early yesterday morning.

As Buck stepped outside, wind, warm and dry, picked up the dust from the street, filling the air with swirling whorls.

Grinning, Che nudged him with his elbow. "See? Here they come." He pointed toward the approaching buggy. "Brrrr," he said, shivering dramatically as he looked at their boss's companion. "Some icy berg, *si?*"

Buck had to agree. Her nose was so high in the air, she'd drown in a rainstorm. He squinted at the twosome. His boss was a handsome White—according to the girls at Tessa's. Buck knew for certain that he enjoyed a good life and didn't like to get his hands dirty . . . at least not physically. His moral character was another matter.

Buck turned his attention to the young woman at his side. She wore a handsome rust walking suit and carried one of those parasol things, holding it away from her like a royal scepter. She sat ramrod straight on the seat beside him, like a preening duchess surveying the peasants.

Buck noticed her hat and almost laughed. Rust to match her suit, it sat perched on the side of her head. It was loaded with frilly geegaws and sported a gray ostrich plume. And damned if there wasn't a small gray bird at the front that appeared to attempt takeoff every time the buggy hit a bump in the road. Buck decided it would serve the woman right if the bird crapped on her. The picture made him smile.

Their boss nodded toward them, then leaned down to

say something to the woman. She turned, just long enough for Buck to see her face. Blood pounded in his ears and his jaw fell slack. He swore under his breath, unable to take his eyes off her, even though she'd quickly turned her face away.

What in the hell was *she* doing here? And it was her, no doubt about that. He'd never forget those defiant hazel eyes or those lush pouty lips. And the hair . . . A vision of the tawny mass blowing wildly in the wind had stamped itself into his brain years ago. She might have it tamed now, but there was no mistaking who it belonged to.

His gaze followed the buggy as it rolled and rocked down the rut filled street. He tried to remember if Campion had ever mentioned the woman by name. Yeah, he'd said something to his sister, something about Margaret's room. Hell, yes, it was Margaret all right, but no one had ever called her that, not when he'd known her. Growing up on the Gaspard ranch, the little hellion had been nicknamed Molly, for there hadn't been hair on her head that could have belonged to anyone sedately named Margaret.

What in bloody hell was she doing here? He swore again. He didn't know what he'd done to deserve this. Now, along with everything else he had to worry about, he had to watch out for Molly.

The three mounted their horses and followed a respectable distance behind the buggy. Buck couldn't wait to get to the ranch to find out how she was going to explain this one.

Molly Lindquist furtively glanced behind her. Oh, damn! It *was* him. What in the name of heaven was Buck Randall doing here, anyway? It was a big country; he could have chosen anywhere else but Texas. Of all the people on the face of the earth, he was undoubtedly the last one Molly wanted to see. Ever, ever again. And then to discover he was one of Charles's ranch hands. Talk about bad luck. All of her life Buck had been her nemesis. Now, seeing him here was like eating a sweet peach pastry, enjoying it immensely, then biting into an annoying, disgusting pit. Buck Randall was that pit.

She tried to concentrate on something else, like the fact that Nicolette hadn't come with Charles to meet her. It wasn't quite proper for them to be seen alone together.

She gave Charles a sidelong glance. "And you said Nicolette will be home in a few days?"

Charles pressed her hand. "Perhaps even tomorrow. Chelsea, her best friend, has a mare that's about to foal. She didn't want to miss it. But as I said, she was torn. She didn't want to miss a moment of your visit, either."

A terrible odor suddenly contaminated the breeze. Molly brought her gloved hand to her nose, trying to filter out the smell. "What *is* that smell, Charles?"

He laughed on a cough and wiped his eyes. "It's from the holding pens for the cattle. We're downwind of it today, aren't we?"

"Will we smell it all the way to the ranch?" She was desperate to keep her mind on something else, even though she still felt Buck's glowering black eyes boring into her back.

"No, of course not. As soon as we head down into the valley, the air will be fresh and clean." He squeezed her shoulders. "Just the way I ordered it."

She glanced briefly at Charles's hand, which possessively stroked her arm. Oddly enough, she suddenly felt uncomfortable. Still sensing, almost *feeling* Buck's eyes on her, she said, "Those ranch hands of yours . . ."

Charles squeezed her arm again. "Don't be frightened, Margaret. They're just Mexicans. And one is a breed. You won't have to talk to them, I promise. They keep to their kind, we keep to ours. That's a little rule of mine. To keep it enforced, I have an overseer. Hiram Poteet. He'll make sure they don't bother you when I'm not around. And they're really quite harmless when they understand their place."

She forced herself to answer his reassuring smile, although the disparaging way he spoke bothered her a little. However, knowing he had many men to keep in line, she excused him. One couldn't become familiar with the hands. He'd explained that to her. Familiarity allowed the help to expect favors. She already knew Charles wasn't a man to grant many. He was a hard taskmaster, but that's what had drawn her to him. He allowed nothing to stand in his way, and it appeared he always got what he wanted. She rather thought they were alike in that respect.

But harmless wasn't a term she'd have used to describe the three men who followed them. They all looked like renegades. But while the other two were simply unshaven and dirty, Buck was lean, hard-edged and dangerous. In spite of the danger—or maybe because of it—she'd always been drawn to him.

She paused, waiting to feel some revulsion. It didn't come, and that realization frightened her just a little.

Charles might think the men were harmless, but she knew better. Buck Randall was about as harmless as a startled rattlesnake, and twice as sneaky.

She'd have to get away and find him as soon as she could. If he so much as hinted to Charles that he knew her, everything she'd worked so hard for would disappear like so much smoke up a chimney.

Trying to forget that Buck was behind her as they rode into the country, she stared at the landscape. It didn't hold her interest for very long. She kept feeling Buck's eyes boring into her back.

They had been descending into a valley since they left Cedarville. "How far to the ranch, Charles?"

He removed his Stetson, revealing his shock of wavy blond hair before he settled his hat back on his head. "Far enough so that we'll have to stop and have a picnic. There's a beautiful place not far from here."

Again, Buck's face loomed before her. She squirmed on the seat beside Charles.

"Anything wrong, Margaret?"

She couldn't begin to tell him. Giving him a weak smile, she shook her head. A vision of the Buck she'd had such a crush on billowed before her like an oversized balloon. Tall, lean, wild and raunchy. He'd exuded a sexual vitality that she, even at fourteen, had found compelling. Feeling herself blush, she realized that she'd tried to get him to notice her often enough. What a silly, reckless girl she'd been. And how lucky she was that she'd been sent away to school before she'd found a way to lure him into—She flushed again. Well, she would have stopped at nothing to get Buck's full attention had she been allowed to stay home.

As angry as she'd always been when he dragged her out of one scrape after another, she'd always felt . . . something. And because he'd obviously felt nothing for her, she'd needed to be as ornery as a mule, just to get back at him for not being interested. Lordy, her wild, headstrong attitude had almost ruined her back then. But no more. She knew better now. She knew that the only safe route was to suppress those wild urges. They were trouble, trouble, *trouble*.

She brought her lips together in displeasure, suddenly realizing that someone like Buck could *never* catch her eye now that she had Charles. *But you won't have him for long if Buck gets to Charles before you get to Buck.*

Shaking the thought away, she tried again to concentrate on the scenery. In the distance, she could see the pastel hues of the canyon walls, which were dotted with the rich dark green of cedars. As they progressed into the valley, they were surrounded by a littering of detached mounds, domes, arches and colonnades, all streaked with muted pinks, reds, yellows and greens.

She saw more rocks than she knew existed anywhere. They came in all sizes, from long needle shaped ones to those as smooth and flat as coins.

"Gypsum," Charles offered at her side. "The rock is gypsum. At first, you might find the drinking water a little bitter, because of it."

In spite of the beauty, red dust pirouetted around them, causing Molly to bring her handkerchief to her nose again.

Suddenly Charles urged the horses off the trail, over the sandy earth. "See over there?" He pointed toward a line of cottonwood, elm and berry trees.

Shading her eyes, she squinted into the distance. "Is there a river?"

He nodded. "A fork of the Red. We'll stop and have our lunch."

The closer they came to the river, the cleaner and cooler the air. She felt as though every garment she wore stuck to her skin; she thought she might suffocate. The water was so tempting, she wished she had the nerve to go wading. Biting back a smile, she realized shucking her shoes and stockings would shock Charles beyond belief.

He stopped the buggy, pulled a blanket from the back and hurried around to help her down. "Come," he ordered, taking her arm. "We'll have a little picnic lunch over here under the trees."

Molly glanced behind her, noticing that Buck and the other two men had unhitched the horses and were taking them downstream to water them. She sat on the blanket, arranging her skirt out around her.

A harsh pecking sound drew her gaze upward to the trunk of an elm. A black and white woodpecker worked furiously on the bark, let out a sharp *pic* sound, and flew away. A little striped ground squirrel scurried through the short grass under the trees and disappeared.

Molly leaned back against the trunk of an elm and closed her eyes, listening to the bubbling notes of a meadowlark. The shade felt heavenly, and there was a little breeze. She could smell the river.

"Lunch is served, ma'am," Charles said, affecting the voice of a servant.

Sighing contentedly, she opened her eyes and looked

down at the blanket. Cold fried chicken, sourdough biscuits and dried fruit were heaped on a plate before her. She hadn't eaten since early in the morning after she'd left the train to take the stage to Cedarville. Her mouth watered as she bit into a dried apricot.

As she ate, she watched for Buck and the others while Charles prattled on about the ranch. Under normal circumstances, she would have hung on his every word. Now, her own thoughts were constantly interrupted by her fear that Buck would give her away and ruin everything. Her gaze kept going to the trees beyond the buggy. She half expected him to walk straight up to Charles and ask him what he was doing squiring around a breed. Knowing Buck as she did, she truly expected the worst.

When they'd finished eating, she looked down at all the food that was left over. Enough to feed the others. Charles helped her stand. "We're not going to just leave all of this food here, are we?"

Charles frowned. "No, I suppose not." He turned as his men broke through the trees, leading the horses. "Hey! Clean up this mess."

She felt a flush steal into her cheeks. "Did they have lunch?"

He shrugged. "No doubt my housekeeper packed them something. If not, it isn't far to the ranch." He bent and gave her a chaste peck on the cheek. "I know how sweet-tempered and generous you are. But one thing you'll have to get used to is that you can't treat these people like you'd treat your own. Unfortunately, if you give them an inch, they'll take a mile, so to speak. Be very, very careful." He gallantly kissed her hand. "Nicolette would kill me if anything ever happened to you." He kissed her hand again. "I'll be right back. Will you be all right?"

Distracted, she nodded and watched him head into the trees. Her lunch sat like a rock on her stomach. She hadn't told him the truth about her family, or herself, but she had a good reason. Shame had nothing to do with it. Practicality did. She'd learned that survival in the White world meant blending with it. The Whites ruled the country. The Whites got the good jobs. The Whites weren't discriminated against because of the color of their skin. She had passed for a White for years. It was the only sensible thing to do. She was determined to survive, and if it meant burying her own heritage, so be it.

Frowning, she thought about Charles's strong prejudices. They really weren't so unusual. She'd encountered them all of her life. But until now, she hadn't thought that Charles might renounce her. Her lunch lurched upward, and she could taste the bitter acid from her stomach. What would he do when he learned about her? And she'd have to tell him . . . eventually. Certainly before she brought her mother down to live with them. It was only fair.

Taking a deep breath, she tried to calm herself. For now, she would do whatever she had to do to convince Buck Randall to keep his mouth shut. She'd deal with the problem in her own sweet time. She didn't need or want a push from Buck.

She glanced up, her heart skipping a beat. *Speak of the devil* . . .

Buck rounded the buggy, his shirt in his hands. They stood and stared at one another. His eyes held angry questions. Hers, she knew, were wary. She tried to remain unmoved by his presence, but it wasn't possible. His face, still handsome, yet different, had haunted her for almost seven years.

The eyes were the same—dark pools of black, each rimmed with a circle of gold. Surprisingly, they were clear, void of the bleary effects of alcohol. They pierced her soul. His cheekbones were high and prominent. Beneath the left one was a scar, accentuating the sharpness. Briefly, she wondered how he'd gotten it. No doubt it had come from a fight for his honor, that tenacious, Indian honor that had mired him in a constant state of battle with the Whites from the time he was merely a teen. He'd always been the defiant one.

His face was no longer gaunt, as it had been those years ago. But it was still keenly honed, angular and intense—and deeply disturbing. His jaw, as always, was strong, hinting at his stubborn nature, and his chin, sporting that maddening cleft, was even more compelling than it had been before. It was the stubble of beard that made him look dangerous and exciting.

Quickly, she averted her eyes, glancing down at his chest. That was a mistake. He was shirtless and had obviously cooled himself off in the river, because his torso was wet. Water ran in tiny rivers over the expanse of smooth corded muscle. There was a faded ragged scar at his left shoulder, and numerous smaller flaws scattered over his chest. He'd been hurt so many times. A slight pang of sorrow stirred her, for she knew he had suffered much at the hands of the Whites. Shivering, she pushed the thought from her mind.

Like nubs of dark chocolate, his brown nipples drew into tight beads right before her eyes. She quickly jerked her gaze away. But something pulled her back, forcing her to linger over the hard, washboardlike ridges of his stomach. Her gaze dropped lower. His jeans were slung low on his narrow hips, and she could see swirls of black hair around his navel.

A long repressed fluttering started in the pit of her stomach, radiating both down into her pelvis and up into her chest. For a moment she felt the breathless seeds of desire, but she closed her eyes briefly and willed them away.

Dragging her gaze up to his face again, she found him watching her. There was a familiar arrogance about him that infuriated her. Sucking in a greatly needed gulp of air, she stumbled away from him and walked as sedately as possible toward the buggy.

* * *

Well, I'll be damned. Buck slid his arms into his shirtsleeves and swallowed a groan. So the little hellion was all grown-up. For some stupid reason, it bothered him that she had developed such rich, ripe curves—curves that turned men's heads and made them drool. He'd have preferred to see her shapeless, washed-out, skinny, maybe. Flat chested, for sure. Why in the name of hell did she have to be such a beauty? She'd even learned how not to sweat.

He buttoned his shirt, amazed that all those years in a convent school hadn't turned her into a plain brown wren. Instead, she still had the beauty of a Lazuli Bunting. Although she'd been an unruly little brat, she'd had a freedom of spirit before they'd shipped her off. Obviously that was long gone, or more than likely, well hidden. The realization brought him a pang of disappointment.

He'd often thought about the times he had to drag her away from her friends. He'd always put on this show of hating to do it, of only doing it for June's sake. He'd really believed that, until Molly was gone. Then, for some stupid-ass reason, his life had taken on a drudgery he couldn't explain.

And now she was here, visiting Campion—a man Buck believed to be secretly dealing in stolen horses with a rag-tag bunch of Mexicans. And she looked at the bastard with such worship, one would think he was responsible for hanging out the sun every morning.

Buck swore. He didn't really want to be around when Molly discovered what a two-faced swindler Campion was, but no doubt he'd have to be the one to tell her.

She won't believe you. Hell, no, she probably wouldn't believe him. Hoping something brilliant would come to him before things went too far, he tucked his shirt into his jeans and went to help Che with the horses.

Once in the buggy again, Molly's brain was inundated with jumbled thoughts of Charles and Buck. Charles treated her like a queen. He always had, ever since that first day he'd seen her teaching piano to his little sister at the school. And Molly had been attracted to him. He was, after all, everything she'd been looking for. He was perfect husband material, and it had surprised her that he hadn't already been snatched up by someone else. She gazed up as the waning sun painted purple-hued brush strokes on the canyon walls.

In spite of the beauty, a feeling of dread nudged her spine, and that feeling had a name. Buck Randall. She briefly squeezed her eyes shut. Oh, she didn't want to think about him. She had never felt guilty about her goals. Never . . . until now. And it was only because deep down, she and Buck were the same. Physically, anyway. Yet here, she was treated like a queen, and he like the hired help. And things would never change, for he was, is and always would be, a proud, arrogant breed who hated the Whites with his entire soul.

Dabbing at her neck with her handkerchief, she thought about the many dreadfully foul names Buck was probably calling her. And he knew many. She'd been on the receiving end of them a few years ago. But she'd have to tell him her plans, anyway. Not that he'd understand them. Oh, no. But she had to try. Unless he'd drastically changed, she knew what his reaction would be down to the impertinent sneer.

She tried desperately to conjure up a way to stop thinking about him, and what he could do to her well-ordered life. First of all, she couldn't let it eat at her. She had to talk with him first. Maybe he wouldn't say anything. Maybe she was worrying needlessly. Nothing got accomplished by worrying about it. Pulling in a resigned breath, she ruefully realized there was nothing she could do about Buck until she got to the ranch.

As they moved deeper into the valley, Molly noticed more pecan, willows and cottonwood growing along the sloping hills.

"Oh, Charles," Molly whispered on a breath. "It's quite beautiful here."

He gave her a broad grin, as though he'd planted the sight just for her. "You haven't seen anything yet, Margaret. Wait until you see the house."

Craning her neck, Molly could just get a glimpse of a tall white structure beyond the trees. "Oh, I see it, Charles, I think I see it!"

The grove parted before them, and there, rising like a white stone castle, stood the ranch house. Deep eaves, high, narrow windows and similar doorways made the place look grand. Rustling cottonwood swayed with the breeze, and the checkerboard dappling of light and shade shifted over the limestone.

It was everything Molly had dreamed it would be, and more. Much, much more. Excitement swelled within her until she got a glimpse of the outbuildings on the south side of the house. Then she remembered Buck, and her stomach briefly sank to the tops of her shoes.

But all of her anxieties disappeared once she stepped into the house. She felt as though she'd walked into a mansion on Nob Hill. She was almost speechless. "Charles, it's beautiful. And the floor." She gasped in awe. "Just look at that floor."

His chest swelled with pride. "It's a Roman mosaic patterned after the floors in Herculaneum and Pompeii."

Properly impressed, Molly's gaze lingered on the ornate tiles before lifting to the three-part horizontal division of the walls. "I've never seen anything like this." She tentatively touched the wooden border.

"They're tripartite."

"Whatever you say," she answered with a smile.

Charles gently pulled her closer. "See this?" He pointed to the bottom third. "This embossed relief paper is the wainscoting. The cornice around the top," he said, pointing to it, "is embossed anaglyph."

Molly had no idea what he was talking about, but it

sounded impressive, and it was beautiful. She could live this way; she had no doubt about it.

Charles gripped her elbow. "You'll probably want to freshen up. Your room is—"

"No," she interrupted. "Please show me the house, Charles."

"You're not too tired from the ride?"

Shaking her head, she answered enthusiastically, "I want to see every room. Right now."

She was given the grand tour, finding large cool rooms filled with furnishings she'd only read about. Marble fireplaces with ornate brass accessories, enormous gilt-edged mirrors, stenciled wall decorations, a sixteenth-century Persian tile wall, and a Brussels carpet, not to mention two Aubussons, an Axminster and a small Oriental rug in front of the fireplace in the library. And a Steinway grand piano in the salon. Her head swam with the opulence of it all. Perhaps it was a little ostentatious, but she didn't fault Charles. He'd worked hard to get where he was; he deserved to spend his money any way he chose.

"Now," he ordered. "Up to your room. I won't have you exhausted your first day here."

She went reluctantly until she saw the room. Holding back a ragged sigh, she stepped inside and stared.

"Nicolette's room is next door, through the bathroom. You'll share it," he explained. "I hope you don't mind."

With a mute shake of her head, she walked into the room. The wainscoting and ceiling were papered in a matching pink floral design, and the walls were done in a coordinated pink with tiny gray dots. The woodwork was all painted gray, and the white lace curtains billowed outward, vainly holding back the breeze from the open window. A dainty walnut armchair with needlepoint upholstery sat in a well-lighted corner near a window, and a small round pedestal table with a frothy pink cloth stood next to it. A delicate gray commode nestled against the opposite wall, next to a small mahogany fold-out desk.

Her gaze fell to the four-poster bed, which was tucked into an alcove. A half-dozen small pillows were scattered over the bed, and the spread was yards and yards of pink and gray froth.

She swallowed hard. "Charles, I don't know what to say."

He nervously cleared his throat. "I have some work to do in the library. Now, please. I want you to be rested for dinner."

She didn't even notice that he'd left as she crossed to the window and looked out onto the yard. Glimpsing Buck as he went into the barn, she made a face. As much as she dreaded talking to him, she knew she had to. And the sooner the better.

Feeling her happiness dwindle, she stepped back into the room. After removing her jacket, she checked herself in the mirror over the commode and went downstairs.

Grateful Charles had some business to attend to, she stepped out onto the porch on the pretext of getting acquainted with her surroundings. The day had been clear, cloudless, the sky a brilliant shade of azure. Now the bluffs, once sharply etched against the sky, were a muted purple.

Trying to act as casual as possible, she stepped off the porch and strolled to the barn. Her heartbeat accelerated when she saw Buck preparing oats for his horse.

"Buck?"

He lifted his gaze and stared at her briefly before going back to his task.

"It . . . it is Buck Randall, isn't it?" *Fool.* She knew it was him as well as she knew her own name.

He gave her a humorless laugh—a familiar sound that dredged up memories she thought were long forgotten.

She swallowed and pulled a sweet smile. "Thank you for not giving me away earlier."

His face was void of emotion as he continued his chores. "Yeah, sure."

Although it had been almost seven years since he'd last

spoken to her, she remembered the sound of his voice as though it were just yesterday. That sexy, throaty, whiskey-harsh voice that had invaded her dreams, her heart . . . her soul. Clearing her throat, she nervously fiddled with the high neck of her Battenberg lace blouse. "I . . . it's been a long time."

His mouth twisted into the semblance of a smile, and the scar beneath his cheekbone she'd noted earlier formed a devilish dent in his cheek.

She reached toward him, then pulled her hand away. "I . . . you didn't have that scar when I left."

"Cow," he answered succinctly.

"Cow?"

He nodded. "I got kicked by a cow."

"Oh, I'm . . . I'm sorry." Wasn't that just typical? Leave it to her to imagine he'd gotten scarred defending his honor.

He shrugged and went about his business, virtually ignoring her.

"I suppose you're wondering what I'm doing here."

He turned, giving her a mocking smile. "I'd say it's pretty obvious, Molly—"

"Shhh!" she hissed, glancing quickly around her. Relieved that no one was nearby, she sweetened her tone. "Buck, it . . . it probably doesn't make any difference to you, but I've worked very hard to get where I am."

He turned away, appearing to be unimpressed with what she'd done with her life. "Haven't we all."

"I mean, I spent years at that awful school where the nuns did their best to break me. But I stayed, I didn't try to run away, and believe me, I sure as h—" She cleared her throat again. "I sure wanted to." Lord, he brought out the very *worst* in her. She hadn't had the urge to really cuss in years.

"And when I finally graduated, they found a position for me at another school for girls. That's where I met Charles and Nicolette. I was teaching her to play the piano. That's what I do, Buck. I teach music. Did you know that? I'm a different person now. I'm . . . I'm—"

"White?"

His expression of loathing made her cringe. He would never understand her reasons. Never. She had to try, but she didn't want to fight with him. Frowning, she decided on another tactic. "I was sorry to hear about Honey's death. I—"

"That was six years ago. And thanks for coming to the funeral," he said with dry sarcasm.

Her gaze fluttered to the ground. She could still detect pain in his voice. It had been a shock to learn that Honey had been raped by the reservation schoolmaster. Until she had bled to death from his forceful entry and his beating, no one had known that she'd bleed so easily. When Molly had been told that Buck had drowned himself in his precious whiskey, drinking even more than he had before, she'd felt a stupid sense of loss, for it had suddenly dawned on her that he'd loved his wife very much. Everyone knew that's how people in love responded—unable to cope with the death of a loved one, they tried to destroy themselves, too.

She kicked at the loose hay with the toe of her shoe. "I'm sorry I couldn't be there. I was in San Francisco." She looked at him as directly as possible. "I believe with your help," she said, adding a little sarcasm of her own.

He glanced toward the house. "You'd better get your tail back up there. The feudal lord of the manor wouldn't approve of you mingling with the hired help."

His derision was palpable, but she still didn't want to fight with him. "Buck," she said, trying not to beg, "please don't let Charles know what . . . what I was. I mean, what I am. Don't even indicate we know each other. I don't want him to know about Pine Valley or . . . or anything else. Not yet." She gave him her most innocent, pleading look.

He swore. "Campion doesn't know you're a breed, huh?"

"My *mother* is a breed. I'm . . . I'm only one quarter." She had the decency to blush. She lowered her gaze to the ground again, embarrassed that she'd taken his baiting so easily. "And, no. I . . . I haven't told him that yet. But I will. Honest, Buck, I will. Just . . . just not yet."

He swore again. "What would your mother think if she knew you were so ashamed of her that you're passing yourself off as a White?"

"It's *for* my mother that I'm doing this," she shot back.

He gave her an insulting snort. "What in the hell is that supposed to mean?"

His anger went so deep, it almost frightened her. "Are you really ready to listen to me?"

"Try me. I can't wait to hear it."

Taking a deep breath, she looked up at the gnarled branch of an oak tree that hung over the roof of the barn, hoping to choose her words carefully. "I want you to understand. I . . . I've got to have some security for mother and me. I can't always depend on Anna and Nicolas to take care of her. I miss her, Buck. I really do. But . . . but I hardly make enough to take care of myself. I—"

"What a crock of shit." He gave her a look of disgust.

Fury surged through her. "You aren't even trying to understand, are you? Why is it so hard for you to believe I'd want to care for Mother?"

"To be honest, I don't give a damn what you do with your life. You can go to hell, for all I care. But from where I stand, it sounds like you're lying to yourself." He snorted a sound of disgust again. "You'd better watch your back, brat. Campion has a real aversion to breeds. He might hire us, but he sure as hell doesn't want us in his family tree."

She remembered Charles's prejudices. "I know he's a bit hard on his help, but he's basically a good man, Buck. He . . . he wouldn't . . ." She couldn't finish. She wouldn't sound unsure or express her fears in front of Buck. After all, surely once she and Charles were married, he wouldn't lock her dear mother in an attic, like some deranged madman. Buck was exaggerating. She could change Charles. Love did many strange and wonderful things. But a niggle of fear crept into her consciousness anyway, and try as she might, she couldn't get rid of it.

His sardonic, lopsided grin told her that somehow he knew what was in her thoughts. "You're pissin' in the wind, brat."

"Oh, don't call me that!" He'd called her that so often in the past, in her mind it had almost become an endearment. But she shrugged off all feelings of tenderness.

"And I'd expect gutter talk coming from you. When you haven't anything intelligent to say, you swear." She turned to leave, then spun around again. "You haven't changed, Buck Randall. I'm really sorry to see that. You haven't changed a bit."

"I've never pretended to be anything but what I am. Unlike you, I have nothing to hide." He brushed past her and strode toward a low, whitewashed building on the other side of the corral.

Frustration welled up inside her, but she pulled in a deep breath. He was here; she couldn't do a thing about it. She'd just have to keep an eye on him, that's all. She couldn't let him be alone with Charles, not if she could help it. Knowing how she and Buck riled each other, it wouldn't take much for him to spill all the beans. And she'd do that in her own sweet time.

Huffing resentfully, she turned on her heels and stormed back toward the house, the crisp swish of her skirts a blatant clue to her own anger.

Buck stared out the bunkhouse window long after Molly had disappeared into the house. He swore and pounded the windowsill with his fist. The glass rattled as though a huge wind had briefly invaded the building.

He dragged his hand over his face. Molly might be all grown-up, but she was still rushing willy-nilly toward self-destruction. He wondered how long she thought she could get by without telling Campion what she really was. And that cock-and-bull story about trying to snag a rich husband so she can take care of June. It was a laughable excuse, typical of Molly.

And of all the Whites in the world she could have chosen, it had to be Campion. He'd learned a great deal about Campion's history, a grisly tale that involved his mother, and knew that Campion would kill any Indian or Mexican who looked at his sister cross-eyed. Campion also believed that any woman who was touched, much less raped, by an Indian should kill herself. Yeah, he was some prince, his boss.

Somehow, he'd have to get Molly to understand the depths of Campion's hatred. But he'd have to be careful—she wasn't ready to listen to the truth. Maybe there would never be a good time. That was a chance he'd have to take. But not because he cared about her. Hell, no. If it weren't for June, he'd let Molly wallow in her lies and stupidity.

She was someone he didn't want to care about, yet he couldn't begin to explain the feeling that crept over him when she'd stood in front of him, pleading her pathetic case. The years had been very, very kind to her. At fourteen, she'd been a reckless, burgeoning beauty. Now, at twenty-one, she was an exquisite young woman who had apparently learned how to tame her wild side. But wild or tame, Molly Lindquist was more woman than any man could handle. He knew that better than anyone.

Pushing out a lusty sigh, he crossed to the cupboard and stared at the door where he knew Che kept a bottle of liquor. God, he thought, dragging his hands over his face again, he sure could use a drink.

❧ Two ❧

Trying desperately to calm herself after her run-in with Buck, Molly took a nervous, solitary tour through the downstairs rooms again. Lamps were lit, further softening the delicate tones of dusk. She ended up in the salon, where the highly polished piano silently beckoned her. Sliding onto the needlepoint bench, she ran her fingers over the sumptuous grand's ivory keys. She cringed. It needed tuning. Badly. At times like this, she found her perfect pitch more of a curse than a blessing. Finding someone to tune the piano would probably be difficult out here. But if Nicolette practiced as she should, the piano needed to be sound. Not just for the player, but for the piano itself. The Steinway was such a beautiful work of art, it was a shame to treat it like it had no heart. And it *did* have heart. Every time someone sat down to play it, it gave back every bit as much as it got. Quality always showed. *Rather like people.*

Yes, like people. And even though Buck didn't believe in her noble reasons for what she was doing, she did. Accepting who she was hadn't come easily. She'd never truly been ashamed of her Indian blood. If she were alone in the world, she might have flaunted it, for she could survive on what she made as a teacher. She might not like it, but she could. But Molly had her mother's future to think about, and she wanted to be with her. Badly.

She caressed middle C, then stretched to play an octave. Yes, she could survive on her own if she had to. But . . . would she? She didn't have the luxury of finding out. Her mother, the sweet, simple girl-woman who had done the best she knew how to raise her, was the driving force behind Molly's practical need to secure a future. But even without that, there was no reason to think she wouldn't have cared for Charles anyway, and accepted his proposal.

Again, that germ of fear about Charles that Buck had planted grew in her chest. Hatred for the Indians was something she understood. Something she'd grown up knowing existed. Something she'd painfully experienced firsthand. Years ago she'd decided that the only thing she wanted from that man who had sired her was his name, and she'd taken it. She wasn't naive. She'd left her naivete back at the vineyard. She was just being practical. She was trying to blend, trying to survive.

Well, she thought, running scales over the keys, she'd show Buck that she wasn't the selfish brat he painted her to be. He hadn't been around for the last seven years, what in the hell did he know about her anymore, anyway? She closed her eyes and sighed. *Hell.* She'd thought the word, which was as good as saying it. It was Buck's fault. He made her so angry, she'd probably blurt out a good juicy cuss word right in front of Charles if she wasn't careful.

Her finger struck a sour A flat. Everything seemed to be going sour. Her life, her luck, her plans . . .

She shook her head vigorously. It was foolish to sink into self-pity. She'd never been one to do so, and she wasn't going to start now.

She tried to block out the occasional unpleasant twang of the keys. It definitely needed tuning. She'd find a way to have it done or do it herself. It wouldn't be the first time. She'd tuned the piano at the school often enough, and had found herself enjoying the work.

Ignoring the sour notes, she launched into one of her favorite Chopin valses. It always buoyed her spirits. Chopin was her composer of choice for piano music. That any mortal could write such beautiful, poetic melodies nearly made her weep. Music had always spoken to her with far more emotion than words ever had—until she discovered Mr. Cooper, of course, and his exciting, dangerous stories about the frontier.

She turned to the piano when she was happy, troubled, angry or out-of-sorts. Whatever her mood, she could find a piece to fit it. The piano was her panacea.

As she came to the end of the valse, she looked up and saw a woman standing in the doorway. She finished and got up briskly, smoothing down her skirt. "I'm sorry, was I bothering you?"

The woman, an attractive Mexican whose coal black hair was pulled back into a severe bun, shook her head. "It was quite lovely," she answered, her voice holding just a hint of an accent. "I'm Mrs. Alvarez, the housekeeper. And you are Miss Lindquist. Nicolette's teacher."

Molly stepped forward and took the woman's hand, grasping it warmly. "Yes. How nice to meet you, Mrs. Alvarez." She looked into the woman's face, noting the hardened experiences that were captured in soft places. Pain and hardship radiated from the tight lines on either side of her mouth and at the corners of her dark, haunting eyes. Knowing that any woman who wasn't white had miseries that could easily have been her own, Molly rarely missed the pain that was stamped with such subtlety on their faces.

A smile briefly flitted about the woman's lips. Molly was sure others wouldn't even notice the overlay of grief in it.

She removed her hand from Molly's and thrust it into the pocket of her crisp, white apron. "You will play often?"

Molly gave her a tentative shrug. "If no one complains. I plan to be available for Nicolette every day. I don't want her getting rusty just because she isn't at school." She waited for the woman to respond. When she didn't, Molly blathered on. "I've been without a piano for weeks, and I have to restrain myself from playing on and on just to make up for lost time."

Mrs. Alvarez merely nodded and left the room, leaving Molly puzzled. Shrugging again, she returned to the piano, launching into a string of preludes and mazurkas before finishing up with her favorite polonaise.

When she'd finished, she dropped her chin to her chest and closed her eyes. The piece always left her drained, satisfied. *Probably like making love.*

The silent voice shook her upright and she blinked, glancing around her. Where in the world had *that* thought come from? As she rubbed the back of her neck, the vision of Buck loomed before her, his black gaze filled with scorn.

Forcing Buck from her thoughts, she looked up at the portrait that hung on the wall near the piano. It looked so much like Nicolette, yet Molly was sure it wasn't. There was a diaphanous quality to the painting, hinting at the subject's delicate fragility. Her beauty was almost celestial.

"Are you sore from your trip?"

Molly jumped at the sound of Charles's voice. He squeezed his thumbs gently along the cords of her neck and rubbed. Even though his touch was a bit more familiar than she had expected, it felt marvelous.

She turned and looked up at him when his hands left her neck. "How long have you been watching me?"

"Not long. As I finished my work, I heard you play. It delights me. The piano needs playing, I know that. Nicolette has been lazy about practicing. I don't think she really appreciates what I've been able to give her."

Molly fondled the highly polished, beautifully carved music stand, then glanced up at the portrait again.

"Who is that woman?"

Charles's fingers suddenly tensed on her shoulders. "My mother. She . . . she died many years ago."

Molly sighed, sensing that Charles still missed her. "She's really very beautiful."

"Yes," he answered tersely. "She was also a lover of the arts. This was her favorite room."

Molly sensed a great disturbance in his words. She decided it was best to change the subject. One day, perhaps, he would bare his soul. She wanted them to share everything.

"I love your home, Charles. I love everything about it. It's more beautiful and grander than I'd ever imagined."

He joined her on the bench and took her hands in his. "I hear an unspoken 'yet' at the end of that sentence."

She shook her head, her gaze moving over his handsome features. She wished she could tell him her fears, and deeply wanted him to comfort her. With the appearance of Buck Randall, her well-ordered life had erupted like volcanic ash. "It's really nothing, Charles. I guess I'm just tired from the trip."

He touched her chin. "How can you be tired and still look so beautiful?"

She felt her heart skip a beat. He cared for her deeply, she knew that. But *damn* Buck. Now that germ of fear had begun to ferment, and no matter how hard she pushed it away, it always came back. *Like Buck. Like a bad penny.*

Charles leaned toward her, his eyes filled with a strange, disconcerting heat. She allowed the kiss. It wasn't invasive or hungry, but as their lips clung, it became so. She pulled back, the change alarming her.

Bracketing her face with his hands, he studied her. "I won't force you, Margaret." He let out an audible sigh. "But you have to know that being with you once again has rekindled some fires."

She pulled back, her alarm growing. That sort of talk was dangerous. "Fires, Charles?"

"I'm a man, Margaret. A gentleman, yes, but still, a man. Your beauty inflames me. You're like . . . like an ache deep inside me that I can temper only because I want to wait until you're ready. Until we're wed."

He bent and kissed her knuckles, and Molly stared at the

top of his head. A dread of a different sort wormed its way into her stomach. For all of her determination to make this match, she hadn't considered the physical side. She'd purposely avoided thinking about it. "Charles, you . . . you know I'm not—"

"I said I wouldn't force you, Margaret." Meeting her gaze, he squeezed her hands. "But do understand that I care for you deeply. Now," he said, getting to his feet, "you go up and get some rest before dinner. I insist."

She gave him a tentative smile, then slid off the piano bench and moved out of the room toward the stairs. As she gave him one last glance, he blew her a kiss. Tempted to lift her skirts and take the steps two at a time, she sedately climbed to the second floor, hurried to her room and closed the door.

His words hammered inside her head as she crossed to the window. She would have to think about them. She wasn't naive about sex, but she hadn't thought much about it. Only when Charles insinuated it. It wasn't something she cared to dwell on. She didn't like the feelings the image of it dredged up.

Pulling the gauzy curtain aside, she stared down onto the yard. Charles was handsome and gallant, but she certainly hadn't been drawn to him *that* way. She'd killed that part of her character long ago, and quite successfully, too.

Or had she? Her pulse raced as Buck rode into sight, his lean body graceful and comfortable astride his mount. Again, like the day before when she'd seen him at the river, old feelings stirred.

Cursing him loudly, she spun away from the window and marched to the bathroom she would share with Nicolette. The roll top tub was filled with bathwater, the bubbles shimmering in the light from the kerosene filled sconces that glowed on either side of the mirror over the sink.

Suddenly feeling tired and dirty, she undressed and sank deeply into the warm, silky water. She sighed aloud. If this wasn't heaven, it was close to it.

* * *

She and Charles dined alone. It was almost comical for the two of them to sit at opposite ends of the long table, but she thought she could get used to it. During her bath, she'd decided that after she and Charles got married, she would try very hard to get used to sharing his bed. It was a woman's duty, after all. There were many things she would have to sacrifice to make a safe haven for herself and her mother. Her last letter from Anna had nearly made her cry. *June sits in her room by the hour, holding your doll, staring out the window.* The stinging, burning threat of tears pressed against the backs of her eyes, as it did each time she thought of her mother's condition. She brought her linen napkin to her mouth and pressed her lips hard against her teeth. It would be foolish and dangerous to let her emotions rule her now.

The silence in the room was deafening. A brief picture of Anna and Nicolas's crowded, noisy dinner table punctured her thoughts. Nicolas hadn't allowed more than one person to speak at a time, but he had insisted on everyone having a turn to voice an opinion or share their day. The memory made her sad, but also made her smile.

"That's not a very happy smile, Margaret."

She cleared her throat, dabbing her napkin over her lips. "I was just remembering our dinner table when I was a girl."

Charles leaned back in his chair and studied her. "You have a Swedish heritage, don't you?"

"My . . . my father is Swedish, yes." It wasn't a lie.

He nodded. "Were there many of you?"

She nodded briskly, pushing away the pang of conscience. "The table was always full. As often as not, someone else joined us." Buck, in the months before she'd been sent away, had eaten with them at least twice a week. She'd often wondered why he wasn't at home with Honey and his little boy. . . . What was his name? Rusty. No, Dusty.

A deep, wild part of her had liked having Buck there. But on the surface, she remembered vividly wanting to eat and run. Nicolas wouldn't let her, so she'd been forced to endure Buck's presence far longer than she'd cared to. Only because he'd brazenly held her gaze when she'd looked at him. She'd always felt he was judging her. Punishing her with his knowledge of her activities, silently threatening her with it. And she'd always wanted him to be dead drunk, so she could throw it in his face. But he never came to Nicolas's table drunk. At least, not while she was there.

Even now, so many years later, she felt the same threat. He still made her feel like she had to prove herself. The idea that he didn't believe what she told him still made her mad.

The sound of muted voices came from the hallway. Mrs. Alvarez stepped into the dining room.

"One of the hands to see you, Senor Campion."

Charles stood. "Show him in, Angelita."

Nodding, she retreated, and Buck sauntered into the room, his spurs jingling slightly against the thick Persian carpet. His dusty, well-worn hat dangled from his long, strong fingers, and his black wavy hair was pushed away from his face, exposing a line on his forehead left by the sweatband of his Stetson. His shirt was plastered to his skin, and his jeans hung low on his hips, reminding Molly that they rested well below his hair covered navel.

After her appraisal, in which her heart thumped uncommonly hard, she looked away and lifted her chin high, hoping to hide the feelings this terrible man activated in her. *Nerves. It's just nerves.* Of course it was nerves. And fear of discovery. Oh, every time she thought about him being here, she just wanted to scream.

"Yes, Randall?" Charles left the table and came around to stand beside her chair.

"They're here with the horses. Just thought you should know."

The raspy, smoky sound of his voice made her heart race

in spite of her anger. She remembered a time in her foolish youth when she could have listened to that sound forever. Lord, what a ninny she'd been.

"They're here? Great! Great news! How many did they get?"

"Eight," Buck answered, his gaze drifting languidly toward Molly.

Molly studied him briefly, then looked away. She hated that look. The one that told her she was still the selfish brat she'd been seven years before.

"All right. You'll start breaking them in the morning, then?" Charles's enthusiasm was almost adolescent.

"In the morning," Buck echoed. Giving Molly a brief nod, he left the room.

She fussed with her napkin, trying to neatly refold it next to her plate. "My, what was that all about?"

"The hands have rounded up eight wild horses. Randall is the best broncobuster I have. If I left it up to him, he'd have them all broken to the saddle in a week."

Molly bristled under the praise for Buck. "What do you mean, if you left it up to him?"

Charles took his seat again and gently rang the tiny bell beside his plate. "The man is almost superhuman, Margaret. Oh," he added with a wave of his hand, "I know he's a breed, but I've never found a white man who could handle a horse like that Buck Randall can." He shook his head. "It's hard for me to admit that he's that good. I mean, he's terrific at what he does. He actually—"

"Oh, Charles, please. Surely he isn't that good." Molly tried to make her voice sound light, but it wasn't easy to do when her teeth were clenched so hard her jaw ached.

"But he is." He leaned forward, his eyes bright. "I can't explain it, Margaret. You'll just have to see for yourself. Tomorrow."

Her stomach dropped. "Tomorrow?"

"Why, yes. You'll have to watch him work." He grinned at her. "You'll have no choice."

"Why won't I have a choice?" She wasn't going to like this.

His grin widened. "Because Nicolette will insist that you watch."

"Why?" she asked skeptically.

His grin turned sardonic. "She has a foolish schoolgirl crush on the breed."

Molly's stomach lurched. "Surely you don't approve, Charles."

He shrugged. "It's just a crush."

"But . . . but how do you know he isn't encouraging it?" Somehow she knew Buck wouldn't, but the words spilled out anyway.

"If he encourages it," Charles said lightly, toying dangerously with the knife he'd used to cut their meat, "I'll kill him."

A fresh jolt of fear washed over her, bringing Buck's warning back to her ears. "You would, wouldn't you?"

"Of course. As I've said repeatedly, Margaret, he's just a breed. The hired help. He can be replaced, and I don't tolerate insolence—from anyone."

Molly listened to his tone. It bothered her. What was it that Buck had called him? A feudal lord. Yes, he rather sounded like the kind of boss who delegated all the dirty work, but she would hardly call his actions feudal. He wasn't medieval, and he certainly didn't expect his help to pay homage to him. That was just Buck, trying his best to make her angry. He'd always been able to do that with such aplomb.

She was grateful when Angelita entered the room carrying a tray of desserts. Charles picked a piece of thick, rich chocolate cake.

Molly was sure she couldn't eat another bite. First, Buck's presence had caused her to lose her appetite. Now, Charles's coldhearted cure for Nicolette's crush made Molly's skin crawl. Should she warn Buck? Surely he wouldn't be so foolish as to encourage Nicolette's advances. He wouldn't contradict his own warning to her. But he was, after all, a drunk. He was an irresponsible drunk, and everyone knew that drunks couldn't be counted on to make sense.

"Please," Mrs. Alvarez said softly as she stopped beside Molly's chair. "Try the flan. It's a specialty of mine."

Molly almost refused, but thought better of it. The housekeeper already didn't seem to care for her. It wouldn't do to reject her "specialty." Nodding slightly, Molly answered, "Then, the flan it shall be. Thank you, Mrs. Alvarez."

"Oh, call her Angelita, Molly. Everyone does."

Molly's gaze locked with the housekeeper's. She couldn't read what was behind those hard, grief filled black eyes. "Would you mind?"

The housekeeper straightened. There was fierce pride in her stance. "No, *senorita*, I don't mind."

When Angelita left the room, Molly turned to her dessert. She was able to get down a few bites, and it was wonderful. Almost as good as Concetta's. "Charles," she began. "I don't think that woman likes me."

He snorted. "Angelita? What difference does it make? She's only the help, Margaret."

She almost asked if he'd kill the housekeeper, too, if she displeased him, but kept her mouth shut. His prejudice was so casual. The sign of something inbred; something he'd lived with a long, long time. She decided it was best to change the subject. "What time do you expect Nicolette to arrive?"

He patted his mouth then laid the napkin on the table. "Since she knows you're here, I expect she'll be here bright and early in the morning."

She had hoped Nicolette would arrive before bedtime. It was an awkward situation, her being in Charles's house without another female companion, especially since he'd voiced his desire for her. She shifted uncomfortably.

"Well," she said, pushing herself away from the table. "I

hope you don't mind, but I'm suddenly awfully tired. I guess the trip is finally catching up with me."

Charles was at her elbow in an instant. "I understand. Here," he added, guiding her toward the stairway. "I'll see you to your room."

"That isn't nec—"

"Nonsense," he interrupted, taking the stairs with her. "I intend to make the best impression I can, Margaret. I only hope your beauty doesn't undo all my good intentions," he added, giving her a sly smile.

Molly swallowed hard. She suddenly hoped there was a lock on her bedroom door. Bidding him a hasty good night, one that gave him no opportunity to kiss her again, she hurried into her room and shut the door.

Examination of the barrier revealed no lock. Biting nervously at her lip, she scanned the room, searching for something to put in front of the door.

She caught a glimpse of herself in the mirror. Worry lines wrinkled her forehead and her mouth was pulled tight. Shaking her head, she stared at her reflection.

"Would you just look at yourself?" she whispered. Whatever made her think Charles would risk everything by barging in on her in the middle of the night? He was too smart for that. He was wooing her, and she knew it. He wouldn't jeopardize his chances by forcing himself on her like some eager adolescent.

Her entire state of mind was Buck's fault. Had he not materialized into her life like a persistent bad dream, she wouldn't have even *considered* locking Charles out of her bedroom, because it was absurd to even think he would seriously enter it against her wishes.

Trying to relax, she undressed and slipped into her white, short-sleeved cotton nightgown, then took the pins from her hair. She combed through the heavy mass with her fingers, stopping periodically at her scalp to massage the blood vessels that had begun to throb during dinner.

Her fingers automatically threaded her hair into a thick braid which she let hang over her shoulder.

Stifling a yawn, she crawled into bed and reached for her book. Although she was tired, she was also anxious to finish *The Last of the Mohicans*. She'd only discovered Mr. Cooper's novels a year ago, and now she couldn't get her fill of them. They were one long death dance of knives, scalps and hatchets, but she adored them. She'd tried for years to read Jane Austen and Louisa May Alcott, but somehow the lives the characters lived pulled little sympathy from her. She realized it was an odd reaction, coming from her, since those women were living the kind of life she'd always dreamed about.

She propped two pillows behind her, leaned against them and started to read. The book was clumsy and lopsided, for she was nearing the end of the adventures of Natty, Chingachgook and Uncas. She became immersed in the story immediately, sharing Uncas's sorrow upon witnessing Cora's death.

> Magua buried his weapon in the back of the prostrate Delaware, uttering an unearthly shout as he committed the dastardly deed. But Uncas arose from the blow, as the wounded panther turns upon his foe, and struck the murderer of Cora to his knees, by an effort in which the last of his failing strength was expended . . .

A furtive knock on her bedroom door startled her so, she gasped out loud and pressed one hand over her thumping heart.

Holding her breath, she listened for the sound again.

"Margaret?"

She frowned at the door. "Charles?"

"Might I come in for a moment?"

His muffled voice beyond the door sounded urgent.

Anxious, she put her book down and pulled the bedding to her chin. "What is it? What's happened?"

"It's about Nicolette."

Alarm spread through her. Pulling the bedding higher, she answered, "Is she all right?"

"Yes, yes. But . . . I'd like to speak with you briefly."

Hesitating, she wrinkled her nose. "Well, all right."

Charles stepped into the room, stopped short, and stared at her, as if he'd been struck dumb.

Molly felt his gaze crawl over her. "Well, what is it, Charles? Is Nicolette here? I didn't hear anything—"

"Margaret," he said on a whisper of breath. "You are a vision." His voice held traces of adoration.

"Charles, please," she urged, trying not to squirm under his heated inspection. "You're making me very uncomfortable, and this isn't proper at all. What about Nicolette?"

The flare of heat in his eyes died slowly. "Of course. You're right. I forgot to tell you to come down early in the morning. I've just gotten word that Nicolette will join us for breakfast."

She sagged against the pillow. "You had me scared to death. I thought something had happened to her."

He took a step toward the bed, then stopped. "I'm sorry. I didn't mean to frighten you."

"Well, you did. Good night . . . again." She waited for him to leave, then scurried from the bed and peered out the window. She hadn't heard anyone ride up. She knew he wasn't telling her the truth. She had the distinct feeling that he'd merely manufactured an excuse to see her in her night clothes.

Leaning on the windowsill, she dragged in a breath, filling her lungs with the sweet night air. She briefly studied the cheesecloth covered mosquito board, grateful to have it, for insects slapped at the screen, attracted by the light.

Glancing outside, she noted that someone moved near the corral. She pulled back slightly and watched him stroll toward the house. Her instincts told her it was Buck. So did the fluttering of her heart, she thought with a wry twist of her mouth. Refusing to leave, she stared at the figure moving beneath her window.

He lit a cigarette, his face suddenly washed in the harsh yellow light of the flame. A slow, lazy smirk slid over his lips before he blew out the match, leaving him in darkness once again.

She wondered what he was thinking, then realized she didn't give a tinker's damn. Pulling herself upright, she turned briskly from the window, crawled into bed and turned out the lamp. But sleep eluded her. She tossed and turned, punched her pillow and considered lighting the lamp and finishing her book. But she was too edgy. Too nervous.

With a disgusted sigh, she threw her bedding off and slid from the bed. A glass of milk sounded like just the thing to lull her to sleep. She grabbed her robe, slipped into it and left her room, careful not to make any noise as she made her way downstairs to the dark kitchen.

Buck took a long drag on his cigarette and watched the smoke as it was released on his breath. When he'd seen Molly at dinner, sitting at that damned long table like a duchess, he'd wondered who she was trying to fool. The trouble was, no matter how much he tried to believe otherwise, she looked right among Campion's treasures. And he had no doubt that Campion thought he was getting another treasure. A trophy. Something to add to his collection. And he was. But Buck knew that if the bastard ever found out the truth, Molly would be tossed aside and disposed of like a crippled calf.

And as much as he wanted to let her get hurt, he knew he couldn't. She was trying so hard to be something she wasn't. That damned prissy visiting music teacher routine was a role she was playing. She'd fool Campion for a while, but she would never fool him.

One side of his mouth lifted in a wry half smile. Prissy

teachers rarely, if ever, hung out their bedroom windows like hungry tarts, the backlight showing every luscious curve of their bodies. As she'd backed away and turned, her breasts had been visible beneath the lightweight nightgown.

He shifted, trying to adjust himself more comfortably. Now, whether he wanted to or not, he'd probably dream about those breasts all night. His mouth watered, and he swallowed, knowing the symptom only too well. Whenever he was upset, randy as a billy goat or mad as hell, he wanted a drink.

Swearing, he crushed his cigarette beneath the heel of his boot and crossed to the back door that led to the kitchen. Angelita always left milk out for him, knowing it was the only thing he drank. He'd learned to crave it, grateful something worthwhile had even halfheartedly replaced his craving for whiskey.

As he pushed the door open, he heard someone gasp from inside. A figure stood at the counter.

"Angelita?"

"Lord in heaven, you scared me to death."

His heart jumped at the sound of the strained whisper. "Oh, it's only you."

"Why are you creeping around in the dark?"

He moved closer, noting that the moon flooded the kitchen, bathing her hair with silver light. "I could ask you the same question."

Molly grasped the collar of her robe, pulling it tightly against her neck. "I . . . I couldn't sleep. I thought a glass of milk might help me."

He smiled in the dim light. "That's my glass of milk."

"Yours? Oh, I didn't know . . ."

"Angelita always leaves some out for me. It's the only thing I drink these days. That, and coffee." He stepped closer still, unable to help himself.

She cocked her head to one side. "Really? I find that hard to believe."

He reached out and touched the thick braid that lay over her shoulder. With his fingers beneath the plait, he moved his hand downward until it rested against her breast. His mouth watered and a lusty itch sprang in his groin. "Believe what you like, brat."

Clearing her throat, she stepped away and thrust the glass at him. "Here," she offered, her hand shaking. "We can share it."

His fingers touched hers, caressing them lightly before he finally took the glass from her. He downed the rest of the milk in two swallows. "I guess that much will have to do." Putting the glass on the cupboard with one hand, he reached out and grabbed the belt of her robe with the other, pulling her close again.

She looked up at him, her eyes wide and wary. When she spoke, her voice sounded strangled. "Why are you doing this to me?"

Unable to help himself, he loosened her belt and pulled her robe open. She was trembling, and her breasts quivered against the thin cloth of her gown. He wanted to touch her, fondle her, bury his face against her soft, swelling curves. He swallowed a groan and his hands shook with need. Although her skin was warm beneath the thin gown, she shivered, her entire body quivering beneath his touch. Suddenly, he pushed her away. "Get out of here."

She stumbled back, frantically closing her robe. "Why did you have to be here?"

Her voice sounded more panic-filled than angry. Or maybe that was what he chose to hear. "It's fate, brat. Someone has to save you from yourself."

Shaking her head, she moved silently toward the door. "But who's going to save me from you?"

She ran from the room, leaving him standing alone in the dark. Balling his hands into fists, he realized she had a point. Somehow he had to get himself under control. Somehow. Swearing again, he left the kitchen and crossed to the bunkhouse. He had no idea that seeing her again would make him want her so.

His hunger returned. The milk hadn't done its job. Needing to clear his head and cleanse his spirit, he went to the well and drew a pale of water. Without a second thought, he lifted it above his head and poured, drenching himself. It wasn't a permanent solution, but it helped.

❧ Three ❧

Molly had just awakened from a restless sleep when her bedroom door burst open.

"Margaret! You're here! You're finally here!" Nicolette ran to the bed and threw herself on the pink and gray coverlet.

Molly yawned and stretched, then pulled her hair loose from the braid and combed her fingers through the tangled mass. Noting Nicolette's barely leashed energy, she said, "No one deserves to be so cheerful so early in the morning."

Nicolette sat back on the bed and sighed. "And no one deserves to be as beautiful as you are so early in the morning."

"Ha! Such flattery will get you anything you want, you little liar." Molly slid from the bed and stretched again.

"It's not flattery, Margaret. You're so . . . so sensuous. So erotic looking."

"Erotic?" Molly frowned at her. "Now, how would you know about a word like that?"

Nicolette made a moue. "Don't think I haven't heard the way Charles talks about you to his friends."

Molly gave her a stern look. "You shouldn't be eavesdropping." But the eavesdropping didn't bother her nearly as much as the picture of Charles talking with his friends about how "erotic" he thought she was.

Nicolette flopped onto her stomach and supported her chin with her fists. "I couldn't help it. And anyway, I didn't hear that much. Only that you had the voluptuous, erotic body of a goddess and the soul of a frightened virgin."

Molly hid her alarm. "And you didn't find that an unflattering thing for your brother to say about me?"

"Unflattering?" Nicolette bounded off the bed. "Oh, I'm sure he didn't mean it as an insult, Margaret. Don't you have any idea how beautiful you are?"

Molly straightened her bedding. "Beauty isn't very important in the scheme of things, Nicolette."

She waved the words away. "Oh, I know. Beauty is only skin deep, and all that rubbish. But I know you're beautiful inside, too."

Molly had to smile, for the girl knew only those things Molly wanted her to know. The rest she would know—one day. She wondered if Nicolette would still find her "beautiful" when she discovered she had Indian blood.

"C'mon, sleepyhead," Nicolette urged, tugging at Molly's nightgown. "It's time for breakfast."

Molly let herself be pulled toward the bathroom. "Just how long have you been up? You're far too cheerful for me."

Nicolette giggled and gave Molly a tight hug. "I don't think I even slept last night I was so anxious to see you."

The giggle was infectious and sweet, and Molly returned the hug, but she'd never been a giggler. She'd never been a lot of things, and though she used to blame her miseries on her heritage, she'd long since realized that if you blame your parents for your failures, you have to give them credit for your success. She was bound and determined to be a success in spite of what she was: A bastard, a breed, and the product of a savage rape. Her father was a stranger and had never known or cared that she existed. Though Nicolas had always been a father figure to her, there had been times in her youth when she'd craved the love of the man who had sired her.

"Well," she said, tweaking Nicolette's nose as she stepped away, "I'll never get ready if you're here. Why don't you—"

"Oh, please, Margaret. Let me stay. There's so much I have to tell you, and I won't bother you, honest."

Molly gazed at the girl. She was a budding beauty, and today, in a peach colored striped gingham with three drop flounces, she looked like a confection. And she was sweet and unspoiled, a realization that had surprised Molly when she'd seen how Charles doted on her.

"Well, then, why don't you find something for me to wear. There's a light green faille dress hanging in the wardrobe—"

"Oh, no, no," Nicolette interrupted. "That's far too dressy to wear to watch Buck break the horses. Here," she added, pulling out a plain linen shirtwaist and Molly's favorite suede riding skirt. "I have a skirt just like this. It's perfect."

Molly eyed Nicolette's gay apparel with a jaundiced eye, but said nothing. Charles was right; Nicolette had a crush on someone, or she wouldn't be dressed for suitors. Smiling to herself, she went into the bathroom. She would have liked to spend some time at the piano with Nicolette this morning, but obviously that would have to wait.

She wasn't looking forward to the morning Nicolette had planned for her. Being forced to watch Buck break horses wasn't high on her list of things to do. And force it would be, for the last thing she wanted to do was watch a grown man grin with glee as he was tossed around on top of a wild horse.

She paused. *Tossed around on a wild horse. Maybe* off *a wild horse . . .* A slightly evil grin creased her mouth. Maybe it would be entertaining, after all.

After a lively breakfast, Charles went on an errand and Nicolette dragged Molly to the corral. Most of the hands milled around, covertly watching them as they waited for the action to begin.

A big, burly man with a heavy growth of black stubble stepped out of the barn. Cruelly muscled, he carried himself like a bully. He pulled his hat down over his eyes and shoved a cigar to the corner of his mouth. He carried a whip.

She shuddered as Nicolette leaned toward her. "That's the foreman, Mr. Poteet," she whispered. "Isn't he scary?"

Molly nodded. Indeed, he was scary, but he dipped his head in her direction, and she hesitantly answered with a polite nod.

Her gaze left him when she caught a glimpse of Buck as he came around the corner of the barn, pulling on a pair of gloves. His hat was pulled down over his eyes, too. But a different feeling entirely washed over her when she looked at him. His shoulders, so wide and hard, drew her gaze. Their accidental meeting in the kitchen the night before swam in front of her. Little shivers of excitement danced along her arms in spite of her efforts to pretend the tryst hadn't phased her.

"Oh," Nicolette whispered, squeezing Molly's arm. "Here comes Buck."

Molly bit the insides of her cheeks to avoid making a face or a wry comment. Nicolette's voice held the awe one saves for *real* heroes. Like Mr. Cooper's Pathfinder.

"Buck! Halooo, Buck!" Nicolette gave him an enthusiastic wave.

He tipped his Stetson in their direction and took his place at the corral.

"Did you see? He winked at me." She clutched her hands over her heart.

Molly gave her a stern look. Buck hadn't winked, Nicolette had just imagined it. And it was a dangerous fantasy —especially for Buck, who might possibly have a completely innocent role in Nicolette's adolescent daydreams.

"Hey, *amigo*," one of the hands shouted. "Let her ride."

Buck dropped onto the horse's back and shoved his boots into the stirrups. The brown stallion twisted sideways and bucked, kicking his hind feet straight out behind him.

Molly's hands went to her mouth and she pressed hard, trying to keep her feelings under control. The stallion was strong and beautiful, and attacked the ground beneath him, belligerently trying to rid himself of the weight on his back.

She stared at Buck. It wasn't entertaining at all. She actually feared for him. But he was graceful and supple as he rode the beast. His thighs, as tightly muscled as iron, clamped the stallion's belly while his torso moved with the animal, thrusting hard, then pulling back. Thrusting, pulling back . . . Thrusting, pulling back . . .

A slow heat seeped into Molly's vitals as she watched Buck work. Each thrust of his pelvis sent a wave of current along her nerves and she caught her breath, fighting the feelings that swirled through her.

The animal's sides heaved with exertion, innocently mimicking Molly's own labored breathing. He continued to pitch, turning in circles, kicking his hooves high, trying desperately to unseat the rider, but Buck held firm.

Suddenly the horse stopped, his head lowered and his sides continuing to heave. Buck nudged the stallion. It lifted its head and walked sedately toward the fence. Buck started and stopped the spirited animal several times, indicating he was in control. After a few turns around the corral, he dismounted.

A roar went up from the hands, Spanish and English adulations mixed with the lusty laughter of weak men who attempt to identify with another man's strengths.

"Let me take 'em fer ya, Buck." An old geezer with a grizzled feed bag beard hobbled up, ready to take the reins.

Buck shook his head and took the stallion into the barn himself.

Molly expelled a breath, unaware that she'd been holding it so long she had the beginnings of a headache. She watched Buck disappear into the barn, blatantly eyeing his back beneath the sweat soaked shirt.

"Isn't he wonderful?"

Clearing her throat, she looked at Nicolette. The girl's eyes were shiny and her face glowed. Definitely a girlish crush. "Well," she answered. "He certainly does know horses. But Nicolette," she continued, her voice scolding, "it isn't wise to be so obvious. The man might be dangerous, and anyway, he's far too old for you."

Nicolette's laughter peeled like chimes. "Dangerous? Buck? He's as gentle as a lamb. And how do you know how old he is?"

"I don't know, of course," she lied. "But your brother—"

"Oh, pooh on Charles," she answered around a pout. "Buck is the most wonderful man I've ever met."

Molly swallowed an unladylike snort. "Surely there are boys your age who are exciting and interesting."

Nicolette made a face. "They're just boys. Buck is . . ." She looked at the sky and sighed. "Buck is so handsome and strong."

"He's also a grown man *and* a breed, Nicolette."

"Breed, schmeed." She turned and glared at Molly. "I didn't think you had the same horrible prejudices that Charles has. But then," she added glibly, "I guess that's why he likes you so much. You're such a prude, Margaret. I suppose you never had these feelings when you were my age."

"I'm going to practice," she said crisply, tossing the words over her shoulder. She flounced away and walked toward the house, leaving Molly feeling older than dirt.

Oh, if you only knew. Molly realized that she had never been able to rid herself of those memorable infatuations with Buck. They had always been there, nudging her memory. And now, when she wanted so desperately to be rid of him both in her head and in her heart, he was practically underfoot.

Glancing after Nicolette as she walked daintily toward

the house, Molly felt the urge to go after her and shake some sense into her. But she knew better. It was wiser to discretely bring the problem up with Charles. But not before she talked to Buck. If Buck was deliberately teasing the girl, he was asking for trouble. Charles had told her as much last night. And, she thought, fear skittering up her spine, even if he wasn't, Charles wasn't the type to let a breed affect his sister in any way, good or bad.

She started toward the barn, then stopped. Why did she care what happened to Buck, anyway? Actually, getting him fired was what she'd wanted from the moment she discovered he was working for Charles. She wanted to be rid of him. She wanted him gone.

But her good sense told her to at least warn Buck of possible trouble. Glancing toward the barn, she decided now was as good a time as any to confront him. If anyone overheard, all they would hear would be her chastising Buck for leading Nicolette on. It would sound innocent and sincere.

The sounds of Nicolette attacking a Bach invention on the piano faded as Molly strode purposefully into the barn. The interior was shadowy. Light filtered in from a window high at the point of the roof, the beacon a shaft of dancing particles of dust. An odor of hay and manure reached her nostrils, but it was faint enough to be merely earthy, not pungent. The darkness and the quiet were provocative, titillating.

Her boots made no noise as she moved over the dirt packed floor, past the empty stalls. As she neared the back of the barn, she heard Buck's voice, seductive, raspy, outrageously sexy. And, she thought, her foolish heart bumping, he was only talking to a horse.

She paused when she saw him and rested her shoulder against the rough wooden doorway. He was shirtless, the muscles in his back moving, bunching, releasing as he curried the brown stallion. He still murmured words of confidence with each stroke of the brush. The animal's ears twitched, as if focusing on the sound of Buck's voice. She wondered what it was about him that had changed. Of course, he was seven years older, but that wasn't it. He seemed more contained now, less apt to fly into a rage. He'd always been so angry. At her, at the Whites, at the world. And, more often than not, working hard at getting good and falling down drunk.

She raised her eyebrows. That was it. So far, she hadn't seen him drunk.

"What are you doing here, brat?"

She jumped, his voice startling her. He still hadn't turned. "How did you know it was me?"

He chuckled, and the raspy, tobacco-rough sound made her breath catch in her throat. "I can tell."

"Impossible," she answered, meandering slowly toward him. "You must have glanced over your shoulder."

"Didn't have to. I've always been able to tell when you're around. I could seven years ago, and I can today."

She snorted lightly. "Have you got an extra sensitive nose or something?"

He still hadn't turned around. "When it comes to your scent, I have."

He could smell her? Well, that was an attractive notion, she thought dryly. Even so, an odd heaviness gathered in her pelvis. "That's ridiculous. I've never worn perfume, and I'm not wearing any now."

He stopped brushing, turned and stared at her. His dark eyes smoldered as his gaze raked over her. "It's not perfume I smell, brat."

She wanted desperately to give him a blazing retort, but found it hard to breath, much less talk. All of her energy was centered elsewhere—in dark, warm places that swelled with unwanted desire. Finally, "That . . . that's bull," she whispered. "And . . . and don't call me 'brat.' "

He merely shrugged and put the currycomb on the ledge near the door. He was closer now, and she could smell him as well. The sweat of man and animal, leather, tobacco, hay, and the dark, secretive odor of the back room in the barn. The erotic overlay of all the scents mingling in the electric air between them made her heart bump and her knees weak.

"What are you doing here?" he asked again.

Finally coming to her senses, she pulled herself up straight. "Are you flirting with Nicolette?"

A humorless sound erupted from his throat. "Why in the hell would I flirt with a sixteen-year-old girl?"

Molly swallowed, watching the corded muscle flex in his arm as he braced it against the wall beside her. She followed the hard, vein-threaded lines of his limb until her gaze met the thatch of black hair under his arm. She tried to control a shiver. "She has a crush on you, you know."

"I know," he answered simply, his gaze never wavering. "I liked your hair better last night."

She wanted to move away but didn't . . . or couldn't, as the memory of his hands opening her robe throbbed behind her eyes. "If Charles . . ." she began weakly, then took a deep breath. "If Charles has any reason to believe you're leading the girl on, he'll kill you."

He moved away, turning back to the horse and stroking the animal's shoulder. She felt a foolish sense of loss. "He really will, Buck."

"I can take care of myself."

Anger erupted inside her. She took a step and grabbed his arm, trying to pull him around. "Don't be a fool. You're the one who warned me about Charles's feelings for breeds. You know it's dangerous to play games with him."

With whiplash speed he turned and gripped her shoulders, his gaze burning into hers. "Listen to yourself. What in the hell do you think he'll do to you when he finds out the game you're playing?"

A stab of fear plunged through her, making her dizzy. "It will be different with me," she heard herself say. "He's in love with me."

He swore, the sound oozing disgust. "There's a name for a woman like you, a woman who marries a man just because he's rich enough to give her everything she thinks she wants."

"It's not like that at all," she spat.

"Then tell me you love him."

She gazed up into his face, his features so taut they looked chiseled from stone. Glancing away, she swallowed hard. "I . . . I care for him a great deal. Love will come. I'm going to marry him, Buck. Love will come later. It will. I know it will." Her words sounded limp and weak even to her own ears.

Buck pushed her away and swore. "You don't know him at all. You think he has this simple little prejudice against breeds and Mexicans. Listen to me, brat. He may hire us to work for him. But a woman like you? Hell, once he finds out what you are, he'll treat you like a whore. Nothing else. He'd never allow his legitimate heir to have even a trace of Indian blood."

Molly was stunned by the hatred in Buck's remark. "Charles would never do that to me. He's a gentleman. He's always been the epitome of charm and good manners. And . . . and he loves me, Buck. When I tell him—and I *will* tell him—he won't care." She was certain Charles loved her. And because of that love, she knew she could change him, if she had to.

Looking back at Buck, she saw the hatred simmering in his eyes. It was so strong, she could feel it. "What's he done to you? What in the *world* has he done, to make you hate him so much? Is it because he's a rich white man with everything in the world you want, but can't have?"

He turned back, concentrating on the stallion, but his back muscles tensed, as with anger. "That's your desire, brat, not mine. Not all breeds lust after the white man's world like you do. Unlike you, I've never envied the white man for what he has. I've just hated him for what he is."

The disparaging remark didn't sit well, but she ignored it. "Then, you will stop encouraging Nicolette?"

He turned again and faced her. "Why in the hell do you care? What I do with my life is my business. I don't encourage the girl, but I'm going to be civil. And you," he snarled, suddenly angry, "can stay the devil away from me and my affairs."

As always, the sparks between them erupted into flame.

"You're disgusting. I've warned you, and if you don't care for your life any more than that, why should I?" Her breath came hard, her anger was so intense. "You've been on a path to self-destruction for years. Oh," she said, watching the flare in his eyes, "I *have* been in touch with people at home. I know things about you, Buck. I know that you pickled yourself with whiskey after Honey died, and you probably still do—"

He slammed her against the wall so hard, he nearly knocked the wind out of her. "*Never* assume to know my business, brat. *Never.*"

When she caught her breath, she hissed at him. "I don't give a flying baboon's butt about your business. I came in here with good intentions. I've warned you about your actions with Nicolette. That's all I can do. If you don't want to listen, then you can go to hell."

They stood, nose to nose, like the combative adversaries they'd always been. She could see his pupils dilate, darkening against the circle of gold that rimmed them. She could smell him, feel him, almost taste him.

Suddenly his mouth was on hers, punishing, tormenting, berating. It took her by surprise, took her a moment to respond. Then, when she did, she knew it wasn't right. Buck wasn't the one who should be kissing her, Charles was.

She struggled against him, pinching her lips together, pushing, twisting and shoving to get out of his embrace. He held her tightly, wearing down her resistance as he continued to press himself against her from mouth to knee.

He was hard all over. His bare chest was a solid surface of warm flesh. She reached up, intending to push him away. Yet when she touched his shoulder, she couldn't resist cupping the skin that encapsulated his muscle.

Suddenly, something akin to a juice-filled fruit exploded low in her belly, sending gushes of hot liquid into her pelvis. Her mouth opened beneath his. It was so good. So hot. So tempting. And fires of hell, it felt right. She allowed him to probe her tongue with his, the heat in her nether regions intensifying.

He lifted her slightly and pulled her close, grinding his pelvis against hers, pressing her against him with blatant familiarity, punishing her with his need. Wanting desperately to melt into him, she wrapped one leg around his, bringing his stiffened manhood closer to the source of her own desire.

A throaty chuckle escaped his mouth, triggering an alarm inside her. With all of her energy and willpower, she turned her head away and shoved at his chest.

He glanced down at her, his eyelids heavy. Smirking, he released her slowly. "So, you've—"

On solid ground again, she slapped him hard across the face. "No. Whatever you were going to say, the answer is no."

He touched his cheek, the old scar denting it devilishly as he smiled. "I don't believe you."

"I don't care what you believe. I—"

"I think you've missed our little battles. I think you've been wondering for years what it would actually taste like to have my tongue in your mouth. I think I should have given you a taste years ago, when you begged for it."

Anger and desire made her gulp back a powerful shudder. "As I said before, you can go to hell. I forgot about you the minute I left the vineyard." Taking a deep, shaky breath, she touched the wild tangles of hair that had come loose from her carefully twisted coiffure and marched toward the door. The sound of his husky chuckle followed her as she rushed from the barn.

Fool. Fool. Fool. How many years had she wondered what his kiss would feel like? How many times, in her secret dreams, had she tried to imagine it? She'd told herself it would never be as good as she'd dreamed. As she licked her lips, finding the lingering taste of him on and in her mouth, she knew it wasn't true. The bubble of anger that had festered since the day before, when she realized Buck was going to be a stumbling block to her happiness, burst into full-blown rage.

After the confrontation with Buck, Molly had stormed back to the house and gone immediately to the piano that Nicolette had just left, pounding out the lusty strains of Chopin's "Revolutionary Etude" to release her anger. It was a grand piece for that, for it took so much effort to play, it got rid of most of her hostility.

Even so, by evening, she still hadn't shaken away the feel of Buck's kiss or the sound of his voice, calmly, huskily telling her he could tell she was around just by her scent. Her education with the sensual had virtually ended the moment she was forced into the rigid school for girls. Her imagination hadn't. She wondered if he could truly smell her. Was there really an essence about her that he could sense? She doubted it. Highly. Even so . . . it was a provocative idea, and it had teased her for the rest of the day.

After dinner, as she and Charles waited in the salon for Nicolette to grace them with a small recital, she broached the subject that had been eating at her since morning.

"Charles, I really think Nicolette's infatuation with your ranch hand is out of control."

Charles appeared amused. "If it's just an infatuation, Margaret, why are you so upset? Because he's a breed? Breeds and Mexicans are expendable. I've told you that before."

Molly moved her fingers along the line of a small wrinkle in the skirt of her green faille dress. "Well, ah . . ."

To him, her hesitation must have sounded like an agreement. "Margaret, Margaret," he said, his voice filled with delight. "I knew you thought like I did. You know I'd never let this foolishness go anywhere. Oh, don't get me wrong. Breeds and Mexicans have their place. Personally," he added, taking a sip of his brandy, "I couldn't get along without them. I've already told you that."

"But, Charles, if he—"

"He won't," Charles interrupted, pressing close to her on the sofa. "Besides, I need him too much, and he knows it. I give him far more latitude to do things his own way than anyone else would. He's almost his own boss, so to speak. He's too smart to get himself killed over a woman. Any woman."

"A *woman*? Charles, she's just a girl."

He leaned over and gave her fingers an affectionate squeeze. "And if I find he's trying to encourage her, I'll get rid of him. Maybe I should give him more time off," he mused, leaning back against the sofa. "Obviously he's not spending enough time in Cedarville."

"What's in Cedarville?"

"There's a—" He shook his head. "No, it's not for delicate feminine ears."

Molly almost cursed. "For heaven's sake, Charles, I'm not an eggshell. What does he do in Cedarville?" She watched as his blue eyes flared with desire.

"You don't know? Can't guess?"

She tried to contain her resentment at being treated like a swooning belle. "If I knew, I wouldn't be asking."

"Margaret, really, I don't think it's—"

"What does he do in Cedarville?" she grilled.

He sighed. "If you must know, there's a particular . . . lady," he said, obviously using the word lightly, "he sees on an occasional basis." He gave her a nervous laugh. "Funny, I thought breeds were lusty bas—" He blushed and cleared his throat. "Sorry, I didn't mean to offend you with such talk."

Molly turned away, her face twisting into a frown. So, Buck had a woman in Cedarville. The realization sat heavily on her chest, and it was not a welcome sensation. Suddenly the memory of his kiss whispered inside her, and she bristled.

"He's probably the lusty stud at some brothel." The minute the words were out, she wanted to gobble them back. She felt herself flush.

Charles spun around and stared at her. "Really, Margaret. Where did you learn to talk like that?"

"Oh, Charles," she said, truly flustered, "I'm sorry if that offended you. It's just that . . . that the man is so arrogant and infuriating."

He gave her a strange look. "I had no idea you'd even spoken to him."

"Well . . . well, I haven't, of course. It's just his attitude. He's cocky and . . . and so self-assured . . ."

"Rather a little too sure of himself for a breed, is that what you mean?"

She expelled a huge sigh. "Yes. Exactly. *Far* too sure of himself—for a breed." *Or any other kind of man.*

"Don't worry about Nicolette's crush on Randall." He squeezed her hand again. "I may find him the most talented horseman I've ever hired, but he can still be replaced. In fact," he added, giving her an intent look, "I'll get rid of him tomorrow if it pleases you."

Her heart jumped against her ribs. "What do you mean get rid of him? . . . Fire him?"

Charles sighed, then quickly looked away. "Yes, I suppose, but—"

"But, what?" Molly felt the stab of fear again. "You wouldn't kill him just because Nicolette has a crush on him, would you?"

He looked at her, his eyes filled with a strange humor. "Would that bother you so much?"

"Well, well, certainly not. No, of course not," she answered, trying not to stumble over her words. "But it wouldn't make any sense to kill him, would it? I mean, he doesn't seem to be encouraging Nicolette's advances. He seems . . . he seems completely oblivious to them."

Charles raised his eyebrows. "Then what has you so upset?" He took another sip of brandy. "Sounds like everything's under control."

She sighed. "Even so, I *do* wish she'd quit ogling him. You never know," she added, turning toward him, "when he'll weaken and do something . . . irrational."

Chuckling, Charles leaned over and kissed her cheek. "A man who weakens under the spell of a flighty, flitty, sixteen-year-old girl is a fool. Randall is no fool."

"Perhaps you're right. But still, it could happen."

"And if it happens, I'll deal with it. All right?"

She nodded, wishing she hadn't brought the subject up at all. Oh, her mouth got her into the most awful muddles.

He chuckled. "I think he's an honorable bastard. For a breed, that is."

Molly turned away again so he couldn't see the relief in her eyes. Lord, she wanted to get rid of Buck, but she didn't want him dead.

Just then, Nicolette entered the room and glared at them, obviously aware that she'd been the topic of discussion, and not liking it one little bit. When she sat at the piano and began playing a sweet Schubert melody, Molly could tell, just by the sharp angle of her spine, that Nicolette was piqued.

Charles barely heard Nicolette play. His mind raced with his feelings for Margaret. He'd never seen her so angry, so disgusted before. It excited him. His blood thickened; there was a pleasant, potent tightening in his groin.

He brought his hand up to cover his smile. He'd thought Margaret was pretty, but bland. A bleeding heart, yes, but certainly passionless beneath that voluptuous body. Now he knew differently. He'd seen the heat in her eyes when she'd found fault with Randall. Her hatred of breeds was nearly as intense as his own. He could feel it. And that fed the flames that had simmered like embers since her arrival. He no longer thought of her as frigid, merely sweet and lifeless.

Her beauty and talent had drawn him at first. She would be a prize for any man, and he'd wanted to claim her for his wife. Beautiful things were his weakness. He'd even decided that when they were married, he'd live in a passionless, loveless union. Hell, there were plenty of hot-blooded Mexican whores who could satisfy his lust, and his penchant for the bizarre.

But now, he thought, the strains of Nicolette's music dancing on the fringes of his thoughts, perhaps his and Margaret's marriage bed would be well used, after all.

Feeling the urge for release, he squirmed and shot a sidelong glance at Margaret. Oh, yes, he wanted her, but he couldn't do anything to jeopardize the relationship. Not yet. Not until he had her at his disposal legally.

He looked at the clock on the mantel. There was still time to find that quivering new maid, Maria. Angelita, that coldhearted bitch, had brought the little bird to him, claiming she was her niece, and needed work. He and Angelita had always had an underlying hatred for one another. She was far too aloof for a woman of her station. It would serve her right if she discovered he was fucking the little tart right under her nose. The thought of Maria's face and lusty brown body floated before him. Swallowing repeatedly, he tamped down the urge to leave the salon in the middle of Nicolette's recital and seek out Maria's taut brown thighs and warm bed.

❧ Four ❧

Buck grabbed his Stetson off the hook by the door, left the bunkhouse and strode toward the barn. The morning sun still hadn't cleared the eastern ridge. He hadn't slept worth a damn, tossing and turning all night thinking about Molly. Finally, at four A.M., when several of the hands had gone out to look for cattle stuck in the bogs, he'd drifted off. Then, dammit, he'd even dreamed about her.

In his waking moments, he'd vacillated between saving her from herself and letting her stew in her pot of mishaps. She'd always been a girl of many talents, but as far as he was concerned, her talent for getting into trouble was one of her most accomplished. And Campion was trouble. Buck would be doing her a favor by telling Campion what Molly was up to, instead of waiting until she'd dug herself a hole so deep, Campion would savor shoveling the dirt in over her.

Buck never had understood her. As if she didn't have enough to worry about when Campion discovered *her* heritage, she was trying to keep him from dying because of his. As cock-eyed as her logic was, at least it wasn't selfish.

But these things hadn't been the only things to keep him awake. The kiss had, too. Each time he thought about it he found himself hungering for more, and that only made him angrier. He didn't want to desire her. And he sensed there was something deep inside her that felt the same way. She could protest until the cows come home, but her own response clearly said something else.

She'd made him so mad, he'd been tempted to take her over his knee. He'd never been that angry with a woman before. Never angry enough to strike. Well, that wasn't entirely true. Now that he thought about it, there had been times when she was a teenager that he'd been inches away from whacking her on the butt. Instead, he'd shouted. Swore. Drank . . .

This time, he'd punished her with his mouth. And she'd fought like a hellcat. He'd hoped that would be enough to stop the kiss before it went any further, but it hadn't. She was no longer that fourteen-year-old hellion, and that was the biggest problem of all. Her answering heat was trouble. He would try his damndest to save her from Campion, but she'd been right to question who was going to save her from him. He'd better damn well get his glands under control.

He had to find a way to send her home, where she belonged. She and June needed each other. Molly's single-mindedness about June's care hadn't spilled over into the reality that June wasn't fit to travel halfway across the country just to be with her. Both of their needs were better met back home.

Needs. He shoved his aside, but the memory of Molly struggling against him, then responding so fiercely the day before set him aflame again. Cursing loudly, he lit a cigarette and pulled the smoke deep into his lungs.

Somehow, he had to divorce himself from his feelings for her. Though they'd been born under the same circumstances, they'd never wanted the same things. He couldn't see that ever changing. She wanted a white life; the idea sickened him. But he still couldn't stop thinking about the fact that he'd know her anywhere, even if he were blindfolded. There was something about her scent that had always driven him crazy. And that scared the hell out of him.

As he approached the barn, Sage Reno, the only ranch hand he trusted at the Double Bar C, strolled up to him. Shortly after he'd arrived at the ranch, he'd discovered that Reno was an undercover agent for the army. His mission was the same as the one Buck had chosen for himself: To discover where Campion held the stolen herds, and how he got them out of Texas undetected.

"Miss Campion and her guest want to go into Cedarville. Campion has ordered us to drive shotgun, and as long as we're there, pick up an extra hand to replace Fidel Martinez."

Buck stopped short. "What happened to Fidel?"

"Don't you remember? He got that infection in his foot. Angelita's been doctoring him, but the foot looks pretty bad."

Buck tried not to cringe at the prospect of spending the day with Molly. "And he wants *us* to ride in with them?"

Sage gave him a canny smile. "I take it you have a problem with that."

"Yeah, I've got a problem with that."

"As long as we're going in, will you see Nita?"

Buck swung around, glared at him and swore. "I can't very well go in and not see her."

Sage chuckled. "Hell, no. You'd probably find your head on a plate if you did."

Buck winced at the picture of the possessive Nita discovering he'd been to town and hadn't stopped by. He'd learned years ago that just because she was a whore didn't mean she didn't have fierce pride. And she *had* been a very pleasant, lusty companion. And, of course, there was that other thing . . .

Sage squinted at Buck in the dim morning light. "You look like hell, by the way."

"Didn't sleep," Buck answered, stifling a yawn.

Sage gentled the team. "It wouldn't have anything to do with that little skirmish in the barn yesterday morning, would it?"

Swearing aloud, Buck felt the fine, sharp edges of fear. "That's something I'd rather not advertise. What did you hear?"

Sage waved his worry aside. "I heard enough to know that if Campion ever found out, he'd have both of you pushing up prairie flowers."

"Yeah, well, that's true enough."

Sage climbed onto the buggy seat. "I didn't mean to eavesdrop, but when I heard the two of you arguing, I thought I should stick around. In case someone else happened by and, you know, overheard you."

Buck sagged slightly, relieved. "Thanks. I appreciate that. The brat's going to be the death of me."

Sage chuckled. "Might well be, but I'd hardly call her a brat. She looks pretty grown-up to me." After a moment, he added, "Want to talk about it?"

Buck pulled off his hat and raked his fingers through his hair. "Hell, no. I don't want to *think* about it, much less talk about it."

But think about it he did. As he watched Sage guide the team toward the house, he could almost feel Molly's lips pressed against his. And her womanly curves, with the full breasts and the seductively rounded hips. And her hair . . . that wild, tawny mane of hair . . . Heaving a ragged sigh, he ground out his cigarette and went into the darkened barn.

As he neared the stall where he kept his own horse, he talked softly. The animal's ears perked up, and he whickered in return. Buck stepped into the stall and pulled out an apple, shoving it gently against the animal's muzzle. With uncommon daintiness, the horse lifted the apple into its mouth with its huge teeth. Buck had broken the gray stallion with the black mane and tail a few months before, and had worked with him constantly ever since.

"You've got to have a name, boy." Marveling at the long, strong lines, Buck thought back to the day he'd first seen the animal racing across the plains. "You sounded like thunder. That's what I'll call you. *Tim-me-la'-le*, the Thunder."

He saddled the beast, soothing him with words as the animal again became familiar with the stricture. As he tightened the flank cinch, he swore he could still smell Molly's sweet scent in the early morning air.

Molly wasn't a bit anxious to make the trip back into Cedarville. Picking up supplies the day Charles had come for her would have made sense, but when she'd mentioned it, Charles had simply told her how much Nicolette enjoyed doing it. He didn't want to take away one of her pleasures. Pleasures? Somehow, Molly didn't see riding back up that steep incline a very pleasant activity.

Nicolette, on the other hand, was ecstatic. And Angelita, who usually accompanied her on these ventures, was suffering from a bad back. As Molly had sliced beef for the cowhands' breakfast earlier, Angelita handed her the list of things she needed from the store. At that point, Molly had no choice but to surrender. After cleaning up the breakfast dishes, she went out on the porch to wait for the buggy.

She was relieved when she saw the big stranger driving the team, for she'd been afraid it would be Buck. There wasn't any way she could spend the entire day with him and pretend she didn't know him at all. Just the thought sent her muscles into spasms.

In spite of his size, the man jumped gracefully from the buggy. "Miss Lindquist?"

Molly relaxed further. He seemed pleasant and his smile was charming. She remembered now that she had seen him briefly at breakfast. "Yes. Are you driving us to town?"

He nodded. "Name's Reno, ma'am. Sage Reno."

She smiled her response. "Nicolette will be out shortly."

"Yes, ma'am," he answered politely.

A seed of excitement swelled within her for the first time all morning. Maybe the trip wouldn't be so dreadful after all.

Nicolette burst onto the porch with a wicker basket dangling from her fingers. "Oh, Sage. Good morning. Angelita packed us a lunch. Are you driving the team, or is Buck?"

Molly's stomach dropped. "Buck?"

Nicolette nodded as she swished past Molly and on down the steps. "Buck and Sage will escort us. Charles doesn't trust anyone else."

Molly tried to hide her dismay. "I do wish Charles were accompanying us."

"Oh, he's far too busy. He says it's just as well that we'll be gone all day, because he'll be too busy to even join us for dinner."

Again, Molly tried to hide her feelings of panic, but as Buck rode toward them on his newly broken mount, she uttered a dejected sigh and followed Nicolette into the buggy.

Nicolette chattered incessantly, splitting her conversation between Sage, who sat beside her, and Buck, who rode beside the buggy. Grateful Nicolette was occupied, Molly stayed quiet in the small seat behind the other two, trying hard not to think about the tense day ahead.

They stopped by the river for lunch. Nicolette didn't seem to be aware of how blatantly Buck and Molly ignored one another. She continued to prattle on, and finally when there was a lull in the conversation, Sage Reno took up the slack.

"So," he began, settling his large, well-muscled frame against the trunk of an elm. "I hear you're from California, Miss Lindquist."

Molly gave him a tight smile. "Yes. I'm . . . I've lived there all of my life."

"A city girl?"

She felt a twinge of alarm, and jerked her glance toward Buck. He appeared uninterested in their conversation, but Molly knew better. He was like a snake, hiding in the grass, waiting to attack. "Well, I . . . no. I grew up in a small community north of San Francisco."

"Where they grow grapes, right, Margaret?" Nicolette interjected from her place beside Buck.

"Yes, my . . . family has a vineyard." She glanced at Buck, who now appeared to be asleep, his Stetson pulled down over his eyes. *Asleep, my foot.* He was probably just waiting for an opening so he could strike at her. *Snake*, she thought, glowering at him.

As Reno moved to slather another biscuit with jam, the sun glinted off the bleached cap of his dark brown hair. He continued to study her. "Lucrative business, growing grapes."

Molly lowered her head. "Well, I—"

"Yep," Buck interrupted sarcastically. "She's just a poor little rich girl."

She glared at him, wishing he were struck dumb. "The vineyard provides jobs for many families. As far as I know, everyone who works there shares in the profits. It's hardly the feudal system." She heard Buck's insulting snort, but ignored it.

"How do you like Texas?"

Smiling, she admitted, "I haven't been here long enough to form an opinion."

"She'll have to like it," Nicolette interjected. "She's going to marry Charles."

For some reason, the declaration embarrassed her. "Nicolette, we haven't . . . haven't announced it yet."

"Well, that's just a formality." Nicolette settled back against the tree next to Buck, who ignored the entire conversation.

Reno nodded, giving her a thoughtful look. "Will you miss California, and your family?"

Molly pulled her gaze from Buck's indolent form. She was grateful, at least, that he hadn't found it necessary to take part in the conversation. "I'm sure I will." No need to explain the grittier details, like bringing her mother down to live with her and Charles after the wedding.

"I've been gone from my family for many years," he said.

Molly jumped on the chance to change the subject. "Where is your family, Mr. Reno?"

"Please," he said, wolfing down the last of his biscuit. "Call me Sage. And I'm from Kansas, originally. My wife's aunt is still living back there."

"So, you're married." She leaned forward to show her interest. "Do you and your wife live close to the ranch?"

He coughed and cleared his throat. "Well, actually, I'm a widower, ma'am."

"Oh," Molly said around a sigh. "Oh, I'm sorry."

He smiled, breaking the solemn expression. "I have a daughter, though. She's just turned one."

He was devastatingly handsome when he smiled. In every way, he was far more physically appealing than Buck. Strangely, she wasn't attracted to him. "She must bring you a lot of pleasure. What's her name?"

Sage's face split into a wide grin. "Annie."

"Does . . . does she live with you?"

He nodded. "I have a housekeeper." He chuckled. "A tyrant, really. But I don't know what Annie and I would do without her."

Molly thought about how difficult it must be to raise a child alone. For some inexplicable reason, she thought of Buck's son, Dusty, and wondered why they weren't together. Her thoughts weren't benevolent. Because of the circumstances of her own birth, she found anyone who rejected or neglected a child about as honorable as pond scum.

"I find that very commendable. Sometimes, for whatever reason, men are afraid to get close to their children. It's like they don't want to let down their guard and show any emotion, or weakness. Don't you agree, Mr. Randall?"

Buck lazily adjusted his hat over his eyes. "Unless you have some experience with children, ma'am, I don't think you're qualified to have an opinion. Have a couple of your lily-white kiddies first, then we can talk."

Nicolette turned on them with disgust. "You two have

been circling each other like wary dogs all morning. I want you to be friends. Anyway, Buck, when Molly marries Charles, she'll be around all the time. I guess you don't have to like her, but you might as well get used to seeing her."

Nervous perspiration sprang out between Molly's breasts and on the back of her neck. "I have no idea what you're talking about, Nicolette. I was merely trying to include Mr. Randall in the conversation. We haven't really spoken at all."

Nicolette sighed. "That's just my point. Buck is every bit as nice as Sage, and you talk to Sage like he's an old friend. Honestly, Molly, I didn't want to bring this up, but just because Buck is a breed—"

"Nicolette, please," she said sharply. "Let's just change the subject, shall we?"

Nicolette frowned again and turned away. "Prejudice is so stupid," she huffed under her breath.

Wishing she could evaporate and reappear somewhere else, Molly busied herself cleaning up their lunch. She sneaked a glance at Sage and saw the tiniest smile playing about his lips. Buck, who had risen from his position beneath the tree, looked angry. Nicolette, for the first time all day, held her tongue and didn't speak to Molly for the remainder of the trip into Cedarville.

They arrived in Cedarville shortly after noon. The wind had picked up, dredging the air with the malodorous smell of penned cattle. Sagebrush tumbled down the street ahead of them, coming to rest against the edge of a raised wooden sidewalk. The awnings over the store windows snapped in the breeze. On the platform of the Devries Brothers General Store, two elderly men sat on a bench in front of the windows, safely harbored from the afternoon sun.

Sage turned to Molly. "We've got some business to conduct for Campion. We'll leave you off here, in front of Devries."

Nodding, Molly glanced at Buck, who was looking at something across the street. She followed his gaze—which came to rest at a second story window of the building that housed the saloon.

Her stomach caved in. Framed in the window was a woman, wearing a bright red robe. The woman waved. Molly swung around quickly and looked at Buck. A smile cracked his mouth, and he touched the brim of his hat, returning the gesture.

The collapse of Molly's insides continued, and the words she'd flung at Charles about Buck came back to haunt her: *He's probably the stud at some brothel.* Her heart drummed uncommonly hard against her ribs, and she felt if she never ate again, it would be too soon. Her emotional response stunned her.

Buck nudged his mount toward the saloon. "I'll catch up with you later, Sage."

Sage looked up at the window and chuckled. "Can you finish your business in an hour?"

Buck glanced over his shoulder, first at Sage, then at Molly. A sultry smile spread over his face, heating his eyes, the look piercing Molly like a weapon. "I can't make any promises." Then he was gone. To his whore. *To his whore.*

Drawing in a shaky breath, Molly scolded herself, mincing no words. It was stupid and pointless to feel this way. But damnit all to hell, every fiber of her being shook with fury at the thought of him sleeping with another woman. It was ridiculous. No, more than ridiculous. It was adolescent, foolish and just plain dumb.

She had no claim on him, and what he did shouldn't bother her. It *shouldn't.* She didn't care, remember? She didn't give a flying baboon's butt what he did with his life. She'd said it, and she'd meant it. And she still didn't give a diddly damn what he did. She had Charles. She had one of the richest, most handsome men in Texas. He was everything she'd always dreamed of.

So why, then, did it bother her so very much that Renegade Randall had a whore in Cedarville? She pulled off her gloves, stuffing them into her purse. Her feelings for Buck were a mystery to her, a ridiculous, confusing, paradoxical enigma.

"Where's Buck going?" Nicolette's voice shattered Molly's ugly introspection.

To hell in a hand basket, I hope. Molly stared up at the window again. The woman was gone—and the curtains were pulled. The peculiar nausea spread through her insides, and she forced herself to look away. In doing so, her gaze briefly met Sage's.

He gave her a curious look, then broke contact. "He's . . . he's got some business to attend to."

"Um . . . ladies, just have them stack the supplies outside on the platform." His gaze drifted to the upper story window of the building across the street, then back to Molly. "I'll be back in about an hour."

Trying to ignore the turmoil inside her, and Nicolette's questions about Buck, Molly steered her toward the store.

"Buck has business in the saloon? That's where he went, you know. Into the saloon." Nicolette frowned. "He shouldn't be there, Molly. He used to drink, you know."

They stepped into the general store. The smells of freshly ground coffee and baked bread hung in the air. "I think Mr. Randall is old enough to take care of himself." Molly tried to sound dispassionate. At the moment, she didn't care if the bastard drowned in a vat of whiskey. Actually, she mused wickedly, he'd probably enjoy that.

Pickles. He'd always *hated* sour pickles. She pictured him flailing around in a giant barrel of vinegar brine with a cucumber crammed in his mouth. A vindicated smile creased her lips, making her feel ever so much better.

Nicolette turned toward the door and looked back across the street, her face etched with concern. "You don't understand. Every time we come to Cedarville, he goes into the saloon and *tests* himself. He orders a drink, then sits there and stares at it. One of these days I'm afraid he'll actually drink it."

Molly found the picture very disconcerting. She didn't want to believe he'd become sober, which would make him honorable. "Now, why would he do something like that?"

"He's an alcoholic, Molly," Nicolette chided. "But he hasn't had a drink in over three years."

Surprised, Molly asked, "How do you know this?"

Nicolette gave her an impatient look. "Well, he *does* talk to me now and then, you know. I'm not a child."

The clerk came from behind the counter and walked toward them. Molly gave him an absent smile, handed him Angelita's list and asked that he stack the supplies outside on the platform.

"Nicolette, has he ever told you what he was doing before he hired on at the ranch?"

The girl gave her a curious look. "Why do you care? You don't even like him."

Molly shrugged casually and strolled toward the tiny restaurant area in front of the windows. "Just being nosy, I guess. Never mind, it isn't important."

"Well, if you must know, he was working for some old man who had a small spread up on the edge of the plains. I think his name was Sully, or Scully, or something like that."

Molly took a seat at a round table, making sure she had a clear view of the saloon—and the rooms above it. She didn't understand why she was punishing herself, but she couldn't seem to help it. Like a homing pigeon, her gaze floated to the covered window. Her stomach pitched downward as thoughts of what they were doing lambasted her.

"Why did he quit?" With effort, she pulled her gaze back to Nicolette.

Nicolette took the seat next to her. A young girl hurried to the table and took their drink order. "The old man died, or was killed, I think."

"Mr. Randall told you all this?"

Nicolette shook her head. "Not exactly. Some of it I've gotten from Angelita. He talks to her all the time."

The daughter of the store owner put a cup of coffee down in front of each of them. Molly stared at hers, watching the steam curl into the air and disappear. Nicolette poured cream into hers and stirred it daintily.

Molly had often wondered what Buck had been up to after he'd left California. Once, when she'd returned home to see her mother, she discovered that Buck hadn't been heard from in three years.

"How long did he work with the other rancher?"

"You mean, the old man?" At Molly's nod, Nicolette answered, "I'm not sure. I think he was with him for years, though. Angelita told me that Buck was really a pathetic drunk when the old man took him in. He dried Buck out and treated him like a son. He's the one who taught Buck how to handle horses. I'm really not sure of the details, but I think the old man was killed by some cattle thieves while they were stealing his herd. Buck signed on at the ranch shortly after that. He's been with Charles since the last time I was home, which was last fall."

Molly sipped her coffee, letting everything Nicolette said to her sink in. Again, her glance shifted to the window across the street. Before she began to feel too sorry for him she remembered what he was doing in that room. Drawn curtains in the middle of the day, in a room above a saloon, meant only one thing. It was disgusting and indecent. No one did that sort of thing during the daytime.

As hard as she tried not to think about it, the vivid picture of the woman at the window removing her scarlet dressing gown for Buck thrummed behind her eyes. And that hot, sultry look of Buck's that marked his territory would be focused on someone else. Swiftly turning her gaze away, she sucked in a breath and realized Nicolette must have asked her a question, for the girl was looking at her quizzically.

"What, dear? I'm sorry, I was wool-gathering."

"I said," Nicolette responded patiently, "why do you dislike Buck so much?"

Molly looked down at her hands. "I don't dislike him, Nicolette. I . . . I don't even know him," she lied. Then, she realized it probably wasn't a lie. She hadn't seen him for seven years. It was very possible she didn't actually know him at all.

An hour later, Sage returned to the store with a young man. They loaded the supplies into the back of the buggy.

Nicolette kept looking at Sage's companion. "I wonder who that is," she whispered to Molly.

Molly watched the young man work. She guessed that he was at least twenty, perhaps older. He was a breed, but darker than most she'd met over the years. His cheekbones were high and sharp, his lips finely shaped and his hair straight and black, cropped to just below his ears. Tall and leanly muscled, he carried his height and weight proudly. He had an energy about him that drew admiring gazes. He was a handsome young man. Glancing at Nicolette, who couldn't take her eyes off him, Molly guessed she thought so, too.

Sage entered the store and tipped his hat. "All packed up, ladies."

"Sage," Nicolette asked, her voice pointedly casual, "who was that helping you?"

"Your brother asked that we pick up an extra hand. To replace Fidel."

Nicolette perked up. "He's coming with us to the ranch?"

"Yes, ma'am." Sage glanced across the street, then back at Molly. "Um . . . I think we'll be ready in five or ten minutes."

Molly noted his discomfort. She didn't doubt for a minute that it had to do with Buck, and his lusty male urges. Surely poor Sage felt he had to cover for Buck in front of

her and Nicolette. She snorted softly. Maybe he could fool
Nicolette, but he certainly couldn't fool her. She noticed
that the damned curtains at the window across the street
were still drawn.

Minutes later, Buck sauntered out of the saloon. Again,
Molly inspected the upper story window. A tumble of emotions hurled through her. The curtains were open, and the
woman stood in her brazen red robe, waving down at Buck.
She even blew him a kiss.

Molly wanted to throw up. She glared at Buck's back as
he responded to the whore's farewell. He'd been with her
the whole time. Molly wanted to run at him, screaming
and scratching, demanding to know what he thought he
was doing. It was a ridiculous urge, she knew it, and she
hated herself for it. He had his life to live, and it certainly
didn't include her.

But somehow, she had to get over the stupid possessive
feelings she had for Buck. She knew they were just leftover
feelings from years before, when her youthful daydreams
had centered around the bastard. She swore mildly. She'd
thought she was over them. She had no claim on him, and
Lord knows, she didn't *want* one. She should be happy that
he had someone, even if it *was* a whore.

Feeling old and tired, she slipped on her gloves, picked
up her purse and made her way toward the door. Everything would have been fine and dandy if the bastard hadn't
gone and kissed her in the barn. She'd hated him for that.
And she'd never forgive him. Ever.

Buck had just pulled himself into his saddle when she
and Nicolette went outside. She glanced at Sage, who had
just given Buck one of those foolish "man to man" grins.

"Everything come out all right?" Sage asked.

Buck tossed Molly a casual look, then returned the
smirk. "Couldn't have come out better."

Molly clenched her jaw and hoisted herself into the
backseat of the buggy, purposely refusing Sage's help.
Oooooh, men were such swine.

Sage turned and hailed the young man who had helped him load the buggy. "Hey, Cody!"

The young man loped toward the buggy, a bedroll under his arm.

"Your first job is to protect these two lovely ladies," Sage told him.

The newcomer gave Molly a brief glance, then settled his gaze on Nicolette. A careless, cavalier smile lifted one corner of his handsome mouth. "I think I am going to like this job." His voice was deep and rich—and meant to charm.

Molly sneaked a peek at Nicolette and found that her cheeks were red and her eyes unnaturally bright, although she was purposely staring straight ahead. As Molly settled back in her seat, she felt the first stirrings of fear. Would Sage and Buck warn this new hand about Charles? If they didn't, she was afraid he wasn't going to be on the job for long, and he certainly wouldn't leave of his own free will.

❧ Five ❧

Molly stood at the salon window, gazing out at the distant cliffs. Green-gray clay swirled mutely into the red rock, and the terra-cotta shale was streaked with white gypsum. The massive canyon walls loomed above the valley, standing guard over the gentle swells of earth and water.

Behind her, Nicolette practiced her scales. Molly winced as she struck the sour middle C. Charles had promised that someone would come and tune the piano, but so far, no one had shown up. She was tempted to do it herself.

Nearly a month had passed since their trip into Cedarville. Molly had discovered that Buck and Sage had been gone much of that time, mending fences and checking on some wells on Charles's more distant grazing lands. They had returned just yesterday. Charles, too, had been extraordinarily busy, leaving Molly and Nicolette alone many days and evenings. Not that Molly had seen much of the girl. She'd grown increasingly concerned about Nicolette's comings and goings.

After helping Angelita prepare meals for the hands, which she continued to do against Charles's wishes, Molly spent much of her time in the library, scouring the bookcases for something interesting to read. Hidden behind some volumes of Shakespeare, she'd discovered a real find: A stack of dime novels she'd carefully confiscated and taken to the privacy of her room. Joyously, she'd immersed herself in stories of *Malaesaka, The Indian Wife of the White Hunter*, the blood and thunder tale of *Bess, The Trapper*, whose long black hair was suspiciously Indian-like, but who the author assured was unmistakingly Caucasian. And her favorite, *Hurricane Nell, The Queen of the Saddle and Lasso*.

Molly was oddly appeased that Bess and Nell had ended up in polite society, married to men with names like "Frank" and men who had upstanding occupations, like "Cecil," who was a lawyer from Philadelphia. It gave her foolish hope that all would be well between her and Charles.

Had Charles been home more, Molly suspected that Nicolette would have, too. But she'd discovered the new hand, Cody, and had spent as much time as she dared with him. Naturally, Molly disapproved, especially since she saw flashes of herself in what Nicolette was doing.

Not two nights before, she'd been in the kitchen getting herself a glass of milk when Nicolette had crept in through the kitchen door, unaware that Molly was there. The girl had nearly jumped out of her skin when she'd heard Molly's voice, but Molly hadn't apologized. And with Sage and Buck gone, Molly had no one to commiserate with. She surely didn't dare tell Charles. She'd warned Nicolette so many times that what she was doing was dangerous, but the girl went blithely off, doing as she pleased. It frustrated Molly, and for the first time since she'd left the vineyard, she realized how much misery she'd put everyone else through while she was growing up.

Nicolette's behavior caused Molly even more concern, for one night shortly after they had returned from Cedarville, she had a disturbing dream. It was like no other she'd ever had, for even now, weeks later, she could remember every detail. And it had awakened her with such force, she'd sat bolt upright in bed, heart pounding like she'd run a mile.

In the dream, with the clarity of reality, she had seen Nicolette rush from the house dressed for riding, climb onto her spotted mare and ride toward the caprock. But she hadn't gotten far, for not a half mile from the ranch, she had been overtaken and kidnapped by a band of renegades. Although Molly knew it wasn't real, she couldn't shake the feeling that it was a premonition. She'd thought to mention it to Charles, but felt foolish putting so much emphasis on a dream.

The scales stopped. "I'm tired of practicing."

Molly swung around, startled. "You haven't even been at it for half an hour."

"I don't care," Nicolette said with a pout. "I'm going riding."

The alarm went off in Molly's head. "Oh, Nicolette. I wish you wouldn't."

Nicolette narrowed her gaze. "I finally find someone closer to my own age, and you *still* don't approve. I love you dearly, Margaret, but your prejudice is not a very attractive trait."

"It's not that, Nicolette, really. I . . . it's just that I had this dream . . ."

Nicolette sighed, tapping her foot impatiently. "You're acting like a worried old woman."

Molly surrendered. "You're right, I suppose. I just think you should at least tell your brother what you're doing."

Nicolette uttered a sharp, humorless laugh. "You know perfectly well what would happen if I did." She picked at the pocket of her split riding skirt, the one that resembled Molly's.

Sadly, Molly knew she was right. Cody was not the kind of boy Charles would approve of for his sister. He could perform deeds of heroic proportions, and Charles still wouldn't find him suitable. She briefly pressed her palms against her eyes. "You're not only looking for trouble for yourself, but for Cody as well."

"But you won't tell on me, will you?"

Molly felt her stomach tense. "I hate keeping these secrets, Nicolette, and I don't like being put in the middle of this. I also worry about you. It isn't safe to ride around out there alone."

"Well, I won't be alone. And anyway," Nicolette mumbled petulantly, "we're not doing anything wrong."

"You're seeing the boy behind your brother's back. That's wrong. And you're asking me to keep your secret. That's unfair." Weeks ago, when Nicolette started sneaking out of the house to meet Cody, Molly had realized that dealing with Nicolette was her penance for her own unruly childhood.

Nicolette looked at Molly long and hard. "If you break my confidence, I'll never trust you again." She slid off the piano bench and ran from the room, leaving Molly fretting in her wake.

Molly sat down at the piano and played a furious Bach invention, all the while telling herself she shouldn't keep Nicolette's activities from Charles. If something *did* happen to the girl, Molly would never forgive herself. But somehow, she couldn't break Nicolette's confidence, either.

As Molly played, she thought of her own predicament: Buck Randall and his Cedarville whore. Try as she might, she couldn't stop thinking about it. She'd successfully avoided the bastard since their return, and sincerely hoped the woman had given him the clap.

Her musings returned to Nicolette and Cody. Surely Sage and Buck had warned Cody about Charles's prejudices. Frowning, she stopped playing and stared at the window. Maybe if she could find Sage and tell him what was happening with the two young people, they could prevent a tragedy.

She slid off the bench and left the salon. As she passed Charles's office, she noted the door was closed, a sign that he was in there with someone. Suddenly, she realized that he was always busy with something or someone else. She had no doubt things would stay that way even after they were married. He'd built an empire, and it required most of his time. Strangely, today she was relieved that it was so.

She hurried outside. The bright morning sky shimmered against the striated canyon walls in the distance. The air was warm, the fragrance from Angelita's little flower garden drifted on the wind. Molly glanced around, then strode purposefully toward the barn, hoping to find Sage alone.

Instead, she found Buck, who was repairing a bridle in the tackroom. He glanced up at her briefly, then returned to his work. "Visiting the peasants again?"

She held her tongue, wishing she'd found Sage. "I think you should know that Nicolette has gone off riding with Cody, and this isn't the first time."

He stopped working. "So that's where he's been going."

"Have either you or Sage warned him about flirting with Nicolette?"

He returned to his task. "That's the first thing we did, Molly."

"But . . . but he didn't listen. Why would he be so careless?"

"He's a randy kid. Cocky, too. And Nicolette feels smothered by her brother's possessiveness. Tell me," he said, turning to look at her. "How many times did you take anyone's advice when you were Nicolette's age?"

Molly faltered. Leave it to him to dredge up her unsavory past. "Not often, as you well know." She nervously paced the tiny area. "I suppose it's because I know how stubborn a girl can be, and how much trouble it can cause, that I worry about her. And she's in far greater danger than I ever was."

He looked at her again, his sultry gaze piercing her. "You're sure of that?"

The question, so soft and deadly, sent a vision through her mind of Buck seducing her. It was a fantasy, of course, but it wasn't unpleasant, and that both frightened and angered her. Suddenly, she was sick of the cat-and-mouse game they'd been playing since she arrived. "Let's get this over with, once and for all. I'm tired of all the innuendoes. Let's just clear the air, all right?"

He hung the bridle on a hook, crossed his arms over his chest and smirked at her. It was nearly her undoing, but she forced herself to continue.

"It's true. I threw myself at you when I was fourteen. It was a foolish, careless mistake, but I learned a valuable lesson from it. That's why I can understand what Nicolette is doing, and know why it's so dangerous and so very wrong."

"Why?"

With nervous fingers, she smoothed back her unruly hair. "It's . . . it's just wrong. She'll get into troub—"

"No," he interrupted.

She shook her head. "What do you mean?"

"Why did you throw yourself at me?"

She squirmed, suddenly remembering clearly every time she'd tried to seduce him. "Because I was just a wild, foolish girl. I was unhappy with who I was. I had . . . had all these *feelings,*" she said, clasping her hands over her chest, "that confused me.

"Don't get too smug," she added, noting his interest. "You represented every terrible value any man possessed. I was lucky I got away when I did. Like I said, I was foolish. Stupid. But, you were wilder than I had any hopes of being. I envied that. You had freedom that, as a girl, I couldn't have. Everything you did and everything you were seemed so exciting. You were forbidden fruit. You were a man, not a boy. You were a drunk. You were married. And . . ."

She turned away so she didn't have to look at him. "And you didn't know I was alive." She was quiet for a long time. "I thought the only way to get your attention was to act as wild as you and pretend to hate you with every fiber of my being."

The quiet was deafening. Molly immediately regretted showing such an intimate part of herself to this man who represented the dangerous side of her youth.

He moved behind her, shifting his weight. "We were talking about Nicolette and Cody."

The cold, hard edge to his voice made her stomach hurt, reminding her that fantasies were foolish wastes of time. "Well, you asked me."

"And I heard your answer. Now let's get back to Nicolette and Cody."

Humiliated, she nodded, forcing out a shaky, "Yes."

"I'll talk to him again, as soon as he gets back."

"You'd better pray they come back," she answered, turning to leave. Embarrassed anger surfaced. "Been in to Cedarville to see your little whore lately?" Her voice had the sharp, harsh shrill of a jealous fishwife's.

"What business is that of yours?"

She swung around and glared at him. "Oh, it's no business of mine. I was just hoping she'd given you a good, juicy case of the clap."

He appeared unaffected by her cruel wishes. "I wouldn't get too nasty, if I were you."

"Oh? And just why is that?"

He smirked, the devil made dent delving into his cheek. "I could still tell your sweet Charles exactly what you are."

She stared at him, unwilling to believe he would do it. But then, why wouldn't he? She hadn't exactly ingratiated herself toward him these past weeks. "Do what you have to do. Perhaps it's time Charles knows the truth—about all of us."

Turning briskly away, she left the barn. She hadn't meant to dare Buck to talk with Charles. But his obvious disinterest in her as a teenager had stung, clouding her thinking. She wondered what she'd expected. That he'd confess that he'd always felt something for her, too? Lord, she was such a fool. All of that had been better left unsaid. All of it. And now, she'd as much as begged him to tell Charles her secret.

With new resolve, she marched to the house, vowing to keep a keen eye on Renegade Randall. She would still tell

Charles what she was, but it would be her way—not Buck's. That meant making sure she was around whenever he came in to talk with the man she fully intended to marry.

Sage emerged from the back of the barn. Buck glanced at him, then at the barn door. "Eavesdropping, again?"

Sage gave him an embarrassed smile and threw up his hands helplessly. "I always seem to be in the wrong place at the wrong time. Sorry."

"Forget it," Buck said. "Better you than someone else. You heard everything?"

Sage nodded. "That damned kid is going to get himself killed."

"Yeah, maybe we should have gone with our gut instinct and found someone older."

"Probably," Sage answered. "But Cody was so enthusiastic about everything." He gave Buck a grim smile. "I guess it was catchy."

"And, don't forget he was the only one of the bunch who was sober," Buck tossed back.

Sage was quiet for a moment. "Why didn't you explain to her about Nita?"

Swearing, Buck swung away from him. "It's none of her business."

"You're right. It isn't. But if she knew why—"

"It doesn't matter. She never will," Buck interrupted tersely.

Sage stared at him and finally shrugged. "You're determined to let her think the worst of you, aren't you?"

"Why not? It gives her so much pleasure," he answered, his voice filled with scorn.

"And you've always wanted to give her pleasure, haven't you?"

That anyone, even Sage, suspected how Buck felt about Molly brought him a twinge of fear. In spite of her venomous words and her obvious disgust at what she viewed was his life-style, her safety was the most important thing to him. If anyone else ever got wind that he knew her, she'd be doomed. "Don't insinuate that ever again, my friend."

Sage brought one hand up defensively. "No harm intended." He gave Buck a grim smile. "My life may not be a party, but I sure as hell wouldn't want to be in your dancing shoes."

Giving him a bleak nod, Buck placed the repaired bridle back on the hook with the others and left the barn.

Molly sat at the small mahogany fold-out desk in her room, finishing a letter to her mother. She'd tried to be entertaining, but the words had come hard. The embarrassment of her encounter with Buck a few days before hadn't dissipated. She wondered if Buck had written his family, telling them she was there. She couldn't bring herself to mention his name in her letter. It was easier to omit all of the unpleasantness than try to reveal something she knew she'd have trouble explaining.

The window near her bed was open, the curtains fluttering in the breeze. Now and then she caught a noise from outside, one that was muffled, yet sharp. Curious, she rose from the desk and crossed to the window, trying to pinpoint the sound. She heard it again, and although she couldn't identify it, the frequency and tone alarmed her. It seemed to be coming from the shed behind the barn.

She hurried from her room, rushed down the stairs and ran through the kitchen to the back door. Angelita stood on the stoop, wringing her hands, staring in the direction of the shed. They exchanged brief glances, and Molly saw rage in the housekeeper's eyes.

Lifting her skirts, Molly ran down the steps and over the grass. As she neared the shed, she no longer wondered what the sound was. The vicious, methodical crack of a whip made her pause, but only briefly. She pulled on the door, almost surprised to find it unlocked.

Light flooded the enclosure, freezing Hiram Poteet with his beefy arm raised, ready to flog his victim again.

"You," he growled, turning to face her. "Get the hell outa here."

Her fury nearly blinded her. "Stop hitting him!" she screamed, hurling herself at the ugly overseer. Fearless, she pulled at the whip, which Poteet held tightly, and tried to wrench it away from him.

To her surprise, the overseer lowered his arm, but wouldn't release the whip. "You ain't supposed to be here, missy."

Molly rushed to Cody and though her fingers shook with angry tremors, she was finally able to untie him. Glancing up into his handsome face, she noted the defiant pain that pooled in his eyes.

"Are you all right?" At his terse nod, she examined his injuries. Raised red welts, some coursing blood, crisscrossed his back.

The door of the shed opened again, and she knew the cruel overseer had left. "This has to be taken care of," she said quietly, sitting down beside Cody.

He refused to look at her, but his mutinous profile told her that he'd born similar indignities in his life, and this was nothing new.

Molly helped him stand, but that was all he would allow. They walked to the door. "Sage and Buck warned you about being with Nicolette. They told you how Mr. Campion feels about such things. Is that why you were beaten?"

"Yes," he answered, his voice strong.

She turned and looked at him, trying to understand. "Why did you do it, then?"

His insubordinate grin surprised Molly. "It was worth it."

His tone sent a shiver of alarm through her, for although he'd just been beaten to within an inch of his life, his voice was laced with unabashed arrogance.

Not wanting to imagine what he and Nicolette had been

up to, Molly shoved the door open and held it for him. "Come with me. Angelita will dress your back."

It was an order, and he obeyed.

Hiram Poteet stood, feet spread wide, in front of the desk where Charles was seated, the whip coiled tightly in his fist. His thick neck was slick with sweat and his heavy pelt of black chest hair pushed out over the top of his collar, and through each buttonhole. He was a bull of a man, which was one of the reasons Charles had hired him. He had no scruples. That had been an asset.

"And she just came in and told you to stop?" Charles asked, almost amused.

"I coulda kilt her with one backhanded slap, but I figgered ya didn't want her dead."

Charles rested his elbows on the desk, tenting his fingers in front of him. "I've misjudged her. I didn't think she'd venture from the house, much less give a damn if a breed was whipped."

"Aw, she's a woman. They don't like nothin' to get hurt —leastwise where they can see it."

"You did the right thing, Poteet. But from now on, take care where you do your whipping. Obviously, in a place where my nosy little fiancée won't discover you. Maybe that old line shack out in field number four. As for the kid, we'll find another way to take care of him." He studied his overseer. "About that other thing. You're sure about what you heard?"

"Yeah, I'm sure. I didn't hear much, but I heard what I heard."

"Tell me again." Charles leaned back in his revolving desk chair.

Poteet shifted his weight uncomfortably. "I seen your woman comin' from the barn. When I went by the door, I heard—"

"When was this?" Charles interrupted.

Poteet looked puzzled. "Coupla days ago."

Nodding, Charles said, "Go on."

"Like I said, I heard someone talkin'. He said the kid was gonna get hisself kilt."

"And what made you think they were talking about the new hand?"

Poteet shrugged. "He's the only kid workin' on the place."

"And again, you're sure you saw Nicolette ride off after him the other day?"

"Yessir, I'm sure of that."

His stomach burned with hatred. "Thank you, Mr. Poteet. You can go."

Poteet hesitated at the door. "What we gonna do with the breed?"

"I'll think of something, then I'll let you know."

Long after Poteet had gone, Charles continued to stare at the door, forcing the hate filled bile back down his throat. The thought of the son-of-a-bitch's hands on Nicolette made him want to pull the breed's filthy heart out through his throat. He had to be disposed of. Permanently.

Molly paused before she got to the office door and took a deep breath. She wondered if Charles had found out about Nicolette and Cody, and that's why the boy had been whipped. Something inside her didn't want to let her believe that. She wanted to believe that Mr. Poteet had done the deed alone, without knowledge or approval from Charles.

She had left Cody with Angelita, who hadn't seemed surprised to see the welts, but whose eyes snapped with anger. It was so strange that in this big, beautifully furnished house there was so little warmth or gentleness. It was the first time she'd actually come to terms with her feelings that despite its opulence, it wasn't a home. It was something she certainly wanted to change once she became Charles's wife.

Fully composed, she moved toward the open study door.

Charles was bent over his desk, studying some papers. She rapped lightly.

He looked up and gave her a brief smile. "Please. Come in, Margaret."

Answering his smile with one of her own, she entered the room. "I've hardly seen anything of you, Charles. I've missed our time together."

"Have you, now?"

She felt a bite of apprehension. "Of course I have. But I have to tell you something. I hope you don't get too angry with me."

He sat back in his chair and studied her. "What is it? You know you can tell me anything."

"Charles, I . . . I must tell you that your foreman is a very vicious man."

"Mr. Poteet? Of course he is. That's one of the reasons I hired him."

"You don't mean to tell me you ordered that poor boy's whipping."

He looked at her quizzically. "Whipping?"

"Charles, I discovered Mr. Poteet whipping that new hand you hired. The one we picked up in Cedarville. Mr. Poteet would have killed him if I hadn't stopped him."

Charles picked up his pen and drummed it distractedly against the desktop. "Margaret," he began. "I don't want to scold you. I'm proud of you. All my cowhands respect you, basically because you seem to think Angelita works too hard in the kitchen and needs your help." He continued to drum the pen on the desk. "I never pictured my future wife working as a kitchen maid. You know I don't like it, but I'll try to get used to it. However," he added harshly, sitting forward and resting his elbows on the desk, "what Mr. Poteet does it none of your business. He keeps the men in line, and since most of them are Mexes and breeds, they have to be ridden hard or they'll become lazy and slack off. You aren't to interfere *ever* again with his activities. Is that clear?"

Molly felt no remorse, even though she'd been scolded as if she were a child. She didn't even allow the germ of fear to intercede. "I don't believe whipping someone into submission is a satisfactory method of punishment, Charles. Your Mr. Poteet is a bully, and I don't like him one bit. I know you must keep your men in line, but isn't whipping rather excessive and cruel?"

Charles sat back in his chair again and studied her for a long time. The small pendulum clock above the mantel ticked away the seconds. Suddenly, almost with nonchalance, he said, "Mr. Poteet tells me he saw you coming from the barn a few days ago."

Her heart leaped against her ribs at his change in tactics. "Am I not allowed in the barn, Charles? Would you prefer I sit about the house and do nothing?"

He smiled indulgently and shook his head. "Don't get defensive, my dear. I would just like to know what could possibly have taken you to the barn, that's all." He gave her a jaundiced look. "I'm becoming aware of your many talents, Margaret. I just didn't know milking cows or feeding horses was one of them. Next, I'll discover you've been in the chicken coop and the pigsty."

She felt herself flush, partly with embarrassment and partly with anger at his condescension. "Did your Mr. Poteet accuse me of something?"

He smiled his beautiful smile. "Of course not. But was he wrong? You weren't in the barn?"

"Well, of course I was," she began. "I wanted to make sure the men who hired Cody had told him to stay in line. I . . . I rather like the boy, but he is a cocky sort, and I just . . . just didn't want him getting into trouble."

He continued to study her. "Obviously he already has."

She forced herself to remain calm. "What has he done to deserve a whipping?"

"He's been seeing Nicolette."

Her heart thudded with dread, but she attempted to

show surprise. "Are . . . are you sure? Have you talked to her?"

"I don't have to verify if with her," he answered testily. "She probably wouldn't tell me the truth anyway. No, she was seen riding off with him."

Molly's knees were weak. She sank into the gold damask easy chair beside the desk. "What are you going to do about it?"

He straightened some papers in front of him, then put them into the drawer. "I haven't decided."

Molly leaned toward him. "Charles, don't be too hard on her. She's just a girl, she's young, impetuous—"

"Yes," he interrupted. "She's young. And I will not allow any filthy little breed to—" He stopped, pushed himself away from the desk and crossed to the window. His hands were clenched tightly behind his back.

Molly discovered she was holding her breath. The seed of fear that Buck had sown when she'd arrived had taken root. But still, she forced herself to give Charles the benefit of the doubt. Of course he was concerned for his sister. She was his responsibility. He adored her. He doted on her. He wanted only what was best for her. And Molly, perhaps more than anyone, knew that what was best for Nicolette was *not* a wild, handsome young breed who could charm the claws off a bear.

She stared at her fiancé's back. He was fit, trim and impeccably dressed. He had some very strong prejudices, and a temper that she sensed could explode into violence, if things didn't go his way. Her fear of him grew a little more each day. But she still felt, or perhaps hoped, that if she had to, she could change him.

The kerosene lamp threw flickering shadows into the room. Campion stared across his desk at the surly, unkempt Mexican who heedlessly moved his fingers along the rim of his filthy hat.

"I don't like threats, Che."

"An' we don' like waiting for our money, senor."

Charles drew in a deep breath. "I can't afford to move the cattle now. They're safely hidden, grazing on land where they won't be found. They've been rebranded with the Double Bar C, and I'll decide when they can be moved, not you. You still work for me."

He was reluctant to do any major dealing with the cattle he'd stolen until Nicolette was back in school. And he wasn't even sure he wanted Molly around. She was a damned curious woman, unable to take anything he said at face value. For all he knew, she could stumble onto the stolen herds by accident. He wouldn't put anything past her, not anymore. Oh, he still wanted to marry her. He would just have to teach her to stay in line. She had no place in his business plans.

As for the ratty bunch of thieves who worked for him, they would not intimidate him. Although they claimed to be descendants of the clever, ruthless *Comancheros*, they were little more than filthy, ragged animals who could be disposed of in the wink of an eye.

"We don' like what's happening, Senor Campion. You might force us to do something we don' want to do."

"You aren't paid to like it. You'll wait until I tell you it's safe. That's final. And don't threaten me."

The angry Mexican stood and glared down at him, the lamplight giving him a fierce, ghastly look. Charles knew it was only superficially intimidating. He could outwit the fool in his sleep.

✠ Six ✠

As Molly dug out her tuning tools from her satchel, she realized it had been nearly a week since her meeting with Charles, and his announcement that he'd learned Nicolette was secretly seeing Cody. Molly knew he wouldn't hurt Nicolette, and as much as she wanted to tell Charles it was normal for the girl to have crushes, she, herself, sensed there might be more to this than was healthy. In the meantime, Nicolette had been sent to visit her friend Chelsea, and Cody was recovering from his wounds, which were healing nicely under Angelita's care. But the whole situation was like a song, written up until the last few bars, then stopped. The end hadn't yet been determined.

After dressing in an old, worn gown, Molly dropped her tools into the pockets of her apron and left her room. She couldn't stand to listen to the sour notes of the piano any longer. The tuner Charles had promised her never showed up, and something had to be done.

As she descended the stairs, she saw Charles enter his study. As usual, he was busy. She momentarily faltered, remembering that his foreman had told him she had been in the barn. She hadn't dared go back, had purposely stayed away from Buck and all of the other hands. It wasn't clear to her what, if anything, Charles had discovered about her. He had seemed satisfied with her reasoning and

hadn't really acted any differently toward her. She hoped
and prayed Mr. Poteet hadn't heard her conversation with
Buck. But she could never be sure. Her inability to finally
confront Charles with the truth about herself was making
her a little bit crazy and suspicious of everyone.

Because of the uproar over Cody, Molly was quite certain Charles wasn't focusing his energy on her. But her
own duplicity had begun to haunt her, and she knew if she
didn't tell Charles everything soon, he would find out another way, and she couldn't let that happen.

And Buck . . . Shaking her head, she moved down the
hallway and entered the salon. After removing her tools,
she immediately went to work on the piano. Ah, yes, Buck
. . . She wondered when he would tire of her smart
mouth and tell Charles everything he knew. He'd already
threatened to do it, and there was no reason why he should
keep her secret. Not after the other day, when she'd not
only told him he deserved a disgusting disease, but had
dared him to go ahead and tell Charles and get it over
with.

In her quiet moments, she reflected on many of the
things Buck had said to her. Almost two months before,
he'd told her she was just marrying Charles to maintain a
white life. It wasn't exactly true, because she honestly felt
she was doing it for her mother, and their future. And no,
she didn't love Charles. But she cared for him and admired
him. She had no reason to believe she wouldn't fall in love
with him once they were married. She hoped she did, but if
she didn't, she would make her marriage work anyway.

Yes, Charles had a temper, and she knew he could be
cruel to his help, but he had a lot at stake, and even more
to protect. Even though she knew all of this, she also felt
he would never hurt her. She felt that whatever else happened, he had fallen in love with *her*, therefore it wouldn't
matter to him once he discovered she had a little Indian
blood. And she fully expected to love him back. She just
knew she would fall in love with him . . . any day now.

For the past two years of her life she'd been determined to marry into money. The calculated plan had never bothered her before; it had seemed quite reasonable. Practical. And she certainly wasn't hurting anyone, she was only trying to help care for her mother. Charles wouldn't be hurt. She would always try to keep him first in her life, if— no—*when* they were wed. She would be a good and faithful wife. But she would have to tell him her secret. It was tempting to wait until he was so much in love with her, he wouldn't care. But she knew she couldn't put it off much longer. She was absolutely convinced that if she didn't tell him soon, Buck would.

Buck . . . yes, if there was a problem, *he* was it. He was toying with her now. Dangling his threat in front of her like a carrot on a string. And, as always, she played the part of hungry rabbit to perfection. He was an odious man, that Buck Randall. Now, more than ever, she was determined to tell Charles her secret and prove Buck wrong.

She'd been working for nearly two hours when she heard Buck's voice in the hallway. She stopped, frozen, barely daring to breathe as she tried to hear what he was saying.

Dropping her tuning fork on the carpet, she inched her way toward the door and peeked out into the hall. Empty. But she heard voices coming from the study. She needed to be close when Buck talked to Charles. As close as a tick on a hound's ear. If Buck began to talk, she wanted to be there to tell the story herself.

She tiptoed down the hall to the study and pressed her ear against the door. If she concentrated, she could make out each man's voice, but she still couldn't tell what they were saying.

"You need something, senorita?"

Molly nearly jumped out of her skin. Stumbling backward, she pressed her hand over her heart as Angelita stepped around to face her. Even though she and the housekeeper often worked side by side in the kitchen,

Molly sensed the woman still didn't like her. Angelita was always cool and abrupt with her.

"Well . . . no . . . I . . ." she bumbled foolishly. "I mean, I was just . . ." Oh, *damn*. Nothing she said was going to make any sense.

"I will announce you, Senorita Lindquist," the housekeeper responded, a dangerous smile forming on her mouth.

"Oh, no . . . please, I—"

Before she knew it, Angelita had rapped soundly on the study door, opened it and announced her.

She was trapped.

"Margaret." Smiling, his white teeth gleaming, Charles let his gaze wander slowly over her. "How . . . provincial you look this morning."

As always, Charles looked fastidious. His blond hair was coaxed into perfect waves, his handsome face cleanly shaven, and his shirt pristine, the sleeves sporting long, crisply ironed creases. It was almost as if he repelled dirt. As if dirt wouldn't *dare* touch his immaculate person. It was irritating. Briefly, she wondered how she was going to like living with and being married to a man who paid more attention to his wardrobe than she did to hers.

"I . . . I've been tuning the piano," she answered, in defense of her own disheveled appearance.

Charles chuckled. "But, my dear, I pay someone to do that."

"Well," she answered, trying to shove stray curls back into the confines of her combs, "he hasn't shown up, Charles. I certainly hope you haven't paid him in advance."

"What am I going to do with her, Randall? She works in the kitchen like a servant, now she's become my handyman."

Buck's gaze slid over her like honey down a pole. "Seems to me you have a real find here, Mr. Campion."

Molly stared at him. A black eyebrow was arched over

one eye, and he appeared to control a smirk. She didn't think the man ever smiled. He smirked. He always had.

And just *look* at him, she fumed silently. There was undoubtedly a two-day stubble of beard growing on his face, his shirt was dusty, and his jeans hung so low on his hips she could probably tug them right down his legs—if they weren't so blasted snug.

"I think so, too. Was there something you needed, Margaret?"

Charles's voice interrupted her gaping perusal of Buck's legs. She quickly fabricated a reason for interrupting them. "Ah, two things, Charles. First, when are you leaving on your chores?"

Charles checked the clock on the mantel. "I have some other errands along the way, so I'll leave here around one o'clock." He studied her. "You're sure you don't want to ride along?"

With nervous fingers, she smoothed back her hair. "No. But thank you anyway. There's still more work to do on the piano, and I want to finish the job before dinner."

He shook his head. "And here I thought I was merely getting a wife. At the time, I had no idea you were so . . . so accomplished." He gave her a humor filled smile. "And the other thing?"

"Other thing? Oh. Oh . . . yes. Well, I need a . . . a *stumpferdoodle*." She winced at the sound of the inane word she'd just invented.

"A *what?*"

She waved her arm in a dismissive manner. "Oh, it . . . it's this German tool I use when I'm . . . when I'm raising the damper pedals." It was a stupid thing to say, but because of the dreadful condition of the piano, she was sure Charles didn't know anything about it anyway.

Buck turned away and coughed. Molly knew he was covering a laugh.

"I'm afraid I don't have a . . . a stumpferdoodle lying around, Margaret," Charles answered around a chuckle.

He was humoring her, and though she deserved it, she didn't like it. "Well, it's very much like a simple pliers, Charles. You *do* have a pliers, don't you?"

"Darned if I know. Randall? There must be a pliers out in the shed. Would you mind—"

"Oh, really," she interrupted. "It isn't necessary for him to get them for me. I'm perfectly capable—"

"Oh, I'm beginning to realize that, my dear." He laughed again, obviously pleased with his wit. "But let Mr. Randall get it for you, just the same."

She'd climbed out on a limb and was forced to either back right into the enemy or fall to the ground. "Well, if you insist."

"I insist," he answered, still smiling. "Randall, would you show Miss Lindquist where the tools are? If she's determined to be so blasted resourceful, she might as well know her way around the toolshed."

Buck picked up his Stetson and cleared his throat. "My pleasure, Mr. Campion." He ambled to the door and held it open for her. He gave her a wide-eyed innocent look, but deep in his dark depths, she saw amusement. "Miss Lindquist?"

Molly clenched her teeth, tossed him a look she hoped would melt rock, and sailed through the doorway ahead of him.

It wasn't until they were outside that she dared speak. "Just point me in the right direction. You probably don't know what I'm looking for, anyway."

His low, whiskey-laugh plagued her. "No doubt you're right. I wouldn't know a . . . a stumpferdoodle, is it?"

She gave him a curt nod, acutely aware that he was making fun of her.

"I wouldn't know a stumpferdoodle if it jumped up and bit me on the ass."

"I only wish it had the ability," she snapped, her voice low enough so no one else would overhear.

He continued to chuckle quietly as they crossed the yard toward the barn.

Walking slightly behind him, she muttered, "This isn't the way to the toolshed."

"There's a pair of pliers in the toolbox, which is on the wagon. Since we can't find you a stumpferdoodle, a pair of pliers will have to do, isn't that what you said?"

"Oh, for heaven's sake, Buck. I don't need a pair of pliers, and you know it."

He slowed his steps until she was beside him. Then, touching her elbow lightly, he guided her toward the barn. The skin beneath her sleeve tingled. The shiver traveled to all the newly found places his kiss had probed weeks earlier.

"I know it, and you know it," he answered, his voice low. "But if Campion is watching from the window, you'd better damned well leave the barn with a pair of pliers."

Her heart jumped. He was right, of course.

"Watch your step, brat."

She knew he didn't mean her footing. "I'll watch mine if you'll watch yours."

"Meaning what?" he answered as they stopped at the barn door.

"*Meaning*, I've changed my mind. I don't want you to tell Charles my secret. I'll tell him myself, very soon."

He stepped inside, returning with a toolbox, which he lifted onto a tree stump near the door. "And if I don't believe you?"

She pushed away the feeling of dread. "If you don't believe me, then stick around. I'll make sure you get a front row seat."

He turned, handing her the pliers, his gaze narrowing as he looked at her. "You can count on my being there, brat. I wouldn't miss this for all the money in your beloved fiancé's wall safe."

She pulled her gaze away and blinked furiously. As always, each time she talked with Buck, the germ of fear he'd so deftly planted weeks ago had a spurt of growth. The roots fanned out a little farther beneath the surface of her consciousness. She tried to ignore it. "Why can't you just accept the fact that I'm not afraid, and that he won't care when I tell him?"

"Because I know him better than you do."

As she massaged her neck, she realized that he seemed determined to fight with her. "It's hard work fighting with you all the time. I don't see why we can't get along."

"Oh, we could get along if you weren't so damned stubborn."

Her frustration with him blossomed. "Why is it always my fault? As far as I can see, you're the one who has always been there to upset my plans."

He shoved his hands into his back pockets and stared at her. "As long as you keep thinking of it that way, I guess things will never change."

Her shoulders sagged. He was right. They were on a collision course and both were too stubborn to avoid the crash. "Just try to be happy for me, Buck. Don't spoil it by going to Charles before I have a chance to."

He snorted a laugh. "Is that why you were listening at the door? To see if I was spilling my guts about your silly, shallow plans?"

"I *wasn't.*" Yes, she was, and he knew it. "All right, I was." She gave him a skeptical look. "How do I know I can trust you not to give me away until I'm ready to do it myself?"

"You don't." He gave her an infuriating smirk, turned and walked toward the bunkhouse.

With the pliers clutched in her fist like a weapon, she stared after him, wishing she had the nerve—and the desire—to plunge them into his back.

It had taken her hours to make the piano sound even remotely as it should. She had tools for minor tuning, but this had been beyond that. She'd done the best she could, given the circumstances.

Wiping her hands on a cloth, she strolled to the salon window and gazed outside. Without warning, her pulse raced, sending her fingers to the base of her throat.

Buck was hauling water from the well. She watched him cross easily to the back of the house where Angelita held the kitchen door for him. She beamed as he approached and gave his arm a familiar squeeze as he entered the house.

Molly continued to stare outside, unconsciously waiting for him to leave. So she could . . . watch him? In a way, yes. Oh, not because she wanted to *watch* him, in the carnal sense. No, certainly not. Only because she needed to keep track of him.

He came out, returned to the well and effortlessly brought Angelita two more pails of water. He had such strength. She looked at him, trying to see him as others did. He was tall and well muscled, but not massively so, like Mr. Reno. Buck was sleeker, like a slightly hungry jungle cat.

Back home, Buck, Jason and Nicolas had stood tall over their people. Most of the breeds did. She wondered if other women thought Buck handsome. To her, he was. Maybe she saw something others didn't. Or maybe the type of man he was—rugged, earthy and sexy—just appealed to her. But when she compared him to Charles . . . Well, Charles was handsome, too. Unfortunately, her pulse didn't thrum wildly when Charles entered a room. She truly wished it did.

She tensed at the window as Buck stood by the back door and talked with the housekeeper. Frowning, Molly felt the now familiar bite of jealousy as he threw back his head and laughed at something Angelita said. She wished feelings could be controlled and tamed, like wild horses. She hated this feeling of yearning that hollowed out her stomach every time she saw Buck with someone else.

Buck and Angelita glanced toward the salon window, and Molly jumped backward, embarrassed that they might have seen her standing there.

Staying a few paces back, she craned her neck, trying to see if they were still there. Suddenly, Buck strolled past the window, looked straight at her, tipped his Stetson and gave her that infuriating smirk.

She made a face at him. He and Angelita had been talking about her, she was certain of it. Molly wasn't one to feel insecure about what others said of her, but now, with the muddle she was in, she wouldn't put it past Buck to tell the housekeeper her secret. She felt a sudden jolt of anger. Angelita didn't seem to care much for her in the first place. Buck had no right making it all worse. But surely he wouldn't tell Angelita that he knew her . . . would he?

Biting her lip nervously, she moved slowly from the window—and came face-to-face with Angelita. A quick stab of fear rendered her uncommonly speechless.

"Senorita," Angelita said crisply. "Perhaps you would like some lemonade?"

Molly gave her a calculated look. "Lemonade?"

"Si, after working so hard on the piano."

Pulling in a deep breath, she nodded. "Yes, thank you. That would be nice."

"Would you come into the kitchen, please?"

"The kitchen? Why . . . ?" Shrugging, Molly sighed again. "Why not." She followed the housekeeper into the spacious kitchen and sat at the long table they used to feed the ranch hands. A tall glass of lemonade waited for her. She sipped, unable to enjoy the sweet-tart drink. This wasn't like Angelita. Despite the fact that they'd often worked together, they seldom exchanged pleasantries. She felt a yawning well of suspicion open inside her, but said nothing. It was probably just her conscience, guilty now because of that blasted Buck.

"You are happy here?" The housekeeper worked at the counter, rolling out piecrusts.

"Yes," Molly answered, slowly moving the glass in small circles. "It's a lovely home."

Angelita nodded. "Nicolette, she is happy to have you here."

"I enjoy her company, too." Molly frowned, wondering where this was leading.

"And Senor Campion? You enjoy his company?"

Uh-ooh. She carefully formed her thoughts into words. "I . . . think Mr. Campion is a very nice, generous man. And the staff . . . all of you have been more than kind to me. I couldn't ask for anything more."

"What is your family like, senorita?"

"My . . . my family?" She took a nervous gulp of lemonade.

"*Si.* Your family." Angelita pressed the pie dough into large round tins.

It *seemed* like an innocent question. Molly thought about the years she'd created her own little fantasy world to protect herself and her mother. How easy it had always been to pretend she was the daughter of Swedish immigrants from Oregon. "I . . . have an ordinary family, like everyone else," she managed to say.

Angelita turned and stared at her. "You are not what you pretend to be, senorita."

Molly's heart nearly dropped into her lap. "I beg your pardon?"

With a shake of her head, the housekeeper rattled off what undoubtedly were a few sharply punctuated Spanish epithets. "You pretend to be white. You are not."

Molly swallowed the lemonade that tried to slither back up her throat. *Buck.* How would she know this if Buck hadn't told her? That's what they were laughing about on the back porch. It had to be. The lemonade continued to form acid in her stomach.

"I have no idea what you're talking about," she lied. Oh, she'd get even with that man if . . . if it was the last thing she ever did.

Angelita clucked her tongue. "I think you are asking for trouble, senorita. Senor Campion is not a very generous man."

Molly's stomach hurt and she pushed away the glass of lemonade. She wanted to ask Angelita how she knew, if Buck had told her, but that would be admitting her guilt. She couldn't do that. She wasn't prepared to ask the question, much less receive the answer. Instead, she sullied Buck's character.

"Drunks are liars, Mrs. Alvarez, and if Mr. Randall said something about me, you can't believe him. I've heard he's a drunk."

The housekeeper looked puzzled. "In that, you are mistaken, senorita. I know him well, and he has never been drunk while working here."

Molly stood, angry and defeated, and steadied herself by clutching the back of the chair. If she wasn't careful, she'd fall into a trap of her own making. Angelita Alvarez was a clever opponent, and Molly had almost been exposed. Now she would have to tell Charles the truth, or he might hear it from yet another source. With forced effort, she walked toward the door, amazed that her knees held her.

"You don't have to worry, senorita."

Molly stopped, but said nothing.

"I will not give you away. I will not tell Senor Campion."

Turning, Molly stared at her. There was no reason to trust her. She'd made it clear from the beginning that she barely tolerated Molly's presence.

"I . . . I still don't know what you mean," she answered.

Angelita shrugged. "Whatever you say."

Molly thanked her for the lemonade and left the kitchen, anxious to get away. As she walked through the rest of the house, her anger mushroomed. She had to find Buck. If everything exploded in her face, he was partly to blame for being unable to hold his tongue. But first, she had to make sure Charles had left on his chores.

After checking the study, she quickly took the stairs, then rapped gently on his bedroom door. When she got no answer, she opened the door and peeked inside. The room was lavishly furnished with heavy, dark, cherry wood furniture. The bed, an enormous four-poster, was covered with a bloodred velvet coverlet. Strangely, it was mussed and wrinkled, as though a child had taken to the bed and used it as a trampoline. A petite Mexican girl was attempting to straighten it.

"Maria, isn't it?"

The maid nodded shyly and lowered her gaze, blushing beneath her dusky skin.

"Has . . . Senor Campion gone?"

Maria glanced nervously at the bed. "*Si*, he gone." She rushed quickly past Molly down the stairs. Lord, even the mousy little maids were afraid of him.

Giving the shy girl no further thought, Molly went into her own room, took a quick bath and changed into her split suede riding skirt and a clean linen waist. In too much of a hurry to redo her hair, she brushed it, gathered it at the base of her neck and bound it with a ribbon.

She hurried out of her room and down the stairs, eager to find Buck before her anger dissipated. As she ran across the yard to the stable, she tried to formulate what she would say to him. The only thing she was sure of was her anger.

Jorge, the stable boy, grinned and stood quickly when he saw her coming.

"I must speak with Senor Randall, Jorge."

His grin widened. "Ah, *si*, Buck." He pointed into the distance. Molly saw a shed, and the figure of a man.

"He's out there? That's Buck out there?" She shaded her eyes, able to make out his hard, muscled form even from such a distance. "Can you saddle me a horse, Jorge? A regular saddle, like Miss Nicolette uses, please?"

The boy nodded eagerly, then disappeared into the stable. In a few minutes, he returned with Nicolette's spotted mare.

She thanked him, allowed him to help her into the saddle and sped toward the lone figure, her anger growing. When she reached Buck, she didn't rein in the horse until she was almost on top of him. Even so, he hadn't moved or flinched.

Surprisingly, *his* face was like a thundercloud. "What in the hell are you doing here?"

She flung herself off her mount and lunged at him, furiously swinging her fists at his chest and shoulders. "You *bastard!*"

He gripped her wrists, pushed her away, then turned toward the shack. "Of course I am. So are you. I thought we'd settled that years ago."

"Don't turn away from me, you . . . you disgusting, dirt-eating worm." She grabbed his arm and held on tightly.

"Dammit, Molly. What's the matter with you? What if Campion sees us out here together?"

"Oh," she yelled. "A lot *you* care."

He swore again. "What are you talking about?"

"Thanks to you, he'll undoubtedly know before I even have a chance to tell him."

"What do you mean?" His black satanic brows were suddenly shoved down over his eyes.

She doubled up her fist again and punched him in the stomach. He barely flinched. "Innocence doesn't become you, you . . . you weasel. I knew I couldn't trust you. I just *knew* it."

Suddenly he grabbed both of her arms. "Will you shut up? Do you want to bring every hand on the ranch running?"

She tried to twist free, all the while burning him with a look of hatred. "You told Angelita about me."

"I what?"

She twisted again, but to no avail. "Oh, don't play dumb. She *knows*, and you told her."

Buck glanced around, dragged her toward the shack and shoved her inside. The interior was dusty and smelled of stale smoke.

"Now start again, and dammit, don't shout. I'm not deaf." He still gripped her arm.

Sucking in a breath, she said, "Angelita *invited* me into the kitchen for a glass of lemonade. She was about as subtle as a black widow beckoning a fly to her web. She tried to get me to tell her about my family, about my background. She was fishing for something."

"How do you know that?"

Molly snorted. "How do I know? Because, you bastard, I saw you talking and laughing with her just moments before. Did it give you pleasure to tell her what a fool you think I am? Did it?"

He took off his Stetson and tossed it aside. "It may come as a surprise to you, but you aren't the only topic of conversation around here, brat."

"Oh, don't give me that. Why don't you just admit you told her and get it over with?"

His study of her was probing. "What did she say, exactly?"

"She . . . she said I wasn't . . . wasn't white."

He snorted softly. "Well, you're not."

"And you told her."

Turning away, he crossed to the small window and glanced outside. "Would you believe me if I told you I didn't?"

"Not if you were on your deathbed, which," she answered fiercely, "I just might thoroughly enjoy."

He turned from the window and stared down at her, his lids dangerously hooded. "Why are you such a shrew?"

The question caught her off guard. She struggled with it briefly. "I wouldn't be if it weren't for you."

"So, I've made your life miserable, is that it?"

"Yes." He always had. Always. She turned away so he couldn't see her. She felt dangerously close to tears. She hadn't cried tears of self-pity in years, and she wasn't about to start now.

"Has it ever occurred to you that you are your own worst enemy?"

"What does that mean?" She stared at the door, trying to separate herself from her topsy-turvy feelings.

"If you didn't make life so hard for yourself, you'd have a much easier time coping with it."

She snorted. "When did you get so philosophical?"

"Oh, you'd be surprised, brat."

She rounded on him. "You've *got* to stop calling me that. You might slip one day and say it around—others." She felt her anger waning, and as hard as she tried, she couldn't fire it up again.

He came to her and ran his hands up and down her arms. His touch was familiar, physically tender yet emotionally painful. There was a softness in his eyes that she'd never seen before. Without conscious thought, she reached up and pressed her finger against the scar on his cheek. His eyes darkened.

He gripped her harder and pushed her toward the door. "Get out of here."

The threat was meaningless. She refused to move. She had an urgent need to be kissed, again. Her lips parted, felt dry, so she licked them, bathing them with moisture.

He swore, low and profoundly, before he dragged her against him and lowered his head to touch her mouth with his.

Boldly, she allowed her tongue to meet his, and the kiss deepened briefly. Groaning, he pulled away, moving the tip of his tongue over her lips, inside her mouth, over her teeth. She shuddered, answering with her own, touching, probing, circling until he clamped his mouth over hers again.

His hands framed her face, and she feared he might push

her away, so she pitched forward, pressing herself against him, feeling the heat of his passion, which matched her own.

Suddenly, he broke the kiss and shoved her away. "I said, get out of here."

She was more bewildered by her need than his anger. It wasn't what she wanted. Of course it wasn't. Desire and passion were empty words, describing vague, empty feelings. Feelings that didn't last. Feelings that were far best buried deep inside. Oh, kissing Buck had felt good. Better than good. But that didn't matter. Allowing her feelings to surface now would ruin all of her plans with Charles. He was right to push her away.

With a firm hand, he guided her toward the door. "Dammit, this should never have happened. *Never*. I want you to forget about it. Forget, do you hear me? And don't come looking for me again. We have nothing to talk about. I won't tell Campion your precious little secret. If you want to tell him, go right ahead. I hope to hell it all works out for you. Now, go. Have your white life. Live it up. Enjoy it. You have my blessing. Just remember one thing, brat," he added with deathly quiet. "You are what you are, and all the money in the world won't change it."

Suddenly his anger filtered through her thoughts. Her feet and her head felt like stone. She couldn't move, could no longer think. Confusion reigned inside her.

Buck shoved her outside and slammed the door. Wincing against the sound, she stood there alone, her bewilderment and confusion growing. All of her adult life she'd known what she wanted. It did no good to admit to the world you were an Indian if you looked white. Whites were accepted. Whites were hired for the good jobs. Whites weren't discriminated against. Why, then, did all of her facts suddenly sound so shallow and wrong?

And even though her head still told her she wanted Charles, her heart wanted Buck. She couldn't ignore it, and she didn't understand it. Everything Buck had just said to her should have been exactly what she wanted to hear. He wouldn't tell Charles. She could live her white life and tell him in her own sweet time. She *wanted* Charles. She wanted the security Charles could give her. She ached for everything he had, and now it looked like she might have it.

So, why did she feel such a sense of loss? She stumbled to the mare and, with great effort, pulled herself into the saddle. *Ride.* She'd ride. It always helped clear her head. Gently kicking her mount, she urged the animal into a lope then a gallop.

The wind hit her face, forcing her tears over her cheeks and into her hair. Somewhere, deep in her soul, she wondered if she really knew what she wanted at all.

Blinded by the wind and her confusion, she didn't notice the riders approaching until they were directly beside her. Startled, she pulled on the reins. A cloth was clamped over her face, and she felt herself falling. . . .

🌣 Seven 🌣

Buck returned to the ranch, cursing himself for being so hard on Molly. He couldn't just let her go off and marry Campion, in spite of what he'd told her. She might be determined to go through with her plans, but she had no idea how shattered she'd be once Campion learned what she really was. Buck could predict Campion's response. The bastard wanted Molly, and he'd find a way to have her without marrying her.

Even though Sage was aware of how dangerous Campion was, he didn't know what Buck did. He didn't know that it was Campion's men who had killed Buck's old friend, Scully. The poor old fellow had been murdered for a meager one hundred head of cattle. If Buck lived to be ninety, he'd never forget finding the old man's frail body slumped over the table, riddled with bullets. And if it was the last thing he did, he'd prove Campion was the ringleader for all of the stolen herds in Texas.

Buck had to vindicate himself for not being there to save the man who had saved him. Even that wouldn't have been an even trade.

As he left the barn, Jorge ran up to him, leading Nicolette's mare.

"Miss Lindquist is back from her ride, I see."

The boy's eyes were large, and he looked puzzled. "No,

senor. She not on the horse." He handed Buck a piece of paper. "This pushed under the saddle."

Buck opened the note and scanned it. Terror seized his heart. *Senor Campion, we warn you. Now we take your sister.* Molly had been riding Nicolette's mare.

"Hurry to the house and get Senor Campion." He watched the boy run off, then let his gaze return to the paper. *We warn you,* he read again. When Campion came outside, Buck jogged over and handed him the note.

Frowning, Campion read it. "They must have mistaken Molly for Nicolette."

They? Buck mused. Campion hadn't even asked who could have done such a thing. It was as if he already knew.

"She went riding on Nicolette's mare? Alone?" Campion dove his fingers through his hair. "Dammit, she knows better than to go off by herself."

Buck knew it was his fault, but he could hardly confess. "I'll go after her."

Campion nodded, seeming preoccupied. "Yes. Yes, you go after her, Randall. Take what you need."

Buck left him standing on the grass near the house, gazing into the distance. He tried to interpret Campion's odd reaction. This was something he obviously hadn't expected, yet wasn't surprised to discover. Hell, Buck didn't trust the bastard, but he didn't have time to analyze him, either. The kidnappers' trail was growing cold.

Molly awakened slowly. She felt groggy and nauseated. Groaning against her discomfort, she lifted her head slowly, then let it fall back again. It ached, pounded. She swallowed the urge to retch. And her arms . . . Had she slept on them? They were numb. She couldn't move them. But it was odd . . . they seemed to be behind her, not under her.

Confused, she opened her eyes. They teared, her headache was so severe. She was suddenly filled with fear.

Where was she? An unfamiliar arch of daylight angrily probed her sensitive eyes, and the light blurred before her.

She tried to get up. She couldn't move. With the panic of one confined against one's will, she tugged frantically, suddenly realizing that she was bound, hand and foot. Sucking in hysterical gulps of air, she looked around her. *Stay calm.* She forced herself to take a few deep, well-measured breaths. All right, she thought, finally gaining control. She was in a cave. And for the moment, she was alone. But she knew that probably wouldn't last, for she heard voices outside, not far away.

Without thinking, she attempted to bring her hand up to ease her pounding head. A sharp pain shot up her arm and into her neck, and she slumped back against the wall. What had happened? She didn't remember anything after leaving Buck and riding off in tears. Except . . . the vague, sketchy memory of riders and a foul-smelling cloth being pressed against her nose. The smell still lingering in her nostrils. Yes, she shuddered, she remembered that.

Glancing down, she discovered she was dressed only in her camisole and her drawers. A brown heap in the corner resembled her split riding skirt, but she couldn't see her linen blouse anywhere. Her boots were by the cave opening.

She attempted to shove herself into a more comfortable position, biting back the pain that shot through her hip as it scraped against a rock. She tried to move her hands, desperate to feel something. They could just as well have been wooden stumps.

She drooped against the wall, pulling in great gulps of air to relieve her nausea. Who had done this to her? Her active imagination moved into high gear, and she imagined herself the victim of the worst kinds of torture. Oh, *damn.* She should have known better than to ride off alone. Had she not been so foolishly bawling over Buck, she'd have had more sense. The hills were full of thugs and renegades. She'd scolded Nicolette repeatedly about riding off by herself. Too bad she hadn't had the sense to heed her own warnings.

Suddenly the cave opening darkened, and someone entered. Startled, Molly slowly eased herself back against the wall. She sagged with relief when she discovered her "visitor" was a woman.

She stood before Molly, her bare feet planted wide and her hands on her ample hips. It took Molly only a moment to discover that the woman was wearing her blouse, but she had it unbuttoned halfway down the front, exposing a deep, full cleavage. Her brown skin showed through the eyelet design at the bosom, and she'd rolled the sleeves up to her elbows. Her skirt was full, similar to that which Molly had seen the Mexican women wear in Cedarville.

As the woman moved toward her, Molly could tell that except for the blouse, she was filthy, covered with the reddish dust that seemed to coat everything. No doubt her skirt had once been colorful. Now, it was torn in several places, and so soiled it was difficult to tell if it had ever been any specific colors at all. There was a fringed shawl tied around her waist.

That it was a woman and not a man who stood before her gave Molly courage. "My hands are numb. You've tied them too tight."

The woman didn't move. Molly wasn't sure she understood English. Probing her own meager Spanish vocabulary, she finally said, *"La mano . . . doler."*

"What kind of stupid Spanish is that? Speak English."

"Then you heard me the first time," she repeated tersely. "My hands are numb; I can't feel them."

The woman sashayed toward Molly, her fists still on her hips. "You will ask nicely. *Por favor.* Please."

Molly glared up at her, refusing to be intimidated. That was a mistake. She was rewarded with a kick in the stomach.

Gasping for breath, Molly tried to double over to protect herself, but she had no sense of balance without the use of her hands. She fell to the side, still unable to catch her breath. She struggled quietly, hoping she wouldn't get kicked again.

"I said, you will ask nicely. You will say 'please.' "

Battling for breath, Molly nodded and finally pushed out a strained, "Please."

The woman grabbed Molly's hip, rolled her onto her stomach, and untied her wrists. Her cheek was pressed into the dirt, and dust clung to the soft, moist area on the inner sides of her lips. She tried to spit out the grit, but her mouth was too dry. Although her hands were untied, her limbs were still numb and her arms flopped to her sides. Slowly she rolled to one side and hoisted herself up on one elbow. With effort, she brought her other wrist up to wipe the dust and dirt from her mouth. Tingling pain, like shards of glass or needles beneath her skin, began as the blood flow returned to her fingers and hands.

She stared up at her captor. "My feet?"

The woman kicked Molly again, this time hitting the lower edge of her ribs. The pain was excruciating, cutting into her ribs, across her chest and up into her neck. Molly groaned, but bit back a cry. "P-please," she murmured.

The woman sniggered. "No. Just your hands." She picked up Molly's stockings, first one, then the other, sliding them up over her feet and calves, rolling them into a knot above her knee.

Next, she took the riding boots and ran her fingers over the soft leather. "Nice," she said around a sly grin. "I think they are mine now." She easily pulled them on and strutted back and forth in front of her. "Look good, *si?*"

Molly didn't respond, but out of the corner of her eye, she glanced at her split riding skirt, which was now a rumpled heap in the corner.

As if reading her mind, the woman crossed to the corner and picked up the skirt. Giving Molly a slow, evil grin, she unfastened her own filthy skirt, letting it fall to the ground. She wore no underwear. She stepped into the riding skirt, grunting and wiggling as she tried to maneuver it up over her ample hips. When she could get it no higher, she spewed an angry curse and shoved it down her legs, finally kicking it away.

"Stupid way to make a skirt, anyway." She picked it up again and inspected it. "What the hell good are these?" She pulled at the wide leggings. "Too hard for your man to get at you and, you know," she said with a whorish smile, moving her hips around suggestively. "What word you use?"

Molly refused to play along. "I have no idea what you mean."

The woman tossed the riding skirt aside and stepped into her own. "Ah, sure," she said, pulling her skirt up over her hips. "You know. Skirt like that too much trouble when you want to play stallion and mare."

Molly didn't show any response, and that seemed to anger the woman.

"Maybe white bitches are too cold to play," she snarled, jabbing Molly's thigh with the toe of her newly stolen boot.

Molly flinched but didn't cry out.

"You a tough one," the woman said, examining her new boots.

Molly decided she was grateful they hadn't stripped her naked, grateful they probably found underwear unnecessary, and certainly cumbersome. Feeling was returning to her hands and fingers, and she gingerly moved herself back against the wall. "Water . . . please."

Her captor crossed to the other side of the cave, picked up a canteen and tossed it at Molly. It fell in her lap, and as she struggled to uncap it, she sensed that if she spilled it, she would get no more. She drank, small sips that she knew would stay on her queasy stomach. She even swallowed the sand that had clung to her lips. Her hands trembled, and she almost dropped the canteen, but she willed herself to hold it tightly.

After she'd finished, she clumsily recapped it and put it on the ground beside her. The woman stood nearby and continued to watch her.

Rubbing her wrists to improve her circulation, Molly asked, "Who are you?" Outside the cave, she heard raucous laughter and loud voices.

"You don't have to know who I am."

"What am I doing here, then? Can you answer that?"

The woman scratched the pendulous breasts that strained against the linen blouse. They moved around beneath the fabric like puppies in a sack. She crossed to the cave opening and quickly peered outside. "Che will tell you what he wants you to know. He comes now."

She stepped to the side as the man entered. He turned and abruptly pulled the woman into his arms, fondling her lecherously. Molly looked away.

The man said something to the woman in Spanish, and they both looked at Molly and laughed lewdly, undoubtedly at her expense. He then swatted the woman on the behind, and she left the cave.

As he moved toward her, Molly had the urge to scurry farther into the cave wall, but she'd gone as far as she could go. The man was dirty and dusty. And as he got closer, his malodorous smell gagged her. When he was mere inches from her, she felt a fresh jolt of fear, for she recognized him. "You," she said in a shaky whisper. "You work at the ranch."

"Si." His filthy, arrogant gaze raked her.

"Charles will kill you for this."

He just grinned, showing wide gaping spaces where his teeth had rotted away. He reached out and fingered the snarled curl that hung over her shoulder. Molly swallowed a shudder and tried not to cringe.

"So, they bring me the wrong woman."

She frowned. *Wrong woman?*

He settled himself on the ground in front of her, squatting to reveal the split seam in his crotch. Like the woman earlier, he wore no underwear. Again, Molly looked away.

He laughed, seeming pleased that she'd noticed. "Si, they bring me the wrong woman," he said, his grin never wavering. "It don't matter. One white bitch is as good as another."

Molly had a deep, visceral feeling that she didn't want to know what he meant.

He put his hand on her calf and moved it slowly to the back of her knee. Fear careened inside her, she jerked herself away and pulled her legs up so that her weight was on her knees.

Laughing, he grabbed her ankles and yanked them out from under her. Her hands were still weak and wouldn't support her weight, and she fell backward, hitting her head against the wall. She saw a brief splash of stars.

"So white. So *clean.* Nice white legs," he mumbled around a grin, moving his hand higher on her leg.

"Wh-what do you want with me?" Because her skin had begun to crawl beneath his touch, she was afraid she already knew.

He continued to grin and stroke her leg. "Oh, I want many things, senorita. Maybe . . . maybe I want *you.*" He groped her breast, pinching her nipple.

She sucked in a painful breath but didn't cry out. She knew he was looking for even a flicker of fear from her, but she wouldn't give the animal that satisfaction. "Who did your men think I was?"

He leaned back on his heels and studied her. "You wear her clothes and ride her horse. They think you are her."

A finger of fear danced along her spine. *Nicolette.* His men had mistaken her for Nicolette. Why would anyone want to kidnap her? For a multitude of obvious reasons, Molly was grateful she'd been taken instead. Suddenly she remembered her dream, the one in which Nicolette had been kidnapped, and she knew now that it hadn't been a dream at all, but a premonition. Not a warning to Nicolette, but a warning to her. But why, she wondered again, had they wanted to kidnap Nicolette in the first place?

His hand moved up to touch her breast again, and Molly pushed it away with her wrist. He caught it and squeezed, pressing hard against the delicate bones. Suddenly a shaft of pain shot through her wrist, and she cried out. Black dots danced before her eyes, and her whole body was filled with pain. When he released her wrist, she pressed her lips together against the burning, unable to stop the tears of agony that coursed down her cheeks. She carefully cradled her painful wrist with her other hand.

"Do you know what we like to do with white women?"

Her heart pounded in her ears and her wrist throbbed, sending more pain into her chest, intensifying her nausea. Never had she felt pain like this. She refused to meet his gaze lest he see her agony and her fear. Instead, she studied the ground, seeing nothing, feeling only the throbbing at the base of her arm.

Abruptly, he gripped her chin. "You look at me when I talk to you!"

Hate tumbled over her fear and her pain. She suddenly found it easy to look at him, for the more she saw his ugly, filthy face, the deeper her hatred grew.

"We like to strip the white women naked and tie them up outside in the sun." He touched the skin on the inside of her calf and an involuntary shudder raced through her. "Whites are so . . . white, you know? The sun burns them to a pretty shade of red. Like the red rock in the canyon walls, or the hot red of the sun as it sets behind the mountains." He continued to touch her. "Then, they blister. Pretty, white blisters that ooze pus. Soon, the insects find them and they feed, sucking on the liquid and laying eggs in the sores."

The picture caused her stomach to heave, but she swallowed repeatedly, trying to gather strength. "Does burning women and seeing them suffer make you feel like a big man?"

He laughed, the stench from his rotting teeth laving over her like spoiled meat. "No, not so much as other things. I think," he said, getting to his feet and massaging his groin, "that I should show you what makes me a *big* man."

Molly was suddenly afraid she'd gone too far. She tensed, feeling new fear when he crossed to the cave opening and shouted.

A moment later, the woman who had kicked her and stolen her clothes stepped inside.

"Blanca," he said seductively, "why don't we show the little white bitch what she can look forward to?"

Blanca snorted a laugh, flung her long, greasy hair from her eyes and lifted her skirt. Her naked hips gyrated seductively. The man fiddled with the front of his trousers, pushed the woman onto the ground, and entered her quickly. They copulated in front of Molly, grunting and groaning like animals.

She closed her eyes, refusing to watch, focusing instead on the pain in her wrist. It was broken, she was almost certain of it.

The woman cried out and the man's lusty groan followed. What they were doing was meant to shock and scare her. It was working. She had no doubt that she would be raped—over and over again, by every man in the camp. Her only consolation was that it was she who would suffer the atrocities and not Nicolette.

✸ Eight ✸

The *llano estacado*. The staked plains. Aching, treeless miles of vast high flatlands covered with tough buffalo grass. A place where men and horses have disappeared, never to be seen again. A place so flat and huge and void of texture and shape, that it could drive a man mad, especially if there was no sun to guide him across it. It was an ocean of grass. A prairie of emptiness. It was the perfect place to hide, yet there didn't appear to be any hiding places at all.

Buck sat astride Thunder and scanned the horizon. It told him nothing; there was nothing to tell. All he knew was that his only desire had been to protect Molly, and now, she was out there somewhere, suffering because of him. He just hoped he'd get to her in time, because he wasn't sure what the kidnappers would do once they discovered they had the wrong woman.

Thunder capered and danced, anxious to get moving. Buck nudged him, and they headed toward the eastern edge of the grassland, where the world dropped away to a yawning abyss.

Cooking smells awakened Molly. She opened her tired eyes, once again aware of the painful throb at her wrist. The woman, Blanca, had wrapped it for her the day after it had happened, but the pain was still excruciating. She was surprised she could sleep at all. She'd fought it every night, trying to catch naps during the day in hopes of keeping her wits about her. The pain helped. It gave her reason to survive the nightmare. Somehow, she wanted to get even.

The dusky light outside the cave proclaimed sundown, and she knew the horrors of the night weren't far behind. She would have thought that one day might blend into another, preventing her from counting the days since her capture. That hadn't happened. She remembered every moment of the long, swelling deadness of time. She was acutely aware that her fourth night in this hell was fast approaching, and she saw no end to the pain, discomfort and humiliation she'd already experienced at their hands. She was grateful for one thing: She hadn't been raped. She didn't know why, for they'd had plenty of opportunities. Perhaps it would come to that. Perhaps. Drawing in a shaky breath, she prayed that she could survive until Charles sent help.

The night before, staked out on the ground like a splayed hide, she had sensed someone at the cave entrance watching her. She'd kept her eyes closed, hoping, praying they would go away. They hadn't. Whoever had been there had stepped inside, moved closer to her and ran his hands over her naked flesh. Her stomach, heart and soul had quivered, she had bit the insides of her cheeks until she'd tasted blood, and held her breath until she thought she might faint. She had expected the worst, as the hand moved over her breasts and pinched her nipples. Then he'd touched the inner surface of her thighs and her privates, open and defenseless because of her forced spread-eagle position on the ground.

Suddenly, to her immense relief, someone else had entered the cave and pulled the man away, scolding him in rapid Spanish. Perhaps it was merely a short-lived reprieve for an inevitable act, but she quietly wept with relief just the same, grateful the humiliation would be put off for another day.

Afterward, she had lain in the darkness, unable to move or cover herself and imagined that if she told them she was not white, they would release her. When she came to her senses and realized it would probably make no difference, she began to think of other things. Anything to keep herself awake and focused. Anything to keep herself from thinking about her degradation and pain.

Strangely, it wasn't Charles's face that loomed before her in her fantasies. It was Buck's, further affixing the notion that she was truly going mad. Each time she dreamed up a situation for herself and Charles, Buck's features, lean and hard, replaced the softer, prettier features of her fiancé. But when she was awake and clearheaded, she knew the first thing she had to do after she was rescued—and she firmly held onto the belief that she would be rescued. She had to make peace with herself, bury her fears and tell Charles everything.

The long, endless nights had given her plenty of time to consider her situation. She admitted to herself that her attraction to Buck was not just a remnant from her past, but a full-blown reality of the present. But it didn't matter. He wasn't husband material. At least, not the kind of husband she'd always dreamed of having.

Now, as darkness approached, she thought of the unbearable night ahead of her. Having almost grown accustomed to the pain in her wrist, she suddenly became aware of the throbbing in her ankles. At first she'd been surprised that they hadn't kept her bound during the day. Then she realized that even if she tried to escape, she had no shoes. They'd thought of everything. She glanced down, wincing at the sight of the raw flesh around her ankles.

For whatever reason, she was allowed to move freely around the cave during the day, wearing her underclothes. At night, when her defenses were down and her fears exaggerated anyway, she was tied to four posts driven into the crumbly rock, and stripped of all her clothing—and her dignity. Her captors were masters of applied humiliation.

The day before, she had gotten as far as the cave opening, just to see what was outside. The cave was merely a hollow in the canyon wall, and the drop to the canyon floor was enough to keep her from escaping, even if she'd tried. She could only visualize the layout of the camp. The men and their women weren't far away; at times she could hear them clearly. And smell their cooking.

Her mouth watered as the cooking smells intensified. They would feed her—snickering as she ate, telling her in graphic words and gestures just what she was eating. Perhaps tonight it would be rattlesnake, rat, scorpion or dog. They hoped to disgust her so much she would refuse, then they could still say they had tried to feed her. But she wouldn't refuse. As long as the food was even remotely palatable, she would eat. She needed her strength. For what, she wasn't sure. But when Charles showed up to rescue her, she knew she had to be strong.

To take the edge off her hunger, she reached for her canteen, jiggling it to make sure there was still some water left. With shaky fingers, she opened it and took a small sip. It was hardly enough to coat her tongue, much less swallow, but it would have to do. She was never sure that she would get any more.

Shimmering stars filled the night sky. There was a half-moon overhead, giving him enough light to see, without being seen.

Buck slid quietly from his mount and tethered him near the horses that belonged to Molly's captors. Silently, he crept around the perimeter of the camp, refilling his canteens and absconding with some packable food. He carried the items back to Thunder and shoved them into his saddlebags. After stuffing his knife and a narrow leather thong inside his shirt, and shoving the metal stake into his belt loop, he slung the coiled rope over his shoulder and quietly made his way toward the cliffs. He'd studied the camp before sundown and sensed that Molly was being kept in a small cave dug into the canyon wall, for one of the camp whores had gone in with a bowl of food at supper time.

Just above the cave and to the left, he drove the stake into the ground and attached the rope to it. He shinnied down onto the narrow ledge on the opposite side of the cave from the camp. Keeping his back against the face of the cliff, he moved along the narrow ledge, stopping occasionally to listen for sounds. There were none other than the normal, eerie songs of night birds and scurrying animals. Moving to the cliff opening, he stepped inside. A low fire burned in the corner, throwing a soft, dull light over the interior of the cave.

He bit back a vile curse when he saw what they'd done to her. He'd never be able to describe the fierce emotions that exploded inside him. Flat on her back, spread-eagle on the ground, she was either asleep or unconscious. Her wrists and ankles were staked to the floor of the cave with leather bindings. And she was naked, every inch of her sweet, flawless flesh coated with dusty red dirt.

He swallowed the bile of his anger and left the cave the way he'd come, then proceeded to the camp. The guard dozed against a rock, his rifle resting on his lap. Taking a deep breath, Buck strode to him, lifted the rifle off his lap and kicked his legs.

The guard grunted and stumbled to his feet.

"What kind of camp is this?" Buck roared, poking the sluggish guard with the rifle. His noise brought other men running. He pointed the rifle in their direction, recognizing Che among them.

"What's this about, *mi amigo*?" Che stuffed his shirt into his pants.

Buck gave him a look of disdain. "Exactly my question. What in the hell kind of operation is this? Your stupid guard was sleeping so soundly I could have put a bullet through his balls."

Che looked at Buck suspiciously, then let his gaze flit nervously about the campsite. "Why didn't you then?"

Buck kept the rifle aimed at Che. "I didn't come up here to kill your men. You have Campion's woman, right?"

Che scratched the scraggly hair that grew on his chin. "What business is that of yours, senor?"

Buck gave him a dark smirk. "Don't you see what you're doing?"

"No, senor, why don't you tell me," Che snarled.

Buck sighed, pretending scorn. He had no proof of what he was about to say, but his gut told him he and Sage were right about Campion's dealings. And Molly's abduction and the note that accompanied it made him sure the Mexicans were getting itchy to move the stolen cattle. "You're putting the focus on yourselves, you fools. Do you want to get caught kidnapping?"

Che finally appeared to be in control. "What do you know about it, senor?"

Buck forced a languid chuckle. "Campion has a reason for lying low. Can't you see that? By taking his woman, you've drawn attention to yourselves."

Che narrowed his gaze at him. "You're working for Senor Campion, too?"

Buck almost smiled. "If I weren't, how would I know what you're up to?"

Che shook his head. "No. We know what we're doing. We don't need your help."

Buck shrugged expansively. "Have it your way, Che. But I think you should know that the sheriff's making noises, poking his nose into places neither you nor Campion want him to. Not only that, rumor has it someone from the army has infiltrated the ranch." He gave each of them a suspicious stare. "How do I know it isn't one of you?"

There was an uncomfortable rumbling among the men. Che shouted at them to shut up. He gave Buck an insolent glare. "How do we know it isn't *you?*"

Buck raised his eyes skyward, as if begging some higher being to forgive them their stupidity. "If it were me, don't you think I'd have turned the whole pack of you in by now?" He swore, shaking his head in disbelief. "Tell you what," he said after a minute. "Let's drink to Campion, his clever, diabolical mind, and his scheme to get all of us rich."

Che snorted a laugh, then gave Buck a hard, calculated look. "Senor Buck, you never drink. I seen you at the whorehouse in Cedarville, pouring good whiskey back into the bottle. And you never join us when we celebrate."

Buck shrugged again. "Hell, one little drink won't hurt. I want to prove to you I'm on your side, *mi amigo*." He watched as Che's face lit up. Buck could read the man like a map. He knew exactly what Che was thinking. *Let's get the half-breed drunk*.

"*Si*. Come," he ordered. "Drink our whiskey."

Buck wagged his finger at him. "No need. I have my own," he said.

"You carry whiskey?" Che was incredulous.

"Every cowman who knows his job carries whiskey, Che."

"*Si*, I know. But you—"

"It's in my saddlebag. I'll get it."

"Hector," Che ordered, giving Buck a sly grin. "Go with our friend here. Make sure he only gets whiskey from his bag."

Buck shrugged, strode to his saddlebag and pulled out the flask of whiskey he always used for snake and scorpion bites. Hector grabbed it from him, opened it and took a swig. He raised his gaze to Buck's face and grinned.

"It's whiskey," he shouted back over his shoulder.

Buck took the flask from him and followed him back to camp, shoring up his resistance. He hadn't taken so much as a sip in three years. But now he must, to prove he was on their side.

The Mexicans settled around the fire and passed the bottle among them. Buck took an occasional sip from his flask, setting his mind against the sweet first rush that whiskey had always given him—and he'd always anticipated.

Che belched and sighed. "So, Senor Buck. You think we are making a mistake by holding the woman."

Buck wiped his mouth with the back of his hand and pretended to have trouble focusing. "The boss doesn't like threats, Che. You ought to know that."

"You think if we let you take the woman back, he'll forget about it?"

With a casual shrug, Buck leaned back on one arm. "He doesn't want the woman hurt, Che. You've already bungled the job by taking her."

Che studied him. "All right. This is my plan. You," he said, pointing the bottle at Buck, "will take her back."

Buck squelched a huge rush of relief. "If that's what you want," he said casually.

A ghastly, rotten-toothed grin split Che's lips. "Oh, it is what I want, *mi amigo*. The only thing is," he added, his expression guarded, "I don't know if I really trust you."

Buck put the flask to his lips and kept it there for a long while, yet allowing only a small trickle of whiskey to enter his mouth. He pulled it away and forced a belch. "What do I have to do to prove I'm on your side?" *You stupid asshole.*

Che scratched his crotch, then wiped his face on the back of his shirtsleeve. "I think . . . I think you will take the woman."

A cool surge of panic broke into Buck's face. He pretended ignorance. "I already said I would take her back to—"

"No, no, fool," Che said with a lecherous laugh. "You will mount her. Here. And we will watch."

Showing his anger, he spat indignantly into the fire, sending a sizzle of smoke into the night sky. "Buck Randall doesn't perform in front of anybody."

"But, senor, if you do not, then I won't believe you," Che answered silkily. "Those are my terms."

Buck studied Che's expression. Damn those Mexicans. They could act stupid and ignorant, but beneath it all, they were sly and crafty. He'd be a fool to underestimate them.

He took a swig of whiskey, more than he'd planned to. He fought the pleasure it gave him. "I have no trouble screwing the bitch," he said, hoping he sounded convincing. "But I've already seen what you've done to her." He pumped out his chest. "You've got her staked out like an animal hide." He leered at Che. "I like my women to have a little bit of fight in them."

Che grinned his rotten-toothed grin. "Si. I know what you mean." He leaned toward Buck conspiratorially. "Let her bite and scratch a little, so you can slap her around, eh?"

Buck nearly smashed in Che's few remaining teeth. "Exactly," he answered, his jaw so tight he could hardly speak.

"Hector! Release the woman."

"Another thing," Buck added. "I want the woman blindfolded. And I repeat, no one will watch." He stood, giving Che a hard stare.

Che snickered. "Blindfolded? Si, so she will not recognize you." He pulled a grimace and shook his head. "But maybe she thinks it is one of us. I don't like that, mi amigo."

Buck forced himself to smile. "Those are my terms, mi amigo," he said, trying to keep the scorn from his voice. "And, I repeat, no one will watch."

Che frowned. "Then, how will we know you do it, senor?"

"You'll just have to listen, and use your friggin' imagination," Buck growled, fast losing patience.

Che looked at his men, pulled in a deep breath, then gazed back at Buck, his foul grin returning. "Make it nice and loud," he said with a lewd smirk. "My men, they do not have much imagination."

Buck held back an audible sigh of relief. Pretending a confidence he didn't have, he capped the whiskey flask and followed Che to the cave.

* * *

Molly swallowed her panic as Hector stood over her, ogling her like he always did. Cringing inwardly, she held his gaze, although she felt her body betray her as deep inside, she began to shake.

He squatted down beside her and moved his hands over her breasts, tweaking the nipples so hard she gasped.

She squeezed her eyes shut. This was it. They'd waited long enough. It would be Hector. Bile burned her mouth, and she swallowed, feeling the burn in her throat. His big, dirty hand traveled down her stomach and over her mound, pausing there. If she were being eaten alive by ants, she couldn't possibly feel any worse.

She twisted against her bindings and screamed, refusing to go quietly.

Suddenly someone shouted Hector's name from outside the cave. He spewed something in guttural Spanish, then proceeded to untie her bindings.

Puzzled, Molly watched him free her. When he'd finished, not caring why, she quickly scooted to the back of the cave, cowering there like caged prey. She wasn't prepared for what he did next. With an evil laugh, he went to the entrance of the cave, gave her an offensive once-over, then left.

She sagged against the wall. So, it wouldn't be Hector after all. The thought should have brought her some relief, but it didn't. Her teeth clattered with fear as she clumsily stepped into her filthy, dusty drawers. Something was happening. She'd never been untied during the night before. She hadn't realized how comfortable she'd become with the procedure. At first she'd been frightened, then, when nights went by and nothing happened, she'd begun to relax, accepting it as routine.

But now . . . Shuddering wildly, she tried to tie the strings of her drawers together, but her broken wrist was useless, and her other hand was still numb from the bindings. She glanced up at the cave entry, and her heart plunged, leaving a cold emptiness in her chest as Blanca and the other camp whore stepped inside.

"Blanca. What . . . what's happening?"

Before there was time for an answer, the other whore held Molly's arms behind her back while Blanca tied a bandanna around her head, covering her eyes. Panicked, Molly fought.

She was slapped so hard across the face, she stumbled backward, against the other woman. She fought for breath, then began breathing so rapidly she felt dizzy. Suddenly, she remembered with clarity Che telling her all of the ways they had of torturing white women. Hell and damnation, she wasn't going without a fight.

She kicked backward violently, feeling avenged when the whore shouted and cursed at her. Suddenly hard, firm hands were on her shoulders, and she was being pressed back, toward the ground. Her arms were free, but her injured wrist throbbed. She tried to fend off her attacker with her good arm, pounding, punching and scratching.

Her fingernails found his face, and she dug in and pulled down the length of his cheek. He cursed at her, throwing his leg over her to hold her down and pinning both arms over her head.

"No!" She bucked against him, kicking at him with her bare feet as he pressed his long, hard body on top of her.

She felt his hand at the waist of her drawers and he tugged, tearing the fabric away. She screamed, pummeling his back with her heels. He came closer; she could feel moisture from his breath on her cheek. With as much force as she could muster, she spit at him.

His mouth was at her ear; she could feel his hot, vile breath. "Goddammit it, brat," he whispered, "I'm trying to save your worthless life."

She tried to catch her breath, gasping wildly. *Buck?* For a moment, she stopped fighting as relief cascaded over her.

"What . . . what are you doing?"

"I said, I'm trying to save your life. Now fight me, and *scream*."

She fought, but only part of it was an act. She couldn't see, and confusion tumbled over her fear. Everything seemed strange and unreal. "Get off me! *Get off*."

"I'm not going to hurt you, brat. But scream. Give me one damn, good scream!"

She took a lungful of air and screamed her rage, fighting against him as though he were her worst enemy. She was so mad at him for scaring her to death, she wanted to kill him.

His mouth was at her ear again. "I'm going to get you out of here. Now, dammit, whether you want to or not, *do what I say*. Do you understand me?"

She boiled with fury, but her good sense forced her to nod in agreement.

"I'm going to leave you for just a minute," he whispered. "But you can't take off the blindfold. Pretend you've fainted. You've got to make it look like I've raped you."

She panted beneath him, then suddenly tensed when he reached down and pulled off her drawers. "Wh—"

"Shhh," he hissed against her ear.

Then she sensed he was gone. Every nerve and muscle in her body screamed to pull off the blindfold and crawl into her drawers again, but she waited, winded from the fight and her fear. It wasn't long before she heard someone enter. She moaned, stirring on the ground, pretending to come around. Her blindfold was removed, and Blanca stood over her.

"You are leaving," she said tersely. She tossed Molly's camisole and split skirt at her. "The man waits to take you back."

Molly lowered her gaze, biting the insides of her cheeks to keep from saying anything at all.

Blanca watched her dress. "You are not curious about who takes you back to your man?"

Molly clumsily tied the strings of her drawers together

over the torn fabric. Her wrist ached, but she refused to ask for help. "What does it matter, as long as I get to leave?"

Blanca snickered, giving her a lusty look. "I should be so lucky to go somewhere with the breed."

Molly pretended ignorance. "Breed?"

"Senor Buck."

"Oh, him," Molly said dully. *Remember what the bastard said.* "Is . . . is he the one who raped me?"

Blanca gave her a wide-eyed innocent look. "Oh, someone rape you? Tsk. We know nothing of that." She clucked her tongue again. "Oh, if that happened, we are truly so sorry, senorita. But we know nothing. Too bad," she said, her mouth curving downward as she shook her head. "It was not one of our men, I can promise you. Be sure to say that to your man, Senor Campion. Our men did not rape you."

Molly gave Blanca a jaundiced look, noticing that she still wore her white linen blouse. Of course, the fabric was no longer distinguishable, and the color a dusty, dirty shade of red, but she would have appreciated having it back, nevertheless.

"May I have my blouse back, Blanca?"

Blanca looked down at her chest and pouted. "No, it's mine now."

"How about my boots? Please?" The thought of traveling back to the ranch barefoot left much to be desired.

"No," Blanca answered lightly. "They are mine now, too."

Frowning, Molly pulled at the top of her camisole in the hopes of hiding some of her bosom. Realizing it was hopeless, she gave up and stepped into her split skirt, fastening it around her waist.

"Here," Blanca said.

Molly looked up, noting that Blanca was untying the flimsy shawl from around her waist. She thrust it at her.

"It is an exchange for what I took. No one calls Blanca a thief."

Molly murmured her thanks, took the shawl, and secured it around her shoulders. As she followed Blanca out into the night, she sucked in a deep breath, grateful to be rescued, but hating her rescuer with renewed vengeance.

♨ Nine ♨

Molly tried to shut out the pain in her wrist as she sat behind Buck, her good arm wrapped around his middle. She knew they probably should have waited for morning, but she was glad that Buck had insisted they leave right away. After all, Che could have changed his mind about letting them go. She was still madder than hell at the way Buck had chosen to rescue her. He didn't know her at all. Had he expected that she'd give him away? Swoon? Get hysterical?

"You could have told me it was you right away, Buck," she groused. "I didn't appreciate being scared out of my wits."

"Hell, how was I to know you'd draw blood?"

"Well, what did you think I'd do? Lie there and let some savage barbarian rape me?"

"You're just damned lucky I convinced them not to watch."

She felt a flash of fear. "What do you mean?"

"What do you think I mean? If they'd insisted on watching, I might have . . . might have . . ."

His unfinished sentence was crystal clear. Good lord, if they'd insisted on watching . . . "Would you . . . Could you have done it?"

"For Christ's sake, Molly. I didn't have to make that decision, now did I?"

She mouthed a prayer of thanks. Heaven, hell and purgatory, she'd really gotten herself into a mess this time. She glanced over his shoulder, into the black night. Although she'd never admit it out loud, she felt safe out on a lonely prairie in the black of night with Buck.

His horse moved slowly over the dark, dry ground. Travel at night was dangerous. She'd learned that even in the daytime, the plains, flat as they were, held treacherous secrets.

Molly was exhausted, but knew she wouldn't sleep. Her wrist still ached unbearably, and she couldn't find a comfortable position for it. Pain shot up her shoulder and into her neck, but she steeled herself against it. It was a small price to pay. She was free! Nothing else mattered. The only thing that rankled was that, once again, Buck Randall was her savior. She should thank him for saving her, but she was still too angry at the way he'd done it.

They rode for hours. She dozed, her head lolling against his back. When she awoke, the sun was just cresting the ridge, and the wind had picked up, pressing against them like a wide blanket of dust. Had they not been so close to the edge, the wind might have been cleaner, for very little dust was swept up on the plains themselves.

Buck handed her a bandanna over his shoulder. She tried to tie it with her good hand and discovered she couldn't. Pressing the scarf over her nose and her mouth, she held it in place with her good hand and leaned into Buck for balance. She felt shrouded in dust. Her eyes and nose were thick with it, and when she attempted to wet her lips, she was rewarded with a mouthful that quickly turned to grit between her teeth.

Sometime during the early morning hours, they had doubled back, and were now pushing against the wind, moving even closer toward the ridge. The horse picked its way through some gnarled mesquite, beyond which was a gully—or arroyo. Buck stopped the animal and dismounted, then lifted Molly down.

"We're going down there," he shouted into the tempest, pointing to the arroyo. "It'll get us out of the wind."

She nodded and followed him, using her good arm and both feet to move down the rocky bank. The rocks bit into the soles of her feet, but she ignored the discomfort, anxious only to get out of the force of the gale. Her broken wrist throbbed incessantly, worse than a toothache. It was almost to the point where the pain had radiated to every part of her body. She ached all over.

As she slid onto the sandy floor of the gully, she felt the wind die away. The ten-foot walls protected them from further buffeting. She stumbled, falling to her knees. She crumpled farther, her knees giving way, sending her flat on her fanny.

Buck squatted beside her and unwrapped her wrist. "Is it broken?" At her nod, he asked, "How bad is it?"

She stared at the black and purple discoloration that encircled her wrist. It looked dead, or like something close to it. "It hurts like bloody hell," she mumbled, allowing him to examine it.

He left her, only to return again with his saddlebags. "How long has it been broken?"

She shivered against the pain, cradling her wrist with her hand. "It happened the day after they took me." She shook her head, unable to remember how many days it had been. Funny, up until now, she'd known almost to the hour.

He swore and dug deep into the bag, pulling out a packet of powder. "I think we should make a splint. We can use some of your underwear, and there ought to be some small pieces of wood around here somewhere."

"You've already made cleaning rags of my drawers," she answered testily. "Now you want to rip up the rest of my underwear?" She looked down at her camisole, which was dirty, and brown with dust. Glancing up, she caught him staring at her bosom. A flood of heat crept into her cheeks. "There must be something else we can use."

He turned away. "I suppose we can use the tail of my shirt. It doesn't matter." He pulled out a tin cup, opened the packet of powder and shook some into the vessel. Then he uncapped a canteen and added water to the powder, swishing it around to dissolve it.

She was so thirsty, her tongue stuck to the roof of her mouth. "Might . . ." She swallowed. "Might I have a little of that?" She took the canteen from him and drank, enough to slake her thirst.

"Here," he said, handing her the cup.

"What is it?"

"Something to dull the pain and help you sleep."

She wanted to argue that she didn't need help, but the prospect of a few hours of blissful, pain-free sleep was too enticing. She drank, then allowed him to help her to his bedroll, which he'd laid out under a small outcropping of rocks.

"Where will you sleep?"

"Don't worry about me. I have a blanket under my saddle."

Compared to what she'd been accustomed to during the past week, the bedroll was as good as a bed. She snuggled into the bedding and gazed up at him, the medicine already working in her empty stomach.

He had pulled out his shirttail and ripped off a length. After rummaging through his saddlebags, he removed a stiff piece of rawhide. "I think this will work as a splint until we get you back to the ranch." He hunkered down beside her and started to rewrap her wrist.

Her pain was already subsiding. Giving him a lazy, sleepy yawn, she mused, "I guess I should thank you for rescuing me, but to be perfectly honest," she added around another yawn, "I'd just as soon split your skull in two."

He shook his head, and a small grin cracked his mouth. "Now you sound like that wild fourteen-year-old kid, high on bad whiskey."

She snorted a little laugh as memories washed over her.

Funny, they seemed almost pleasant now. Suddenly she wasn't angry anymore, but she knew it was because of the medicine. In the morning, she could hate him again. "That sure was bad hooch. Bad, bad, bad."

"And we both drank enough to pickle a barrel of cucumbers," he answered with his infamous smirk.

She laughed again, snorting again. "Maybe if they'd been pickered . . ." The word didn't sound right. "Pickered . . ." She gave him a questioning look.

"Pickled," he offered.

"Right. Well, maybe if cucumbers had been *pickled* in whiskey, you would've liked 'em."

His God-given grin widened; his cow-made dimple deepened. "Maybe."

She truly did hate the man, but she loved the way he looked, even when he didn't smile. All of a sudden, she wondered why she'd always been so angry with him. Her mind was fuzzy, but she knew there was a reason. Nothing made any sense right now. She snuggled deeper into the bedroll. Her arms and legs were loose; it felt as though she were floating. The throb in her wrist was dull, bearable. He finished her splint and continued to watch her.

She tried to touch his cheek, where she'd scratched him, but her arm felt like a noodle. "I didn't like the way you did it, mister, but all things considered, you're a pretty good rescuer. Sorta like Pathfinder, I think. You know Pathfinder?" Her mouth felt all rubbery, so the words sounded odd. She laughed, a sound that strongly resembled a giggle. But that was ridiculous. She'd never giggled a day in her life.

He nodded. "In *The Last of the Mohicans*. But didn't he have another name?"

Her head was swimming, but she was enjoying their conversation so much, she fought sleep. They had rarely ever talked without arguing. She wasn't sure, but she had a feeling that was her fault. "Y'mean Natty Bumppo?"

Chuckling as he stood, he answered, "Now I see why he changed his name."

She loved his laugh. She thought she was laughing, too, but she didn't hear any sound. Sighing deeply, she felt her eyelids grow heavy. As she drifted into sleep, she wondered what he'd said to Che to get him to let her go.

She'd dreamed of water, drinking glass after glass of cool water, but somehow, her thirst was never satisfied. When she awakened, she had a mild headache, her wrist throbbed anew, and she was very, very thirsty. She sat up slowly and groped for the canteen.

"Here," Buck said, handing it to her.

She drank deeply, ignoring the bitter taste. When she'd finished, she wiped her mouth with the back of her hand and carefully handed the canteen back to him. He stopped what he was doing and took it from her.

"What are you working on?"

"I killed a couple of rabbits. I'm just tanning their little hides."

"Why?"

He gave her a brief glance. "You'll see."

She sniffed, suddenly smelling the cooked meat. "Are we having rabbit for breakfast, then?"

"That would make sense, wouldn't it?"

She ignored his sarcasm, noting only how dusty and tired he looked. His face and hair were almost the same color, as was his shirt and his pants. Everything was coated in reddish brown powder. "Do I look as bad as you do?"

He gave her a long, slow perusal, one that made her feel as though he were marking his territory. Obviously she was reading something into it that wasn't there. Even so, it was exciting. And frightening. Suddenly he grinned, breaking the spell. "Worse."

She touched her hair. It was a mass of snarls. "The sad thing is," she answered remorsefully, "I don't even care."

He delved into his saddlebags. "So, it sounds like you've

forgiven me for my crude rescue methods," he said as he pulled out a tin plate.

"I'm grateful you rescued me, I just thought the way you did it was . . . was dumb." She looked at his face, noting the long, reddened scratch marks on his cheek. "I am sorry I scratched you. Do you have something to put on it so it doesn't get infected?"

"I've taken care of it." He took the tin plate to the fire. "Hungry?"

Her stomach growled. "I could eat a bear."

He put a strip of meat and a biscuit on the plate. "This will have to do."

She grabbed it from him and devoured it like a coyote on a carcass.

"I brought you a few things I thought you might need, but if you don't care how you look, I don't suppose you'll want them."

"What? What did you bring me?" she asked eagerly, setting down her empty plate.

He produced her hairbrush, a leather thong to tie back her hair, her toothbrush and tooth powder, and a tin of camphor for her cracked lips.

She fell upon her toothbrush and powder first, cleansing her mouth. "You are a saint," she said around the small mouthful of water which she used for a rinse.

"I'd sure like to get that in writing," he answered dryly.

She tossed him a dry look as she tried to comb out her snarls. It was too much effort. She slumped against a rock.

Buck was watching her. "Want me to do it?"

She gave him a weary nod. "I'd appreciate it. I don't know why I'm so tired."

He moved in back of her, took the brush and began carefully pulling out the snarls. He was so gentle, Molly nearly fell asleep again. She tried not to. "Do you think they'll follow us, even though they said they wouldn't?"

He paused, then he pulled the brush through her hair again. "Maybe, for a while."

She wanted to tell him her captors had mistaken her for Nicolette, and ask him if he knew why anyone would want to kidnap her. But she was so relaxed, she didn't really want to talk anymore. After all, there would be plenty of time for that.

Buck worked the tangles from her lavish hair. Earlier, he'd watched her sleep, finding her beauty almost painful to him. She'd been given such natural bounty, yet even at the ranch, she hadn't seemed to know what to do with it. Against her flimsy camisole, her breasts were lush and full, rounding up over the tops as she slept. Her hair, her curves, her mouth . . .

Everything about her was ripe and ready to be plucked. She was the kind of woman who deserved a slow, careful seduction. A teasing, coaxing, kissing, stroking kind of thing. Her breasts were made to be adored, deluged with tender flicks and deep, sucking kisses. A loving, anxious tongue should lap the insides of her velvet thighs, tease the sweet, swollen nether lips until they were wet and hot, and she was shaking with violent need.

A frenzied bite of jealousy nipped him. Campion didn't deserve her. Buck couldn't imagine Campion having her. The bastard would never appreciate all of the complicated layers that went into knowing Molly. And it hurt him to think that once Campion discovered what she was, he'd have her, and use her like a common whore. He'd destroy her. Buck couldn't let that happen.

She'd truly become a fine woman. If she'd been a beauty to behold at fourteen, she was magnificent and breathtaking now. She'd haunted his thoughts since the day she'd leaped so gracefully into womanhood. Hell, even if June had never pleaded with him to save Molly from herself, he would have anyway. He hadn't been able to stay away from her.

But he didn't dare get too comfortable with his feelings. His attraction to her meant little. Even if he'd wanted to, he couldn't marry her. First of all, she wouldn't have him, which was a blessing for both of them. And his first marriage had been such a miserable failure, he'd vowed never to try again. He wasn't suited for it. Hell, he couldn't even care for his own responsibilities. If he wasn't careful, though, Molly would become an addiction harder to overcome than alcohol.

He swore. Even the *thought* of the word sent a craving to his brain. Che had shoved a bottle into his saddlebag before he left, but once they'd ridden away, he'd tossed it, anxious, yet grateful when he heard the bottle break against a rock. He'd become comfortable with his little flask of emergency whiskey, using it wisely and sparingly when he had to. But a whole bottle, that was a temptation.

Molly leaned back and gave him a lazy, contented smile. For a long, foolish moment, his heart swelled, reveling, wallowing in the glory of that smile. As far back as he could remember, he'd thought about that look. The look she'd given so freely to others. The look that held no anger, no defiance, no suspicion. The look that said, "I'm comfortable. I like being with you, spending time with you. . . . I could love you."

But she couldn't be feeling that way about him. Even so, every once in a while he desperately wanted to imagine what a future with Molly would be like. But hell, the possibility was too terrific and delicious to think about in any depth, for he knew it would never happen. There was no sense in purposely causing himself more pain. There had never been any hope for them. A future for the two of them wasn't like a puzzle, but more like that glass back there, smashed upon a rock. One could be pieced together; the other could not.

In spite of his earlier resolve, he had the urge to bury his face in her hair. God, it would be so much easier if he learned that she really hated him.

☒ Ten ☒

They moved on down the twisting arroyo, Buck leading his mount, which Molly had learned he'd named
Thunder. She sat astride. It was nearly sundown
when they stopped again.

Buck picketed Thunder near a patch of buffalo grass and
mesquite and made a small fire, using cow chips he'd
brought with him. He'd already explained to her that there
probably wasn't enough dry wood on the entire expanse of
the plains to make a decent fire. After drinking some perfectly vile coffee, which she thoroughly enjoyed, they ate
biscuits, jam and rabbit, again.

Molly had little to say. Every time she looked at Buck,
there were twinges of emotion fluttering around in the pit
of her stomach. She'd gone and fallen in love with him,
really in love. Heart-pounding, soul-wrenching love. Oh,
damn, but that would never do. Never. She didn't want
this.

So, he'd become a fine man. A good man. So what? He
still couldn't accept responsibility. And he lived a life she'd
vowed never to return to. A life she'd worked so very hard
to forget. They no longer had anything in common. And
why was she thinking about him, anyway? She had
Charles, and that was what she'd wanted from the beginning. Wasn't it?

She felt his gaze on her, and all of the secret places he'd

awakened weeks ago came to life again. Even though her discomfort was pleasant, she knew she had to stop it.

"Buck, about the kidnappers. They thought . . . they thought they'd taken Nicolette." She looked at him, puzzled. "Why had they wanted to take her in the first place?"

He fed the fire, seeming to struggle with his answer. "Molly, I think it's time you learned exactly who Charles Campion is."

She strained to laugh. "I know perfectly well who he is, Buck."

"No," he argued. "No, you don't."

She felt that germ of doubt take root, its tendrils coiling around her heart. "Then you'd better tell me who *you* think he is. I'm not saying I'll believe you, though."

He leaned against his saddle, but he appeared tense. "I think he's involved in stealing cattle, rebranding them and moving them across the boarder into New Mexico where he sells them as his own."

She was stunned. A wide gaping blackness opened inside her. "I don't believe it. No," she said, shaking her head slowly. "It's nonsense. Do you have any proof? Do you?"

He poked at the fire. "Sage Reno is with the army. He's working undercover, trying to find the proof we need to stop Campion's operation. Molly, it's only a matter of time."

"So . . . so you don't have any proof, yet. How long have you two been looking? Weeks? Months? Don't you think if there had been something to find, you'd have found it by now?" She was desperate to find holes in Buck's story. Desperate. This was so unexpected. She'd never dreamed . . . But it was still possible it wasn't true. She clung to that hope with fierce urgency.

"Why had those men decided to kidnap Nicolette?"

"They're working for Campion in some capacity. Two of them do, anyway."

Yes, she distinctly remembered the one. She gnawed at her lower lip. "I can't imagine Charles hiring any of those men. Maybe they're working against him. Have you given that any thought?"

He snorted softly. "Not really."

Anger swelled within her. "You're so quick to paint Charles black. I doubt that he had anything to do with any of this."

"Dammit, Molly, when Nicolette's horse came back without you, there was a note attached to the saddle. They'd planned to use Nicolette as leverage to get something from Campion. Something he was withholding from them. I don't think discovering they had the wrong woman made any difference."

"Well, if that's true, then why did they let me go?"

He picked up a twig and broke it into tiny bits. "I convinced them that if they wanted something from Campion, they were going about it the wrong way."

"And they believed you," she said, snapping her fingers. "Just like that."

"Not entirely. First I had to introduce a little distrust among them. Then, I had to get into their confidence."

"By doing what?" she grilled. "Taking a lying, cheating, renegade's oath?"

"No," he answered softly. "By raping you."

The words, so softly spoken, might as well have been razor sharp. Suddenly she realized how petty and ungrateful she'd been. "Oh, I . . . I see. And . . . and all of this came about because of something they wanted from Charles?"

"It's true, Molly."

Suddenly, everything Buck had told her about Charles brought other fears to the surface. Even if he hadn't warned her about Charles's prejudices, she'd have discovered them on her own. That much she knew. She thought she could change him. Maybe it was foolish. Wishful thinking. But if that was the only fault Charles had, she still felt they could have a successful marriage.

But this other thing . . . She felt sick to her stomach.

Buck could just as well have punched her. If Charles truly was a crook and a thief, there was nothing she could do. Nothing would change that. She couldn't in all good conscience live with a man who cheated others. It wouldn't matter if he were the richest man in the world and welcomed her half-breed mother with open arms. If he was a cheat and a thief, he was a poor excuse for a man. She could never live with that. Never.

Without speaking, she crawled into the bedroll and turned away from Buck. His wisdom came back to haunt her, preventing her from putting everything out of her mind. Maybe she *had* unconsciously thought she could hide her heritage in order to better herself in the white world. Perhaps her sensible reasoning had only been a tool to convince herself that she wasn't ashamed of it. Not since she'd run from the line shack in tears had she felt such confusion.

"Molly—"

"No." She felt his hand on her arm and tried to brush it off. "Don't touch me, and don't say anything."

He swore. "I'm afraid there's more."

She buried her face in the blanket. Lord, what else could there be? "And I suppose you feel obligated to tell me," she answered bitterly.

"Dammit, I'm not hurting you on purpose. If you still think you're going to go through with this hellish marriage, you have to know everything."

She turned and glared at him. "And why should I believe you?"

"Because . . ." He reached out and stroked her thigh. Shivers raced over her leg, into her pelvis. "Because, I've only wanted what's best for you. You'll just have to believe that."

"I suppose you've somehow convinced yourself of that," she said tightly. "Well, go ahead, but I can't imagine there's anything worse than what you've already told me."

"Believe me," he answered. "It's worse. For you, anyway."

She rolled to her back, stared at the black night sky, and waited.

Buck faced her, resting on his arm. "Not long after Nicolette was born, when Charles was eleven or twelve years old, Sylvie Campion, their mother, was abducted by a band of renegade Indians."

Molly's stomach dropped, and she turned toward him. She didn't say anything; holding her breath, she waited for him to continue.

"Oh, they got her back. The Indians didn't kill her, but she probably wished they had. Charles's old man wasn't a very supportive husband, from what I understand. Although he realized that by marrying her she was his responsibility, he apparently couldn't bring himself to . . . to be intimate with her after that."

She interrupted him, huffing impatiently. "Who told you all of this?"

"Someone who's been at the ranch since Campion's father started it. An eyewitness, if you will. And Angelita was there, too. All right?"

She nodded grudgingly.

"From the moment she was returned to her home, Sylvie was unable to take up any of her old duties. She sat in her room, ignoring her children, crying and rocking, day after week after month. Eventually, she pulled herself together and tried to pick up the pieces of her life. She wasn't a weak woman, but she needed strength and support from her family, which she didn't get.

"About four months after she'd been rescued, she discovered she was going to have a baby. An *Indian* baby. A filthy little half-breed that she knew her husband would kill. In her state of mind, she wasn't even sure he wouldn't kill her, too. She'd wanted to secretly get rid of it before he found out.

"Unfortunately for her, she confided in the wrong person. Old man Campion *did* discover her condition and found a doctor who was only too happy to rid the world of another dirty little Indian baby.

"By the way," he added, almost nonchalantly, "he took his wife *and* his son with him when he burned the aborted remains."

Molly swallowed hard, fighting a rising panic. "He made Charles watch? Why? Why would he do such a thing to his own son?"

"To make sure the boy understood just how filthy Indians were. To make sure he knew just what should be done with them. The old man had hammered his own deeply rooted prejudices into his son. And little Charlie-boy was a quick study."

She heard the derision, and finally understood why Buck hated Charles with such passion. "What happened next?"

"Sylvie went mad," he said simply. "From that day until the day she died, she had to be cared for like a child."

Molly curled into a ball, hugging her knees. "The picture in the salon. She was so beautiful. Surely Charles doesn't blame his mother for what happened?"

Buck was quiet for a long time. Finally, he said, "I was told that he, like his father, felt his mother should have killed herself rather than submit to . . . to rape."

Molly was shocked. "*Submit* to rape?"

"These are his words, Molly, not mine. He's hated Indians ever since. Oh, he'll hire them and sleep with their whores, but he doesn't want one in his family tree."

Horror and dismay drenched her. Surely Charles wouldn't feel that way about her. She understood the emotional trauma he'd undergone as a child. Of course she did. But those feelings had been instilled in him by his father. Perhaps they weren't really his own, not completely, anyway. All of this really had nothing to do with her. Charles loved her. He adored her. Love would change him, she was sure of it. Why, then, was her heart pounding so hard she could feel it in her ears?

Without speaking another word, she turned her back on Buck, again, shutting him out. *Damn* him. If he hadn't shown up in her life, none of this would be happening. He confused her. He always had. It was all his fault. All of it. Until now, she'd been confident of every decision she'd ever made. That he could so effortlessly turn her life into absolute mayhem made her madder than hell.

Early the next morning, Molly was awakened by the sound of distant thunder. The air smelled different, too. Buck's mount whinnied and shuddered, as if expressing his elation at the coming rain. Molly sat up and looked around her. A small fire had been made, and coffee cooked over it. Buck rested against his saddle, working on the rabbit hide.

He glanced up, then stood and stuffed the hide into his saddlebag. "You'd better appreciate the dryness now. Things are going to change."

She was still angry with him. Every time he came into her life, it became complicated, chaotic and confusing. She was through letting him tell her what to do. From now on, she'd disagree with everything he said, no matter how much sense it made. "I've never minded a little rain," she said with a casual air as she stretched the kinks from her back.

Chuckling, he handed her a biscuit and jam sandwich. "We're not going to get just 'a little rain.'"

She took the biscuit and tried to eat it slowly. She had a feeling they were running out of food. "Still," she said around a mouthful, "I'll be grateful when it rains. I'm getting tired of all this dust."

He threw sand over the fire, then rolled up the bedroll. "We've got to get out of this arroyo and back up onto the plain."

She felt a twinge of disappointment. "Well, I feel safe here. You can go wherever you want. I'm walking down here."

He laughed again. "It's a riverbed, Molly."

She immediately realized the implications, but still didn't want to admit she was wrong. "So, it's a riverbed. Obviously," she added sarcastically, "there's no river."

He looked at her over the top of the saddle, which he'd just tightened on Thunder's back. "There will be."

"I find it hard to believe a little rain could fill up a gully this big."

"Are you willing to find out?"

She gave her shoulders a haughty shake. "Well, maybe not. But if I really wanted to, I would." Feeling vindicated, she hurried through her meager breakfast, then went behind a scraggle of mesquite to relieve herself.

Later, as they rode on, the wind came up from the north, soft with the promise of rain. By late afternoon, deep, gray clouds had gathered overhead and everything, including the earth, seemed to shiver with anticipation.

Buck nudged her, pointing toward a grove of cottonwood. "We'll stop there for the night. It's too hard for Thunder to go on in the dark."

During the night, they were awakened by the wind as it sputtered through the trees. Suddenly, an intricately woven web of lightning lit up the plains, outlining the flatness of the horizon. Molly glanced at Buck, who was merely a black and white silhouette sketched against the night sky. For a brief instant, she could see him as clearly as if it were noon, then, just as quickly, everything was enveloped in darkness. The thunder followed, shaking the ground, roaring over them like a stampede of cattle.

Buck stood and went to his mount, soothing him with his touch as he tied down the picket pin. Molly sat, shivering and hugging her knees, and watched the natural turbulence crash and boom over them. Even though she was still angry, she was grateful when Buck came and sat down beside her.

Large raindrops battered them, few and far between at first, then faster as the wind pushed the line of the storm past them, leaving in its noisy wake only the rain.

Buck unrolled a large poncho and put it over them. It hung to the ground, like a huge parasol without the ribs. They sat, silent, huddled together against the rain.

Though she would never admit it, Molly felt safer with Buck than with any other man she knew. Even Charles. Maybe, at this point, *especially* Charles. *No.* She forced the thought away. It wasn't that she wouldn't have felt safe with Charles, it was just that Buck was so capable. He knew exactly what to do to survive. And Charles was no fool; he'd sent Buck because he knew that Buck would get the job done. What Charles couldn't know, was the mixture of elation and frustration Molly had felt when she discovered it was Buck, and not Charles who had come for her.

She nudged Buck with her shoulder, and he automatically put his arm around her, pulling her close against his side. It wasn't that she really wanted his arm around her; it was because she was cold, and maybe a little bit afraid. The steady hissing of the rain continued relentlessly. A feeling of warmth, so strong that it made her hurt, swelled within her. Uttering a ragged sigh, she turned her head and pressed her face against his chest. She could hear the strong thump of his heart against her ear, and she breathed in, capturing his scent.

She didn't know how she could love him and hate him at the same time. But she began to realize that's what her feelings had always been: equal measures of love and hate. Never had she felt neutral toward him. Not even now, when she should have no feelings for him at all, except indebtedness and obligation for saving her life.

She must have dozed. When she woke up, she was alone under the poncho. Pushing it aside, she looked out from beneath it and found Buck holding his hat, allowing Thunder to drink from it. Rain plastered his hair to his head. The hard muscles of his back were visible beneath his wet shirt.

An ache, deep inside where she hadn't had any feeling

before, began to form. She wanted so much for things to be different between them. She had a feeling that if she made any unladylike advances, he'd reject them anyway. He always had. He'd rejected her advances from the first time she'd made them, over six years before. It would be stupid to try again. She wasn't so dense that she hadn't learned her lesson. And his kisses, she rationalized, had been merely punishment. Hadn't he pushed her away each time, ordering her to get out of his sight?

"Think you're going to stay under there all day?"

The rain splattered against the poncho, but she was already wet. Tossing it off, she stood, raised her face toward the rain and swung in a circle. Mud squished up between her toes. She'd always loved the rain. That hadn't changed either.

He handed her a biscuit. "That's breakfast. Now, come on. I'll walk Thunder for a while." He helped her get into the saddle.

"I feel kind of guilty," she said, glancing down at her bare feet. "If I had my boots, I wouldn't have to ride."

"Don't worry about it." His answer was terse as he took Thunder's reins and walked him carefully over the muddy ground.

They traveled in silence. Molly's thoughts were filled with her stupidity, and her inability to finally put all of Buck's rejections and even those she invented into proper perspective. The only sound was the wet, monotonous sound of rain, sheeting down upon them in drenching waves. The earth beneath them became thick, a sucking clay that hampered every step they took. They moved away from the riverbank, for it was slippery, offering a fast route into the bed of the river.

Buck stopped, halting Thunder with his hand. "Listen."

Molly turned, trying to hear something other than the sound of the rain. "What? What do you hear?" She sat quietly, suddenly hearing a thundering roar somewhere behind her. He lifted her off the horse and put her on the ground. "I want you to see this," he said, picketing Thunder by a wet clump of mesquite.

He glanced at her feet. "Can you walk a few steps?"

Nodding, she stepped gingerly through the muck. As they neared the arroyo bank, the noisy rumble became so loud, she almost put her hands over her ears.

Then she saw it. Her breath caught in her throat, and she gasped out loud. The very riverbed where, just the morning before, they'd slept and ate, was suddenly a deluge of frothing, foamy rust-colored water. It pitched and tossed from side to side, relentless to destroy whatever lay in its path.

Thunder snorted and whinnied behind them. They both turned in time to see a rabbit scuttle out from beneath the mesquite bush, having obviously startled the horse.

Buck touched her arm. "I'll be right back. Don't get any closer."

Mesmerized by the raging flood, Molly found herself drawn to it. It eddied and rolled, carrying with it sticks, twigs and even entire uprooted mesquite bushes and large branches from fallen trees. Without thinking, she stepped closer, standing on the rise of the riverbank. The ooze crept between her toes, and she wiggled them, loving the mushy feeling. For a silly, inane moment, she was reminded of her childhood when they'd played, naked and barefoot, in the rain.

Suddenly, the earth beneath her caved in, and she lost her balance, skidding down the other side of the sodden, muddy riverbank. She screamed Buck's name, the sound high and piercing in her ears as she plunged toward the angry water. The back of her riding skirt caught on something, slowing her fall. With her good arm, she flailed around, touching the object that gripped her skirt. It was a root. She grabbed it, throwing herself up against the muddy wall, digging her feet into the embankment, holding on for dear life.

Through the mud that coated the hair covering her eyes,

she looked up at Buck, who was on his stomach, reaching toward her. "Hang on, Molly. Hang on."

"*Dammit,*" she shouted between gasps. Her fingers burned, and she felt herself slipping. "Hurry up! I c-can't hold it!" She shoved the toes of one foot into the muddy embankment, bent her knee and flattened the other foot against the wall, trying to relieve some of the pressure on her arm. The next chance she had, she looked up again. Buck was gone. *He'll be back. Don't panic, fool. He'll be back.*

What seemed like a lifetime later, Buck returned above her with a rope. There was a noose on the end of it. "Here," he shouted into the sounds of the raging river. "Can you get it?"

Still gripping the root, she slowly raised her other arm, allowing the loop to fall over her head and under the arm. The pain in her wrist pounded as she tried to move the rope into place. She pulled herself up as far as she could and felt the rope tighten around one upper arm and beneath the other.

Finally, Buck pulled her up. She tried to help by walking her feet up the slippery, slimy sides of the riverbank. Then he hauled her onto the muddy, sloping side beyond the river. She lay there, her heart pounding, wrist throbbing, feet and the hand that had held the root burning. Her cheek was pressed into the mud as she tried to catch her breath.

He hunkered down beside her. "Are you all right?" At her weary nod, he added, "I told you not to move, didn't I?"

"Sorry," she mumbled into the mud.

He took her good arm and helped her stand. "God," he said, giving her a miserable look. "You're a mess."

She glanced down at herself. Mud. Reddish brown mud from head to foot. But she was alive, and again, Buck had saved her hide. How many times would it take before he'd tire of it? As she trudged through the muck, her skirt so heavy it hung to her ankles, she realized she didn't ever want to find out.

The rain slacked off and the sky loomed brighter, offering patches of blue in the distance. She didn't want to dwell on her misery, but it was hard not to think about it. Never in all her born days did she ever imagine herself being captured by a band of ragtag renegades, stripped of her clothes, staked to the ground like a buffalo hide, and treated like an animal. Then, to be rescued, not once but *twice* by a man to whom she didn't want to owe anything, much less her life . . . Lord, that was the stuff dime novels were made of. If she got out of this alive, maybe she'd write one of her own. After all, Hurricane Nell and Bess the Trapper had *nothing* on her.

🎕 Eleven 🎕

Toward evening, they came across a pool of fresh water. There were many, dotted here and there over the plains, short-lived remnants of the rainstorm. They wouldn't last long. By the next day, most would have evaporated. Buck suggested they stop so they both could clean up.

While he left her to look for something with which to build a fire, she stripped and lay her muddy skirt out to dry. After rinsing out her underwear, she washed her hair, using a small chip of soap Buck had produced from his saddlebags. With only one good hand, nothing was going to get very clean, but anything was an improvement.

It wasn't possible to wring the water from her underwear; her wrist still throbbed and she had no strength in it. She still had no power to grip in those fingers. She was twisting and pressing the moisture from her torn drawers against her thigh with her good hand when she heard Buck come up behind her. Though he could only see her back, she felt herself flush.

"Having a little trouble?"

Her elbows automatically came together to cover the sides of her breasts as she glanced at him over her shoulder. He had his shirt off and shoved it toward her. He'd obviously found a similar pond, because his hair was wet and his face and torso clean of mud and dust. "Here, put this on."

She let her gaze fall briefly to the hard ridges of his stomach and the hair circling his navel before she grabbed the shirt and slid into it. Taking a deep, dizzying breath, she managed to thank him.

"I . . . I can't seem to wring the water from my things. My wrist still hurts too much."

He pulled her camisole and drawers from the pool and twisted them repeatedly until they were just damp. After shaking them out, he laid them on the ground near the fire.

His shirt was big and long, and it hung to her knees, despite the fact that he'd ripped a strip off the tail to use on her wrist. It was anything but clean, but she found strange comfort in wearing it. She slipped the buttons through the buttonholes with difficulty. "I guess I could put on my underwear, anyway. At least they're cleaner than they were."

Shaking his head, he answered, "That's foolish. They'll be dry by morning."

He turned and squatted over the fire, her gaze following. As he nursed the small flame that tried desperately to peter out into a puff of damp smoke, she studied him. Muscles bunched over the wide expanse of his back. Hair, black as pitch yet wavy from the moist air curled to his shoulders. His jeans hung low as he hunkered near the fire, dropping into a V at the small of his back. His skin was lighter there. The mystery of what lay beyond gave her the shivers.

Drawing in another deep breath, she crossed to his saddlebags and rummaged around for her brush. Finding it, she sat down on the rubber-coated blanket and started pulling the tangles from her wet hair.

He joined her and examined her feet. "They must be sore." His hands were gentle as they moved over the cuts and scrapes she'd received during her struggle at the river. Suddenly, he lifted her leg and gazed at the back of her knee. Another shiver of pleasure sped through her.

"What are you doing?"

Looking up at her, he gave her a small smile. "Just thought I'd check to see if those three little moles still lived back there."

She laughed in spite of herself. "You make them sound alive." She gave him a curious look. "How did you know I had moles back there?"

His lazy grin spread. "You and Martha used to cavort in the rain, remember?"

"I remember," she answered, briefly looking away as she remembered how casually they'd sported their nudity as girls.

He tweaked her toe, and she wrinkled her nose at him, then peered at the sole of one foot. "I don't think my poor feet will ever be the same again."

He didn't respond, but reached over and dragged his saddlebags toward them. "These might help," he said, pulling out something from the bag closest to him and handing it to her.

Puzzled, she took the article from him and unfolded it. She let out a ragged gasp as two rabbit skin moccasins fell into her lap. Gazing up at him, she said on a breath, "You did this for me?"

Appearing embarrassed, he nodded, then went back to tending the fire.

She slipped her feet into the slippers and gave up a luxurious sigh. So soft . . . so warm. Tears threatened behind her eyes, and she blinked, hoping to hold them back. That he'd gone to the trouble to make them for her bewildered her. It was a gesture she couldn't comprehend, coming from him.

"They're wonderful, Buck. Thank you."

The fire swelled from his ministration. "It's nothing. Don't read anything into it."

There was a resurgence of her anger. "Oh, heaven forbid that I might read something into it. Don't worry, I surely won't think you did it because you cared a diddly-damn for me."

She saw his shoulders shake suspiciously. "You'd better not be laughing at me, Buck Randall."

He turned, his face a bland mask, but the laughter still glimmering in his eyes. "Heaven forbid that I would ever laugh at you, Molly Lindquist."

It was a truce, of sorts. She relaxed and tried to wrap her broken wrist. Then he was there, quietly and seriously doing it for her.

"Then there was the time you and Martha were playing on the roof of that old pig shed," Buck said with a shake of his head. "I was slopping the hogs. One minute you two were there, the next Martha was skidding down the side of the roof and you were gone."

Molly tried not to laugh. "*Through* the roof. Lord, I remember how scared I was."

"The next thing I knew, that old sow came squealing and snorting out of the shed with you hanging onto her back for dear life."

She laughed out loud. "Priscilla."

"Priscilla?"

Nodding, she answered, "Priscilla Pig. That's what we'd named her."

"No one could pry the two of you apart."

"Me and Priscilla?" she asked lightly.

"You and Martha," he answered on a drawl. "You did everything together. Until Nicolas and Anna sent her away to school."

She looked at him across the tiny fire. "I remember you being around a lot in those days."

"I wanted to be near Jason—he was still TwoLeaf then—he was my hero."

And you were mine. She looked away, the thought almost causing her pain. When she looked at him again, he seemed far away, deep in thought. "What are you thinking about now?"

He gave her a rugged smile. "Do you really want to know?"

"I asked, didn't I?" He was quiet for a while. Molly wasn't sure he would share.

"I was thinking about the last time I saw you before they shipped you off to San Francisco."

Toying with the buttons on his shirt, she said, "I don't really remember much about that night."

"I can believe that. You were drunk."

A wash of embarrassment warmed her cheeks. "What an awful child I was."

"No," he argued. "Not awful. Just very determined to get into as much trouble as you could without getting caught."

"No, I was awful." She couldn't look at him. "I remember going to the old shed with some of the others that night. We had three bottles of bad hooch and couldn't seem to pass them around fast enough."

"Do you remember me being there?"

Her embarrassment deepened. "Yes," she said softly. "You kicked in the door."

"Anything else?"

"I remember fighting you. You made me feel foolish in front of my friends." She glanced up at him. "I hated you for that."

"Do you remember the ride back to the house?"

She frowned, trying to think. "No. I can't remember anything after you threatening to throw me into the river if I didn't behave."

"You don't recall turning around in the saddle and facing me? Tossing your legs over mine?" His voice softened, became a tantalizing seduction.

Secret parts of her suddenly came alive, but she shook her head. "I . . . I can't believe I did that."

"Then you kissed me."

Gasping, she threw him a look of shock. "I didn't!"

"Oh, but you did," he said, continuing the verbal seduction. "And when I didn't respond to your liking, you said you thought I could do better than that. That maybe we'd try it again before we got to the house. Then," he added on soft laughter, "you passed out."

It couldn't be true. She wouldn't have done such a thing. Even drunk, she'd thought she was in control of her faculties. "I can't believe I would have done that," she answered, utterly mortified.

"Well, what do you think?"

She looked at him, puzzled by the question and the lazy, provocative smile. "About what?"

"Has my kissing improved?"

It was agony, this whimsical little game he played with her. It was tempting to respond, to tell him she wasn't sure, he'd have to kiss her again. But it was a source of amusement for him, and it wasn't for her. His kisses had opened the floodgates on her emotions, and it was all still too painful to take any of it lightly.

Desperate to change the subject, she quickly asked, "How's Dusty? I'm surprised you don't have him with you."

Suddenly, Buck was on his feet, fists balled at his sides. He looked beyond the fire, past her, into the distance. "Dusty is better off where he is. With Ma and Sky."

Carefully, Molly asked, "Don't you want him with you?"

Buck swore. "What do you think? Of course I'd like to have him with me. But hell, I don't have anything to offer the kid. What kind of life is this, anyway? He's living in a stable home. He's going to school, he has his friends. I can't possibly give him anything better."

"But . . . but you might marry again someday—"

"No," he shot back, cutting her off. "That won't happen. He had a mother, and now she's gone. No one can replace her." He paced in front of the fire. "Marriage isn't something I intend to try again. I don't like making the same mistake twice."

For some foolish reason, his words were like a physical

blow to her stomach, squeezing something vile up into her throat. In spite of that, she could feel his pain. It bracketed him like iron strictures, making him tight and miserable. "What are you afraid of, Buck?"

He didn't answer. She knew he was shutting her out.

"Every child needs his father," she said softly. "I think Dusty would rather live with you than with anyone else in the world."

He sucked in a deep breath that was released on a shudder. He wanted to believe her, but he remembered with haunting clarity the morning he woke up from a week-long drunk to discover that Dusty had almost died searching for him. The guilt still ate at him. It always would. Every time he thought about almost losing his son, and being responsible for it, he felt as though his body had turned inside out and every nerve was exposed to the air.

"Forget about the past, Buck. You were a different man then. You wouldn't disappoint him again."

He suddenly felt tired. The shit-load of guilt and miserable secrets he'd been carrying around with him all these years felt like a ton of rocks. "Do you want to know what really happened all those years ago?"

She stood and crossed to his side of the fire, sitting down beside him. She touched his arm. "If you want to tell me."

He pulled in another deep breath before he began. "I killed Honey."

Molly gave him a startled look. "Oh, Buck. You . . . you don't mean—"

"Molly, I've never told anyone this. Are you sure you want to hear it?"

She nodded, her gaze never leaving his face.

"That morning . . ." He hated the pain the memories dredged up, because it was like it had happened just yesterday. "I was supposed to meet her at the school in the afternoon to pick up Dusty. We were going to take him over to Ma's. She'd made him a cake. It was his birthday." He stopped briefly, wallowing in the self-pity that comes with the pain of loss. "I told her I'd be there on time. I had good intentions."

Her hand moved toward his. He clasped it, holding it tightly. "Honey and I had been arguing for months. She'd begun to get on my nerves. 'Nag, nag, nag,' was all I thought. She'd complained that I spent more time with my drinking buddies than I did with her. Kept saying if she hadn't been pregnant with Dusty, I never would have married her."

"Was it true?"

He closed his eyes and raked his fingers through his hair. "Hell, yes. I guess it was true. I didn't want to admit that, even to myself. I sure as hell wouldn't admit it to her. She wasn't a bad woman. She was a good mother—and as good a wife as she knew how to be. But she . . . she always wanted something I couldn't give her. I never made enough money to satisfy her. She liked pretty things, bracelets, bangles, you know. All the things only money can buy. And she . . . she crowded me. Always accusing me of cheating on her."

"And did you ever cheat on her?"

He glanced down at Molly, her wide hazel eyes staring into his. *Only in my heart*. Shaking his head, he looked away. "No, I didn't cheat on her."

She pressed closer to him, leaning against his side. "What happened after you promised to meet her?"

Fighting the urge to pull her close, he gave her a miserable laugh. "I went out drinking. Missed our meeting by hours. By the time I finally got there, she was dead. Raped by that son-of-a-bitch schoolmaster."

"What happened to Dusty? Did he see her like that?"

The guilt continued to eat at him. "I don't think so. I . . . I found him at Honey's sister's cabin. She lived on the reservation."

Molly was quiet a long time. "But you can't continue to take the blame. It wasn't really your fault."

"The hell it wasn't. If I'd been there when I said I would,

we'd have gone on to Ma's, and everything would have been fine."

"Oh, Buck," Molly answered, her voice filled with sadness. "You don't know that for sure." She was quiet again, then asked, very tentatively, "Could . . . could she have . . . No. I'm sorry. I didn't—"

"You mean, could she have been unfaithful to me?"

Molly looked at him, her face pinched with pain. "I'm sorry. It's not a fair question."

He shook his head. He'd occasionally suspected she was seeing someone else. The horrible thing was, he hadn't cared enough to find out for sure. "I don't know. It happened, I know that. Most of those Whites always had something to lure the Indian girls away. Hell, to some, any kind of life was better than the life they had." He gazed at her. "You saw it as much as I did."

"Yes," she answered softly. "I saw it."

"You were lucky Nicolas and Anna were so strict with you."

"I can't thank them enough now, but then . . ." She took a deep, quivering breath. "Putting all of that aside, couldn't you and Dusty still have a life together? So, all right. You weren't there when Honey needed you. But . . . but you could make it up to Dusty now."

He turned to find her watching him. He touched her hair, smoothing the tawny curls down over her ears. Her beauty continued to make him ache. God, he wondered if he'd ever get over it.

"You're right. I wasn't there for Honey, dammit, and I'll never forgive myself. But what you don't know is . . ." He wasn't sure he could continue.

"There's more?" she asked, surprised.

"Ah, Christ, Molly." He couldn't say it. He couldn't tell her how ironic it was that he'd always been there for her. *Always.* It made him feel like a worthless piece of shit. He hadn't the decency to meet Honey when she'd asked him to, and because of it, she died. He wished to hell he could change all that. Molly hadn't wanted him watching over her, and he couldn't seem to stop himself from doing it. Why had he cared so much? There was no sense to it. None.

"What? What is it?"

"Never mind. It's nothing." He'd never let her down. Even when he was a falling-down drunk, he was somehow able to go out and look for Molly. He would never have let her slip between the cracks into that rotten place that he'd become so familiar with. He remembered how painful it was to learn that she'd been sent to San Francisco. He'd known it was the only solution, but when she was gone, something special had been taken out of his life.

He loved her. He always had. The horrible, tragic truth was, that if he'd loved Honey even half as much, he wouldn't have let her die. If he'd cared enough and had been sober, she would still be alive.

Molly watched the pain drench Buck's features. So much. He had told her so much. Letting go of all his guilt regarding Honey had taken its toll. He looked weary and tired.

She stood and moved her bedroll next to his blanket. She wanted to be close to him. That's all. He needed her strength, perhaps even her touch. After all they'd been through, there was no reason not to spend the night within touching distance.

Buck fed the fire before lying down beside her. She turned toward him, wanting to comfort him if he needed it, but he turned away, presenting her with his back.

It was all right. She knew he was in some horrible place, whipping himself with guilt he shouldn't feel. All those years of doing penance for a crime only his mind had indicted him for. It was no wonder he'd fled California, leaving all of his traumatic memories behind. Then she showed up, unconsciously, and, sadly, sometimes consciously, stirring up his hurt.

His back was bare; she still wore his shirt. She pressed herself against him and shyly snaked her arm around his middle. He tensed, but didn't move away, finally relaxing beside her.

Pressing her cheek against his back, she closed her eyes and tried to sleep, but sleep wouldn't come. She couldn't get the things he told her out of her head. It hurt so much to think he'd been quietly punishing himself for so long. It was a miracle he could stop drinking at all. Whiskey undoubtedly had numbed his pain for years after Honey's death. No doubt it had been the only escape that had kept him sane, but he'd been wise enough to know it would also kill him. She was grateful he hadn't wanted to die. She would have missed him. . . . oh, God, but she would have missed him.

She remembered the first time she'd gone home after Honey had died. She'd asked about Buck, and Jason's wife, Rachel, had told her Buck hadn't been seen sober for almost a year. Then, he'd disappeared. Of course Molly hadn't known it, but he'd come to Texas, no doubt to try to forget his painful past. At the time, she'd felt some concern, but she hadn't known the extent of his pain. Maybe she couldn't have understood it then, either. She was admittedly pretty wrapped up in herself back in those days.

She listened to him breathe. He hadn't moved, but she was almost certain he wasn't asleep, either. She flattened her hand against his stomach. He sucked in a breath.

"Molly, don't tempt me."

Ignoring him, she rubbed her lips over his warm skin, tasting the slightly salty tang from his sweat. She pressed her nose against him, breathing in his scent. She touched his chest, marveling at the hard ridges and the firm knobby nipples.

"Molly, don't—"

"I . . . I just need to be close, Buck. Please," she begged softly. "Don't push me away."

His breathing was ragged as he turned toward her and

pulled her into his arms. She let out a small cry as the wonder of his touch washed over her. They lay that way for a long, quiet moment, her head in the crook of his neck, and the rest of her body pressed against his. He was hard beneath the fly of his jeans. She waited for him to move away. He didn't. She pushed, aching to rub herself against it. She'd thought that just being near him would be enough. What a fool she was. Now that she had that, she wanted more. Whatever it was, she wanted it all.

She boldly pushed against his groin. He groaned and stiffened, then suddenly his hands were everywhere, in her hair, at her neck and down her back. He lifted the shirt and splayed his palms over the skin at her waist and her buttocks, rubbing, touching, seductively teasing. She bit her lower lip when his fingers touched her bruised ribs, determined not to let their moment be spoiled.

She felt his sharp intake of breath when she threw one of her legs over his hip, pulling him closer. His hand moved down over her bottom, moving beneath and beyond to her soft, swollen nest. She gasped softly, shaking with wild need.

All those years, she thought, on the verge of tears. All those years of hiding these feelings. Of refusing to acknowledge they existed. But it was only for Buck that she felt them. Never anyone else. She felt her heart thump greedily as the place between her legs became wet and hot. He stroked her, pressing her against the rising thickness of his own desire.

When his hand left her, she nearly cried out.

"Patience, Molly," he whispered.

"Oh," she moaned. "But . . . but . . ."

He sat up, pulling her up with him. He looked down at her, his gaze hotter than the fire that glowed beyond them.

Slowly, he unbuttoned the shirt, exposing more and more of her flesh. Cool air touched her, drawing her nipples into tight buds.

"It's your last chance, Molly. If you want me to stop, tell me now."

She shook her head, unable to speak. It was so hard to breathe. Her body shivered with anticipation.

He pulled the shirt wide and gazed at her in the dim light of the fire. His hands shook as he touched her breasts, holding them, lifting them. She held her breath, forcing herself to stay passive. Every nerve inside her bounced and throbbed, heavy with a desire she'd never known and wouldn't have believed existed.

The fire danced off their bodies. His gaze lowered, finding the bruising at the lower edge of her ribs. With gentle fingers, he caressed the area, then bent low to kiss it. Butterflies exploded inside her, and she touched his head, feeling her tears of joy dampen his hair.

He moved to her breasts, planting soft kisses on each. With a low, guttural groan, he pulled one of her nipples into his mouth, sucking on it, flicking it with his tongue.

"Oh, lordy," she said, her voice shaking with desire. "Wh-why do I feel this everywhere?"

His fingers moved between her legs. He stroked, finding a spot that made her gasp. "Do you feel it here?"

"Y-yes," she moaned, squirming beneath his magic touch. She gripped his hair, twisting it in her fist as he continued to touch her. Shards of pleasure burst deep inside her, and she spread her thighs wide, pushing lustily against his fingers.

"Oh, I . . . I itch down there, Buck, I itch."

He groaned against her breast, pressing his fingers deeper, causing her to gasp again.

Suddenly, he pushed her to the blanket. Through a hungry haze, she watched, waiting for him to do *something* to relieve her of the ache that so gloriously assaulted her. She felt a funny stab of fear, but pushed it aside. "Buck, please. Help me," she murmured.

He loomed over her, looking like the very devil himself.

He sat rigid, his gaze moving over her. "It's . . . it's still not too late to stop, Molly."

Stop? She was almost in tears with her need, ready to fly into a million pieces, and he wanted to stop?

She wasn't tutored at all in the ways of love, but she knew she couldn't bear another night of this. The hunger inside her was so intense, she felt brazen, wicked. With her good hand, she reached out and touched his groin, gripping the thick root, moving her palm over it.

He jerked, letting out a hiss of breath, but he didn't push her away. She felt him grow further beneath her hand, but he still hadn't moved away.

"Dammit, Buck," she whispered shakily, getting to her knees to face him. "It's *already* too late. It *is*. You've got to do something—"

Suddenly she was in his arms, and he kissed her, deep, long and hard, kisses that were wet and slippery. He dragged her back and forth against him, her nipples grazing his chest. His hand moved down to unfasten his jeans, and suddenly that hard part of him was there, pressing against her belly.

Reaching down between them, she touched him, felt the heat of his root, the moistness of the tip and knew that from this moment on, her life would be changed.

With a cry of pain-filled pleasure, she tumbled backward onto the blanket, bringing him with her. He touched her again, rubbing the wet folds gently until he found the spot that nearly sent her skyward. She cried out again, shaking with a need she would never understand, until finally, *finally*, he lowered himself over her and pressed into her.

Some vague feelings of discomfort centered inside as he pushed against her virginity, but she plunged upward, voicing a small cry at the brief, sharp burst of pain. Then he was inside, moving deeply, stroking slowly. She caught his rhythm and moved with him, wrapping her legs around him to hold him close.

Suddenly an incredible intensity began low in her pelvis,

drawing her toward something wonderful, breathless, yet frightening. She knew it would relieve the incredible itch, but she also sensed she would lose control.

"Don't fight it, Molly." Buck continued to pump slowly, in and out. He reached between them and touched that wildly sensitive nub again, sending her skyward.

Her body tightened as wave after wave of ecstasy rolled over her. He plunged on, driving deep, his movements becoming more rapid until finally he, too, tensed above her.

She threw herself at him and held him tight, suddenly unable to speak. No matter what he did to her from this night on, he could never hurt her. He'd given her something she would remember for the rest of her life. If she never tasted such pleasure again, she would be satisfied.

She felt him tuck the blanket in around them and pull her close against his chest. His hand came around her and caressed her breasts. She thought it would be soothing, but all it did was make her want him to love her again.

❧ Twelve ❧

Molly awakened before dawn, wrapped in a cocoon of warmth. She felt wonderful . . . The feeling didn't last.

Guilt suddenly invaded every pore. Moving to leave the sleeping roll, she winced, sucking in her breath at the soreness between her legs. She stood and went to what remained of the rain pool so she could wash herself. After ripping off another piece of Buck's shirt, she dipped it into the water and pressed it against her womanhood.

She gasped quietly as the cold water touched her raw skin. Soon, though, it became soothing, and closing her eyes briefly, she sighed. She brought the cloth away and saw the blood. The visible, viable remains of her night of passion. It wasn't that she'd hoped it had all been a dream; she knew herself better than that. But now, as daylight approached, she was filled with shame.

She slipped into her underwear and skirt, all the while asking herself how last night could have happened. What kind of woman vows to marry one man, then, without a conscious thought, sleeps with another?

Charles. Heaven help her, she hadn't even given the man a thought. Not once. *Not once* while she and Buck were making love had she even considered Charles. If she had, she certainly would have stopped. Probably dead in her tracks. Even now, she was filled with guilt at her shameless behavior. It didn't matter that on some deep, hidden level she'd always wondered what making love with Buck would be like. She'd betrayed Charles's trust, and she hated herself for it.

But the deed was done. She couldn't go back and change it, and she couldn't pretend it hadn't happened. She pulled on her new rabbit moccasins and clumsily tied the thong around her ankle. Her wrist still hurt. She was afraid it was healing wrong. It had recently dawned on her that she might not be able to play the piano again. At least, not the way she'd played it before. She didn't want to think much about that just yet. She just hoped there wasn't too much damage. Speaking of damage . . .

She glanced at Buck. He was still asleep. She allowed herself a lazy look. His black stubble was darker this morning. But last night . . . She shuddered, remembering how it had scratched the soft places he'd kissed. *Stop it.*

She crept to his saddlebags and dug around for something to eat, finding a dry biscuit and a dried up apple in the bottom of one of the bags. As she nibbled on the biscuit, she took the apple over to Thunder.

The animal nickered as she neared, and she pressed the apple against his large soft lips. He gently took it from her, brushing her palm with the soft hairs that surrounded his mouth.

"You'll be his friend for life."

She jumped at the sound of Buck's voice but didn't turn. She couldn't face him. Suddenly she felt him behind her, so close the hairs on the back of her neck stood out.

"Don't touch me, Buck." It was an order that she truly meant, for if he touched her, she wasn't sure she could push him away. And if she couldn't push him away, she would be destroying what little self-respect she had left.

He swore on a hiss of breath, then walked away. "I hadn't intended to."

She left Thunder and went in search of her hairbrush. The first thing she had to do was bury her feelings for

Buck. *Just like that?* Oh, it wouldn't be easy, but she'd have to find a way.

As she brushed the snarls from her hair, she knew what she had to do. She couldn't wait any longer to tell Charles about herself. It had to be the first thing she did when she got back to the ranch. She hit a huge snarl, and the brush flew out of her hand. She made a face. Telling Charles would be the first thing she did *after* she had a bath and a shampoo. Once she'd told him, if he still wanted to marry her, she would promise to make him a good wife. She'd seen his prejudices firsthand and knew they existed. But deep in her heart, she still didn't want to believe that Charles was a thief and a crook. She tossed Buck a bitter glance, angry at him for concocting that story.

Buck poked at the fire and stole glances at Molly's stiff back. They'd made love three times during the night, and each time she'd been eager and delicious. Hot and sexual. Carnal, if he were really to describe it. In spite of what she tried to be, Molly Lindquist was a woman who could enjoy passion, both giving and receiving. But then, buried somewhere deep in his mind, he'd always known that.

All during this trip back to the ranch, he'd watched her. She'd become an addiction, and hell, if there was one thing he knew inside and out, it was addiction. Every morning, the first thing he thought about was her. How she moved, how her sweet fanny jiggled inside her drawers when she walked. How her bountiful breasts surged above the modest neckline of her camisole. How arousing the soft, inner surface of her arms were, and how he'd always wanted to plant kisses there—as well as many, many other explicit places.

His dreams had been riddled with seductions, yet no matter how enticing they'd been, he'd thought that since they were only dreams, they would never withstand the harshness of reality. How wrong he was. . . .

Now, as he watched her, his gaze moving over her gently flared hips, desire sprang into his groin again. Before last night, he could always stifle the physical urge he had for her. But after loving her, tasting her, feeling the exquisite softness of her body, he wasn't sure he'd ever be able to quash his feelings again. She was no ordinary woman. No matter how wild she'd been as a girl, he'd known she was a sensual thing. He'd been damned pleased that no one had tasted her sweetness before he had. Especially pleased that "Campion the Ass" hadn't gotten past her prim exterior to plunder what he didn't deserve. Buck knew he couldn't have her, but he sure as hell didn't want Campion to have her, either.

On some visceral level, he'd known what she would feel like beneath him. He'd known how she would taste, what little sounds she'd make as she neared her climax. He'd buried himself in her, wanting to brand her with his own scent, mark her for himself. Once they'd begun, there had been no turning back. Even as he'd told her it wasn't too late to stop, he'd known it already was.

And now, there would be nothing. There could be nothing. He'd somehow have to be content with memories of the night they'd just shared. He swore as he thought about it, knowing it wouldn't be enough. Hell, it would never be enough. But somehow, it would have to be. He wondered how two people who seemed to be so right for each other could be so wrong.

All day they'd ridden in silence. Thunder had carried both of them, and Buck had appeared anxious to get back to the ranch, for they moved quickly over the ground, not even stopping for lunch.

It wasn't possible to ride behind Buck and not touch him. Molly leaned into him, her head resting in the middle of his back, telling herself it was only to keep from sliding off. She sighed. So, this would be the end. They'd never even had a beginning. That should have told her something. When there's no beginning and no end, there's nothing. In spite of her good intentions, she found herself thinking about him one last time.

He'd been gentle with her but had become impassioned at her invitation. Even now, when she professed to despise him for everything, the memory of their night together made her want him again. Maybe . . . maybe if she thought about it enough, she'd get it out of her system. Maybe then, she'd get sick of thinking about it and get sick of him. . . . Then again, she thought on a shaky sigh, maybe she wouldn't. But she could want him until hell froze over, and he was still the wrong man for her. He'd told her that before. And she knew it. Yet, there was a part of her that wanted to fight for him, because what they had together was so rare, so complete, so . . . permanent. But she had her plans. If they didn't work out, maybe . . .

Resting her forehead against his back, she let her mind return to the night before . . . again. He'd touched, probed and stroked her everywhere. He'd been gentle and forceful, savage and tender. Every part of her had come alive, even as it was coming alive now, just thinking about it. The last time they'd made love, he'd lifted her up, and she'd straddled him. His hands had fondled her breasts, and she'd bent over so he could take each nipple into his mouth. Oh, never in her wildest dreams had she imagined such bliss. The untamed, uncontrollable urge to ride him was natural, like she'd been waiting a lifetime to do it.

She squirmed behind him, letting her hand drop below his waist. A thrill shot through her; he was hard. Quickly she pulled her hand away, settling it sedately above his waist. But she'd already heard his sharp intake of breath.

"Watch where you put your hand, Molly." His voice was raspy and harsh. The sexy sound nearly drove her over the edge.

She squeezed her eyes shut, forcing herself to behave. She tried to think about Charles, and what she would tell him. It wasn't possible to rehearse a speech for Charles, not when she was pressed so close against Buck's back.

Suddenly, she wanted to bawl. For herself, for Buck, for what might have been. How simple it would have been for her to feel for Charles what she felt for Buck. It didn't seem quite fair that things hadn't worked out that way. For all of Charles's handsomeness and graciousness, his overtures had turned her cold.

She had to rid herself of these feelings, and soon. She needed her strength to face Charles. Everything she felt for Buck had to be expunged, erased. Even if she felt no desire for Charles, she had to admit she'd have to pretend, once they were married. She allowed herself to think the worst: What if she discovered he truly *was* a crook, what then? The future she'd planned for so long would disappear. She'd have to start over . . . somewhere.

Tears pressed the backs of her eyes, the weakness making her so angry, she punched Buck's back with her fist.

He jumped, surprised by the attack. "What's the matter with you?"

"*Damn* you! I was fine until you came along," she accused, swiping at her eyes with the back of her hand. "I'd hidden all of these disgusting feelings for years. I didn't have any trouble burying them and keeping them buried, until *you* showed up in my life, ruining all my plans, making me not even trust the man I planned to marry. Damn you, Buck Randall." She gulped back tears. "And another thing. I *hate* all the crying I've done these past weeks. Do you realize how long it's been since I've cried? Do you?"

He mumbled something she couldn't understand, then pulled Thunder to a stop. "Get it out of your system, Molly. It's not far to the ranch." He turned slightly and stared at her.

"What's wrong? Why did you stop?"

He studied the bare expanse of flesh above her camisole. "I can't take you to your fiancé like that. Where's that shawl the whore gave you?"

She glanced down at her very visible cleavage and blushed. Funny how it hadn't bothered her until he mentioned it, although she'd felt him eyeing it often enough. "I think it's in the saddlebag."

"Hell, let's hope so." He dismounted and dug through the bags until he found it. He handed it to her.

She took it and draped it over her shoulders. "Thank you for thinking of that," she said quietly.

Sucking in a shaky breath, she wondered how in the bloody hell she was going to live the rest of her life without this infuriating, thoughtful, exasperating, tender, angry man.

All of her tears, tantrums and carryings-on had turned her into someone she didn't even like. She didn't deserve Charles. She didn't deserve the things he wanted to give her. She didn't deserve the happiness she had yearned for. She was, without a doubt, the most awful kind of woman. She lusted after one man, and still planned to marry another. How had this happened?

Pulling herself together, she sat up straight, held on to the back of the saddle and prayed they'd get to the ranch soon.

"Molly?"

"Now, what?" she asked wearily.

"Don't say anything to Charles about Che. Let me take care of it."

She nodded, almost gratefully.

The minute the dogs heralded their arrival in the yard, Sage Reno came from the barn to greet them. He ambled toward them, grinning like a fool.

"Goddamn, Buck, I'm glad you're back." He helped Molly down. "You all right, ma'am? We sure were worried about you."

"Thank you, Sage. I'm . . . I'm fine, thank you." She looked toward the house, relieved, yet confused when Charles hurried down the steps.

Behind her, Sage spoke quietly to Buck. "A message

from Nita," he said under his breath. "She needs to see you right away."

Something inside Molly collapsed when she heard Sage's words. The tenuous facade she'd put in place just moments before crumbled, and when she saw Charles racing across the yard toward her, she met him halfway and flung herself at him, hugging him tightly, hoping to block out her feelings of emptiness.

"Charles! Oh, Charles, I thought I'd never see you again!" Charles was solicitous and caring. His concern compounded her own personal guilt.

"I knew you could do it, Randall!" Charles held Molly against him. She closed her eyes, trying to feel grateful to be back in the safety of Charles's embrace. But it was hard. Hard to ignore the hollow feeling in the pit of her stomach.

"Where's Nicolette?" she asked against his chest. "I've missed her, too."

Charles pulled away and gently steered her toward the house. "She's still visiting Chelsea. She should be back in a few days."

It might have been Molly's imagination, but she felt unspoken tension burning between them. Maybe it was just her incredible feelings of frustration and guilt.

"We have much to talk about, darling," Charles whispered, squeezing her waist.

Oh, he didn't know how much. "But, Charles, I'm . . . I'm exhausted, and I'd love a bath. Couldn't it wait until later? Perhaps tomorrow morning?"

"Of course, darling. I'm sorry. Of course you're exhausted. How selfish of me." He squeezed her again, bringing her close. "I've just missed you more than you'll ever know," he whispered against her ear. "They didn't . . ." He seemed unable to get the words out as he looked at her shawl-covered shoulders. She was grateful Buck had thought to cover her. "They . . . they didn't . . . hurt you, did they, darling?"

Though he'd generously tiptoed around the question, she felt herself flush anyway. "No, Charles. They didn't . . . hurt me." *But Buck did. That bastard Buck, who, after awakening all my desires, is now on his way to see his whore.* She was sick to her stomach, and so mad she wanted to throw things.

He glanced up the stairs. "The women are filling the tub. Go. I'll talk to you later."

Grateful, she dragged herself up the stairs.

Angelita was waiting in her room. "Here, senorita, let me help you." She took Molly's ragged underwear and helped her pin her hair on top of her head. The woman's eyes were warmer than they had been the last time they'd talked. She sucked in a hiss of breath when she saw Molly's bruised ribs.

"What happened, senorita?"

Molly looked at them in the mirror, noting the bruises were a positively vile shade of yellowish purple. "Oh, it's really nothing. It doesn't hurt that much anymore."

Angelita muttered angrily. "No, I don't think it is nothing. I think it is something. Something very bad happened to you."

"Don't worry about my bruises, Angelita. They're already healing. But," she added unwrapping the filthy bandage from her wrist, "I . . . think this is broken."

Angelita frowned as she probed it, causing Molly to gasp. "*Si,* I think you are right. I will set it properly after your bath."

"Thank you, Angelita."

The woman nodded. "You have been through much, I can tell."

Suddenly, Molly felt the inane, helpless tears slide down her cheeks. "Yes." She'd been through a lot of anguish, but much of it had been of her own making. She gave herself a hard shake and stepped into the tub.

"I will leave you to soak, senorita. Would you like me to wash your hair in a few minutes?"

Molly nodded, leaned against the back of the tub and closed her eyes. She sighed as the warm water caressed her. "This is wonderful. Yes, thank you, Angelita, I appreciate everything you've done for me."

After her shampoo, she dozed in the tub. Awakened by a sound that came from the doorway, she opened her eyes and gasped. Charles was standing there, watching her.

"Charles!" Frantically, Molly scanned the room for her towel. She stood, only long enough to grab the towel that was folded over the back of a chair. She tried to wrap it around her, but her broken wrist hampered her movements. "What are you doing here? Charles, this isn't proper at all." Fear and confusion tumbled over her.

He gazed at her, desire flaming in his eyes, his breathing erratic. "God, Margaret. You're so beautiful. . . . Your breasts . . . so plump and sweet. I knew it. . . . I knew you'd be a seductress. Dammit, Margaret, I'm ready to burst, I want you so badly."

With the towel pressed in front of her, Molly backed away from him. "Charles, please." Panic seized her. She'd never imagined him like this.

He moved toward her. "Margaret, Margaret. It's only a matter of time. Come," he urged, his voice still shaking as he reached for her towel. "I want to marry you more than anything in the world. What does it matter if we jump the gun a little? God," he said on a harsh intake of breath. "I want you. I don't want to wait to bed you."

His heightened arousal continued to frighten her. She hated what she saw in his eyes, that irrational, heated lust that made him too strong and determined to listen to reason. She tried to scoot around him, but he caught her and pulled her toward him. It was more than revulsion that she felt at his touch. A feeling more ridiculous than anything she could have imagined snaked into her thoughts. A sense of unfaithfulness to Buck.

"Charles, please. We have to wait. We . . . I have some things I have to tell you—"

He ripped off her towel and pressed himself against her, grinding his pelvis into her abdomen. He shook with desire. His hands were everywhere, groping her breasts, her back, her buttocks. She pushed at his shoulders with her good hand, anxious to be free of him. But he was too strong. He shoved her toward the bed, all the while trying to unbutton his fly. Molly continued to fight, but she was no match for him, not when he was like this.

Suddenly someone pounded on the door. "Senor Campion?" The knocking became insistent. "Senor Campion, por favor. Someone to see you downstairs. They say it is urgent."

"Goddammit!" he roared. "How dare you interrupt, you stupid bitch!" he shouted at the closed door.

"Please, senor. They say it is urgent."

Molly held her breath, quietly thanking Angelita for the timely interruption.

With another wild curse, Charles flung himself off the bed and buttoned his fly. He angrily pulled open the door and slammed it behind him, leaving Molly quaking with relief.

She rolled off the bed and slipped into her bedclothes, still shaking with fear. She'd very nearly been raped by her own fiancé. She wondered why fear had been her first response. Why hadn't her body been aroused, just knowing she was arousing him? She shouldn't have fought him. She wouldn't have, if she were really in love with him. She'd have welcomed him into her bed, and her body—as she'd welcomed Buck the night before.

Crawling under her covers, she shuddered, the thought of sleeping with Charles suddenly repulsing her. But it was the shock she'd just experienced. That was all. Surely, once she and Charles were married, she would feel differently, and Charles would be different, too. He'd lost control, yes. But she knew it was because he'd been so worried about her. So concerned for her safety. Obviously, he'd just briefly snapped when he'd discovered he'd been worrying needlessly. And she would welcome him into her bed once they were married. She would have to. She'd do anything to purge her guilt for sleeping with, and loving, Buck Randall.

She had to face Charles with the truth. Everything had slowly become clear to her. Charles loved her and desired her. He'd been wild with worry during her capture; it was no wonder he'd lost control once he discovered she was all right. But now she knew what she had to do. The first thing tomorrow, she would tell him everything. If Buck was right, and Charles turned against her, she'd just have to return to San Francisco and find herself a better paying job so she could move her mother in with her.

She really hoped it didn't come to that. From Charles's response to her just a while before, she was certain he loved her enough to ignore her heritage. But the other thing Buck had told her still bothered her. She still didn't want to believe Charles was involved with crooks. In that respect, she truly hoped Buck was dead wrong. But if he was right, her decision was made. She felt a strange sense of peace.

There was a quiet knock on the door. She held her breath, fear suddenly twisting inside her.

"Senorita?"

Molly relaxed. "Come in, Angelita."

The housekeeper entered with a small splint and some clean linen. She came to the bed and quietly worked on Molly's wrist.

"Thank you for that very timely interruption, Angelita."

Angelita gave her a knowing smile. "Fortunately, Mr. Reno had to talk to Senor Campion immediately."

"Maybe with some help from you?"

Her smile widened, and they exchanged wicked little knowing glances. "Maybe with just a little help."

"I want to ask you something," Molly said, resting back on her pillows.

"Si, go ahead."

"Did . . . how did you know I wasn't a White?" It was a dangerous question, but since Molly fully expected her secret to be out in the morning anyway, it made little difference.

Angelita gave her a soft smile and put her hand over her heart. "In here I know. I see in your eyes when you first come here that we are sisters, of a sort." She shrugged slightly. "I have no logical proof; it's just a feeling, and I'm never wrong."

"And Buck didn't . . . didn't tell you about me?"

"Senor Buck? Why would he tell me anything about you?"

Molly tried to relax against the bed, but the memory of her shrewish behavior that day in the line shack came back to haunt her. "It isn't important now." She glanced down at the clean, fresh wrapping around her wrist. "Thank you, Angelita."

"You want I should brush your hair to dry it?"

"Oh, yes. That would be lovely," Molly answered.

While Angelita brushed her hair, Molly probed again. "Why do you stay here when Charles treats you so badly?"

"I come here after Nicolette's mama died. The *nina* was only three years old." She stopped brushing momentarily, as if remembering. "She was an angel," she began, pulling the brush through Molly's hair again. "Her papa, he don't see how she turns to me for comfort. He had none to give her. He was a cold, heartless man. The boy, he didn't seem to need or want anything from me. But Nikky . . . she needed loving. I gave it to her. I stay because of her."

When Molly's hair was dry, Angelita left her. She thought again about her behavior these past weeks. In many ways, she'd become a woman she didn't like very much. It was partly because she felt guilty lying about her heritage, and partly because she hated herself for loving Buck. Hopefully, after tomorrow and her confession to Charles, she would like herself once again. She hadn't realized how heavy a burden lying was. She was ready to stop lying—to herself and to Charles. But she wondered if she would ever stop loving Renegade Randall.

A brief picture of him with his red-robed whore burst before her, and she tried to rekindle the fires of her hatred. She couldn't. All she felt was that tightness in her chest, and the sick, hollow feeling that had come over her when she'd known he'd left her to go see the other woman, and how easy it had been for him to do it.

🦋 Thirteen 🦋

The morning sun woke Molly, as did the throbbing in her wrist. She'd slept in spite of it. She slid from the bed and went to the wardrobe, rifling through her dresses until she came to the yellow embroidered silk-organza with the two-tiered skirt. She had to look her best for the difficult meeting with Charles.

Angelita came in and helped her dress and fix her hair, then left on a quick errand. When Molly was ready, she stepped to the mirror and scrutinized herself. She sighed helplessly when she looked at her hair. It had become sun bleached, much like it had been when she was a girl. And her skin . . . She gave herself a doubtful look. That, too, was a color she remembered well. While she was growing up, by the end of the summer season, she had been browner than her mother. Although she wasn't that dark now, she certainly was not fashionably pale. She gave herself a wry smile. *Not very stylish, Molly-girl.* Bleached hair or not, she was beginning to look like a breed. She shook her head and shrugged. What did it matter now?

Taking a deep breath, she left her room, and, after a small breakfast of biscuits and berries with cream, she went to look for Charles. She found him in his office. The minute he saw her, he was on his feet, his face creased with remorse.

"Darling," he said, taking her hands as he met her in the

middle of the room. "Please, you must forgive me. My behavior last night was abominable." He kissed her hands, suddenly noticing her splint.

"What happened?" He cradled her wrist in his palm.

"I broke it," she said simply. She was tired of the inconvenience, and even sicker of explaining how she got it.

The concern he'd already shown deepened. "Oh, Margaret," he said on a sigh. "What you've gone through . . . can you ever forgive me?"

She gave him a little laugh. "Forgive you, Charles? It wasn't your fault I was abducted . . . was it?" She remembered clearly that the kidnappers had thought they'd taken Nicolette.

Unreadable changes crossed his face. "I . . . I hope not. But a man in my position, well, anything is possible. Blackmail is quite common when one has money and power."

At least he hadn't denied he could be responsible. But that didn't mean he was a crook, either. "I do believe that's what happened. They thought I was Nicolette."

He groaned and led her to a chair by the desk. "If anything had happened to you—" He shook his head, unable to continue.

"I'm all right, Charles. And if someone had to be taken, I'm glad it was me and not Nicolette. I wouldn't have wanted her to go through what . . . what I did."

Charles slumped into the chair behind his desk and put his head in his hands. "I don't deserve you, Margaret." He looked up, his face filled with longing. "I hope my behavior last night didn't ruin what we could have together. I want to marry you, Margaret, and the sooner the better. I promise I won't dishonor you ever, ever again. You were just . . . just so beautiful, and I'd missed you and worried about you for days . . ."

His sincerity gave Molly courage. "Charles, please. I believe you. But . . . but I have something to tell you."

Even though her stomach twisted into knots, she knew she couldn't back out now.

"Anything, my sweet. Anything."

She took a deep breath. It was now or never. "I know you love me, Charles. And, love . . . love is a strong and wonderful thing." Briefly, she thought of his mother's tragedy, but she pushed it away. Sighing again, she said, "This isn't easy, Charles."

"Margaret, Margaret. Please," he said with a nervous laugh, "you're beginning to scare me. What is it? You don't want to marry me after all? If my actions last night were to blame—"

"Oh, no. No, Charles, that's not it at all. I've . . . I've just been keeping something from you, and I think you deserve to know the entire truth about me and my family before you truly commit yourself to me and . . . and to them."

He tried to laugh, but it was strained. "Don't tell me, Margaret. Is your father a politician? Or maybe it's your mother. She's an ax murderess, right?"

Her stomach quivered and the contents of her breakfast pressed up into her throat. She tried to give him an answering smile. "No, no, it's not that."

He leaned forward, concerned. "Well, what can be so awful that you can't tell me?"

"It's . . . it's my . . . my mother. She's a half-breed."

The room was shrouded in silence. Molly stared at her hands, hearing only the thumping of her heart. She'd never been ashamed of what she was. She'd only been ashamed that she hadn't told him sooner. She looked up to find him watching her. A shiver of fear turned her insides to ice.

Finally, he said, "That isn't a very funny joke, Margaret."

She glanced away, her apprehension growing. "It's no joke, Charles. It's the truth. Not only is my mother a half-breed, but she's quite simple. She's sweet and warm and beautiful, but she's . . . she's childlike. And," she added, purging herself completely, "I'm a bastard. My mother was raped. Not by an Indian, but by a white soldier."

She paused, waiting for him to respond. He didn't, so she stumbled on. "I've heard about what happened to your mother. It seems . . . it seems we have something in common, after all. Don't you think?" She didn't know if she felt relief or fear.

Charles expelled a deep sigh, rose from his chair and crossed to the window. Molly followed him with her eyes, watching . . . waiting . . . holding her breath until her head throbbed. It was a long time before he finally spoke.

"Margaret, Margaret . . ." His voice was a whisper, but Molly sensed the strained energy behind it. "Just what is it that you think we have in common?"

Molly swallowed anxiously. "I think it's rather obvious, Charles. Both of our mothers suffered at the hands of . . . of cruel and heartless men."

He made a sound that she couldn't identify. "Do you know anything about Texas law?"

She frowned, wondering what the law had to do with it. "Of course I don't."

He continued to gaze out the window. "It's against the law for a white man to marry an Indian or a Mexican, Margaret."

Her frown deepened. Was this true? She didn't know. Maybe it was just an excuse.

"We could both go to jail. Did you know that?"

She laughed nervously. "Oh, Charles, really. Aren't you exaggerating, just a little?"

He turned on her, his eyes snapping fire. "It's the law. If you don't believe me, check with someone else." Suddenly he changed, his charm resurfacing. "I still want you very much, Margaret. My desire for you hasn't changed."

Want. Desire. Not love. She couldn't believe how wrong she'd been about him. She hid her feelings, still foolishly groping for something she knew she'd lost. "But, surely, if

we love each other, we can find a way around the law,
Charles."

He stepped closer, raking his gaze over her body. Desire
flared hot in his eyes. "I'm afraid that's not possible. Not
now. But I do have a proposition for you."

"A . . . proposition? Why don't I like the sound of
that?" She tried to act glib and casual, hiding her anguish.

He touched her chin, raising her face to meet his gaze.
"Such beauty." He shook his head in disbelief. "I wouldn't
have imagined you were a breed. But I think I can see it
now. Yes," he added, nodding slowly. "Your coloring from
the sun is most unfashionable. But very, very . . . interesting." Desire continued to flare in his eyes. "Stay, Margaret. Stay and become my mistress. I'll give you everything
you would have had as my wife."

Mistress? She stood, listening to the pounding of her
heart as she moved slowly away from him. Oh, no. She
would be mistress to no man. If she had been good enough
for marriage yesterday, she was good enough for marriage
today, despite her confession. So. Buck had been right all
along. Charles had no strength of character. He was weak,
shallow and assumed that whatever he wanted, he could
buy.

All of the men she'd ever looked up to in her life—
Nicolas, Sky, Jason and Buck—were breeds, like she was.
But she'd been blind to their values and beliefs in her
frantic race to become something she wasn't. Something
she could never be, no matter how hard she tried. And
now, she realized it hadn't been worth the effort.

She turned, noting the anger behind Charles's suave
facade. How had she allowed all of his material wealth to
blind her so? She wondered if she'd known on some unconscious level that he wasn't the man she'd hoped he was.
She'd allowed her foolish dreams to interfere with reality.
She, who'd always claimed to be so realistic.

His prejudices were too embedded. She knew that now.
There was no way anyone would change them. Perhaps

there was a law that prohibited marriage between Indians and Whites, but since no one else knew she had Indian blood, they could have married and kept her secret hidden between them. If he'd loved her as he professed he did, he would have moved heaven and earth to marry her, in spite of her heritage. Now she was relieved that he wasn't going to try.

So, her blood in his precious family tree would be a disaster, would it? Ha! He should *be* so lucky as to have the blood of her proud ancestors flowing through the veins of his pale children. Yes, Buck had spoken the truth. Had he been right about the illegal cattle sales, too? She could find out. It was something she could do for Buck and Sage, as she had greater access to the house than anyone else. But she needed time. She needed a plan.

"Mistress, Charles?" She paused at the door, pretending a casual interest.

"Yes, Margaret. I can still make you happy." He seemed eager, but his eyes were angry. She saw that clearly now.

Sighing dramatically, she said, "I'll have to think about it. It isn't exactly what I'd planned to do with my life."

"But you'll consider it?"

She opened the door, wanting more than anything to call him the sucking swine that he was. "Yes, I'll consider it."

Charles watched her leave. His features relaxed, the facade dropped. His eyes glazed over with hatred and his mouth curled into a snarl. The *bitch*. She'd almost pulled it off. Deception undoubtedly came easy to a woman like her—a lying breed. A damned beautiful one, but a lying bitch just the same.

Fury knotted his gut. He crossed to the desk and kicked his chair, sending it clattering against the wall. Oh, the times he'd kept his hands off her, wanting to wait until it was legal to press himself between those lush white thighs. *Fool*. He'd put the bitch on a pedestal, for god's sake, treated her like a goddamned queen, bragged about her beauty to his friends. And, dammit to hell, he'd *panted* after her to bear his children. His *white* children! And all along, he thought, tasting the bile in his mouth, all along she was just a filthy, deceitful *breed*.

He went to the window again and stared outside, seeing nothing. His jaw was so tight his neck ached. Hell, while she was gone, she'd probably slept with every dirty Mexican in the state. Who did she think she was, playing the modest virgin with him the night before? Oh, he still wanted her, all right. He wasn't going to let her go without giving her a great deal of what she deserved. No one. *No one* pulled something like this on Charles Campion and got away with it.

An evil grin cracked his mouth. He'd get into her bed one way or another. And now, since she wouldn't have the benefit of being his wife, she'd get what he liked to give best.

The angrier he got, the more his loins itched, aching for release. At that moment, the door opened, and the little Mex maid, Maria, poked her head in.

"Oh, senor, I'm sorry," she said, quaking deliciously. "I was going to clean. I didn't know anyone was in here."

He gave her a lavish, lusty smile. "Come in, Maria. Come in and close the door."

The timorous little mouse did as he asked and walked toward him, her face downcast, hidden by the long black fall of her hair.

Charles reached into his desk drawer and pulled out his special leather thongs. "Come here, whore." His voice was soft, seductive.

Maria's expression told him she remembered the last time he'd used the thongs, and she hadn't liked it. But she wisely said nothing.

"Are you wearing drawers, Maria?" he asked silkily.

She shook her head, still looking frightened. "No. You . . . you tell me not to, so I don't."

"Good girl." He pulled her to him and reached beneath her skirt to fondle her. Her crispy Mex hairs were already wet, in spite of her fear. He shivered with anticipation. "Now," he said, "get out of your clothes, then clean off the top of the desk. You know what to do after that, don't you, whore?"

She nodded, but tears streamed down her cheeks. Good, he thought, his root swelling. So good. Fighting was better, but it was also satisfying when they cried and whimpered.

Molly changed her clothes and left the house. She wanted to be alone in a place that didn't have the look, smell and feel of Charles Campion. On one of her earlier wanderings, she'd discovered a copse of cottonwood trees hidden behind a rocky knoll. It was an unlikely thicket of greenery tucked away in a landscape of dust and colored walls of sand, and for some reason it always made Molly feel safe.

She sat beneath the trees, her chin resting on her knees and her arms wrapped around them, and listened to the wind music. Suddenly, after her revealing meeting with Charles, she saw her life with such clarity. What a fool she'd been to think she could stand to live a lie. She couldn't even imagine why she'd wanted to try.

Charles had wanted to marry her—until he discovered her Indian blood. Now he still wanted her, but as a prize. Something to add to his collection of beautiful "things." After what had happened earlier, all she wanted was to be gone. To leave Texas and never come back. If she had any sense, she'd do it now, before she thought too much about it. But she'd committed herself to helping Buck, even though he hadn't asked for it. And truthfully, she wanted to know if Charles was a crook. And if he was, she wanted to help put him away. It would give her *such* satisfaction.

Lifting her face to the breeze, she closed her eyes, amazed at how quickly her feelings for Charles had changed. All it had taken was for her to see him as he really was—behind the handsome facade. She'd known all along that she hadn't loved him, but in the beginning, she'd thought she could learn to care. She'd even foolishly dreamed of falling in love with him.

She shuddered, once again wanting to leave and never have to look at him again. But she knew she couldn't. There was Nicolette to consider. She couldn't just leave without setting things right with the girl. She would have to tell her why she wouldn't be marrying her brother. Unless, of course, Charles got to her first. Poor Nicolette. All the girl really wanted was a family, people to love her, to be there for her. It wasn't fair that she couldn't have such simple, honest pleasures.

Letting her mind wander back a few weeks, she thought about Nicolette and Cody. She winced, recalling the terrible beating he'd gotten from Mr. Poteet. She gazed up at the leaves, studying the variety of colors and shapes, allowing herself to wonder what had happened to the boy. Charles hadn't mentioned him, which was a good sign. But she hadn't seen Cody leave the kitchen after breakfast with the other hands either.

She tamped down her fear. He was probably just out mending fences or windmills. The men were often gone weeks at a time doing those lonely chores.

She glanced down at her splinted wrist and made a few weak fists. At least she could move her fingers. She'd have to continue to exercise that hand, or she'd never play the piano again. A harsh ache spread through her when she thought of not being able to play. It had always been such a strong force in her life. Although she'd never expected to play at the concert level, she'd fully intended to use her skills teaching. Hopefully, she still could. She'd neither had the discipline nor the talent to become a concert star. Nicolette had the talent. But so far, she had no discipline.

Molly continued to press her fingers into a fist, ignoring the constant ache in her wrist.

"How is it?"

She jumped, pressing her hand over her heart as Buck

stepped in front of her. "I thought you were in Cedarville," she groused.

"I was, now I'm back." He hunkered down beside her and examined her wrist. "Nice job. How is it?" he repeated.

"It will be fine once it's healed," she answered abruptly. She looked up at him, assuming she'd see that his visit to his whore had given him some relief. Oddly, he looked more tired than before.

"Well, how is she? Did she miss you?" Again, she sounded like a jealous fishwife. But that wasn't it entirely. Just the fact that he was still sleeping around in brothels told her he hadn't changed completely. No matter how much she might love him, she didn't want a man who, at nearly thirty years of age, hadn't embraced his responsibilities and settled down.

He sat down beside her. "I'm assuming, by the tone of your voice, that you really don't want to know."

"Oh, please," she begged dramatically, "*please* tell me how eager she was to have you back in her bed. *Please* tell me that she wore that whorish red robe, flicking it open to show you her naked body the minute you walked through the damn door." Tears clogged her throat, and she turned away, hating herself for letting her jealousy get the best of her.

He said nothing in his defense. "You're in my secret place."

She turned and glared at him. "Is that all you have to say?"

He gave her a careless shrug. "You seem to have it all neat and tidy in your little pea brain. I suppose it wouldn't matter if I told you it was a mercy visit."

She snorted a tear filled laugh. "Oh, please."

"Just as I thought," he said, leaning back against a tree.

They sat side by side, listening to the wind hiss through the trees.

Finally, he asked, "What brings you out here? You look

lonely. Your first day back with your wonderful fiancé not what you expected it to be?"

She didn't want to play any more word games. "I told him about my mother this morning."

There was a harsh intake of breath, on which he uttered a curse. "I won't say 'I told you so.' "

She managed a wan smile. "You already did."

"I'm sorry," he said simply. "I suppose you'll be leaving, then."

"Oh, that would suit you just fine, wouldn't it?" She felt her anger flare and couldn't rein it in.

"What in the hell is that supposed to mean?"

She shook her head, hating the tears that threatened. "Never mind."

"No," he insisted. "Tell me what's on your mind, brat."

Oh, wonderful, she thought miserably. So he was back to calling her that. Suddenly, now that they were back at the ranch, everything that had happened between them the past week was forgotten. Even though she'd known nothing would come of their lovemaking, it still hurt to think he could so easily forget what they had shared. Now she had no one. Nothing. She didn't have Charles. Of course, she didn't want him, anyway. But she didn't have Buck, either, and the secret part of her soul wanted him more than he would ever know.

"There's nothing on my mind, honest. I'm . . . I'm just upset, that's all. But you weren't right about everything. Charles still wants me. Oh, yes," she said vehemently. "He definitely wants me." She sucked in a breath. "As his *mistress*," she finished, the word tasting like bile in her mouth.

He pulled her to him. "Ah, Molly. I'm sorry. I'm really sorry this didn't work out for you."

She knew it was foolish, but she pressed herself against him, reveling in the comfort, knowing it was a transitory thing. Suddenly his scent awakened memories of their night together, and her body began to respond, swelling and throbbing with need. She pulled away briefly and looked up at him.

"Buck?" It was a question that needed no verbal answer. His mouth came down on hers, hard and explosive. She responded with pent-up longing, accepting the brutal kiss. His tongue pressed against her teeth, and she opened for him. For a brief, palpable moment, with their mouths open, their lips merely touched. Anticipation made her quake with desire. Slowly, deliberately, his tongue entered her mouth, and she drew him in with greedy force.

As their tongues made love, his hands moved along her ribs until they reached her breasts. His thumbs circled her aching nipples, causing heat to explode in her belly. He pulled her onto his lap, and she ground against him; he was already hard beneath her. She twisted, bringing one leg around so that she sat astride, her knees on the grass.

She rose slightly, then settled herself over him, rocking against the long, firm ridge beneath his fly. Pleasure flooded her as potent desire radiated up from her core. She continued to move, pressing hard, drawing back slightly, only to return to press against him again. The heated delta between her thighs was engorged, swelling with hunger and melting her bones, leaving her weak with pleasure.

She rocked against him, shuddering with a desire so strong, she thought she might burst into an explosion of hot sparks. She pulled her mouth away and pressed her nose against his neck, then back to his mouth, where they kissed again. She moaned, losing focus as shards of pleasure shot through her, bringing her to release.

She slumped against him, resting her head on his shoulder.

He smoothed her hair and patted the back of her head. "Well," he said lightly, "a little dry humping never hurt anybody."

Shame and humiliation made her flare with anger. She pulled back and punched him hard in the chest with her good fist, then rolled to her feet. "You *pig!*" She stood and glared at him. "You really *are* a bastard, aren't you?"

Without a backward glance, she ran toward the house, not stopping until she knew he couldn't see her anymore.

Buck collapsed against the tree and rubbed his face, cursing his lack of self-control. But hell, he couldn't let her think what they'd had together meant anything. It was far better that she think he was an unfeeling pig, than a man who might care for her. Every damned time he saw her, he wanted her. He'd known having her for one night wouldn't be enough. If only she'd leave now that Campion had rejected her. If she would, everything would be fine. She'd be safe from Campion . . . and from him.

As it was, he thought, reaching into his pocket for a cigarette, Campion had no reason to wait to get into her bloomers now. If he knew the bastard as well as he thought he did, he was already plotting to do just that. Buck had meant to warn her about it, but . . . hell. She'd given him that *look*. The one that had made him want to rip off her clothes and make love to her on the grass. Just one time . . . Just once he'd like to love her in the daytime, so he could watch her face, kissing the flush that would sprout on her chest as she reached her climax. . . . He wanted to touch her everywhere and see just exactly what he was touching.

Instead, he had to act like she meant nothing to him. He had to *make* her hate him, because loving him would hurt both of them and get her nowhere. Now, when she probably needed him the most because of Campion's rejection, he had to make sure she didn't want him at all.

As he lit his cigarette, drawing the smoke deep into his lungs, he forced himself to think of something else. Nita. Ah, hell, he thought, his stomach twisting into knots. Thinking of her didn't do any good, either.

❧ Fourteen ❧

Molly had stumbled to her room after the fiasco with Buck and spent the rest of the day there by herself. For hours she tried to sift through her feelings. She thought back to their escape and how caring and considerate Buck had been throughout the entire episode. Without complaint he'd come to her aid, nursed her broken wrist and her cut and scraped feet. He'd confided his miseries to her, using her to help ease his own personal demons about Honey's death. He'd been gentle, tender and vulnerable. He'd needed to talk to someone, and he'd chosen her. She'd been a most willing and compassionate listener. After all, she loved him.

She had no idea what had changed him once they returned to the ranch. It amazed her that she could still love him so much, considering the crass way he treated her. She should have known he'd never change. A person couldn't go from a drunken, whoring bastard to a kind, caring lover —not in a lifetime.

She closed her eyes briefly, remembering her frantic response to his touch. Likewise, she thought, a person couldn't go from loving one man all of her life to simply not loving him at all, in spite of what he was. It hurt that he could cast her aside so easily, but she'd be damned if she'd let him know it.

The next morning, she rose early to help Angelita prepare breakfast for the ranch hands. Dallas, the toothless old man with the feed bag whiskers, had come in early and was regaling the women with stories about his youth.

"Yep, yep," he said, nodding slowly. "Well, back'n them days I was workin' way south to the border. One of the best things I ever et was called s.o.b."

Molly couldn't help laughing. "Sounds pretty nasty, Dallas. What was it?"

"Well, ya take a yearling—that's a small calf, missy—and kill it, o'course. Ya take the small intestines," he added, pronouncing the second *i* long, "marrow, gut, heart and liver, chop it into pieces, add tallow and a little beef and cook the devil out of it." He smacked his gums. "Top it off with chili powder, enuf ta set yer mouth ablaze, and chow down."

Molly made a face. Angelita just shook her head, obviously having heard the recipe before.

Dallas cackled with delight. "I burned the insides of my mouth raw the first couple 'a times I et it."

Molly was glad she hadn't been hungry when she came down to help. If she had been, she wouldn't have been after that story. But the old geezer was such a sweetheart. His escapades always lifted her sagging spirits.

She was busy cutting corn bread into large, square pieces and heaping them onto a platter when one shiver chased another along her spine. Without turning toward the door, she knew Buck had entered the kitchen.

Gathering her poise, she shifted the platter onto her forearm and tried to lift it off the counter.

Sage saw her dilemma and was at her side immediately. "Here, now, ma'am," he said, taking the platter and putting it on the table. "That broken wrist is sure an inconvenience, isn't it?"

She gave him a grateful smile. "I wouldn't wish it on anyone, Mr. Reno." Except Buck, she thought, narrowing her eyes in his direction. He ignored her as he heaped scrambled eggs and beef sausage onto his plate.

Dallas split a biscuit and slathered it with butter. When he chewed, his toothless gums smacked together, drawing his chin nearly up to his nose. "Hey, Buck. Who ya gonna git to haul freight now't the kid's gone?"

"Why not Saul?" one of the other men interjected. "Hell, the last time he did it, he did a fine job." All the men laughed.

Dallas snorted. "Yeah, after he got the lead mule in the right spot. 'Afore that, the ornery critters ripped off the wagon yard gate and tore up the side of the poultry house." He cackled, his eyes watering. "Last time I seen so many damned chickens screechin' and squawkin' was when there was a fox in the henhouse."

Another hand nodded, laughing. "Never saw that much hay fly off'n the back of a wagon, neither."

Saul, a quiet boy who blushed easily, continued to eat, obviously trying to ignore the jibes.

"Ain't got nothin' to say fer yerself, Sauly?" Dallas always enjoyed teasing the younger men. Early on, Molly had noticed that he didn't do much work himself. She was surprised that Mr. Poteet hadn't sent him packing.

Saul skidded two more pieces of corn bread onto his plate and smothered them with syrup. "I ain't much for haulin' freight, I admit that, but I can heap a pile of cow chips higher'n anyone here, I reckon," he answered, poking a little fun at himself.

Dallas laughed again and slapped the kid on the back. "That you can, boy. That you can."

While the men ate, Molly hovered nearby in case there was something they needed. The men generally ignored her, and she appreciated that, for she didn't like to call attention to herself, and the men seemed to respect her. Initially, Charles had hated her helping Angelita, but now that he knew what she was, he'd probably encourage it. It didn't matter. She rather enjoyed it, except for mornings like this, when there was so much tension between her and Buck, she could almost slice it with a switchblade.

After the men had eaten and left to attend their chores, and the kitchen was cleaned up in preparation for another meal, Molly sat down at the long table with a cup of coffee. She'd barely taken a sip when Nicolette burst in through the back door. She stood and stared at Molly, her face crestfallen.

"Oh, Margaret . . . I'm so glad you're all right. I'm sorry you had to go through such a terrible thing."

Her genuine concern and dismay touched Molly's heart. She wished, for Nicolette's sake, that things could have been different for them. "It's over, and I'm fine, honey. Let's not dwell on it."

Nicolette hurried to her and gently touched her splint. "And this. They did this to you?"

Molly reached out and tugged Nicolette toward her. "Come and sit with me."

The girl slumped onto the bench. "Oh, Margaret. Things just seem to be falling apart." She looked at Molly, her brow pinched with worry. "Is . . . is it true that you're not going to marry Charles because you have Indian blood?"

Molly pushed a wayward curl off the girl's shoulder. "It's true. But it's really the other way around, Nicolette. It's because of my Indian blood that your brother chooses not to marry me."

Nicolette's eyes filled. "I don't want to believe he's really that . . . that much of a bigot." She rested her elbow on the table and put her chin in her hand. "I . . . I really thought he loved you to distraction."

Molly was still weary from the kidnapping ordeal, and hadn't yet gathered strength enough to toil in the kitchen without tiring, much less do verbal exercises with Nicolette. "Well, I'm afraid it's true. All of it," is all she said.

"Why didn't you tell me? You know I don't care about those things."

Molly swung her gaze from her lap to Nicolette's face. "But your brother does," she answered softly. "And I . . .

I thought I had to be sure of his love before I said anything about myself to anyone. It was really foolish, I know that now. I don't know what I was thinking. Even if I had never told him, he'd surely have figured it out once my mother came to live with us."

Nicolette gave her a puzzled look. "Your mother?"

"He probably didn't mention her," Molly said with a weary sigh.

When Nicolette shook her head, Molly added, "I somehow thought that since I didn't look Indian, I could live my life without acting like one. I was a fool to think that could happen. My mother is a dear, dear woman. She's a beautiful, delicate half-breed, Nicolette, and although she's almost thirty-eight years old, she still acts very much like a young girl."

She told Nicolette about her mother's rape, about the people who loved both of them and helped raise her. She mentioned her secret need to become successful, to marry well, all because she desperately wanted to help care for her mother.

When she'd finished, Nicolette sat quietly for a while, then suddenly stood and ran from the room, her hand over her mouth as if she were trying to keep from bursting into tears.

Molly gave her a few minutes, then followed her. When she reached Nicolette's room, she saw her on her knees in front of the chamber pot.

She rushed to the girl and knelt down beside her. "What's wrong, honey? What is it?"

Nicolette lifted her head and gave Molly a look of pure, abject misery. "I don't know what's happening to me," she whimpered through her tears. "For no reason at all, I get sick to my stomach. I'm perfectly fine," she added, "then suddenly . . . suddenly I'm so sick I think I'm going to die."

Dread twisted in Molly's chest, curling around her heart

and pinching her stomach. "Oh, dear. When was the last time you flowed?"

Nicolette gave her a pitiful look. "I don't remember."

Molly slid to the floor beside her and closed her eyes. *No, not this. Anything but this.*

"What's . . . what's wrong with me, Margaret? Do you . . . do you think it's serious?"

Molly looked at Nicolette's chalky face, her wide blue eyes and quivering mouth. She smoothed back the girl's hair. "It's serious, all right." When Nicolette collapsed into tears, she added, "But it isn't fatal."

"I'm not going to die?"

Smiling grimly, Molly shook her head. "I think you're going to have a baby."

Nicolette blanched whiter, then she flushed.

Molly got to her feet, pulling Nicolette up after her. "Come on, little one. Tell me all about it."

She grudgingly followed Molly into her room and sat down beside her on the bed. "It's . . . it's Cody."

"Yes," Molly said on a sigh. "I rather thought it was."

"He's gone, Margaret."

Another stab of fear entered her chest. "Gone? You mean, he just up and left?" She realized now that the "kid" Dallas had referred to at breakfast was Cody.

Nicolette closed her eyes, tears pearling on her cheeks. "He . . . we were so close. I love him, Margaret. Why would he leave me like this?"

Molly shuddered. She knew that kind of love well. It was spelled *l-u-s-t.* She'd experienced it herself—although fortunately it hadn't been consummated—at least not then. But this . . . She'd instinctively known there would be trouble from the moment Cody hired on.

She looked at the girl again, wondering if perhaps the boy hadn't been forced to leave. Another thought assaulted her. Maybe Charles had killed him. It was an awful thought, but knowing what she did now, and knowing that Charles knew of Nicolette's trysts with Cody, she was almost certain the boy was dead. Gone. But her gut feelings wouldn't help Nicolette. She pulled the girl into her arms, having not the slightest idea what they were going to do about this.

"We'll keep this from Charles as long as we can," she said. "Unless . . . unless you want to get rid of it." She held her breath, knowing it was the practical thing to do, yet foolishly hoping it wouldn't come to that.

Nicolette shook her head violently. "No. No. I don't care about Charles. He can't make me kill Cody's baby. He *can't.*"

Molly wondered how much she knew of her mother and what had happened to her. "Well, then, let's make sure he doesn't find out. When were you supposed to go back to school?"

"I thought I'd stay here until the last week in August. Now I don't know." She gazed up at Molly. "How big will I be by then?"

Molly pinched the bridge of her nose. She didn't think Nicolette could be more than two months pregnant, not unless Cody had successfully seduced her almost immediately. "If we're careful, we might be able to hide it until then."

Nicolette snuggled close. "I don't want you to leave, Margaret. Not until I do."

Molly smoothed the girl's curls, hiding her own selfish disappointment. If it were up to her, she'd be on the first train to California. But she had other things to do. At least she'd be around for Nicolette—for a while. She shuddered to think about what Charles would do if—or when—he found out his baby sister was going to have a half-breed's baby.

"What's going on here?"

Nicolette froze in her arms. Molly glanced up to find Charles standing in the doorway. "Nicolette has a bug of some sort. She's sick."

He gazed at them for a long time. "That's odd. She seemed fine when I picked her up this morning."

"Well, she's not fine now, Charles. She's miserable."

He sighed impatiently. "All right. Feed her some warm milk or something and put her to bed. I don't have time for this. I'm expected in Cedarville this afternoon."

When he'd gone, Molly let out a long, pent-up breath of air. "Why don't you crawl into bed, honey?"

"Can I sleep in yours?"

"Of course. Here," she said, "let's get you undressed." She helped Nicolette get out of her clothes, then tucked her into bed in her drawers and camisole. She bent down and smoothed back the girl's hair.

"I'll go down and see if Angelita has something for your stomach." She debated telling the housekeeper about the baby. She thought she would; she needed the woman's help to deal with this.

Tears slid from Nicolette's closed eyes. "I really love you, Margaret."

Molly's insides twisted with emotion. "And I really love you, too, honey." She moved toward the door.

"Margaret?"

She stopped and turned, giving the girl a gentle smile. "Yes, sweetie?"

"Why are all these terrible things happening?"

Molly leaned against the door frame and sighed. "Bad things happen. All we can do is deal with them the best we can." She left the room, wondering how this was all going to end, and dreading the outcome.

Molly stood at the window and watched Charles ride off on his blood bay. She waited a few minutes, then crossed to the study, opened the door and slipped inside. As she leaned against the closed study door, she listened to the noisy thump of her heart. It seemed to echo in the quiet room. But she had to do this. Somehow, she had to find out if Charles was dealing in stolen cattle, and the only place she could think of looking was in his study.

Pulling in a deep breath, she crossed the blue and gray striped Venetian carpet to the mahogany desk and studied the drawers. Each one had a beautiful, leaf-carved wooden grip. She grimaced. And each drawer also had a keyhole. She tugged on each of the nine drawers. They were all locked up tighter than strung piano wire.

She sat down in the chair and studied her problem. Naturally he wouldn't keep any incriminating papers out in plain sight, and she had a feeling that even if she somehow got into the drawers, she wouldn't find what she was looking for.

She bent down and studied the panels on the inner walls of the desk. Nothing. The outside? Maybe. She went around to the outside panel closest to the fireplace. Nothing there, either.

The quiet room was giving her guilty jitters. She'd thought about including Angelita in her search, but she didn't want to get the woman into trouble in case they were caught. But she didn't want to get caught snooping, either.

She glanced at the pastoral painting on the wall over the Empire sideboard. Charles's wall safe was back there; she'd seen him open it in front of her before. That was the likely spot for something he wanted to hide, but there was no way for her to get into it.

Pushing out a frustrated sigh, she walked toward the door, stopped and turned. With an eager sprint, she returned to the desk and checked the other side panels, those closest to the wall—close enough so that they couldn't be seen clearly from any angle in the room.

Her heart leaped as her fingers pushed the back panel. Although she couldn't find a keyhole, the panel jiggled. Pushing back her excitement, she pressed her fingers along the edges. Suddenly she heard a *click*, and the panel popped open.

With her good hand, she reached inside and pulled out everything she touched. Sitting on the floor next to the window, she went over every item, stacking each carefully beside her when she was finished. On the bottom, she found a small envelope. As she opened it, her heart surged with discovery. It might be nothing, but then, it might be just what Buck and Reno were looking for. It was a map, and there was a series of Xs scattered over the surface.

She dug into her pocket and pulled out a piece of paper, laid it over the map, and traced the outline of the map and the markings.

Anxious to get out of the study, she clumsily stacked everything back into the cubbyhole, shut the panel and crossed to the door. Hearing no movement in the hallway, she quietly left the study and crept down the hall toward the stairs.

"Afternoon, ma'am."

She stopped, her heart beating a wild tattoo against her ribs. Turning, she looked straight into the sweaty, ugly face of Hiram Poteet. "Mis-Mister Poteet," she managed to say, hoping she sounded calmer than she felt.

His beady gaze flicked to the closed study door. "The boss in?"

She swallowed hard, hoping guilt wasn't written on her face. "No. Ah . . . I think he went into Cedarville this afternoon."

He nodded, his gaze moving from the door back to her. "Thought mebbe he was in since you come out of his study."

She nervously touched the pocket that held the map. "He's not in, Mr. Poteet. Now, if you'll excuse me, I have something to take care of."

She hurried to her room, her guilt escalating. The foreman had frightened her. He'd obviously seen her come out of the study, and no doubt would tell Charles. Pulling in a deep breath, she realized she had to relax. She hadn't taken anything. Even if Charles were to discover she'd been in there, he wouldn't find anything missing.

She pulled out the map and studied it, hoping it would help Buck and Sage. Later, after it was dark, she'd try to find one of them and show them what she'd discovered.

Charles hadn't returned by dinnertime, and Angelita surrendered to Molly's request that she and Nicolette eat in the kitchen. Nicolette toyed with her food, but managed to eat a fresh hot biscuit and some flan. When they'd finished, Molly urged the girl to practice for a while. She joined Nicolette in the salon and listened to the beautiful strains of a Chopin nocturne. Each time she heard a noise, she jumped, hoping Charles wouldn't come home until she'd delivered her message to Buck or Sage.

Finally, Nicolette begged to stop, claiming fatigue. When the girl had gone up to her room, Molly pulled on a light woolen shawl and stepped outside. Night sounds swooped upon her. Crickets *chirruped* under the porch beneath her feet. Somewhere in the distance, a horse whinnied, and if she listened very closely, she could hear cattle lowing in a nearby pasture.

Lifting her skirt, she stepped off the porch and made her way carefully over the uneven ground. Suddenly she stopped, realizing that it would be foolhardy to go to the bunkhouse and ask to see either Buck or Sage. Spying a flicker of light from the barn, she made her way there and quietly stepped inside. Again, the familiar smells gently assaulted her, reminding her of the day she'd confronted Buck after he'd broken the stallion.

Giving her head a stern shake, she stepped farther into the barn and walked toward the light. It wasn't relief that she felt when she saw Buck moving around in the back room. She would have preferred to find Sage, but she didn't have the luxury of time to go looking for him.

"Slumming again, brat?"

She jumped, rolling her eyes at her skittish behavior. "I suppose you smelled me this time, too."

He chuckled quietly. "Something like that."

She watched him work, the kerosene lamp throwing grim light on his task. His hands were capable, strong. Briefly, she remembered how they'd worked their magic that one night they'd had together under the stars. A lump formed in her throat, and she flung away the memory, hating the havoc it played with her emotions.

"What do you want?"

Clearing her throat, she dug out the map she'd drawn earlier and stepped closer to him. "I thought you might be able to use this."

He turned and glanced at her, then at the paper she offered. He put down the saddle and took the map, bringing it closer to the lamp. His forehead furrowed as he looked at it. "Where did you find this?"

She studied the top of his head, loving the way he pulled his hair to the back of his neck and tied it there. "I found it in a hidden panel on the side of Charles's desk."

He looked at her and frowned. "What in the hell were you doing in there?"

"Well, you're entirely welcome," she answered sarcastically.

"You could have been . . . He could have—"

"Charles had left for Cedarville. No one saw me, and I put everything back the way I found it." She held his gaze, deciding not to mention that she'd run into Mr. Poteet in the hallway. "Do you think it's important?"

Buck leaned into the light again and peered at the map, his index finger moving rhythmically over his lips. "Could be. By the outline, it looks like all of the land Campion owns, plus some that he doesn't." He traced the marks with his finger. "These Xs could be . . . could be where he's hidden the stolen cattle."

A bolt of excitement shot through Molly. "You really think so?"

He gave her a jaundiced look. "Do you realize what he'd have done to you if he'd caught you?"

She nodded, feeling her excitement dwindle into fear. "But I knew he'd be gone for hours, Buck."

"Just the same," he replied, rising from his workbench. "You aren't the precious commodity you once were. I think you'd better remember that."

She knew her status had tumbled in Charles's eyes. She hadn't thought of the consequences of her intrusion into his private study until now. Her stomach quivered.

"But you did good, brat," he said softly. "Sage and I will get on this as soon as we can."

She suddenly remembered the conversation she'd had with Nicolette in the general store. "Is this a personal vendetta, Buck?"

He glanced away and rubbed his neck. "Sort of."

"That old man, the one you lived with. Do you know who killed him?"

"I have a pretty good idea," he answered.

"You think it was Charles?" When Buck nodded, she added, "Why would Charles have bothered to have an old man killed?"

"Because . . . because that old man knew what Campion was up to. Somehow, he knew." He paused for a moment then added, "Haven't you noticed how Campion seems to deal with his problems? He gets rid of them and if the 'problem' happens to be human, he kills it." Something in his stance changed. He looked vulnerable.

"Was the man very special to you?" Molly asked.

He turned and looked at her, his expression carefully masked. "He saved my life. Yeah, he was pretty damned special."

His words, his voice worked magic on her, but she hid it from him. At least she thought she had.

"Dammit, girl. Don't look at me like that."

Swallowing hard, she let her gaze drop to the hay and dirt packed floor. "I . . . I don't know what you mean."

"Oh, you know all right," he said on a hiss of breath.

She squared her shoulders. "All right, maybe I do. I won't hide my feelings for you, Buck. I love you. It's the dumbest, most foolish thing I've ever admitted to anyone in my life, but God help me, it's true. I don't like the feeling, either. Why I'd subject myself to loving you makes no sense, especially since you treat me like a worn-out shoe." Her knees felt like pudding, and her heart jumped wildly in her chest at her admission.

Buck turned away and swore. "Love? Hell, brat. Love is only a word. One that can suck the feelings from you and kill your spirit. Believe me, I know. Love is . . . is some intangible emotion that can be blown away by the wind. Or killed by an unfaithful mate. Or smashed by the realities of a cruel, hateful world. Love," he scoffed. "It isn't worth the pain, Molly. It isn't worth the pain."

She sucked in a wild, shaky breath, turned and hurried out of the barn. Maybe one day she'd learn to keep her mouth shut. Maybe . . . For once again, she'd bared herself in front of this man, and he'd craftily poured salt into her wounded heart.

Buck noted the ramrod state of her spine as she hurried away. His gut still had knots in it every time he saw her. So, she thought she loved him. Hell, he knew he loved her. But loving was the easy part. The hard part was the reality of what loving another person meant. It meant exposing those raw nerve endings to the air. In the long run, it meant disappointment and more often than not, at least in his case, death. Besides, he didn't have a pot to piss in, yet his responsibilities continued to build.

His life was filling up with burdens he hadn't wanted to deal with, but deal with them he must. But, like breathing, no one could do it for him. And as provocative as sharing his troubles and his life with Molly sounded, he knew he had to handle them alone. Hell, Molly was just in love with the idea of being in love. He'd saved her sweet behind

more than once. She was beholden to him. For some stupid-ass reason, women got all misty-eyed when men played
the hero. It wasn't reality. It was a feeling based in fiction
and had no place in the grueling day-to-day world. She'd
get over it. As he bent over the map, he knew that he'd be
sorry when she did.

❦ Fifteen ❦

Three mornings later, after helping Angelita feed the hands, Molly ran into Charles in the dining room as she was setting the table for his breakfast. Being in a room alone with him suddenly made her flush, and she felt a burning ache in her chest. He had such an imperious look about him. Why hadn't she noticed it before? Perhaps she had, but *before*, she'd found it appealing—in a twisted sort of way, she decided. It was their first meeting alone since she'd told him the truth.

"Join me, Margaret." He seemed to sense her hesitation. "Please." His voice was warm, but his eyes were not.

She reluctantly sat down across from him, watching him with wary eyes as Angelita served him sourdough biscuits, a small steak and scrambled eggs. The housekeeper gave her a sympathetic look as she left the room.

"Well, my dear," Charles began, as he cut into his steak. "Have you given any thought to my proposal?"

Molly watched the blood ooze from the piece of rare meat, and her own breakfast pressed upward. She swallowed hard. "Of course I have, Charles. I've thought of little else." It wasn't a lie.

He gave her a benign smile. "And have you come to any conclusions?"

Pretending confusion, she studied the gold-tinged Lincrusta wallpaper and the scroll shaped brass sconce on the wall beside the window. What she really wanted to do was dump his plate, bloody meat and all, into his lap. "You'll have to forgive me, Charles. I . . . I need time." If nothing else, she *had* to convince him of her sincerity—even though the only thing she was sincere about was that she loathed him so much, she could barely stand to look at him.

He sipped his coffee, assessing her. "Time is running out, you know."

Her stomach plummeted. "Running out? What do you mean?"

"I mean, you must decide by the end of the week."

Her stomach dropped farther. "Why—" She swallowed, her mouth dry as dust. "Why by the end of the week?"

Chewing a piece of meat, he continued to study her. He swallowed, dabbing his mouth with his napkin. "Because I have a feeling if I don't give you an ultimatum, you'll never decide."

"Oh, Charles. That's ridiculous." She looked at him, noting the shuttering of any emotions behind his eyes. "Certainly you can understand my dilemma. Really, you . . . you proposed marriage in February. *Marriage*, Charles. That's something quite different from . . . from simply being one's mistress."

He gave her an infuriating patronizing laugh, then looked away. "Maybe for most women, Margaret, but I wouldn't think a woman like you . . . a woman in your position, would pass up the opportunity to live in this kind of luxury," he said with a sweeping motion of his arms.

A woman like you. In this kind of luxury. How quickly she'd come to realize that warmth and comfort aren't automatically found amidst luxury. How quickly she'd found everything he had to offer hollow and empty. "I'm a woman like any other, Charles. I don't want to be considered any man's property."

He gave her a look of disbelief. "But, Margaret. You're a

breed. Breeds are always someone else's property. It's the law."

She couldn't believe she hadn't seen through to his ugly soul before. "Who created this law, Charles?"

"Why, the government. And, of course," he added, nodding confidently, "God."

It was useless to argue. His twisted beliefs were so deeply entrenched, she'd be a fool to try. Gratefully, her gaze left him and found an incredibly interesting spot to study on the ceiling.

"I'm offering you something I'd never offer another woman like you." He flung up his hands in a gesture of incredulity. "I don't understand what there is to think about."

She stood, unable to tolerate being in the same room with him another second, much less breathing the same air. Still, she hid her fury and maintained her facade. "All right," she said with a forced sigh of acceptance. "You'll have your answer by the end of the week." She just hoped Buck and Sage had some answers then, too.

The rest of the day dragged. But she knew better than to go looking for Buck before dark. To make time go faster, she helped Angelita put up wild plum preserves, then sat with Nicolette as she practiced the piano.

As Nicolette played, Molly studied the wood paneling on the far wall. The unusual combination of square panels topped with a small border of arched panels intrigued her. Or maybe it was just something to take her mind off her own worries about not ever being able to play the piano again.

She automatically clenched her fist, finding some small measure of victory in the fact that each day, her fist appeared tighter, harder, stronger. There was still occasional pain, and always discomfort. The ache was deep inside and often radiated up into her elbow, and when she was very tired, even into her shoulder.

She listened to Nicolette play, yet part of her considered the other deep ache she felt daily. The ache of Buck's rejection. He'd hardened himself against loving again. He'd told her that over a week ago, and obviously, even though they'd shared a magical night together, he hadn't changed his mind. It was frustrating, but not nearly as frustrating as her own feelings. Still unable to understand how she could love a man who couldn't or wouldn't love her back, she tormented herself by imagining what life with Buck would be like—if he ever did change.

She fantasized about it. She allowed her mind to go into full, rapturous ecstasy thinking about it. How wonderful it would be to curl up against that hard, wide chest every night, to press herself against him and find him wanting her as much as she wanted him. To experience nightly what she'd experienced only one night. . . . To be loved, adored, satisfied, all by the same man. In full view of the world. Proudly. Openly. And it wasn't just that she hungered for him in a sexual way. She wanted to be his mate, to share his pain, to celebrate his successes. She envisioned them going back to California and raising Dusty together. In spite of everything he'd said and done, she knew that deep down in a place no one had yet touched, he was a good man.

Nicolette suddenly stopped playing, also bringing a halt to Molly's daydreaming.

The girl scooted off the bench. "I'm gonna be sick," she mumbled, running from the room.

Molly briefly closed her eyes and massaged the tension in her neck. Hopefully, Nicolette's morning sickness wouldn't last too much longer. "Morning sickness" was rather a foolish term, she thought, for the poor girl seemed to be gripped with nausea at odd times throughout the entire day.

With a weary sigh, Molly stood and stretched her back. Ever since her meeting with Charles at breakfast, she'd experienced an edgy sense of panic. She hadn't seen Buck or Sage for almost three days and wondered if they were checking on the map locations, or if Charles had sent them to do other chores. Even if he had, she was sure they would find a way to look into the possibility that stolen cattle were being held at the marked sites.

She crossed to the window and gazed outside. The days were getting warmer as they pushed deeper into summer. Even so, the house was cool. So cool, that Molly shivered. Or maybe that was just a response to what was happening in her life.

Angelita's daughter, Carmen, had come over earlier in the morning to give her mother a hand in the kitchen, as she often did. This morning she'd brought Estella, her eight-year-old daughter, with her, who was now playing in the yard with a little boy. Molly hadn't seen him before. He didn't appear to be any older than two, or at most three. She smiled at how the girl mothered the boy. She was currently teaching him how to pet one of the many dogs that roamed the ranch. Molly's grin widened as the dog lifted its head and licked the boy on the face. Both children laughed gleefully, and Molly felt a strange tugging that made her want to cry.

It had been crazy, this strange urge to begin a family. It had started when she and Buck had spent so much time together coming from the camp to the ranch. They were strange, deep twinges that left her wanting something, someone to care for and love.

She felt a wry smile lift one corner of her mouth. Who would have thought that she, Molly Lindquist, would have felt such a strong, aching pull toward motherhood.

She continued to watch the children, wondering who the little boy belonged to. He was a sweet thing, giggling engagingly as the dog continued to lap away at his cheek and ears. She knew it wasn't Angelita's grandson, for Angelita had despaired repeatedly about her daughter's inability to have another child. Like her, she had told Molly, her daughter was only able to conceive once.

Still feeling chilled, Molly left the salon and went outside. The heat felt wonderful as she lifted her face to the sun. Ever since she'd returned from her abduction, she'd scorned wearing a large brimmed hat and gloves, having decided it didn't matter anymore whether her skin was tanned or not. Of course, it wasn't fashionable, but she was already so dark from that week on the plains with Buck, that it didn't matter.

The children quit playing with the dog and watched her come toward them. Molly waved. Anxious to use some of the Spanish she'd practiced with Angelita as they prepared meals for the ranch hands, she called, "*Hola!* Estella." When the girl waved back, Molly asked, "*Quien es tu amigo paquito?*"

"*El se llama Tomas,*" the girl answered.

Molly squatted down in front of him and smiled. "*Hola!* Tomas."

Gravely, Tomas studied her through eyes as round and shiny as black buttons. His hair, lighter by shades than Estella's black braids, curled around his ears and his brown skin had a beautiful golden undertone. He reached out and touched Molly's hair, then turned and lisped something in Estella's ear. She nodded sagely.

"He say your hair look like dried wheat."

Molly bit back a laugh. "Well, sounds to me like he means it looks like straw." The children didn't understand the humor in that, but Tomas continued to stare at her. Suddenly, he glanced over her shoulder, and his face lit up.

"Papa," he said, almost in awe.

Molly turned, curious to know who the child belonged to. Nausea spread through her, for she saw Buck coming toward them astride Thunder. She stood slowly, turning to face him. Their gazes locked briefly before Buck looked away and dismounted.

"Papa!" Tomas held out his arms toward Buck, who smiled, going down on one knee as the boy threw himself against his chest.

Molly couldn't move. She couldn't speak. In truth, she could hardly breathe. Raw hurt battered her insides. Even if she could have spoken at this moment, she didn't know what she would have said. But she could see, and what she saw sent her emotions spiraling.

Little Tomas clung tightly, his chubby brown arms wrapped around Buck's neck and his face hidden against his father's shoulder. Buck hiked the boy against his chest and stood, running his fingers through the child's soft, curly hair.

When Molly met his gaze again, she saw something in his eyes she didn't understand. She would have thought he'd have broken eye contact, but he didn't. His look challenged, dared her to ask. But she wouldn't. Couldn't. Right now, she didn't even want to think about the possibilities.

Blinking back tears of frustration, she turned and walked to the house, hurrying to her room only after she was out of Buck's sight. Pressing a cold cloth against her eyes, she cursed her recent stupid urge to bawl.

Sighing with disgust, she crossed to the window and stared down at the yard. Buck had put Tomas on Thunder's back, instructed him to hang onto the saddle horn, and was now leading the horse toward the barn. Molly's insides continued to ache. She could make no sense of the whole situation. Who was the child's mother? Surely not the whore. And why hadn't she seen the child around here before? Tomas obviously knew full well who his father was, that had been very evident by the way his eyes lit up when he spotted Buck ride in. This wasn't a new relationship.

She continued to battle her confusion, wondering why he hadn't mentioned the child when he was telling her every other gut-wrenching thing in his life. What difference would one more little indiscretion have made? She couldn't imagine that he'd have given a diddly-damn what she thought anyway. He hadn't cared for her opinion regarding Dusty. But she wondered, too, if he planned on becoming Tomas's permanent father. A horrible thought snagged the coattails of that image. If he was Tomas's permanent father, was there also a permanent mother?

She felt a quick sense of anger. Dusty needed him every bit as much as this little boy. She couldn't imagine how he could reject one child so soundly, only to turn and embrace another.

She watched them disappear into the barn, then turned from the window just as Nicolette poked her head around the door. The girl still looked pale.

"How many times have you been sick today?"

Nicolette flopped onto Molly's bed, moving her arm up to cover her eyes. "I've lost count."

Molly edged toward the bed and sat down beside her, smoothing Nicolette's hair away from her face. "Things will get better, honey. Believe me."

"I try to keep telling myself that."

Molly continued to soothe Nicolette's forehead. "What do you know about the little boy Tomas?"

"You mean Buck's boy?"

Molly's stomach dipped, and she frowned at her instinctive response. "Yes. How long have you known he had a son?"

Nicolette shrugged, her eyes still closed. "For a while, I guess. Although he'd never brought him out here before."

"Do you know why he's out here now?" Molly tried to sound casual, but her heart was in her throat.

"No. I can't imagine why."

Molly toyed with the grosgrain ribbons that adorned Nicolette's yellow summer silk gown. "Who . . . who's the boy's mother?"

Nicolette shrugged again. "Probably some whore in Cedarville."

Molly felt a pang of jealousy. "Why do you say that?"

"Well, if it were some decent woman, I'm sure Buck would have married her."

Molly rose from the bed and wandered back toward the window. She should be vicious and explain to poor Nicolette that Buck wouldn't know a decent woman if one popped him in the nose. But it would do no good to verbalize her petty thoughts on the subject of Buck Randall. It was still best that no one knew that she and Buck had known one another all of their lives. Then again, at this point, what did it matter? Still, she couldn't imagine what purpose it would serve, either.

There was a gentle tapping at the bedroom door, and Angelita stepped inside. "How is my little Nikky?"

Nicolette gave the housekeeper a wan smile. "Margaret tells me I'll live."

Angelita returned the smile. "I'm sure she is right, *nina*. I will bring you some special tea and flat bread. You have not been eating enough to keep a bird alive, much less *un bebe*."

Nicolette groaned. "Even the thought of food makes me want to puke, Angelita."

The housekeeper clucked her tongue. "It will pass. In the meantime, you must try to keep something down." She turned to Molly. "Senorita Lindquist, please, would you help me for a minute?"

Nodding, Molly followed her downstairs to the kitchen. She was glad she'd told Angelita about Nicolette's condition; she needed an ally in this house. She watched as Angelita went to the window, peered outside, then came back to the table, where Molly stood. "I have a message," she said in a hushed voice.

Anxious excitement swelled through her. "From whom?"

"Senor Buck. He ask me to tell you to meet him later tonight at the place you were before you were kidnapped."

Molly didn't want to face Buck, but she knew she must. "I see," she said with more calm than she felt. "Did he say what he wanted to see me about?"

She gave her a casual shrug. "That is not for me to know."

So, Molly thought, pulling in a long, quiet breath of air.

This was it. Either he and Sage had found something important, or they hadn't found anything at all.

After dinner, Molly claimed a headache and went to her room. She changed into a pair of boyish twill trousers and a dark shirt that she'd found at the bottom of the wardrobe. After knotting her hair on top of her head, she turned out her lamp and quietly left the room. As she tiptoed down the stairs, she could see the light flickering faintly from beneath the study door. Holding her breath, she opened the front door and slipped outside.

Although the line shack was over a quarter of a mile away, she knew better than to cause any commotion by saddling a horse. She walked, then ran the brief distance to the shack. It was dark; no lamp was lit inside.

She crept to the door. It opened swiftly, and she was pulled inside. A scream forced its way into her throat. A hand covered her mouth.

"Shhh, brat," he whispered against her ear.

She closed her eyes and sagged against him. "Is all this drama necessary?" she asked, when he took his hand away.

"I thought you thrived on it."

She forced herself to pull away from the wide comfort of his chest. "No more than you, obviously." She turned, and although the moon shone into the room, she was unable to see Buck's face. "Have you found anything? Was the map any good?"

"It was exactly what we needed. Sage and I checked out a few of the marked spots and found hundreds of head at each place. We even checked the brands. Most of them had the Double Bar C brand, but we could tell it had been branded over something else."

"So, what do we do next?" In spite of her confusion toward Buck, she enjoyed being a coconspirator.

"*We* do nothing. In two or three days, I want you and Nicolette out of that house."

"Why? What's going to happen?"

"Sage has gone to report to his superiors at Fort Elliot—"

"It will take days for him to go there and back, won't it?"

"That's why at least for now, I want you to make sure nothing appears different at the house. Campion can't suspect a thing. But somehow, you and Nicolette have to be out of there by the end of the week."

Giving him a humorless laugh, she crossed to the tiny window and looked out into the night. The moon outlined the bleak landscape, making the distant cliffs seem like dour Goliaths, keeping everything beneath them prisoner. "It appears that the end of the week will be a turning point in my life. This morning Charles told me I had to give him my answer about being his mistress by the end of the week, too."

Buck shifted behind her. "He said that specifically?"

"Yes," she answered, turning toward him. "Why?"

"Something's in the wind, then. He's up to a few tricks of his own."

They were quiet for a few moments. Molly wanted to ask him about Tomas, but she couldn't. She didn't want to know—not yet. Maybe not ever. "I think you should know that Nicolette is pregnant."

Buck swore. "All things considered, I guess I'm not surprised."

"Do you have any idea where Cody is?"

"No. He hasn't been around for a couple of weeks." Buck was quiet again, then added, "Doesn't sound good, does it?"

Molly felt a flash of fear, and in spite of her topsy-turvy feelings toward Buck, moved closer to his warmth. He enfolded her in his arms, against his chest, as if it were the most natural thing in the world. She felt those damned tears again. "Charles had him killed, I can just feel it."

"I know that's what it sounds like but don't count the kid out yet."

She snaked her arms around his waist, loving the nearness of him so much, she knew she couldn't broach the subject of Tomas, for it would break the spell. "How can you say that? Charles knew he was seeing Nicolette, and he'd been warned, Buck. That whipping he took was a clear, concise warning to stay away from her."

"Yeah, I know all the signs point to that." His chin moved back and forth on top of her head.

She stepped back and looked up at him. The moon shone in through the window behind him, making him look like a gray outline against the light. "Do you know something I don't know?"

He shook his head. "It's just a hunch. I think if Campion would have had him killed, we wouldn't have heard another word about it. As it is, I hear he's got a couple of his men out beating the bushes for the little bastard."

Hope surged through her. "You mean he might be alive?"

"I wouldn't doubt it."

"Then . . . then he doesn't even care what he's done to Nicolette. I'd hate to think he left her on purpose." The picture of Nicolette gagging over the slop pail made Molly cringe, and she wanted to shake the lusty boy until his britches cut off the circulation to his potent, youthful genitals.

"Maybe he doesn't know."

Aware that she could do nothing about it now, she snuggled farther against Buck's chest. She lifted her face, searching for his mouth. It met hers, and they kissed, gently, tentatively at first, then hard, deep and long. She could feel his stubble around her mouth, and the roughness drove her to demand more. She pressed close, rubbing her breasts against his chest, shuddering as the drag coaxed them into hard buds. She came alive, pulling his tongue into her mouth, stroking, teasing, offering herself to him, silently pleading with him to take all of her.

His hand came around her back, slid down her buttocks and pulled her tightly to him. He was hard and ready, moving suggestively against her. Then his hand was at the fly of her britches. He deftly unbuttoned them and dipped his fingers inside her drawers, into the dark, soft wetness of her aching flesh. She moaned, her knees giving way as she clung to him while he stroked her.

With shaky fingers, she undid the front of his pants as well, finding the hard length of him. Her fingers moved over him, discovering the ridge beneath, the hot, wet tip, and finally, the warm, hairy sac below.

Suddenly he shoved her gently away from him. "Get out of those," he whispered, his voice thick with desire.

The moon shone in through the tiny window, bathing them in light. Every nerve in her body was alive and pulsing as she stepped back and began to undress. She flung off her shirt, then pulled her camisole off over her head, tossing it aside. She stood in front of him, her breasts quivering beneath the forceful beat of her heart.

His gaze moved over her, devouring her. He reached out with one finger and slowly, erotically circled her nipple, flicking the pebbly nub gently. A stab of desire struck her deep inside, and she bit her lip to keep from moaning out loud.

"The rest," he said succinctly.

She pulled off her boots, then slid the britches down to the floor, kicking them off.

"Is there a slit in your drawers?" he asked silkily.

She quaked with desire. "Y-yes," she stuttered.

He crooked a finger at her. "Show me."

With knees as mushy as oatmeal, she moved toward him. When she reached him, she boldly took his hand and brought it between her legs, catching a sigh in her throat as his warm fingers pressed inside, stroking her. He was bringing her close to the edge, but she wanted it to last, so she pulled his hand away.

"Now . . . now you," she said in a choked whisper.

He grinned, the scar beneath his cheekbone denting his cheek. "You do it."

In spite of her shaky desire, she felt a wicked answering smile. Moving her hands up over his chest, she began undoing the buttons of his shirt. With each open buttonhole, she reached inside and stroked him, then leaned into him and licked his skin. When she heard his sharp intake of breath, her own desire burst into flame, and she slowly made her way down to the opening of his jeans. She pulled off his shirt and threw it aside, then stepped close so she could rub her nipples across his bare chest. Their shuddering responses merged, lighting the magnetic fuse between them.

She quickly moved away, hardly daring to breathe as she ran her fingers over his hair-covered navel, and on down to the thick thatch of hair beneath.

"Get out of your jeans, breed." She felt brazen, hot and wicked.

"Yes, ma'am," he answered, his husky voice threaded with desire. She saw a dangerous light shining in his eyes as he stripped for her. When he'd finished, he stood in front of her, his jeans dangling from his fingers. The light wasn't good, but she let her gaze wander over his hard, flat stomach to the throbbing manhood that stood firm against his belly.

"Touch me." His voice was a suggestive caress. "I won't break or bite—unless you want me to."

With reluctance, she moved her gaze to his face, seeing his dark, serious eyes, no longer filled with humor, but with an intense burning that she was sure was a mirror of her own. "But I might," she answered on a whisper. "I might . . . might break into a million pieces and never . . . never—"

"Touch me," he ordered again.

She reached out and gripped his hot length, moving her hand up and down the shaft, listening to his shuddering breath. Her own desire soared, and she felt a burst of wetness soak the crotch of her drawers.

She shivered, swaying dizzily as he pulled her hair from

its topknot and combed his fingers through it. He brought her face to his, holding her firmly so he could control the kiss. It was hard, wet, passionate as he forced his tongue into her mouth and drove deep. They moved as one toward the cot, and he pushed her down gently before lowering himself on top of her. Her legs came around his back as he pressed into her through the slit in her drawers. She clung to him, matching his movements as he drove deeper and deeper. Scintillating sparks rocketed through her as his potency grew. Her legs tightened and her pelvis pushed against him as she felt the burst of desire explode within her.

He quickly kissed her, covering her sobs of delight. It wasn't long before he, too, began to reach his peak, and she, in turn, pulled his head toward her and quieted his deep, fulfilled cries with her mouth.

They lay quietly, breathing heavily. Buck shifted himself off, taking her with him so they faced one another on the cot. He threaded his fingers through her hair. "Your hair is beautiful," he said huskily. "I've always wanted to touch it, to bury myself—"

The cot creaked dangerously, moving and cracking beneath them.

"Buck, wh—" Molly sat up, ready to leap from the rickety bed, when the frame suddenly snapped, plunging them to the floor with a hard thud.

They lay there, stunned. Molly felt a bubble of laughter in her throat. Beside her, Buck was on his back, his chest and shoulders shaking quietly. She tried to swallow the sound, too, but she suddenly snorted, and they both began to laugh until tears coursed down Molly's cheeks.

Still chuckling, Buck pulled the dusty old blanket around them and they rolled onto the floor, over and over again until they hit the wall. When they stopped, she looked up and saw the bright, dazzling humor stamped in his eyes and on his face. She thought that if she were never to see him again, this is how she'd always remember him. Oh, lord, she loved him so much she ached with it.

"Buck," she said, her voice catching in her throat.

"Shhh," he whispered. "Don't say anything, brat. Just feel," he added, pressing into her again. "Just . . . just feel," he finished, loving her one more time.

Afterward while they dressed, Molly threw him nervous glances. She wanted to ask him about Tomas. She needed to know.

"Buck?" When he answered, she forged ahead. "About . . . about Tomas." She held her breath, waiting for him to speak.

"What about him?" He buttoned his shirt, then stuffed it into his jeans.

She shrugged into her shirt, her heart pounding. "He's your son?"

"He called me 'papa,' didn't he?"

"Yes, but . . . but why didn't you tell me about him before?"

"Because he doesn't concern you."

She felt a fierce hurt deep inside. She wanted him to confide in her, tell her everything, like he had that night they'd spent together on the plains. She wanted to hear that Tomas was just an orphan he'd adopted, that it wasn't his seed that had gone into making the boy. She didn't want to know that there was another woman out there, somewhere, waiting for him to come and make a home, a family.

"I know it doesn't, but . . . but I was just so surprised when I found out he was yours." She let the words fade slowly, hoping he'd tell her about it, yet knowing he wouldn't. He'd very efficiently closed himself to her once again. Disappointment filled her chest.

"Are you . . . are you going to raise him?"

Shoving his hat on his head, he flung himself away from her and stepped to the door. "I don't quite know what I'm going to do with him."

She swallowed the lump in her throat. "Where's his mother?" Actually, a part of her wanted desperately to know *who* his mother was, but another part of her didn't.

He pulled open the door and held it for her. "It can't possibly be any concern of yours who, or where, his mother is, Molly."

She felt the sharp sting of tears. Those damned tears that she'd held back for years and years. He wouldn't confide in her. Nothing had changed.

"Get going, brat. I'll wait here until you reach the house. I'll get another message to you through Angelita."

Realizing she wouldn't get any more out of him, she hurried into the darkness and made her way to the house. She opened the door quietly, slipping inside as quickly as she'd slipped out earlier. With her back to the hallway, she stopped and listened, hoping everyone had gone to bed.

"Where in the hell have you been?"

Her heart slammed against her ribs. She turned and came face-to-face with a very angry Charles.

🌿 Sixteen 🌿

"**W**h-why, Charles," she managed to say. "What are you doing up so late?"

He glowered at her, the light from the lamp casting macabre shadows over his face. "What am *I* doing up so late? What in the hell are you doing, wandering around this time of night?"

He'd been at his brandy; he reeked of it. She ran nervous hands over her hips, hoping she didn't look as disheveled as she felt. "I . . . I couldn't sleep, so I went out for a walk."

He clearly didn't believe her. His licentious gaze started at her boots, moving slowly over the rest of her until it reached her face. Never before had he given her such an open, lusty, almost dirty look. "In *britches?*"

She was seeing the real Charles Campion now, she was sure of it. Refusing to let him intimidate her, she answered, "Why not? They're far more comfortable than my skirts and all those petticoats." With more confidence than she felt, she brushed past him. In his state of mind, she didn't doubt that he would ferret out the smallest scent of fear. "Really, Charles, you're acting crazy. It isn't as if I've committed a crime."

He grabbed her arm, pinching it so hard between his fingers that she bit her lip to keep from crying out. "And where did this little walk take you, Margaret? The barn?"

With a fierce tug, she tried to pull her arm loose from his grip, but he was too strong. "Of course not. Why would you think I'd been in the barn?"

He plucked something from her hair and dangled it in front of her nose. It was a spear of straw. She swallowed hard and bravely met his gaze. "It's windy tonight, Charles. I'm surprised I don't have more odd things clinging to me."

He briefly relaxed his fingers and she slipped from his grip, darting quickly up the stairs. He was so close behind her, she could almost feel his breath on her neck. She ran to her room and tried to shut the door, but he forced it open, shoving her back toward the bed.

"You won't deny me any longer, you little breed whore," he snarled, seizing her arm.

She fought him, shoving at his face with the flat of her hand. "Charles . . . Charles, please," she gasped, still pushing against him. "You've been drinking. Don't do this, you'll regret it, you know you will."

"Shut up, whore," he answered, pushing her down on the bed with one hand while the other worked furiously at the fly of his trousers. "No doubt every hand on this ranch has dipped his stick into your little honey pot. No reason why I shouldn't, don't you agree?"

He could have been talking about the weather, his voice was so calm. But his eyes . . . his eyes were wide and glassy, and there was a sneer on his lips that made him ugly.

It was useless to scream, and she didn't want to awaken Nicolette. But Molly wasn't going to just give up, not without a damned hard fight. She tried to fend him off with her lame wrist, but pain shot through it, landing high in her neck and hammering into her skull. With a frustrated yelp, she brought her knee up, but he rolled to the side, grabbed the waistband of her britches and her drawers and ripped them down the front, exposing her nudity to his hungry gaze.

With a violent twist she moved away from him, shoving

her heel against his groin, where his own pulsing manhood was now exposed.

He roared with pain, clamping his forearm across her neck, nearly cutting off her ability to breathe.

"Ch-Ch-Charles," she croaked. "Please, I . . . I can't br—"

"Shut up, whore." He was astride her now, atop her thighs, pinning her down. One hand gripped her wrists, holding them over her head. His fingers crushed her bad wrist, and another explosion of pain shattered through her. Tears of agony sprang into her eyes.

He briefly removed his arm from her throat, pulled open her shirt and ripped away her camisole, leaving her breasts bare to his gaze. He pressed against her throat again, an evil grin creasing his once handsome mouth as he stared down at her bosom.

She tried to keep her gaze focused on him, fighting for breath, and suddenly, with painful clarity, she understood what Charles Campion was all about. He enjoyed the fight, savored the battle. And he always wanted to win.

Black dots danced before her eyes as he continued to press against her windpipe. She glanced briefly at his pale manhood, swollen, hot and pink as he thrust it toward her.

"It's my turn now, my beautiful whore." His voice shook with lascivious need.

A low, garbled cry sprang from her throat and she tried to twist away again.

Suddenly the bathroom door swung open, hitting the wall with a bang.

"Charles! Charles! Stop it, please, stop!"

Through a haze, Molly saw Nicolette at the bedside, pulling on Charles's arm. He swung at her, hitting her across the chest. She stumbled backward, righting herself before she fell.

Fighting to stay conscious, Molly saw Nicolette fling herself at him again. "Charles! Please, stop it!" She pulled his arm from Molly's throat and clung to it.

With a deep, agonizing growl, he threw himself off the bed and turned away from them.

Nicolette grabbed Molly's dressing gown off the chair, went to the bed and helped her into it. Molly gripped the girl's hand and they sat on the bed, quietly watching Charles. Her heart continued to pound painfully against her ribs and her throat was sore. She ached all over; there was a new, throbbing pain in her wrist. She finally understood that Charles was a sick, sick man. She hoped the knowledge hadn't come too late.

Nicolette finally spoke. Her voice was soft, filled with pain and confusion. "Charles, what . . . what were you thinking?"

Charles turned, fully composed. "Get out of here, Nicolette."

"No, I won't. I—"

"Get out of here," he repeated. "I have to talk to Margaret."

"No." Her voice was firm with anger.

"Oh, for Christ's sake. There will be no more raping or pillaging tonight." His voice was snide, filled with venomous sarcasm.

Molly still hadn't completely caught her breath. Her head ached from the lack of air, and her wrist continued to throb all the way up to her shoulder.

"I don't care what you say, Charles. I'm not leaving Margaret." Nicolette crossed her arms over her chest and held her stubborn chin high.

On a disgusted sigh, Charles strode to the door and pulled it open. He turned and glared at Molly. "This isn't the end of it."

Molly didn't answer. She gripped Nicolette's hand and looked away, aching for him to just leave. He slammed the door, the noise echoing in the quiet room.

"I'm so sorry, Margaret."

Molly gave her a wobbly smile and patted her hand. "I am too, sweetie." She clasped one of the long curls that hung over Nicolette's shoulder, threading her fingers through the silky mass.

They were both quiet. Molly realized that now, more than ever before, she had to leave. Charles wouldn't stop until he raped her. She remembered the look of excitement that gorged his features when she'd fought him. She shuddered against the memory. He was one of those men who got his pleasure from hurting women.

Yes, she had to leave, but until she could, she'd have to avoid Charles like a cluster of locusts. Somehow, she must never find herself alone with him. As much as she wanted to turn to Buck for help, she knew she couldn't risk getting him involved. Charles was already suspicious. It was about time she learned to get out of her muddles herself. Buck had saved her miserable hide too many times.

Suddenly she remembered Buck's warning that she and Nicolette must be out of the house by the end of the week. Molly wanted her out of danger. "I think you should go and visit your friend for a few days, Nicolette."

Nicolette turned, worry lines creasing her smooth brow. "I can't leave you now. I won't."

Moving toward the edge of the bed, she took Nicolette's hands in hers and squeezed them. "I'm going to ask you to do it as a favor to me."

Nicolette gave her a wary look and pulled away. "Why? What's going to happen?"

Molly leaned close. "Do you trust me?"

Nicolette hesitated, then nodded quickly.

"I can't tell you exactly what's going to happen, because I don't honestly know. But I want you safely away from here."

"What about you?" Nicolette asked.

"I won't be here, either."

Nicolette's face held panic. "You're not leaving, are you?"

Molly shook her head. "No, but please, Nicolette, just trust me if you can."

She stared at Molly for a long while. "This has something to do with Charles, doesn't it?"

Molly refused to lie to her, but she didn't want to hurt her, either. "Yes, but—"

"Wait," she interrupted, raising her hands to her ears. "I could demand that you tell me, but I won't. I . . . I don't want anything to happen to him, but . . ." She gave Molly a look of despair. "He's my brother, but these last few months, he's become someone I don't even know anymore."

Molly was exhausted. Every bone in her body ached. "I'm so sorry, Nicolette. I'm so sorry." She crawled to the pillows, pulled back the covers and slid into bed.

Nicolette stood beside her, a worried frown on her pretty face. She rubbed her arms, as though she were cold. "I think I should sleep in here with you, Margaret."

Molly gave her a sleepy smile. She didn't think Charles would come back, but it wouldn't hurt to thwart him if he did. "I'd be happy to have the company."

The morning sun captured flecks of dust left by the messenger's horse as it galloped away. Buck stood at the door of the barn, his gaze drifting to the letter that had been delivered. "To Buck Randall, open in the event of my death," the envelope read. He'd know Nita's barely intelligible scrawl anywhere. God, he thought, absently hitting the letter against his palm, he hated surprises.

He thought back to the last time he'd seen her. It had been the day he'd returned to the ranch with Molly after the kidnapping. He remembered well the pain on Molly's face when she'd heard where he was going. Even after everything they'd shared, Nita and Tomas were two people he couldn't talk about, couldn't explain. He'd rushed to the whore, finding her small, thin body more wasted than ever. . . .

* * *

"How are you?" He came to her and sat down on the bed, taking her hands in his.

She pulled one hand away, covering her mouth as she coughed. "I'm not getting any better, Buck. I'm tired all the time. I can't . . . can't take care of Tomas anymore."

He glanced around the familiar room. "Where is he?"

"Tessa took him."

Buck swore. Of all the women in the world, Tessa Black was the last one he wanted to take care of his son.

"Don't be angry, Buck. She's good to him."

Buck stood and crossed to the window, remembering his reaction three years before when Nita had told him she was going to have his child. God, how he'd hated to hear that! He couldn't take care of the one he already had. How in hell could he take care of another? But she'd assured him she would not ask much of him. She'd known he didn't love her.

But over the years, he'd come to look forward to visiting them. Tomas, the handsome boy with the light brown hair and dark brown eyes, had called him "Papa," innocently finding a place for himself in Buck's heart.

But now Nita was dying. She'd tried to hide the bloody sputum from her cough in her handkerchief. Another mother of another one of his children was going to die, and this time he couldn't do a damned thing about it.

"Buck, come and sit with me."

He went to her, taking her hands in his again. Most of her beauty had been ravaged by the disease. Her eyes no longer drooped seductively. They were weary, flat and looked enormous above her prominent cheekbones. "I remember the first time I saw you," he said, trying to smile.

"Oh, but I saw you first." She touched his chin before her hand fell limply back onto the bed. "I liked the way you looked. So cocky and sure of yourself. I knew that under all of that was a good, kind man."

He continued to look at her. "You saw all that, did you?"

For a brief moment, her eyes flashed with intensity. "Yes, I saw all that."

He remembered their lusty relationship, although they hadn't been lovers for more than a year. Not since Nita had become ill. He'd paid Tessa, forcing her to let Nita stay on in her room, even though she no longer had a source of income. He continued to feel responsible for Tomas, too, but he refused to consider Nita might die and leave the boy motherless. If that happened, he'd begin to wonder if somehow he was a curse to women who bore him children.

She coughed, doubling over in bed.

"Dammit, I wish I could do something for you."

Sighing, she collapsed against the pillows. "You can, you know."

A feeling of panic coated his stomach. "I . . . I can't do that, Nita. I've failed before."

Her dark eyes filled with pleading. "You're all he's got in the whole world, Buck. It's all I'll ask of you."

He sighed, feeling himself weaken. He didn't know what he'd do with the kid, but he sure as hell couldn't let him grow up in a whorehouse.

"All right," he finally said, hoping she didn't hear his reluctance. "Where is he?"

Nita relaxed. "He's in Tessa's room, down the hall. Go. Take him with you, now."

"Don't you want to say good-bye?"

She shook her head. "I already have. He's waiting for you."

If Buck hadn't been so miserable, he might have laughed. "You were pretty sure of yourself, weren't you?"

"No," she whispered, her eyes filling. "I was pretty sure of you."

Swearing silently, he picked up his hat and strode to the door. He stopped, turned and looked at her. "I'll see you soon."

Smiling through her tears, she nodded. "Of course."

Buck left, realizing they both knew it wasn't true. . . .

* * *

Giving himself a violent shake, he ripped off the end of the envelope and let the letter fall into his hand. With slow deliberation, he unfolded the paper and gazed down at Nita's scribbly print. A sudden pain gripped his gut, twisting it fiercely as he read the meager lines.

He shoved the paper into his pocket and dug at his eye with the heel of his hand. Christ. Damned clever woman. And he was pretty damned stupid. Stupid and naive. How had he let that slip by him?

He stood by the barn unable to move, barely noticing as Sage rode up and dismounted.

"Well," Sage said dryly, leading his mount past Buck into the barn. "I'm glad to see you, too."

Buck pulled in a deep breath, trying to block out what he was feeling. "I'm glad you're back. Let's talk in the barn."

Sage gave him a stern once-over. "What's wrong?"

"Nita died sometime yesterday."

"Hey, I'm sorry, man. She'd been sick for a long time. Too bad no one could do something for her."

Cursing, Buck pulled out the letter and handed it to him. He watched as Sage's face took on a look of pure disgust.

"What are you going to do about it?"

Buck swore again. "What can I do? It's over. Done with. What good would it do to get mad? That she played me for a fool isn't the kid's fault." But he was angry. Deep inside, he felt an angry eruption forming. Somehow he had to work through it. It was time to let the past die.

Sage let out a long, low whistle. "As if you don't have enough on your mind."

"Yeah, yeah. Now, tell me what you learned at Fort Elliot. Will we get any help cornering Campion?"

When Sage was sure they were alone, he pulled out a letter of his own and shoved it at Buck. "This will put the last nail in his coffin. And all the help we need will be here the day after tomorrow."

Molly prayed for the time to fly. As she dressed for dinner the next evening, she wondered if she could bear another night in the house, much less another meal with Charles. She left her room and descended the stairs just as Charles's voice rang out in the hallway below. Her stomach pitched, causing her to grab the railing for support. Stopping for a moment, she pulled in a deep breath, and gathered her confidence.

Suddenly Angelita came rushing toward the stairs, her face lined with worry. "Oh, senorita," she said quickly. "There is much sickness at my daughter's house." She looked around wildly. "I feel I must go to her, but . . ." She glanced toward the dining room. "You know, Senor Campion must have his dinner, and I cannot leave until that is done."

Molly was already making her way to the door. "I'll go over now, Angelita," she said, pulling her shawl from the coat tree in the entry. "You come when you can."

"Oh, thank you, Senorita Lindquist, thank you." Tears streamed down Angelita's cheeks as she pressed her fingers over her lips. She was roughly pushed aside.

"Where in the hell do you think you're going?" Charles held a half-full snifter of brandy.

Molly was already out on the porch. "I'm going to care for some sick children. Don't wait up," she added, trying to hide her sarcasm.

"I forbid you to go!"

She got to the bottom step and turned. "Charles," she said with quiet strength, "I don't think you're in a position to forbid me to do anything." She held his glowering gaze, then turned away, running quickly toward the barn.

Angelita's daughter, Carmen, showed promise of exotic beauty. She was softly curved where her mother was round.

Her eyes, the deep, nearly black sloe-eyes of the Spanish, were warm as fire.

"These are not all my children," she explained, holding one baby against her breast and cuddling Tomas to her side. There were two other young children besides Estella in the room, one asleep on a cot near the fire, and Estella holding another. "They are left to me by their mothers who have died or have been killed by the whites."

The child in her arms coughed, a deep croupy sound that shook his little body. Tomas began to cry. "All the children," Carmen said with a weary sigh, "are burning up with a fever. And they have this cough that comes up from their toes."

Molly tossed her shawl on a chair and surveyed the chaos. Carmen gave her a hopeful glance, then went back to soothing the children.

Rushing to her side, Molly asked, "What can I do?"

Carmen shook her head. "I don't know what else there is to do. I have done what I can." She shrugged helplessly. "I have bathed them with cool water, yet their fevers don't break."

Molly pressed her fingertips to her temples. "There must be something else we can do." She forced her head to clear, trying to think back to her childhood. Suddenly, she remembered something.

"Carmen, are there any rocks nearby?"

Carmen thought a moment, then nodded. "Many outside, near the cabin."

"All right. All right," Molly answered, her thoughts whirling. "I'll go out and gather some. And we'll need as many extra blankets as you can find, and some . . . some poles or sticks."

Carmen gave her a puzzled frown. "What are we going to do?"

Molly was already on her way outside. "We're going to build a steam hut!"

Less than two hours later, a colorful blanket-and-robe

teepeelike structure had been erected in the middle of the room. The fireplace roared, the fire heating dozens of rocks. Inside the teepee, piled on an iron grate, were hot rocks that were cooled slightly with a spray of water, sending hot, wet steam into the air, filling the small, dark tent.

Molly felt sweat trickle down her temples and between her breasts as she held Tomas. His hair was damp, curling lightly around his face. His black button eyes, once wide with curiosity, were dull and his cheeks chapped from fever.

Estella peeked into the tent. "More rocks?"

Molly nodded. "Can you handle them?" Estella gave her an answering nod, then was gone.

The air was as thick with tension as it was with steam. There had to be a way for them to relax while they waited. The apprehension she and Carmen felt surely was passed on to the children.

"Carmen, do the children understand any English?"

"*Si*, most understand some."

Molly gazed down at the languid Tomas and brushed a curl from his forehead. She pulled the child close, fighting back tears when she considered the child might not survive. Oh, but she couldn't let that happen. She couldn't, *wouldn't* let him die! A deep, hidden part of her wished that Tomas was hers and Buck's. Something to bind them together. Anything to keep a part of Buck with her always. "Tomas," she whispered, smiling brightly down at him, "do you want me to tell you a story?"

The child blinked slowly and nodded.

Estella entered the tent, lugging a makeshift sling that held some hot, steaming rocks. Carmen rose and helped her shift them to the pile on the grate, then they poured water on them, sending a fresh hiss of mist into the warm, wet air.

Molly snuggled Tomas close, ignoring her own discomfort. "This is the story of His-sik the Skunk. You know what a skunk is, don't you?" She wrinkled her nose, pretending to smell something bad. It brought a small smile to the child's mouth, and lifted Molly's sagging spirits.

"His-sik was a selfish, greedy skunk," she began, speaking slowly. "He often went hunting for elk with his son-in-law, Gray Fox, but it was Gray Fox who had to do all the work. All His-sik did was spray the elk herd with his stinky scent, and poor Gray Fox was left to kill them all. And old, lazy His-sik made Gray Fox not only carry the elk home, but His-sik as well, for he always claimed to be too tired to walk. But he was never too tired to dance, often dancing on poor Gray Fox's back on the way home.

"His-sik would tell his people to skin the elk and hang the meat out to dry, always promising to share. But when his people had done all the work, His-sik refused to give them any of the meat. If they complained, he turned as if he were going to spray them, and everyone was afraid, so said nothing more.

"Each time he and Gray Fox went out hunting, the same thing happened. Each time he promised to share meat with his people, who did all the work, and each time he went back on his word. The people were getting very angry, but they were afraid of him, for they knew his scent could kill them.

"But one day, Too-wik, the badger, said he had a plan. While His-sik watched his meat so no one would take it, Too-wik dug a big hole and built a fire in it. When someone asked why he had done this, he said, 'Skunk is a great dancer and loves to dance. We will have fire in the hole and cover the top with sticks and leaves and earth so he can't see what's beneath. Then we will send for him and ask him to dance for us. When he dances, he will break through, fall into the hole, then we shall kill him.'

"The people were still afraid, but they wanted to get rid of the lazy, good-for-nothing His-sik, so they agreed. When it was dark, they sent for the skunk and asked him to dance for them. Because he was a vain, pompous skunk, he could not refuse. He danced, harder and harder, for he was proud of his dancing skills. Soon, the sticks broke and he fell into the hole. The people were ready. They got a big rock and pushed it into the hole on top of His-sik, holding it down on him so he could not get out.

"The hot coals burned his feet and made him dance. But now he was angry, and shot his scent so hard against the sides of the hole, he pushed mountains up all around him. After his scent was gone, the coals burned him and killed him. Then, all the people were happy, and the next day they had a great feast and ate all the dried meat they wanted."

Estella had squatted down beside her mother. "That's a sad story," she said quietly.

"Oh, my people don't think so," Molly answered.

"Your people? Who are your people, Senorita Lindquist?"

Nicolas had told her that story so many years before, Molly was amazed that she remembered it at all. But it had felt good to tell it out loud. It had made her proud to be a part of such old customs and myths. "Some of my people lived for hundreds of years in a great valley called *An-wah-nee* in a place called California."

Estella snickered. "But you are a white."

"I am also an Indian, Estella. My mother is a half-breed. Her people came from this valley."

"And your papa? You know your papa?"

Molly shifted Tomas in her arms. "No," she answered, waiting for the foolish, painful memories to return. Surprisingly, she felt nothing. "No, I didn't know him at all."

"But you do not look like an Indian, senorita. He was a white man?"

Molly sighed and glanced down at the sleeping Tomas. "Yes. A white soldier. And I wanted to be white once, Estella. I tried very hard to be a White. But believe me," she added, remembering her miserable experience with Charles, "that got me into more trouble than you can imagine."

One of the other children awakened, coughing. It was still deep, but what was in her chest had begun to loosen.

Molly opened the blanket Tomas had been wrapped in. Her heart leaped with joy, for he was soaked with sweat, and his skin was cool.

"Quickly, Estella. Don't let the heat die. Bring more stones and make more steam. I think we've performed a miracle!"

❧ Seventeen ❧

A bright, yellow sun heralded sunrise. Molly stepped outside, stretching the kinks from her back and squinting against the morning light.

Angelita had come during the night, but had gone back to the ranch to prepare breakfast for the hands. Molly had wanted to help her, but Angelita had insisted she stay with the children, claiming she had other women who would help in Campion's kitchen.

As Molly stood outside, listening to the rapid-fire Spanish exchange between Carmen and her daughter in the cabin, she felt a wonderful sense of peace. The children had pulled through. Fevers were down, coughs loose. All had been fed a soupy porridge earlier, and most were already asleep again.

She closed her eyes briefly, bringing forth the face of little Tomas. He'd been completely comfortable sleeping in her arms all night. She wanted to think it was because he felt a special kind of bond because of his father, but she knew that wasn't the case. She could have put him down once he was asleep, but she'd wanted to hold him, feel his sweet baby breath against her cheek, savor this part of Buck before she left both of them behind for good.

And, she thought, with a heavy heart, it was time to leave. In spite of all the reasons she could think of to stay —Buck, Tomas and Nicolette—she had to leave because of

Charles. Whatever Buck and Sage had planned, she hoped it would be over soon. She had the strongest urge to go home. She was actually homesick. It hurt, this urgency to see her mother and tell her how much she loved her. It was time to make up for all the lost years.

She went inside, picked up her shawl and said good-bye to Carmen and the children. Feeling sentimental tears in her throat, she crossed to the tiny cot where Tomas slept. His plump fist was curled loosely beneath his chin, and his mouth was open slightly. She allowed herself a tearful smile when she heard his tiny snoring sounds. Bending over the cot, she placed a long, loving kiss on his cool forehead.

After embracing Carmen and Estella one more time, she left and rode slowly toward the ranch astride Nicolette's mare. There was another ache deep inside her, one she'd tried not to dwell on. Leaving Buck would be like leaving her soul to fry in the Texas sun. It didn't seem quite fair that she should love him as she did. Until they'd been alone together on the harsh plains, she'd firmly believed he had only a very few redeeming qualities. Even then, she'd loved him. Then, as they spent those days and nights together, she'd discovered he was a thoughtful and gentle man. And he could tease, making her laugh and smile. She knew he had depths that had never been touched. But had he changed? A secret part of her wanted to believe that he had, that he was no longer the angry renegade who would never settle down and accept his responsibilities. After all, now there was Tomas, and there would always be Dusty.

But what of it? She wasn't a part of Buck's life. He would tell her nothing. It was only in her hidden heart that she wanted to believe he was taking on the responsibility of caring for the boy, and therefore, that he'd changed. For all she knew, it was a temporary thing. Or, she thought, her heart sinking like a rock in her chest, he might finally do the right thing and marry the boy's mother.

She pulled in a shaky sigh. That was another reason she

wanted to leave. It would just be her luck that he'd finally settle down and marry again, in spite of his harsh vow not to. The irony would be that it wouldn't be her. He'd done his very best to let her know that her questions about To-mas and the boy's mother were intrusive and none of her business.

But, he made love to me. And their lovemaking had been wonderful. Beautiful. She would never know that beauty with another man, and she refused to believe he hadn't felt the same thing. But he was stubborn and proud. And maybe, she thought, her heart aching again, just maybe he would never love her. After all, if he hadn't learned to love her after all these years, he surely never would.

She shook herself from her maudlin reverie as she approached the ranch. Except for the dogs, it was exceptionally quiet. Frowning, she dismounted and led the mare into the barn.

"Jorge?" The stable boy didn't appear to be around. She felt a chill creep up her back. All this silence was eerie.

After feeding and watering the mare, she hurried to the house, choosing to enter through the kitchen. "Angelita?"

Quiet. The house was so quiet. The creepy chill stayed with her, spreading into her chest. Bread was rising on the table, and the smell of freshly baked berry pie filled the air. Angelita had been back to do her chores, but where was she now?

She crossed to the door that led into the hall, worrying her bottom lip with her teeth. As she moved closer to Charles's study, she could hear the *chung* of the chime clock that sat on the mantel over the fireplace. The study door stood open. She stopped and peered inside, breathing a sigh of relief when she found the room empty.

She moved toward the stairs.

"Good morning, Margaret."

A clammy wash of fear expanded in her chest. With her hand clutching the rounded curve of the wooden railing, she turned. "Charles," she said, hoping her voice didn't shake. "I . . . I didn't hear you. You frightened me." Which was exactly what he'd meant to do, she decided.

"You must be exhausted. Here, let me help you to your room." He was solicitous, taking her arm and moving with her up the stairs.

She gave him a covert, sidelong glance. She didn't trust him any further than she could throw him. "I'm not helpless, Charles, but thank you for your concern."

"Angelita told me how you helped with the children." He looked at her and chuckled. "I'm not up to anything, Margaret. You can wipe that suspicious look from your face."

She felt a scornful smile lift her mouth. "You read me only too well."

"Yes, I know I've given you reason to distrust me."

She stopped at the top of the stairs and gave him a hard look. "You've given me many reasons to distrust you, Charles."

He nodded impatiently. "I know, I know. But for now, Margaret, just go into your room and rest." He brought both hands up, in a gesture of defeat. "Truce?"

She studied him further. "And . . . and later?"

"Later, there will be plenty of time to talk." He gazed at her, laughing softly, his blue eyes deep and warm. "I have many things to ask you to forgive me for, Margaret. I've been a cad and a worm. I don't deserve you, but I hope you'll hear me out, anyway."

She still didn't trust him. She glanced into her room before stepping inside. Everything appeared to be just as she'd left it. Suddenly she ached with fatigue, and her wrist, her constant barometer for pain, throbbed. Her bed looked so inviting. . . .

"I'd like to sleep for a while, Charles. I guess we can talk later." All the talk in the world wouldn't change how she'd come to feel about him, but if he wanted to talk to her, there was no way she could stop him.

"Sleep well, Margaret." He stood in the hallway until

she closed the door. She listened, waiting until she heard him walk away. When he was gone, she undressed and crawled into bed. She immediately slipped into sleep.

Wind rattling against the windowpane awakened her. Through eyes that still felt grainy from lack of sleep, she glanced at the curtains. She felt groggy, and her head had that dull ache that she often got when the room was stuffy.

Yawning, she slid from the bed and crossed to the window. She reached down to slide it up, but it didn't move. Odd, she thought, as she tried it again. It had never stuck before.

Shrugging, she went into the bathroom to wash her face. She cleaned up as best she could, put on fresh underwear and a dark blue cotton gown, and squared her shoulders, ready to meet Charles. There was no point in putting it off.

She moved to the door and turned the knob. Nothing. A wiggly shard of panic stabbed her. Grabbing the knob with both hands, she shook it and pulled it, but to no avail. *The door was locked from the other side.*

She moved back toward the bed, then turned and rushed to the window, pulling on it futilely. Sucking in great gulps of air, she studied the window, suddenly spying the nails that had been driven into the frame to prevent it from opening.

She whirled around, breathing deeply. "Charles," she said on a hiss of breath. She hurled herself across the room and pounded on the door. "Charles! Damn you, unlock this door!"

"Ah, Margaret." His voice was annoyingly pleasant on the other side of the door. "You're finally awake. Good. But that language. Tsk, tsk. And here I thought you were a lady."

Resting her forehead against the door, she clenched both hands into fists, trying to ignore the pain in her injured wrist as she pressed against the wooden barrier.

"Charles, what is this all about? What do you want from me?"

"Well, darling," he said, "it isn't so much what I want from *you*. It's what I want from your rescuer, Randall." He was quiet for a moment then added, "Did you fuck him, too? Along with every other disgusting outlaw from here to the Mexican border, my sweet?"

Her heart pounded hard in her chest. "Charles, you're talking crazy. Please. Just tell me what you want."

He chuckled. "You're avoiding my question. Well," he said on an exaggerated sigh, "never mind. You probably did. I wonder if he thinks enough of you to make a little exchange."

"What . . ." She swallowed hard, trying to sound calmer than she felt. "What do you want from him?"

"It isn't necessary for you to know, my darling. Just make yourself comfortable in there. By the way." His voice was so soft she had to strain to hear it. "What did you take from my study, Margaret?"

Cool fear spread through her. She didn't answer him.

"It doesn't matter now," he said conversationally. "But I know you were in there, snooping around. For whom, Margaret? For the breed?"

Mr. Poteet had done his job well, she decided.

"No answer for me? Well," he said, "never mind. You just rest now. I'll see you again . . . very soon."

She pressed her fist against her lips to keep them from shaking and briefly closed her eyes. There was nothing to prevent him from finally accomplishing what he'd tried to do twice before. For that reason, and for that reason alone, she didn't want to rile him. "Am I a prisoner, Charles?"

"Oh, I hate to think of it in such harsh terms." He was quiet again, then added, "But we do have some unfinished business."

Her stomach pitched downward. She didn't doubt for a minute that they were alone in the house. If he tried to rape her again, he'd probably succeed. Invisible crawly things scurried over her skin, and she shuddered.

"Not to worry, my sweet," he said in response to her silence. "At least for now."

Clasping her hands prayerlike to her chest, she paced the room. She marched into the bathroom, foolishly hoping he'd forgotten to lock the adjoining door to Nicolette's room. She tried it; he hadn't.

She went back into her room, glancing nervously at the window. It was nearly dusk. He would come to her sometime during the night, of that she was certain. He had to know by now that she wasn't going to stay with him under any circumstances. In his sick little mind, he will have convinced himself that he deserves to take her just once before he lets her go—or, she thought, her heart pounding, kills her.

Shuddering again, she tried to imagine fighting him off. She didn't have the strength. Interruptions had kept him from completing the act before. There would be no interruptions tonight.

Thank heavens she'd slept earlier. She would stay awake and hopefully alert throughout the night—or however long it took. . . .

As she stood in the middle of her room, she studied everything in it. Perhaps she'd have a snowball's chance if she had a weapon. A weapon and the element of surprise. Her gaze went from the desk to the chair, the chair to the wardrobe to the bed to the bedside cabinet, and slowly back to the bed.

With her fingers crossed, she stepped to the bed and lifted the end of the mattress. One of the slats that held the bedding was visible, and she pulled on it, unable to move it with the mattress in place. She pushed the mattress aside, lifted the long, flat slat out and shoved the mattress back where it had been.

She studied the piece of wood. It was too long to be of any use to her. It would make noise if she broke it off, so she had to make sure Charles wasn't camped outside in the hall.

Crossing to the door, she called out sweetly, "Charles? Are you there?" Nothing. No sound, no movement. Frowning, she stood back and considered that he might just be there, hoping she'd do something foolish.

She moved back into the room and went to the window. She felt a sigh of relief when she saw him coming toward the house from the stable. Moving quickly, she stood the slat upright, slanted it to one side, and stepped on it, cringing as the wood snapped loudly into two pieces. The piece on the floor was shorter, easier for her to handle. After kicking the longer piece under the bed, she practiced swinging the other, finding the best way to get the most out of her thrust.

Then she went to the bed, hiding her weapon in the folds of her skirt. She pushed her pillows up behind her, leaned back and studied the darkening room. It was only the element of surprise that would save her.

In spite of her good intentions, she dozed off and on all night. It was when the shadowy fingers of dawn snaked in through the curtains that she heard the first sound. A board creaked on the stairs, followed by faint footfalls in the hallway.

Her heart hammered in her chest, the sound echoing loudly in her ears. She scooted down slightly, pushing the pillows onto the bed. The fingers of her good hand gripped the smooth end of the broken slat at her side. She wished she could still her thumping heart, for she feared it was draining her of much needed energy.

A key scraped the lock. Molly turned her face toward the window and pretended to sleep. She knew when the door had opened, for a breeze stole over her, forcing her to swallow a shudder.

She lay there, barely daring to breathe, as she tried to sense his nearness. He'd stopped at the side of the bed; she could almost feel his body heat. She sensed that he was leaning over her, for she swore she could feel his breath on her face.

Opening her eyes, she lunged quickly, swinging the wooden slat at him, catching him on the side of the head.

He screamed a wild curse, but she was already rounding the end of the bed, on her way out the door. Without glancing back she tore down the stairs, tripping over her skirt and sliding roughly to the floor below. She picked herself up and raced to the front door, pulling it open and propelling herself outside.

Her plan hadn't gone any further than her escape, and once outside, she ran, willy-nilly over the ground, finally rushing toward the barn. She ran into a thin, wiry chest.

"Hey, there, girlie."

Relief weakened her. It was Dallas. Lovable old Dallas. His feed bag whiskers brushed against her forehead. "Oh . . . oh, Dallas, am I glad it's you. Please," she huffed, trying to catch her breath. "Please, would you help me saddle a horse?"

"Well, now, missy," he said seriously. "Where ya gonna go so early in the mornin'?"

"I . . . I have to get over to Carmen's to see how the children are," she lied blithely.

Dallas looked over her shoulder and grinned. "Mornin', boss. Got kind of an ugly bash there, ain't ya?"

"Good morning, Dallas. Thanks for stopping her."

Molly's stomach dropped to her knees. How could he sound so calm when she knew he probably wanted to kill her? She didn't even want to turn around to see what damage she'd done, but Charles grabbed her shoulders and turned her toward him. The entire side of his head was bleeding. His neck, his ear and his cheek dripped with blood. It had even soaked into the collar of his shirt. She must have caught him good with the ragged edges of wood. He carried a bloody towel.

His eyes narrowed at her, tiny cold, blue slits that bore

into her. "That wasn't a very smart thing to do," he said in a quiet, unpleasant voice. She sensed the depth of his anger. His need to possess had been thwarted.

"Need anything else, boss?"

Charles didn't take his eyes off her. "Saddle my horse. Margaret and I are going for a ride."

Dallas shuffled off to get the mount, and Molly looked around wildly, wondering if she had any chance at all.

"Don't even think about it," he warned.

She pulled herself up straight. "Can you tell me where we're going?"

He blotted his neck with the towel, never taking his eyes off her. "I can, but I won't. After what you did, you don't deserve to know."

She turned away, unwilling to let him see the fear in her eyes. Well, she'd really gotten herself into a muddle this time. Clearing her throat against the urge to cry, she said, "You can't really blame me for defending myself, can you?"

Dallas shuffled out of the depths of the barn, leading Charles's mount. Charles tossed him a long leather thong. "Tie her hands behind her back."

Without question, Dallas did as he was told. Molly sucked in a breath, then pressed her lips together against the pain in her wrist. In a matter of moments, she was in the saddle. Charles had gone to the shelf beside the window and was coming back toward them.

Dallas looked up at her and gave her his stupid, toothless grin.

"Dallas, I thought we were friends," she said, giving him a sad smile.

"Woulda been, if'n ya'd gone an' married m'boy, here."

She shook her head. "Can't you see the kind of man he is? What's he ever done for you?"

Dallas cackled. "Ain't what he done fer me, it's what I done fer his pa. Years and years ago, now. Women generally ain't to be trusted, missy. His ma weren't, and you ain't."

Charles swung up behind her, and as they left the ranch, she felt strongly that Dallas was the one who had informed the elder Campion of his wife's Indian pregnancy. If Molly had discovered that sooner, she would have known not to trust the old man at all.

They rode deeper into the canyon. The caprock loomed ominously on either side, shading the crimson walls from the hot morning sun.

Molly sat straight, not wanting to touch Charles at all. That wasn't possible, of course, for the front of his thighs automatically moved against the backs of hers. The contact made her skin crawl.

They rode for nearly an hour; neither spoke. Molly tried to focus on the landscape, noting an occasional wild turkey sprinting into the air from its hiding place among the bulrushes along the creek. The lilting whistle of a meadowlark broke through the sound of the whining wind, and from far away, she thought she heard a coyote bark.

They stopped abruptly. Molly studied the cliffs around them, seeing nothing. Suddenly, her heart nearly sprang from her chest. Buck appeared about fifty feet from them, a rifle slung over his shoulder.

"All right, Campion," he shouted. "Let's get this over with."

Charles dismounted, then pulled Molly down, holding her in front of him. "Show me what you've got, Randall." He dragged Molly with him, edging closer to where Buck stood.

Buck pulled out a piece of paper, unfolded it and held it by one end. "This is what you want."

Charles let out a cross between a laugh and a scoff. "You could be holding anything there, Randall. Read it to me."

Molly listened as Buck read the letter.

" 'Charles Campion, owner of the Double Bar C Ranch, blackmailed me into leasing him my land for the use of hiding cattle which he admittedly stole from neighboring ranchers. I saw for myself the rebranding process. I was forced into helping on more than one occasion.' It's signed 'Tom Hansen.'

"He used to be your neighbor. Anything to say for yourself, Campion?"

Charles's hold on Molly tightened. She knew he was angry.

"That little pissant Hansen died in jail. That's a forgery, and you know it."

Buck shook his head. " 'Fraid not. It was signed in the presence of the sheriff and two of his deputies." He gave him a knowing smile. "You didn't have him killed soon enough, Campion."

"That's bullshit, Randall, and you know it. I was nowhere near that jail," he snarled.

"I didn't say you did it yourself. I think we can all agree that you paid someone else to do it." Buck was silent for a moment, then added, "Isn't that the dirty little way you do business?"

Charles pressed his arm across Molly's windpipe, nearly cutting off her air. "Watch what you say, breed. It would be all too easy for me to snap the squaw's neck."

Molly's stomach quivered. How things had changed. Less than five months ago, he'd put her on a pedestal, begging her to have his children. Now, she knew she was of no further use to him. He'd called her a squaw, denigrating her to what he felt was the lowest possible level of womanhood. To him, a whore was more useful.

Buck dangled the paper. "Snap her neck, you bastard, and this piece of evidence is entered against you."

Charles gave him an evil chuckle. "She means that much to you, does she?"

Buck gave him a careless shrug. "Personally, she doesn't mean jackshit to me, Campion."

Molly cringed, his words hitting her like a physical blow. She hoped it was just a ploy, but she didn't know for sure. For all she knew, Buck had gotten sick and tired of hauling her sorry butt out of trouble.

"Then why do you care what happens to her?"

Buck shifted the rifle, resting it across his knee. With casual nonchalance he removed his hat, wiped his forehead with the sleeve of his shirt, and settled his hat back on his head. "I know her ma, Campion. She's a special friend of mine. I've promised to get the girl back home, where she belongs. Nothing more."

Molly's stomach continued to sink. She wanted to believe he was just saying this, that it wasn't really the truth at all. But she was afraid it was just her heart creating a false hope, overriding her sensible mind.

"So," Campion said nastily, "you screwing the mother, or what?"

Molly had the violent urge to shove her heel into her ex-fianceé's groin, but his arm was so tight against her windpipe, she was afraid to move. She watched Buck, waiting for his answer, seething inwardly.

Buck looked away, appearing thoughtful. Molly knew that kind of crack would cut Buck deeply. She knew he loved her mother, and she knew exactly *how* he loved her. Charles's vile remark had to be hard for Buck to swallow.

After a long sigh, he said, "I'll forget you said that, you dirty sack of shit."

Charles squeezed her throat so hard, she yelped and her eyes began to water. "I don't like being made a fool of, Randall." He moved his weapon, pointing toward the cliffs. "I can kill the bitch and have you dead at the drop of a hat at the same time. The cliffs are full of my men, just waiting for me to give them the signal to fill you full of holes."

With frantic urgency, Molly searched the hills. Her stomach ached when she saw a few heads pop up from behind rock formations. Lord, Buck wouldn't have come out here alone, would he, expecting to take Charles by himself? A tiny voice told her he wouldn't; a louder one screamed that he would.

"Molly," Buck said quietly. "I'm sorry things turned out this way. I tried, and I've failed."

Her heart flew up, hovering in her chest like a wild bird. He wasn't going to try anything. He wasn't going to *do* anything. Suddenly she heard croaking, gasping sounds, and she realized they were her own.

"I just want you to do one thing for me, Molly. Molly? Are you listening to me?"

She blinked, trying to put his face in focus. "Y-yes," she answered, the sound barely audible.

"Get on with it, Randall," Charles shouted impatiently.

Buck ignored him. "I want you to remember the time I hauled you out of that barn, when I caught you kissing that homely, snaggle toothed runt from Pine Valley. Do you remember, Molly?"

In spite of her diminished ability to breathe, she wanted to lunge at Buck and claw his eyes out. What was he doing, dragging out her foolish antics in front of a man who would just as soon cut her throat as look at her?

"You . . . you *bastard*," she croaked, pressing dangerously hard against Charles's forearm.

"Molly, shut up and think."

Furious, Molly thought back to that fateful day. She'd been so angry that Buck had tracked her down, when he pulled her to her feet, she . . . she'd *bit* him! Blood zinged through her veins. A burst of energy replaced her fury. She knew what he wanted her to do, yet with Charles's arm where it was, she couldn't do it.

"Ch-Charles," she rasped. "I can't breathe."

"I don't really give a damn," he snarled.

Her wrists were bound behind her back. With her good hand, she stiffened her fingers, then dug furiously at his groin. The moment he reacted, she sank her teeth into his forearm, further crippling him. As she hurled herself to the ground and rolled away, she heard a shot, and Charles stumbled forward, clutching his chest.

Through a fuzzy red-dusted haze, she saw Buck standing

over him. In another instant, the area was crawling with the cavalry. Pulling herself to her knees, she watched as more soldiers filtered down from the rocks, shoving at gunpoint all of the men Charles had planted there.

Weak, she sank to the ground and watched Buck drag Charles to his feet. There was already a wide circle of blood on his shirt, not to mention the blood she'd drawn with the ragged bed slat.

"God," Charles mewled. "I've been shot, dammit. I'll get you for this, Randall."

"Like you got my old friend Scully?" Buck's anger was barely leashed.

Charles tried to laugh, but he coughed instead, the exertion making him double over. "That old fart? He had a big mouth, Randall. A big, big mouth. He didn't . . . have to . . . die, you know," he said, the words coming in gasps. "But . . . but he wouldn't shut . . . shut up. The old geezer wouldn't shut up." He panted and groaned, sinking to his knees in front of Buck.

Sage helped Molly to her feet and untied her wrists. "Are you all right, ma'am?"

She nodded, gently rubbing each chafed wrist. She looked at Buck, hoping for some little sign from him that now everything would be all right. He ignored her. Totally. Completely. She might as well not even have been there.

"Ma'am?"

Blinking furiously, she turned as Sage stood beside a small buggy.

"Can I give you a ride back to the ranch?"

The awful, disgusting urge to bawl crammed the back of her throat. "Yes," she was able to get out. What else could she do? She would never beg any man for his affections. It was clear to her that whatever she'd felt she and Buck had, was completely one-sided. It had only been her foolish heart that had imagined there ever would be something more.

With a weary sigh, she allowed Sage to help her into the buggy. Closing her eyes, she leaned back against the seat and wondered when the sadness inside her would get so big, her body would just cave in around it.

⚱ Eighteen ⚱

She wandered through the big, opulent rooms, remembering how naive she'd been the day she arrived. How anxious and excited she'd been to have all of these beautiful and expensive "things" to one day call her own. She knew better now, painful as it had been to learn. Everything Charles had stood for was wrong. But even if he'd been an honest man without prejudices, she knew she wouldn't have been able to marry him. She'd never loved him. And if she'd learned one thing from this mess, it was that marriage without love was a waste of precious time. Life was just too short. However, she wondered if it was also a precious waste of time to pine away for a love that didn't love you back.

Finding herself in the salon, she went to the piano and sat down on the bench. She stared at the inscribed *Steinway*, drew in a breath and bravely poised her fingers over the keys. Clumsy strains of a soft Brahms lullaby wafted into the air, and she expelled a groan and stopped the melody, smashing the keys with her fists.

Tears came. Honest, painful tears that had nothing to do with self-pity, but everything to do with loss. Loss of everything she'd worked so hard to achieve—her ability to play. It had always been one of the strongest forces in her life. It wouldn't be easy to cope with, but she was sensible enough to know that even if she forced herself to practice, the bones in her wrist were healing wrong, and she would never play as she had before.

She got up swiftly and hurried from the room. She knew the feeling wouldn't last forever, but for now, she didn't even want to look at the piano. Just as she didn't want to look at or think about Buck. Why deepen the wounds? It did no good. It only made everything worse.

She entered the kitchen and was fixing herself a cup of tea when Nicolette hurried in the back door. They stood and stared at one another. Finally, Nicolette asked, her voice soft and breathless, "Is it true? They've arrested Charles?"

Molly sat down at the table with her tea and gave the girl a silent nod.

Nicolette moved around the room in a daze. "I can hardly believe it. What's going to happen now?"

Molly toyed with the handle on the cup. "What do you want to happen?"

"I . . . I don't know. Chelsea's folks said that if Charles goes to prison, the ranch . . . everything is mine." She gave Molly a look of panic. "What am I supposed to do with it?"

Molly took a sip of her tea, studying the girl over the rim of the cup. It sounded like an awful burden to place on such a young girl. "What do you want to do?"

Nicolette stared out the window and toyed with a plump golden blond curl that hung over her shoulder. "Chelsea's dad suggested I find someone to run the place for me," she said on a sigh. "I don't even know who to trust after everything that's happened."

"There are a few you can trust, you know that," Molly answered, not willing to mention names.

She nodded. "Yes, Buck and Sage. I know." Sighing again, she left the window and plopped herself down next to Molly at the table. "Did you know that Sage is with the army? I didn't know that. He suspected Charles all along, that's why he was here." She was quiet, studying the print on the oilcloth that covered the table. "I can't ask him. He already has a job."

"And . . . and Buck?" Molly held her breath. For what reason, she couldn't say. She knew he would be the best man for the job, but she also knew it meant she'd never see him again.

"Yes, Buck. I guess if I'm expected to do something, I'll start with him. Gosh," she said, frowning, "I hope he'll stay, at least for a while. Angelita will stay, and I really wish Carmen and Estella would come, too. I think they will, if Charles goes to jail."

She gave the room a wistful look. "It's such a big house, and there's so much to do. I've just started to realize how much of a burden Charles put on Angelita. She's always done the work of four women around here." She looked up, embarrassed. "It was while I was staying at Chelsea's that I realized how many women it took to run the house of a big ranch." She was quiet for a moment, then added, "I don't even know how to do the wash. I've never ironed or even cooked."

"Don't punish yourself, honey. You've been away at school. You can't be expected to know these things."

She hung her head, unmoved by Molly's words. "I've been no help at all. In fact, I've been blind to everything but my own selfish little needs. But that's going to change. I'm going to do everything I can to help, and if Buck will take the job of managing the ranch, I'll give him free reign to hire whomever he chooses. I trust him, Margaret." She laughed pensively. "I trust him more than I ever trusted my own brother, and that's sad. Really sad."

Even though Molly's stomach caved in at Nicolette's announcement, she was proud of how much the girl had grown up over the entire affair. Still, she felt those godawful tears press into her throat. "Yes," she managed to say. "He's the best choice."

She glanced at Nicolette, noting her healthy, pink complexion. "Have you been feeling better these days?"

Nicolette smiled, her face aglow. "Oh, yes. Much."

"Are you going back to school in San Francisco?"

Nicolette bobbed her head from side to side, as if she couldn't decide on her answer. "It's funny. The other morning I woke up and decided I wanted it all. I want this baby, Margaret. I want it desperately." She sniffed and giggled. "I also know that I want to study music. I don't breathe without thinking about the piano and how much I love it." She reached into her pocket, pulled out a handkerchief and blew her nose. "Is that foolish? Is it possible for any woman to have everything she wants in this world?"

Molly couldn't hold back a sad smile. "I guess anything is possible if you want it badly enough." Which wasn't true in her case, but she wouldn't burst Nicolette's bubble.

"Well, I'm going to stay here until the baby is born. Angelita would kill me if I let anyone else take care of me, I know that. Then," she added on a sigh, "then Chelsea's folks have offered to take the child and raise it for me, at least until I'm out of school. They've already started writing up an agreement, and their lawyer will go over it to make sure it's all legal and everything."

Molly couldn't help but wonder how this giggly, boy-crazy, scatter-brained, sweet but spoiled girl had grown up so fast. "I'm going to miss you like crazy, Nicolette."

Nicolette's face crumpled into tears. "I know," she answered, her lower lips quivering. "I'm going to miss you, too. I just wish . . ." She drew in a deep breath and wiped her eyes with the back of her hand. "I just wish you could stay, too, but I know how much you want to see your family."

Molly stood and squared her shoulders. "Well, that doesn't mean we'll never see each other again. After all, once the baby is born, you'll be back in San Francisco, right?"

Nicolette stood, too. "Absolutely. Now, do you want me to help you pack?"

"Yes. I don't want you to leave my side for a single minute. Not until I leave for Cedarville to catch the train."

Arm in arm, they left the kitchen and went upstairs. Molly still felt miserable, but she was going home. *Home.* She felt a fluttering of hope in her chest, and a determination not to let the past drag her down.

Once she was packed, Molly took a solitary stroll to some of her favorite places. Her first stop was the barn. As she stepped inside, all of the memories of Buck came rushing back at her. This time she didn't try to push them away.

She wandered through the dark, cavernous building, the smells and sounds dredging up the picture of Buck, busily currying Thunder, his broad, bare back exposed to her gaze.

What are you doing here, brat?

How did you know it was me? Have you an extra sensitive nose or something?

When it comes to your scent, I have . . .

Shivering, she rubbed her forearms with her hands and stepped to Thunder's stall. A stab of anticipation gripped her, for the animal was there, laconically munching oats. That meant that Buck was around somewhere. She didn't want to see him, but she entered Thunder's stall, speaking to him softly.

"I'm going to miss you, boy," she said, rubbing his dark gray forehead. He whickered and probed her other hand with his muzzle. "So, you remember, do you?" She reached into the pocket of her apron and pulled out a small apple, offering it to him in her palm.

"Take care of him, Thunder. And Tomas, too." She scratched the animal's rump, eliciting a shuddering, sidestepping movement from the mount. She was a real dilly, wasn't she? Talking to a horse. . . .

Pulling in a deep sigh, she left the barn and wandered slowly down to her hiding place among the trees. She sat down beneath one, closed her eyes and rested her chin on her raised knees. She listened to the wind. Each time she was here, she heard something different in the wind music. If she was angry, she heard Chopin's "Revolutionary Etude." If she was feeling wistful and sad, as she was today, she heard . . . She wrinkled her nose. Yes, there it was. The·"Funeral March."

She certainly was a morose little wretch. Raising her face to the breeze, she thought about the last time she'd been here. Buck had shown up, fresh from his whore. Oh, how that had hurt.

And try as she might, she couldn't forget how she'd embarrassed herself, throwing all caution to the wind and deliberately finding her own pleasure in his arms. But the worst of it had been his departing remark. *A little dry humping never hurt anybody.* So callous. So shallow. So aggravating. So . . . very much like Buck. Just when she'd begun to think he'd changed, he proved that he hadn't.

She stood, brushed off her skirt and walked back toward the house. Angelita's garden beckoned her. Or maybe it was just that she didn't want to go back into the house. She stepped in among the rows of string beans, squatted and began pulling those that were ready off the vines. She made a dent in her apron and dumped the beans there, continuing through the rows until she had a lapful. Carefully drawing in the corners of her apron to make a hammock for the beans, she stood and trudged slowly toward the kitchen door.

Her gaze caught bits of color flapping in the breeze. She turned to see someone's wash on the line and recognized one of the shirts as Buck's—the one she'd worn that night they made love.

Glancing around to make sure no one was about, she crossed to the line and pulled the shirt off, rolling it into a ball and hiding it in her apron, on top of the beans. It was a spur-of-the-moment decision, but she felt this incredible need to have something of Buck's with her.

She lingered on the back steps, wondering why she just

didn't get on with things, change her clothes and leave. Of course, she couldn't go anywhere until Sage came for her, but here she was, wandering around like she wanted to stay. She didn't, not really. Part of her wanted to see Buck one more time. She made a grimace. Must be that part of her that enjoyed pain, she thought.

She shoved the kitchen door open, went inside and dropped the shirt on a chair. She dumped the beans into a bowl. As she passed the window, she saw Sage drive up with the buggy. Her stomach did flip-flops; Buck was with him.

She stood with her arm around Nicolette's **waist** and glanced around the room one more time.

"Sure you've got everything, ma'am?"

Sighing, she nodded. "I'm sure, Sage." She turned to Nicolette. "Are you coming downstairs with me?"

Nicolette bit her lip, but it quivered in spite of her efforts to still it. Tears sprang to her eyes. "I can't. I don't want to see you ride away."

Her heart heavy, she felt a tear run down her cheek as she pulled the girl into her arms. "I understand. Oh, honey, please take care of yourself. Promise?" She felt Nicolette nod against her shoulder.

Drawing in all of her strength, she pulled away from Nicolette and marched toward the door, unable to look back for fear she'd bawl. Properly attired in traveling clothes, she pulled on her gloves as she took the stairs. She stepped out onto the porch. Buck waited by the buggy. Her heart surged, then dropped. Continuing to dig deep inside herself for strength, she tried to give him a cool, composed smile. It faltered when she saw the faded white lines on his cheek, the remnants of where she'd scratched him when he'd rescued her. All that they'd shared came back at her in heart-stopping swells, and she vividly remembered each word, each kiss, each tender, sweet and loving touch.

"That's a dangerous look, brat."

Blinking furiously, she looked away, hating the fact that with him, she always seemed to wear her heart on her sleeve. "Not that it matters anymore," she said bravely, "but I'll try to remember that."

He stepped close enough to touch, but she clenched her fists, resisting the urge. She memorized his face—not that she hadn't already had his image emblazoned in her mind. That had happened years ago. Still, she wanted to remember the lines that bracketed his mouth, the cleft in his chin, the cow-made dimple and his hot, black eyes.

He reached out and touched her hair. "I'm no good for women, Molly. I'm no good."

Fighting the knot of tears in her throat, she looked away again. "I'm just beginning to realize that," she answered, knowing that deep in her heart it was a lie.

"Go home," he said, his voice a husky whisper. "Go home and have a life."

She forced herself to step back and move toward the buggy. She didn't know what kind of life she would have without him. She knew for certain that it wouldn't be easy to simply erase him from her thoughts. She hadn't been able to do it before, and now, she was sure it would be impossible. She stepped into the buggy, refusing to take his outstretched hand.

"It . . . it was nice to see you again, Buck," she said, looking at him one last time. Her glance immediately slid away. It was too painful to realize that she'd probably never see him again.

Something flared in his eyes. "Say hello to June from me."

She tried to smile, but had to turn away, because her mouth felt all wobbly. She sniffed. "Of course. Take care of yourself, Buck. And . . . and Tomas." Praying that Sage would hurry, she kept her gaze away from both men, clasped her hands in her lap and waited to leave.

As the buggy pulled away, she glanced up at her bedroom window and saw Nicolette gazing down at them in the yard. She could tell the girl was crying. It made her want to cry, too. So she did.

❦ Nineteen ❦

Dr. Jason Gaspard poked his head around the door to Molly's room. "You decent?"

She stood from the chair by the window and stretched her back. "Have I ever been?" She met Jason in the middle of the room and let him guide her toward the bed. "Do we have to do this?"

He waited until she was on her back, then opened her dressing gown and gently probed her stomach. "Every pregnant woman I care for goes through this. Even Rachel. So believe me, you're no exception."

She stared at the ceiling while he did his examination, forcing down her anticipation. "You're sure I'm pregnant?"

He glanced up, his expression sardonic, obviously feeling the question didn't deserve an answer.

Almost immediately upon her return, she'd begun to feel a bit queasy. Fortunately for her, she hadn't suffered with morning sickness nearly as severely as Nicolette. Even before Jason had done his initial examination, she'd known in her heart she was carrying Buck's child.

She felt a twinge in her chest, trying to force her thoughts to focus on Nicolette alone, and not on Buck. It wasn't possible. She had intermittent feelings of elation and despair whenever she thought about her pregnancy. Thinking about the baby made her feel warm, almost giddy —until she remembered how she and Buck had parted. It still hurt to think he hadn't loved her enough to want to be with her.

On the way to Cedarville that day, Sage had told her that Nita, Buck's whore, had died. Molly had felt immediate remorse for all of the terrible things she'd both thought and said about the woman. She'd wanted to ask about Tomas, to find out for sure who his mother was, but she hadn't been sure she wanted to hear the truth. At this point, she could have understood if it had been the whore. But if it wasn't, then there was still someone in Texas who had a strong enough hold on Buck to keep him there.

Jason closed her dressing gown and straightened beside the bed. "Any problems?"

Forcing her thoughts back to the present, she gave him a light smile, hoping to hide her topsy-turvy feelings. "Other than the sad fact that you, my doctor and a happily married man, know my body better than any other man alive?"

He glanced at her abdomen, a look that slid craftily to her face. "Apparently *someone* knows you quite well. I wonder if we'll ever know who the father of this child is."

"You won't know unless I tell you." She had no intentions of doing so. She hadn't heard from Buck, she hadn't expected to. She knew that he periodically wrote to Dusty, and to his mother and Sky, but she seldom probed, even though she desperately wanted to know how he was doing. If she happened to be around when Shy Fawn brought one of his letters over for Anna or Rachel to read, she listened greedily, if discretely, for she didn't want anyone to suspect.

"By the way, how is Rachel this morning?"

He raised a black eyebrow at her. "Clever tactics, changing the subject like that."

"Don't be silly. I really want to know." And she did. His wife, Rachel, had become one of her best friends. Although Rachel and Jason lived in town, close to his practice, Rachel brought her children out to the vineyard house often.

"She's doing much better." Jason's eyes softened; a tinge

of pain entered them. "This pregnancy is a little harder for her than the other three, but I think she's over the worst of it."

Molly reached up and squeezed his arm. "She's lucky to have you . . . in so many ways." She'd seen so much love in her extended family while she'd been home. Of course, it had always been there, but she'd taken it for granted. It wasn't until her fiasco with Charles that she realized what she'd turned her back on all those years ago.

He walked to the door. "You could have someone, too, you know."

Laughing quietly, she sat up and dangled her legs over the side of the bed. "I'm getting that impression." Because everyone in her family had been busy, the new sheriff, Clint Brody, had been sent to meet her at the station the day she'd arrived from Texas. He'd come courting almost immediately.

"He's a good man, Molly."

She felt a pang of guilt. She enjoyed Clint's company, and appreciated his attention. He was tall, well muscled, handsome, fun to be with and attentive. It was nice to be openly admired by a man again, but she hadn't wanted to lead him on. "I know he is. And," she said around a sigh, "his children are sweet."

"But . . . ?"

"But . . . I'm just not ready." No matter how hard she'd tried, she couldn't put Buck's face out of her mind. How easily he'd ruined her for other men—even decent, attentive, law-abiding men.

"He wants to marry you under any circumstances, Molly."

It seemed that everyone within fifty miles knew she was pregnant. She felt an angry pinch of resentment. "And that's supposed to automatically make me feel grateful?"

Jason shook his head and hooked his thumbs into the waistband of his trousers. "It's not gratitude he wants, you know that."

Tossing him a frustrated look, she flung herself off the bed. "But don't you understand? That's all I'd have to offer. It isn't fair to him." She was quiet, remembering that Buck had told her to get on with her life. She couldn't, because he still occupied most of her thoughts. "Marriage without love doesn't work, Jason. I thought it could. That's why I went to Texas in the first place. But . . ."

"You'd be foolish to let him go. There aren't many young, good-looking widowers in these parts. Clint's being chased by every unmarried woman for miles around."

Closing her eyes, she pressed her fingers to her temples. "I know that. Why doesn't he let one of them catch him?"

"Because he wants you."

"He doesn't even know me," she spat.

Jason sighed and shrugged. "All right. I tried."

"Rachel put you up to this?"

Amusement filled his eyes. "My wife, the matchmaker."

Molly crossed to the window. "Tell her 'thank you, but no.'"

He was quiet a long while, then said, "Buck has been informed of Sky's condition."

Just the mention of Buck's name sent her pulse pounding. His stepfather, Sky, had been ailing since the initial harvest. "Do you think he'll come home?"

"Does he have something to come home to?"

She swung around and stared at him. He knew. Somehow, he knew.

Buck reread the letter.

Nicolette poured him a cup of coffee and motioned him to sit down at the table. "Bad news?"

Buck sat and doctored his coffee with cream. "My stepfather is ill. I've been offered his job."

Nicolette eased herself into the chair across from him and folded her arms across her pregnant abdomen. "Your mind hasn't been focused on your work, Buck. I think you should consider it."

He slid the letter through his fingers, letting it come to rest on the table. He'd been taken by surprise a few weeks back when the Double Bar C lawyer had informed him that his old friend, Scully, had made him his heir, stating in his will that all of his holdings were to be sold off, and the proceeds to go to Buck. It wasn't a fortune, but it was more than Buck had dreamed Scully could possibly be worth. It was more than enough to start a life for him and his son . . . sons. In the back of his mind, he'd been thinking about taking Tomas and going home. With the money from Scully's estate, he'd wanted to buy some horses. Find a way to get a small spread and raise them.

With Sky ill, Nicolas could use Buck's help, too. He had legitimate reasons for going home. But the driving reason was still Molly. He'd discovered just how bleak his life was without her. The biggest fear he had was that she'd taken his suggestion and started a new life—without him. It would serve him right, but he was desperate to believe it wouldn't happen.

"Are you still considering selling the ranch?"

Nicolette's gaze meandered over the room. "I think it's the smartest solution, don't you?"

He nodded. "Especially if you're going back to San Francisco. You'll have enough on your mind without worrying about this place."

She gave him a soft smile. "So, when will you leave?"

"I can't leave until I know you're settled, Nicolette," he argued, frowning into his cup.

She reached across and touched his arm. "It's already being handled. I want you to pack up and get yourself home before Christmas." She waited a beat. "No doubt Molly's as miserable as you are."

Giving her a rueful smile, he shook his head. "When did you put all that together?"

"Once I quit obsessing about myself and took a good, hard look at two of my best friends."

A heavy weight left his chest. Excitement coursed

through him. His mind was already filled with plans to return home and claim what was his—and he didn't just mean Dusty.

Examination day, again. Jason listened to her heart and her lungs, then pressed the stethoscope against her stomach. "Dusty brought news from Buck."

Molly's pulse quickened, but she kept her eyes focused on the colorful quilt that lay across her bed. "That's nice," she answered blandly. "And what did he have to say?" Her pulse continued to thrum.

"He's coming home."

She felt a surge of panic. She hardly dared breathe. She didn't dare speak.

Jason slung the stethoscope on the bed, pulled her dressing gown closed then sat down beside her. "You had me fooled for a long time, Molly."

She looked away, toward the window. "I don't know what you mean."

"Don't you think that I, of all people, didn't notice that every time Buck's name came up, you clammed up? Honestly, girl. I remember how it was with you. You chased after him with a vengeance."

"Oh, Jason. Don't remind me of my wicked ways," she groused, moving off the bed and to the window. She didn't *need* a reminder from anyone else. Everywhere she looked, she remembered something that brought her a little shame —and a lot of confused memories.

"Molly, Molly. Even if I haven't seen Buck for many years, I still think I know him better than I know my own brothers and sisters. He was sweet on you when you were just a girl. Hell," he added, shaking his head. "He was even sweet on you when he was married to Honey." He snorted softly. "Not proud of it, though."

Her breath came in ragged gasps and she had to force a calm she didn't feel. "Then you don't know him as well as you think you do, Jason."

"What in the hell happened in Texas, anyway?"

Shivering, Molly rubbed her arms and tossed him an impatient glance. "Don't you have something better to do? Like deliver a baby? A calf? A porcupine? Something?"

Jason chuckled and went to the door. "Why did I think you'd let it all out once you discovered he was coming home?"

"As far as I'm concerned," she said on a shaky breath, "we didn't have this conversation."

"We'll do it your way," he answered, stepping out into the hall, "for now."

"Jason?" When he turned, she asked, "When?"

He thoughtfully rubbed his chin as he studied her. "Your 'when' sounds like 'how long do I have to make my escape.'"

Looking away, she couldn't help smiling. "No, I'm not running anymore."

"He'll be here by Christmas."

She turned away until she was certain her feelings wouldn't show. "Dusty must be ecstatic."

"And a little scared. He hasn't seen his pa since he was a tad."

She wanted to ask if he was coming alone, but couldn't. "Is he staying?" She held her breath, not sure she wanted to hear the answer. In some ways, she'd become comfortable not having him around. It was easier to cope when she didn't have to think about him.

"Says he is." He came back and touched her arm. "Are you going to be all right?"

"Yes," she said, nodding vigorously. "Of course."

After Jason had gone, she returned to the window and stared out at the rows and rows of bare grapevines that grew over the sloping hills. So, he was coming home. Not because of her, but because of Sky. Well, at least that was something. Even though the knowledge did little for her own selfish needs, she hoped he was finally becoming the man she knew he could be.

Christmas was only a month away. After she'd dressed, she left the room, unable to decide if that month would pass like the blink of an eye, or drag like a lifetime.

She met her mother on the stairs.

"Did Jason say you're all right, Molly?"

The woman's beauty still amazed her. Taking her mother's arm, she drew her back down the stairs. "Yes, Jason says I'm doing fine."

"I'm gonna be a granny, Molly. Just like Anna." She beamed at her daughter, who returned the smile.

"And a better one I'll never find anywhere." They descended the stairs and went out onto the porch. There was still an hour before it would be time to start supper. Nicolas was out in the fields and Anna was down at the school.

Molly settled into the porch swing and watched her mother page through the flower book. She felt such peace, being here with everyone. Nicolas and Anna had been wonderful, taking her back in. She felt as though she hadn't even left. And there was just nothing more wonderful than being with her mother again.

"Molly," her mother asked, shoving the book toward her. "What's this word?" June had been determined to learn to read better. It had always been a struggle.

Molly leaned over and studied the word. "Why, Mama, you know what it is."

June frowned and looked at the book again. "I do?"

"What's the blue flower that grows wild and free, in the meadows and under the trees?" she asked lyrically, remembering the way Anna had taught all of them to read.

June looked puzzled, then suddenly her face lit up. "Lupine?"

Molly leaned over and squeezed her hand. "Exactly."

June put the book down and gazed at her daughter, a certain strain on her beautiful face. "I'm so happy you came home to me, Molly. Are you gonna stay?"

The fear in her mother's eyes frightened her. "We'll always be together, Mama, I promise."

June frowned and picked at the pocket of her apron. "But are we gonna stay here?"

"I don't want you to worry about it," Molly said, rubbing her temples.

"But are we?" June persisted.

"Of course. Yes," she answered. "We'll stay here."

Her mother visibly relaxed. Molly had wanted to add "for now," but knew it would alarm her.

Molly knew what the problem was. Her mother was afraid to leave. No matter how much Molly wanted to care for her mother and be responsible for her, the woman was terrified of change. She'd truly wanted to independently take on her mother's care, but Anna had argued—gently but firmly—that June wouldn't weather being uprooted and moved to San Francisco, or possibly even to Pine Valley. Jason had agreed with her. Although June had perked up considerably since Molly's return, that could all change if her routine was altered, even if that change included Molly. Looking at it from that point of view, Molly realized she didn't have many places in which to look for work.

She made a fist. Her wrist had healed, but Jason had told her, as she'd suspected, that the bones weren't where they should be. Unfortunately, he'd said, she couldn't expect to ever have full use of it again. But he'd encouraged her to exercise it, even play the piano, if she could. Oh, she thought, still disgusted, she could. But she hated the fact that she didn't sound like she had before. And she'd found a job teaching music, both at the reservation school and the school Anna ran on the vineyard property, although she suspected Anna had been instrumental in creating both jobs just for her. It was something, but it wasn't enough to support her and her mother.

She occasionally had nightmares about her kidnapping. They were almost as real as the dreams she still had about Buck. Dreaming was such a frustrating thing. She hated not having any control over her thoughts of him. But it wasn't just the dreaming that bothered her. Being home, here, where she'd grown up, infatuated with the young, wild Buck, had made blocking him from her mind impossible. Every time she turned around, there was something there to remind her of his existence. And now, of course, there was her pregnancy. A person couldn't have much more of a constant reminder than that, she thought wryly.

She'd strolled through the yard shortly after she'd returned home and saw the dilapidated old pig shed, now standing alone, unused by the pigs since their new little shed was built. It brought back her night with Buck, when they'd reminisced. The memory of that bittersweet night still brought her pangs of heartache. How perfect they had been together. She would never know if they'd had a chance at all.

Even now, when she'd discovered he was coming home, she felt more dread than excitement. There was that feeling of constant restless anticipation. It wasn't pleasant.

What she would say or how she'd react when she saw him eluded her. Suddenly, she again remembered his circumstances, and the feeling of panic pressed against her heart. Yes, he was coming home. But was he coming alone, or was he bringing Tomas, and possibly the boy's mother?

Two days later, Molly sat picking through a basket of wild blueberries when Dusty ambled up the path toward the house.

He waved and grinned. Molly waved back, swallowing the catch in her throat she always felt when she saw him. He was dark, darker than his father, but tall, straight and handsome. As yet, he hadn't honed the many heart-catching traits he'd gotten from his father, but he was on the verge of manhood. One minute he was a young man, serious, moody and silent. The next minute, he was talking in an animated fashion and his voice would change midsentence, squeaking until he forced it back down again. He'd been a joy to Shy Fawn and Sky. In that respect, Buck had done them a favor.

"Good morning," she shouted.

"Mornin'." He smiled and settled down across from her at the table. "Josh home yet?"

Josh was Nicolas and Anna's youngest son. Though two or three years separated them, she'd discovered that he and Dusty had always been inseparable. Much like Buck and Jason had been years ago. "I think I heard Nicolas say he was going in to pick him up today." She studied Dusty. "Missed him, have you?"

He shrugged. "Sure. Willy'n me were going fishin'. Thought Josh might be back so he could come along."

"You boys have finished your chores?"

"All except those that have to be done tonight."

Molly had noticed Willy, the quiet boy, with Dusty, often. She'd thought he was merely shy, until she heard that he couldn't speak. He'd apparently been orphaned very young, and one day, many years ago, after some traumatic incident, Dusty and Josh had discovered Willy cowering in a cave. He'd lived at the vineyard ever since.

She couldn't help smiling. That was the way these people were. There was always enough love for everyone. It was an ever widening circle, a remnant left over from tribal days when the family was always extended to include one more.

She looked up and caught Dusty's confused gaze. "What is it?"

"My pa's comin' home."

Molly understood. No doubt the look in his eyes mirrored the look in her own. Excitement and fear. Anticipation and dread.

She sighed and bent over her basket, sorting the blueberries. "So I've heard." She gave him a brief glance. "How does that make you feel?"

"I don't know. Me 'n Grandfather talked about it a lot last night." He grabbed a handful of berries and popped them into his mouth. "He's bringin' home a surprise," he said around his mouthful.

Her stomach dipped. "Oh? What do you think it is?"

He turned in his chair and put his feet up on the porch railing. "Well," he said confidently, "I'm kinda hopin' it's a new rifle or a pair of boots 'n spurs, him comin' from Texas and all." He leaned back and put his arms behind his head. "I've been readin' a lot about Texas lately."

Molly smiled in spite of herself. Unfortunately, Buck's "surprise" was probably Dusty's little brother. Now *that* would be a terrible disappointment. Oh, not that Tomas would be a disappointment, but it surely wasn't the kind of surprise a twelve-year-old boy bursting to be thirteen would enjoy, especially if he'd dreamed of something different. Something *very* different.

In spite of the fact that Buck had basically abandoned Dusty, the boy had a positive, happy outlook about his father. That was Sky and Shy Fawn's doing. And Nicolas, Anna and Jason always told Dusty stories of his father. Dusty had once related some of them to her, and she'd had to bite back a smile, for suddenly Buck appeared to take on ultraheroic proportions, doing deeds one only reads about in books. Though she knew they were probably embellished by Dusty's active imagination, she knew that Buck *could* perform heroic feats. He'd done so when he'd come to rescue her. It had been hard not to tell him *her* stories, adding to his repertoire of Buck fables. As angry as she'd been with Buck because she'd loved him and he hadn't loved her back, she had to admit that no one else could have done what he did.

She glanced at Dusty again. "Will you be disappointed if it's something else?"

He turned, and when he looked at her, giving her an adolescent version of Buck's hard gaze, her stomach fluttered. She briefly looked away.

"Like what?" he asked, his face stamped with a familiar frown.

"Oh, I don't know," she answered, forcing herself to

look away again. "But it isn't always a good idea to get your hopes up. It's better to be surprised."

"Ha. That's what Grandfather said last night."

"Well, your grandfather is a pretty wise man, wouldn't you say? By the way," she added, "how is he feeling?"

He took another handful of berries, popping them into his mouth by twos. "Jason was by last night. Said he's doin' real good." Suddenly he chuckled—another sound that was so familiar, Molly shivered.

"What's so funny?"

"Grandmother, that's who."

"Is she excited about Buck's return?"

"Oh, she tries not to be, but every once in a while when she doesn't think anyone's lookin' she gets all teary-eyed and her face gets this soft look . . . I dunno. Grandmother's always so firm. So . . . stern. It's kinda nice seein' her this way."

In her youth, Molly had always felt Shy Fawn was a humorless woman. Now, since her return, she'd discovered the precious cache of warmth that Shy Fawn shared with all of those she loved.

Molly stood, almost reluctant to stop her chat with Dusty. "Well, I think Concetta is ready for these blueberries. Are you coming in?"

Dusty shook his head. "I think me 'n Willy will go fishin' without Josh."

Molly left the basket of blueberries in the kitchen, then went to check on her mother. She peeked into her room, found her napping, so she sat quietly in the rocker and gazed openly at her beautiful mother, although her thoughts were elsewhere.

There had been such a flurry since the news of Buck's pending return. A big family dinner was planned for that night. And since Nicolas and Anna had the biggest place, the gathering would be here.

She wondered how she could avoid it. She probably couldn't. Anyway, if she tried, it would just make it more obvious to everyone that something had gone on between them. Lord of mercy, she thought with a sigh, Jason already suspected.

It was odd that no one had pointedly asked her who had gotten her pregnant. She'd told everyone that she'd traveled to Texas to see her fiancé, but that it hadn't worked out. None of what she'd said was a lie. She knew the unspoken answer to everyone's silent question was that her ex-fiancé was the baby's father. Well, thank the high heavens *that* wasn't true. Memories of Charles were so unpleasant, always leaving her with a sour taste in her mouth.

Buck would know who the father was. Every time she approached their first meeting in her mind, she refused to follow through. She had no idea how he would react. And anyway, she thought, feeling that sick, empty sensation in the pit of her stomach, what would it matter if he had a new wife in tow?

Molly stood at her window in Buck's old shirt. She'd used it as a sleep shirt ever since she'd arrived at home. She'd also discovered it had become something of a "security blanket." Although she had some nice, warm nightgowns, she couldn't get to sleep in any of them. She'd always gone back to wearing the shirt with the torn tail, and falling asleep immediately. It was probably a silly, girlish thing to cling to, but she was hurting no one but herself.

Studying the winter flowers that bloomed in the garden below, she thought about the rest of the day. For the past two weeks, everything anyone had said had been prefaced with "The day Buck comes home . . ." Well, for better or worse, like it or not, "The Day" had come.

She gave herself a stern shake. There was too much to do today. She couldn't afford to stand around moping, hoping, and not coping.

Unbuttoning her shirt, she crossed to the mirror and studied herself. Her breasts were larger, although her stomach barely showed a change. She'd felt some discomfort from her petticoats, but it wasn't too bad yet.

Molly had forced herself to be happy. Unlike Nicolette, she felt that a woman couldn't have it all. She had so much, she felt selfish wanting more. After all, she was going to have the child of the man she loved, and would always love. She had home, family, and their love in return. There was hardly anything more she could expect.

In spite of her resolve, she felt a selfish twinge in her chest. No matter how many times she told herself what she had was enough, she knew that deep in her heart, she still wanted Buck Randall.

🎔 Twenty 🎔

The kitchen smelled wonderful. Nicolas and the boys had dug a pit out back, and the delicious smell of roasted pig wafted in through the windows. Pies lined the table. Beans bubbled on the stove. Freshly baked tortillas were kept warm inside soft cotton cloths. Hot fry bread was heaped into baskets.

Jason and Rachel's oldest son, Lucas, crept to one of the baskets and stole a piece of bread, laughing with glee as Concetta, old but still crusty, pretended to chase him with a broom. He escaped outside, unscathed.

Lucas's sister, five-year-old Faith Twilight, was snuggled next to her Auntie June in an easy chair by the window. She read aloud, though she was barely heard above the din.

Her younger brother, Lyle, sat on the floor near the table, playing with—and eating—whatever bounty fell his way.

Jason had come out and dropped the children off, claiming they'd been wild to come out before their mother was ready. Promising to return later, he'd given Molly a chaste kiss on her worried brow, whispering that she should be brave and that Buck's return certainly wasn't the end of the world.

Molly had shoved at him, scolding him for teasing her. But all in all, she was grateful for the distractions. Even so, she had to purposely relax her jaw every so often, for she'd clenched it so hard, she had an ache down into her neck.

She'd just finished washing some dishes and was wiping her hands on her apron when Josh trotted in through the back door.

"They're coming! Buck's coming, and he's got a kid with him."

The tension in Molly's neck got worse. Desperately needing to escape, she crossed to where her mother sat with Faith Twilight. "I'm going to run upstairs for a minute. I'll be right back, all right?"

"All right," her mother answered with a smile. "But hurry back. Buck is coming!"

After giving her mother a wan look, she rushed upstairs to the private fortress of her bedroom.

Once there, she dropped into the rocking chair, leaned her head back and briefly closed her eyes. Her heart hammered against her ribs, and it had nothing to do with her sprint up the stairs. Her stomach alternately quivered with excitement and churned with nausea.

She tried to keep herself together. For a month she'd tried to convince herself that it wouldn't matter whether Buck came back or not. It had been a shield against further pain, and now she realized it hadn't worked at all.

Without even thinking, she caressed the tiny bulge that pooched out beneath her clothing. Four months now, Jason had said. Yes, that was about right. Buck would find out —sooner or later. Then what?

"Buck, you son-of-a-gun," Josh said, striding up to him and slapping him on the back. "It's sure great to have you back."

Buck studied the boy, amazed at how he, too, had grown. Nothing had prepared him for all the changes. His tall, handsome son who was now standing across the room, his new Stetson set at a cocky angle on the back of his head, had been the biggest shock. He didn't know how he was going to make up for all the lost years. And he was a good kid. A damned good kid. He'd only shown brief surprise when Buck had introduced him to his little brother.

"I'm beginning to think you really mean it, Josh. That's only the fourth or fifth time you've said it."

Josh threw his head back and guffawed. "Jeez, I love family get-togethers. Say," he added enthusiastically. "My pa and Uncle Sky are planning the next Big Head ceremony. Dusty and I get to dance this year. Will you be there?"

An intense feeling of warmth centered in Buck's chest. "I wouldn't miss it for the world."

"Great! I'll tell Pa." His mother beckoned him from across the room. "Hey, I'll be right back."

Buck smiled and nodded, running his fingers through Tomas's hair. He glanced down at the top of the boy's head. Tomas still had a tight grip on his thigh. He'd been a good traveler, curious and surprisingly patient for a child his age.

He surveyed the room. His heart swelled with love and pride. Until he'd stepped off the train and saw his parents and his son, he hadn't realized how much he'd missed his people. He'd lightly teased Jason about his heroic ability to produce such fine, sturdy children, and drew Rachel into his arms, hugging her gently, seeking penance for what he'd put her through those many years ago.

Tomas clutched his leg. He glanced down. One of Jason's boys—Lyle, he remembered—stood in front of Tomas, studying him carefully. They were very close in age. Lyle thrust a piece of fry bread at Tomas, who looked up at his father.

"Go ahead, son. I know you're hungry." He'd spoken English all the way home, hoping to get the child used to it. The boy was bright, a quick study.

Tomas tentatively took the fry bread, a gesture that sent Lyle back to Concetta, who gave him two apple slices. He returned to Tomas and shared.

June wove her way through the crowded room, stopped at Buck's side and put her arm around his waist. He hugged her gently. Even now, at thirty-eight, she was still one of the most beautiful women he'd ever known. Somehow, her simplicity had prevented her from aging, for he swore she didn't look any older than she had when he'd left.

She looked at the boys, then put her hand out, touching each of them on the head. "One, two," she counted, then pointed toward the stairs, "three." She repeated the sequence, always ending by pointing toward the stairs.

"What are you doing, Junie?" It still tore at his heart to see how she had to struggle with life.

"We have one baby," she said, pointing to Tomas, "two baby," she added, patting Lyle on the head, "and Jason says that in the spring, we'll have another baby." Her face suddenly lit up. "Oh, Buck. I'm gonna be a granny. Just like Anna. I'm gonna be a granny. Molly's gonna make me a granny."

Buck felt an odd, uncomfortable lump in his throat. There was a knot in his stomach as well. She was pregnant. . . . The question that arose in his mind was cloaked; he didn't even dare think about it. "Where is Molly, anyway?"

"She went upstairs to rest. I told her you was coming, but she didn't care." June frowned.

A cold wash of panic spread through him. His final words to Molly had been to go and find a life. He'd meant it, although he had never considered the consequences. Now she was pregnant. The thought that it might not be his left a painful gash inside him.

He caught Dusty's eye and motioned to him, then squatted in front of Tomas. "Will you stay with Dusty a little while?"

The child was immediately concerned. "Where you goin', Papa?"

"I'll be right upstairs, Tomas. I won't be gone long."

Dusty hunkered down in front of his new brother. "Hey, Tomas, why don't we go out and find grandfather?"

His eyes lit up. "By the big meat?"

"That's a good idea," Buck answered, remembering how intrigued Tomas had been when he's seen the roasting pig. He helped Tomas into his jacket. "By the big meat."

Tomas started to leave, then turned and reached out his hand to Lyle. Grinning a cute little boy grin, Lyle tagged along, trailing after them. At the door, Concetta stopped him and pulled a thick, warm sweater on over his head.

Shoring up his courage, Buck headed up the stairs. He felt a hard flash of betrayal. He'd ached for Molly daily. Hourly. Ah, hell, she'd become an itch he couldn't scratch. Every night when he fell asleep, he saw her face in his dreams, heard her laugh, recalled the love they'd shared beneath the stars.

He often remembered thinking that he'd thought having her once would slake his desire. Only a fool would think that, especially after what they'd shared. He'd felt he'd done the right thing by sending her home. At the time, anyway. And now . . . now when he finally *had* that proverbial pot to piss in, he might have lost her. What had he expected? He'd told her and showed her in cruel little ways that she'd meant nothing to him at all.

Molly had tried to leave her room many times. She hadn't been able to do it. Suddenly she realized that her very own thoughts were holding her prisoner. The knowledge didn't seem to help much.

Stepping to the mirror, she studied herself. She was still lightly tanned from her summer in the harsh Texas sun. She removed her combs, running her fingers through her hair and massaging her scalp. The top layer of her hair was still bleached from the sun, the layers beneath darker, variegated shades of blond and light brown.

As she worked her fingers through her hair, she felt her breasts strain against her bodice. And her nipples itched. She grimaced. Oh, the discomforts and annoyances of pregnancy.

Briefly closing her eyes, she ran a brush through her hair, pulling the heavy mass over her shoulder. She was putting off the inevitable, hiding up here, but she still couldn't force herself to leave.

When she opened her eyes, her gaze caught Buck's reflection in the mirror. A rich stew of emotions swelled within her. Her pulse strummed, vibrating like harp strings. There was a wild flowering in her chest. Her hands shook, and she was suddenly unable to hold her hairbrush.

Although it had only been four months, somehow she thought he would have changed. He hadn't. He was still tall, rangy and lean. Hard. Handsome. Dangerous. His hair was pulled back, leaving his face open and, she chose to think, almost vulnerable. There was a very slight stubble of beard on his cheeks. She bit her lower lip, the knowledge that he would never be completely tamed sending a frisson of desire through her. Everything about him took her breath away, leaving her faint, weak and deeply, hopelessly in love.

He leaned against the door frame and studied her, his gaze moving over her, stopping at her stomach.

She felt a quickening, a fluttering deep inside. She couldn't move. He knew. Someone had told him, and he knew. He moved toward her slowly, deliberately. He stalked her. She wanted to run. He stopped, his thumbs hooked into the pockets of his jeans as he continued to inspect her.

"I hear you're pregnant."

She carefully put the hairbrush down on the vanity, hoping to hide her feelings. Had he been a man hopelessly in love, there would have been some emotion in his voice. Clutching the side of the table, she suddenly realized that all of her stewing and worrying about this meeting had been for nothing.

Bolstering her courage, she faced him. "Yes, I am."

He scanned her abdomen again. "You don't look like it."

She allowed his blatant disinterest to nudge her worry

and concern aside. As always, he got her back up without even trying. "Well," she answered, wanting to hurt him, "I hardly think it's any of your concern."

Something flared in his eyes. "Then it's not mine."

She let out a long, harsh breath and tried to finish her hair, although her fingers were suddenly clumsy, and she shook all over. She hadn't known what to expect, but of all the images she'd conjured up, this hadn't been one of them.

"No," she said sharply. "It's *mine.*" She was *not* going to beg for his affections.

Hurrying to finish her hair, she turned back to the mirror. As she tried to loop her hair into a roll, she saw Buck move away toward the door. Before leaving, his gaze caught hers, and he burned her with a look more dismal than death.

"You didn't waste any time, did you?"

She scowled. "What do you mean?"

He swore. "Hell, I told you to find a life. You obviously have. It's ironic, isn't it? You never bothered to listen to my advice before. What made you take it this time?"

Like a winter storm, cold fury raged through her. He actually believed she was carrying someone else's baby. "You mean . . . you actually think . . ." She was so angry, she couldn't speak. "You . . . you dumb, stupid *ass.*" She grabbed her hairbrush off the vanity and hurled it at him, missing him by inches.

"Get out of here. Get *out.*"

He barked a laugh. "Well, I see some things haven't changed. You still can't control your temper." Though his tone was familiar, the look he gave her wasn't. It was different from anything she'd seen before, and it pierced her skin, leaving dark, ragged scars all the way into her soul.

Buck returned to the party, forcing himself not to think about Molly. He met the new sheriff, a widower he decided was probably in his middle thirties. He reminded Buck of his good friend, Sage, for he was tall and massively built. As they talked, he scanned the yard, spying Tomas and Lyle playing in the sandbox.

"Are you planning to settle around here then?" Sheriff Brody asked.

Buck turned his attention back to the group of men. "I brought some horses with me. Had them shipped on the train. I'd like to find a spread and raise them."

Nicolas stood with them, stroking his chin. "There's plenty of land here that we don't use for the grapes, Buck."

Buck turned, interested. "If I can use it, I'll buy it."

"Fine," Nicolas answered. "We'll take a look at it soon."

Buck had his back to the house but caught the sheriff's smile.

"Molly." The man's voice was filled with pleasure.

Buck's stomach churned. Turning, he stared as Molly made her way down the porch steps. Her beauty made him hurt like hell. When he'd seen her in the mirror, all of his feelings of love had been reaffirmed. But nothing had prepared him for the intensity of those emotions.

She met the sheriff and took his arm. So. That's the way it was. He observed them, trying to stay impartial. That lasted about as long as the thought itself. A fierce stab of possession lanced through him. He suddenly realized that she hadn't said, in so many words, that the baby wasn't his. Betrayal and a bite of jealousy had colored his thinking.

He thought back to her reaction. Fury. Anger. Disbelief. She hadn't blushed, or hung her head in shame, or even turned away. With sudden clarity, he knew the child was his. As he watched Molly and the handsome sheriff, he also knew that if he didn't assert himself, he'd lose her and their child forever.

Giving Buck a covert glance, Molly clutched Clint's arm. She felt no guilt at using Clint, for they'd come to an understanding weeks ago. When she learned that Buck was coming home, she'd told the sheriff where they stood. She hadn't elaborated, hadn't told him what was in her heart, but he had accepted her reasons for wanting to be just friends.

She caught Buck staring at them. The deep probing gaze burned a path across her skin, but she refused to let it touch her heart. The odious ass needed to learn some manners. He looked almost envious as he studied her and Clint. Good. *Good*. Let the ass stew. She was still absolutely livid that he could even *think* that she'd turn to someone else. She had told him she loved him more than once. Had he thought she wasn't old enough to know the difference between a mad crush and deep, burning, urgent love? Just because he didn't know what it was didn't mean she didn't.

She spied Tomas and Lyle in the sandbox. Tomas looked up and saw his father, nearly stumbling in his effort to get to him. He attached himself to Buck's leg and looked up at her shyly.

The warmth she'd felt that day at Carmen's returned. She bent down and smiled. "Tomas, I'm so happy to see you again."

He continued to look at her, his eyes suddenly twinkling. Wrinkling up his nose, he said, "His-sik."

"You remembered," she answered around her smile. Glancing up, she noticed Buck's puzzled look. "Private joke," was all she said.

She allowed Clint to be at her side most of the afternoon and into the evening. It was safer than trying to imagine how differently things would have been if Buck weren't such a stubborn, mule-headed dolt. What ever had made her believe that he could change?

At first, when she realized what he'd been thinking, she'd thought self-pity would drown her. It hadn't. She'd been too shocked and angry at his response to think about herself.

Now, as she prepared for bed, she eyed Buck's worn shirt with disdain. She could certainly do without *that*. Striding to her dresser, she yanked open a drawer and pulled out a flannel nightgown.

After crawling into bed, she tried to get comfortable. The heavy gown smothered her. She twisted and turned, tugged the gown down over her knees, only to find it back up around her waist.

With a sigh of disgust, she threw back her covers and groped around for the shirt. Like it or not, she thought as she changed, she couldn't get through the night without it. It had become a crucial part of her routine. The soft, worn fabric clung to her, seductively embracing her like the arms of a lover. And because she no longer had one, it was the next best thing.

A dream, a sensual fantasy she frequently had, awakened her. As usual, she felt an urgent need for release. Also as usual, she forced herself to ignore it. Although Buck had awakened her sexually, she was pragmatic enough to realize that these urges could be stifled. After all, before she'd met Buck again in Texas, she'd stifled them for years.

Tossing back her covers, she left the bed and put on her dressing gown. It was barely dawn. She slipped into her rabbit moccasins, remembering the day Buck had given them to her. Old memories hurt, but with so many things around her to remind her of him, she would just have to acquire a tough skin. She left her room, yet when she stepped to the landing, she heard no movement below.

She padded quietly down the stairs and hurried into the kitchen, anxious to start a fire in the stove. To her surprise, the room was already toasty warm.

❧ Twenty-one ❧

The kerosene lamp was lit on the table, casting a shadowy light into the room. Molly crossed to the stove and warmed her hands over the heat that rose from the surface. Suddenly a shiver darted up her spine, standing the hairs at her neck on end. She wasn't alone. Turning slowly from the stove, she found her gaze going to the far corner of the room to the chair that sat by the window. He was there. She said nothing, felt everything. The night they'd met in the Campion kitchen those many months ago, fighting over a glass of milk, rose before her. She shuddered, automatically pulling the edges of her dressing gown together.

"I remembered it, too," he said, his husky, sexy voice sliding at her from the darkened corner.

Turning briskly, she attempted to start a pot of coffee. "I don't know what you're talking about," she answered, grabbing the Biggin coffeemaker off the shelf near the stove.

"I don't believe you." His voice was still hushed, but he was closer now, for all of the nerve endings along her back came alive.

Forcing herself not to shake, she put the innards of the coffeemaker together, then grabbed the tin of coffee off the back shelf on the stove, opened it and scooped the grounds on top of the finely strained bottom. As she reached for the kettle of hot water, his hand came around and stopped her.

His touch was stirring, as she knew it would be. "Don't flatter yourself. I've learned to put you and everything about you out of my mind."

He gently shoved her aside, lifted the kettle off the stove and poured hot water slowly over the coffee grounds. "Yeah," he said, his tobacco-rough voice working the magic it always had. "I can tell by the way that little pulse at your throat is throbbing that you've recovered from our many sweet, hot, delightful little skirmishes."

Her fingers automatically went to her throat where her pulse fluttered and she stepped away, just in case their bodies touched. She had a feeling that if they did, she would singe her clothing. "That's not fair," she murmured. "You startled me, that's all."

He waited for the water to filter through the grounds, then added more. "I remember that night, brat. Your pulse was pounding then, too. At first I hadn't known if it was from fear or desire. All I knew was that in either case, I was probably the cause."

Pulling the lapels of her gown closer, she asked, "You thought I was afraid of you?"

He gave her a brief glance before returning to his task. "On some level."

He'd been right, of course. She remembered clearly how her heart had hammered at his nearness. But it hadn't been fear of him exactly, it had been fear of what she felt for him. Reluctant to move away from the warmth of the stove, she turned, warming her backside. The entire front of her body was suddenly cold as it was robbed of the heat. A feeling not unlike being sent away with an order to find herself a life without him.

"It's my baby, isn't it?"

The question took her by surprise. She swallowed the apprehension that gathered in her throat. "I told you before," she said, forcing a calm she didn't feel. "It's mine and only mine."

He gave her a husky chuckle. "It's been a while since womankind has been able to pull that off."

She looked at him, noting the dimple that delved into his cheek. How she'd grown to love it. How silly she'd been, thinking he'd gotten it in a fight for his honor, only to discover he'd been kicked by a cow. In any case, she'd envied the cow. It had put a permanent mark on him. Something she wished she could have done, she thought, a softness settling over her.

"There's that look again, brat."

Blinking, she pulled her gaze away and clasped her stomach with her arms. "You have a vivid imagination, Buck Randall. I was merely looking at you. I had no feelings about it one way or another."

He laughed, a sound tinged with bitterness. "When are you going to give it up and finally see what's best for you?"

She turned and studied him, knowing her eyes were filled with pain. *When are you?* He met her gaze, and she quickly looked away.

Buck finished pouring water into the upper cylinder of the coffeepot and set the kettle back on the stove. In the quiet room, the sound of the water, as it dripped through the grounds into the cylinder below, was magnified.

They stood side by side. She felt Buck's gaze as it wandered over her face, her neck. She suppressed a shudder of delicious pleasure. Suddenly his fingers were at her lapel, and he pulled it aside.

"So, that's where it went. I wondered what happened to it."

Embarrassed that he'd discovered she slept in his shirt, she tried to shrug off his touch, but he turned her toward him. She felt a blush creep into her neck and cheeks as he opened her robe, his penetrating gaze searing her skin. Her breasts tightened and her nipples suddenly itched. She sucked in a breath, hoping to stifle the urge to rub them against something.

"I always liked it better on you than on me," he said in a husky whisper.

She couldn't meet his gaze. "Again, don't flatter yourself. It's simply more comfortable to sleep in, that's all." She tried to pull away, but he held her firmly. The itch became unbearable, and she wrenched herself from him, turned away and brought her forearms to her chest, rubbing hard.

Buck's hand pressed her shoulder. "What is it? What's wrong?"

She shook her head, hoping he didn't hear her shudder of relief.

He turned her around quickly. "No. Something's wrong. Is it the baby? Is something wrong?"

A mortified chuckle escaped her, and her cheeks grew hotter. "No," she said, trying not to laugh. "It's not the baby."

Grabbing her by the shoulders, he shook her gently. "I don't believe you. Tell me, dammit. I have a right to know."

She looked up into his face, surprised to see such deep, honest concern. Her nipples tingled, signaling their desire to be rubbed again. She tried to hold back a nervous laugh but didn't succeed. He wanted to know? Well, fine. "It's my nipples," she said boldly. "They itch."

His eyes, already nearly black in the dimly lit room, darkened further. His nostrils flared. His gaze moved to her chest where her feisty nipples gave him the desired reaction. They pouted, pressing their hard points into the soft, clingy fabric of his shirt.

She saw his Adam's apple bob nervously at his throat, then he uttered a rough sigh and shoved himself away from her. "You're going to marry me."

All humor gone, her stomach dropped, leaving an empty hole in her chest. "Is that your decree, Oh, Exalted One? Well, be still my heart," she drawled, fanning herself dramatically with her hand. "How could a girl refuse such a sweet-talkin' fool."

Turning, he pinned her with a hard glare. "You're going to marry me," he repeated.

Fury laced through her pain. "Just like that?" she asked, snapping her fingers in his face. "I'm not that desperate. If I'd merely wanted a father for this child, I could have been married already."

His gaze narrowed dangerously. "I was afraid of that."

"Although it's none of your business," she snapped, "you don't have to be. However, I will say that my other proposal was a lot more enticing than yours."

He swore, the sound raw and savage. "What in the hell do you want? Flowers? Champagne? Little sweet messages written on heart-filled paper? Dammit," he swore again. "That isn't me. You should know that better than anyone."

Briefly closing her eyes, she walked numbly away from the warmth of the stove. The cooler air assaulted her, keeping her focused on her anger. Her feelings infuriated her. She loved him. She wanted him. She'd marry him in an instant—if only he would tell her he loved her. Even if he cared enough to make a life with her—that would almost be enough. But she wasn't going to marry him just because she was carrying his child.

"Tell me something, Buck."

He turned, raising an eyebrow in her direction. "What do you want to hear?"

Frustration gnawed at her. "Anything. Anything that will make me want to do this."

Sighing, he turned away and lit a cigarette. "The baby is mine. Unlike before, now I can provide for my own."

She pressed her lips together. It wasn't what she'd wanted to hear. Not at all. "I almost made a mistake once, Buck." She turned, shaking her head. "I don't intend to make it again. I decided before I left Texas that marriage without love just doesn't work."

Turning, he studied her for a long time. The moment

stretched to the point of pain. Flickering changes passed over his face, as if he were having a multitude of quiet conversations in his head. Suddenly he grabbed the lid lifter, lifted the stove lid closest to him and tossed his cigarette into the fire.

He crossed to where she stood, continuing to watch her. "Don't be too quick to turn me down, Molly. Despite what you might think, I can give you and the baby a decent life."

She watched him go outside, hunching slightly against the cold winter morning. It had finally happened. He'd become the responsible man she knew he would be one day. It had been the day she'd waited for. Now she knew it wasn't enough. She'd learned of his inheritance. Yes, he could take care of her and the baby and Dusty and Tomas. "But can you give me your love?" she asked quietly, wishing she could have said it to him. She went back to the warmth of the stove, huddling near it, and was certain she'd never be warm again.

Astride their mounts, Buck and Nicolas studied the land. It was a brisk, cold morning. Frost cloaked the ground like an icy cape. Buck sucked the cold air into his lungs, watching the mist dissipate onto the breeze as he exhaled.

"There, Buck," Nicolas said, pointing toward a grove of pecans. "From that point to the edge of the vines and back to where we're standing is about twenty acres. I know it doesn't sound like much, but—"

"It sounds like a lot. Let's get back to the house and iron out the details."

Startled, Nicolas said, "No dickering? No trying to get the price down?"

"No." He gave Nicolas a knowing grin. "The price is more than fair, and you know it."

Nicolas chuckled and nudged his mount with his knees. "In the meantime, I still want you to take over Sky's responsibilities. It will help me, and it will also give you a little extra income."

Buck turned Thunder around and followed him. He would gladly help at the vineyard, although he didn't really need the money. But it would be best to keep busy. Keep his mind off other, more frustrating, things.

He let his gaze move slowly over the acreage Nicolas was willing to sell him. It was perfect for raising horses. It was perfect for raising his sons. It would have been perfect for everything. Damned changeable woman. He should have known that what she'd felt for him in Texas had been a fleeting infatuation. And damn Campion for making her marriage-shy.

The two men took the road slowly back to the ranch. Buck's thoughts were filled with Molly as he'd seen her earlier in the morning. She'd sounded strained, like she'd wanted to ask him something but hadn't dared. Her beauty stole his breath, his reason . . . his sanity. That he hadn't swept her into his arms and kissed her senseless had been a surprise, even to him.

The moment he'd seen her again, after so many months, he knew he loved her. But he still wasn't completely convinced he was good for her. He hadn't had much luck with women. His track record was terrible. He'd promised himself he'd never marry again, yet even before he discovered Molly's pregnancy, he'd decided his luck had changed, and marrying Molly would be worth any price he, alone, had to pay. As long as it didn't jeopardize her.

And Dusty . . . Hell, the boy had only praise and adoration for her. He'd told him of their talks, and how she'd always treated him like a "man," and not like a little kid. He'd waxed poetic on her beauty and her kindness and her willingness to listen to his dreams.

Discovering that she wore his shirt to bed had planted a seed of hope in his chest. Her admission that her nipples itched had planted other feelings elsewhere—where his own itch had yet to be scratched. Her bluntness made him smile.

"You're deep in thought, Buck. Are you making plans?"

He swung his gaze to Nicolas. "It isn't as easy as all that."

Nicolas chuckled. "Women never are."

"Are we both so obvious?" he asked with a bitter chuckle.

"You must remember, we are your family. We know both of you perhaps better than you know yourselves. I remember many years ago when the two of you glared at each other across my dinner table. Mutinous. Even then, Anna and I knew that your supposed hate for one another would one day become a love just as strong."

Buck gave him a rueful smile and shook his head. "I hadn't known we were that obvious."

"Keeping Molly from getting into trouble with her friends was only one of the reasons we sent her away."

"And I was the other?"

Nicolas nodded. "You were the other."

Buck was quiet for a moment. "I would never have dishonored my marriage, Nicolas. And I wouldn't have acted on my feelings for Molly."

"No, perhaps not. But Molly was the one I was most concerned about. She was wild and reckless and determined to get what she wanted. And though she never said it aloud, Anna and I knew she wanted you."

Buck pulled out a cigarette and let it dangle from the corner of his mouth. "I've always lived with the guilt that had I loved Honey even half as much as I've always loved Molly, she wouldn't have died."

Nicolas gave him a sharp look. "That's a foolish waste of energy. I think it's time you talk to Jason about Honey. I think it will finally put your guilt to rest."

❧ Twenty-two ❧

After dropping Anna and Josh off at the church for the Sunday service, Buck stopped in to see Jason. What Nicolas had said to him the day before about erasing his guilt had kept him awake most of the night. He couldn't imagine Jason held that key, but he'd wanted to find out.

"Have a chair," Jason said, sitting down across from him on the sofa.

The house was quiet. Buck had seen Rachel and the children waiting for Anna and Josh at the church entrance.

He glanced around the room. It was homey, snug. Something he wondered if he'd ever have. Again, he was reminded just how lucky Jason was to have found a woman like Rachel. The looks that still passed between them confirmed Buck's intuition that their love had grown over the years. He still felt a bite of envy for what they had. And although Rachel had absolved him of his guilt, he still felt pangs of remorse for the way he'd treated her years before.

As he lowered himself into a high-backed easy chair, he found Jason studying him. "It's great to have you home, Buck."

"It's good to be here."

"And you're here to stay?"

"Of course. This is where I belong." He noticed Jason's slightly sardonic expression. "Don't you believe me?"

Jason chuckled softly. "Oh, I believe you. What about Molly?"

He suddenly felt uncomfortable. "What about her?"

"Are we finally going to get the truth about the baby she's carrying?"

Buck frowned. "What do you mean?"

Jason sighed and leaned against the back of the sofa. "I've been examining her for months, and she still refuses to tell me who the father is."

"Hell," Buck muttered. "That's no secret. That baby is mine."

Jason grinned. "I know that. What are you going to do about it?"

Buck threw his head back and groaned. "Whatever I'm doing, I'm not doing it right."

"You'll figure out something," Jason said around another chuckle. "I don't doubt that." He poured them each a cup of coffee. "Something else on your mind?"

Buck straightened. "What do you know about Honey's death that you haven't told me?"

Jason showed brief surprise. "Why are you concerned about that now?"

Buck drew his hand over his face, then rubbed his neck. "Nicolas seems to think I'm carrying about some guilt I shouldn't feel."

"Are you?"

"Am I carrying around guilt? Hell, yes. As to whether or not I should feel it . . . I don't know. Maybe you can tell me. Nicolas seems to think you can."

"You're serious," Jason said, assessing him briefly before sampling his coffee.

"Of course I'm serious. Dammit, Jason, I was supposed to meet Honey at the school that day. If I hadn't gone out and gotten drunk, I would have. And she'd still be alive today." He often wondered what different turns his life might have taken if Honey hadn't died. Taking a slow pull on his coffee, he settled back and watched Jason.

"Are you telling me you've felt responsible? That your drunken orgies after she was dead were because you thought you'd killed her?"

In his saner, now sober moments, Buck recognized the irrationality of his thoughts and actions. The guilt had been with him so long, it had been hard to see beyond it. Even at the times when he'd come to terms with his remorse, fresh guilt at loving Molly even before Honey was killed shoved all reason aside.

At Jason's question, he shrugged. "Yeah, something like that."

Jason stood and went to the window. "Christ, man. If I'd known . . ."

Frowning, Buck studied his friend's back. "What do you mean?"

Jason turned abruptly. "There were things I found out about her I thought were better left unsaid. Especially after she died." He grew thoughtful. "You weren't getting along very well at the time, were you?"

"Hell, no. But it was my fault, I—"

"No, it wasn't," Jason interrupted.

"But I was supposed to meet her—"

"And maybe that one time you could have prevented the inevitable," Jason finished.

"Inevitable?" Buck felt an odd sensation spread into his gut. "What do you mean?"

Jason swore, then returned to the sofa. He sat forward, his elbows on his knees. "This isn't going to be easy to say, Buck."

"Nothing can be worse than what I've gone through. Believe me, *nothing.*"

Jason nodded, appearing to make a decision. "All right. Honey had come to see me once, not long after you were married. She was somewhat embarrassed, but quite provocative as well."

"Provocative? What in the hell is that supposed to mean? That she came on to you?" Buck felt a stir of anger.

"Dammit, are you going to listen before you pass judgment? Don't leave her on that pedestal, Buck. Don't glamorize something just because it's gone and you think you're responsible."

Apologizing, Buck settled back. He hadn't really thought he felt that way. He'd admitted that they had problems. He'd taken on the guilt for her death. Had it been safer than admitting he knew, deep down inside, that she wasn't just a nagging wife, but an errant one as well?

"All right. Go on, tell me everything."

What he heard sent him reeling. She'd come to Jason because of her own uncontrollable addiction—to sex. She'd admitted to him that one man could never satisfy her, and though she'd tried to remain faithful to her marriage vows, that had lasted only a few months. After Dusty was born, she'd become quite promiscuous, but only with the Whites who could give her money and gifts in return.

"So, don't go beating yourself up, claiming a guilt you don't deserve, Buck. I'm not even sure why she told me. She had no intentions of trying to change. Maybe you could have saved her that day, but eventually, she'd have ended up the way she did."

Buck waited for the numbing pain to come. It didn't. For so many years after her death he'd felt guilty for even thinking she'd been unfaithful. He'd thought it was just a safety valve, something to mollify his own feelings of ambivalence toward her and their marriage. If there had been honest signs of her unfaithfulness, he hadn't noticed them. But then, he realized sadly, he hadn't bothered to look too hard.

Something inside him, the guilt and anxiety he'd fed on for so many years, began to dissolve. A peace stole through him. He'd always be sorry he hadn't been there for her, but he knew that in order to save someone from addiction of any kind, that person must want to be saved.

"And you're sure the schoolmaster, Harry Ritter, killed her?"

"He'd gotten drunk one night and all but admitted it to someone—I can't remember who. But you know, who in the hell cared if a squaw was murdered?" Jason added bitterly.

"Yeah, who in the hell cared . . ." In spite of what Buck had learned, he finally had put everything in perspective and was at peace. Of a sort. At least that part of his life was behind him once and for all. Hopefully, he'd never let himself wonder about "what might have been." Hell, he spent more than enough time thinking about Molly, and "what was going to be."

Molly heard Anna, Buck and Josh returning from church. She'd felt a bit too queasy to join them and had been dozing on the sofa. She'd had some bouts of dizziness as well, but as long as she rested, they didn't last long. The house had been empty save for her. June had gone to Sky and Shy Fawn's earlier to work on a quilt. Concetta was spending the weekend with her daughter.

As Josh and Anna entered the kitchen, Josh was laughing, holding his sides.

"It isn't as funny as all that, Joshua Gaspard," his mother scolded.

Molly glanced at Anna, still beautiful at fifty, and noticed the blush that had colored her cheeks. She looked beyond Anna toward the door, a twinge of disappointment infiltrating her relief when she realized that Buck hadn't come inside with them.

Josh saw Molly at the table. Still gasping for breath, he announced, "Ma and Rachel got a fit of the snortin' giggles in church."

"We did not snort," Anna answered primly.

Molly bit her lower lip to keep from smiling. "What happened?"

"We were standin' for a hymn when Ol' Mrs. Crabtree, who was in front of us, farted—"

"Passed gas," his mother interrupted tersely. "Don't use that other word in the house."

"Yes, ma'am," he answered, taking the stern correction with a good-natured nod. "Anyway, Mrs. Crabtree, *passed gas*," he said, obviously only to please his mother, "and Rachel was sittin' next to Ma and cleared her throat, but she kind of hiccupped at the end, like she was tryin' to keep from laughing. And then—"

"And then," his mother said firmly, "that's the end of it, Joshua."

Still chuckling, Josh left the room and bounded up the stairs.

Anna removed her gloves and her cape, laying them over the back of a chair. As she wove her hat pins into the brim of her hat, she gave Molly a careful look. "Are you feeling any better?"

Molly yawned and stretched, unwilling to mention her bout with dizziness. "Much. I'm sorry I missed the excitement," she added around a smile.

"Honestly," Anna said, her face still flushed. "I can't believe I did that. What kind of example is that for the children? Jason's three youngsters were sitting right there with us, and I do believe they were stupefied to find their mother and their granny giggling and snorting into their hankies like a couple of girls at a basket social." She shook her head with dismay. "Thank heavens Reverend Toland is such a saint. He just talked on and on as though nothing had happened, when in reality, we upset the congregation far more than poor Ella Crabtree did. And that rascal Josh," she said, clucking her tongue. "The stinker started laughing so hard at *us*, he had to leave the church."

With a resolute shake of her head, she mumbled something and went into the pantry.

Unable to help herself, Molly chuckled quietly. Oh, how she'd missed all of this. It was the funny, madcap day-today incidents with her family that made her happy to be home, in spite of her troubled feelings about Buck. She pushed the complicated problems away, preferring to enjoy the day instead.

Anna, now composed, stepped out of the pantry with a cloth covered basket. "Molly, would you do me a favor?"

"Of course. I feel perfectly fine now." And she did. She'd never experienced two bouts of dizziness in the same day.

"Well," Anna began, "on our way back from church, we saw a couple of the hands cleaning out the brush by the line shack back in the woods near the river. They looked so tired, I just know they're hungry. I thought it might be a good idea to bring them some lunch." She slipped the basket handle over her arm and wrung her hands. "I'd send Josh, but after he changes into his work clothes, Nicolas wants him in the barn. I'd go myself, but I—"

"Say no more." Molly stood slowly, just in case the vertigo returned. It didn't. "I'd love the ride. I'll change my clothes and take one of the mares."

"Oh, you are a lifesaver." Anna sounded so grateful, and strangely enthusiastic.

It was a beautiful morning. Unseasonably warm, as had been the entire month. A small grove of sycamores snuggled at the edge of the vineyard, their smooth, light green leaves forming irregular crowns atop the rather colorless trunks. A swallow took flight from within the leafy mass, cutting an erratic path across the road, leaving only a sweet twittering in its wake.

Molly guided the mare off the road onto the path that led to the line shack. A wash of memory made her ache. This was the shack where Buck had found her drinking with her friends that night before the family decided to ship her off to San Francisco.

A flush stole into her cheeks. Had she really kissed him so boldly all those years ago? For all she knew, he could have made the story up, but knowing how she'd been in those days, he probably hadn't.

The line shack stood in the distance, settled comfortably beneath a grove of gnarled oak. Shading her eyes, she looked for the hands. No one was around.

Nudging the mount gently, she drew closer to the shed, but still saw no one. Then, out of the corner of her eye, she saw something move.

She turned; the familiar stew of emotions filled her. Buck had his back to her, clearing away some of the dead grapevines. Her pulse quickened, her pelvis thickened with desire, and she felt an incredible, insane, sense of elation. How she loved this stubborn, straight-talking man.

He turned, the surprise briefly etched on his face quickly masked. "What are you doing here?"

She snorted softly. So much for romance. Glancing around, she said, "Anna told me there were workers here who needed lunch." She raised the basket in his direction.

He stood, leaning on his shovel, and gave her a probing gaze. "There's no one here but me."

To avoid his analysis, she looked down at the basket. "Maybe you want this anyway. Would you mind taking it?"

He placed the shovel against a tree and crossed to where she sat. He looked at her for a long time, his gaze somehow poignant.

Her insides continued to hurt. A wave of nausea swelled upward, she pressed her fingers to her mouth and moaned. Her other hand clutched her stomach, and she briefly realized that she'd dropped the basket.

Everything happened within seconds. Her nausea pressed into her throat, a cold sweat broke out over her skin, and familiar black spots danced before her eyes before she pitched sideways into thin air.

Molly breathed in a long sigh and opened her eyes. She was lying on a cot in the line shack, a soft pillow under her head and a quilt spread over her. One hand was free, resting outside the quilt. The other, she realized, was clasped tightly between Buck's calloused palms.

Turning, she caught his gaze. Her heart expanded, the richness of emotions warming her. His beautiful gold-rimmed eyes were no longer closed down from the inside. Concern, compassion, devotion, kinship, warmth . . . They were all there.

".I guess I fainted." She gave him an open, loving smile.

He brought her hand to his lips and kissed it, drawing it to his cheek where he pressed it against his skin. "If anything ever happened to you . . ." His voice was husky, and he cleared his throat. "Is there . . . do you think . . . is the baby all right?"

She traced her fingers over his dimpled scar, her emotions brimming. "I'm sure the baby is fine. I fainted, Buck. It's happened before. I just have to be careful—"

He uttered a ragged curse. "If it was my fault—"

"Stop," she interrupted softly. "I forbid you to assume any more guilt. Do you hear me?"

A touch of humor softened his eyes. "Still the feisty, bossy brat, I see."

"And you're still stubborn and mule-headed," she answered around a smile. "I've loved you forever, you know." She was no longer afraid to share her feelings.

He bent close, so close she saw every detail of his dangerous, handsome face. "And before that, I loved *you*."

Goose flesh, thrilling and exciting, raced over her skin. Tears of relief surged forth, rimming her eyes, brimming over onto her cheeks. "Oh, thank heavens for that." She pressed her lips together to keep them from quivering.

He lowered his face to hers and they kissed. A sweet burst of pleasure splintered through her as their mouths opened, softly, slowly, and their tongues teased.

He pulled away, looking down at her with an intense look of possession. His gaze roamed her face, her hair, her neck. "I don't want to hurt you, but dammit, I've got to at least hold you."

She scooted to the far edge of the cot and turned on her side, throwing the quilt back as an invitation for him to join her.

He gave her a lusty, lopsided grin. "Think this one will hold us?"

Remembering the one they'd broken, she answered his smile with one of her own. "We'll be careful. But I think I'll dry up and blow away if you don't hold me."

He gingerly lowered himself next to her and took her in his arms. They sighed together, a deep, twin sound that made them laugh again.

Her ear rested against his shoulder, yet she could still hear and feel the pounding of his heart. She thought her own would burst, she was so happy.

"You *will* marry me," he ordered, his voice soft against her hair.

She put her arm around him and stroked his back. "I thought you'd never ask—again."

His hands moved over her, tracing the lines of her body beneath her clothes. "I have some things to tell you."

Her insides rose, then settled gently, leaving her a little anxious.

"The first thing we talk about is Honey."

Frowning, she pulled away slightly and looked at him. "What is it?"

He drew her close again. "I stopped in and talked to Jason this morning. He told me many things about my late wife that I hadn't known. One day, maybe we'll talk about it, but for now, just know that in many ways I feel exonerated."

She brightened. "You don't feel guilty anymore?"

"Well," he said on a harsh sigh, "I guess I'll always feel some guilt, but Jason convinced me I shouldn't waste my life—and yours—worrying about it."

Warmth burst inside her. "Someday I'd like to hear what he told you."

"Someday you will."

She waited for him to continue. When he didn't, she asked the question that had been gnawing at her for months. "Buck, who is Tomas's mother?"

"Can't you guess?"

She nodded, and for the first time, felt no jealousy. "It was Nita, wasn't it?"

"I suppose we should talk about her."

A queer sensation cloaked her stomach. "Yes. Please, just tell me the truth. My imagination has already done enough damage." She snuggled closer, if that was possible, feeling him draw her against him.

"She was a whore, Molly. It wouldn't have bothered me to hear you say it."

"I'll always be sorry for what I said and thought about her."

"She was my woman for a lot of years. You should know that. I think she loved me, in her way, but she also knew I never loved her. Not like she wanted me to. And," he added, gently, "by the time you'd come to the ranch, we hadn't shared a bed in over a year."

Relief tumbled over her guilt. "And I was such a shrew whenever I thought about the two of you together. It was unforgivable, Buck. I'm so sorry."

"I was partly to blame for not leveling with you in the first place." He stroked her hair. "I think the last thing we should talk about is Tomas."

The memory of cuddling him through a night of fever came back to her, reaffirming her feelings for the child. "I love that little boy, Buck."

He let out a whoosh of breath, yet still appeared tense. "I'm real glad to hear it."

"And it doesn't matter who his mother was. I'll love him as if he were my own." She waited for him to respond. His silence was curious . . . nerve-wracking.

"That's what I plan to do, too."

Startled, she pulled away and looked at him. "What?"

"I'm not his natural father, Molly."

She swallowed hard. "But, Buck. He . . . he calls you 'Papa,' and . . . and you said he was your son . . ."

Buck laughed, a bitter, tragic sound. "Hell, I thought he was. Never had a reason to believe he wasn't. But the day after Nita died, I got a letter from her. One of those to be delivered only in the event of her death. In it, she told me I wasn't the boy's flesh and blood father. She asked me to forgive her for deceiving me all these years."

Molly was stunned. "You mean you had no idea? No idea at all?"

He shook his head. "None. And I'd come to look forward to visiting him. I saw what I'd missed with Dusty, and I knew I couldn't let it happen again. Actually, having Tomas made me realize how much I wanted to come home."

Emotions tumbled inside her. "She told you all this in a letter. Did she tell you who Tomas's real father is?"

"Yes."

"But . . . but why would she keep it a secret all those years?"

He sighed into her hair, the sound filled with so much sorrow, she almost wept.

"Probably because his real father was a son-of-a-bitch who would have either killed him, or kept him as a slave because he had mixed blood."

Cold fingers of terror marched across her heart. She felt clammy, sticky with shock. "You don't mean . . ."

"Oh," he said, his voice filled with quiet outrage, "but I do."

"Charles," she barely whispered. Suddenly, all of the implications reached her brain. "Oh, my God. Oh . . . my . . . God."

She clung to him, needing to give him strength and draw it from him as well. "I can't even imagine how you must feel."

"At first I hated her for the deception. I'd been sucked in

to loving Tomas so easily. It was hard for me to believe I could be fooled like that."

"But how do you feel about Tomas, now?"

He was quiet for a moment. "There was a brief period of resentment. But, hell. I'd already grown to love the kid. And what was I supposed to do? His mother was dead, and his father—his flesh and blood father—would have . . . Ah, hell. I didn't want to think about what he might have done if he'd ever found out. I'm sure Tomas wasn't Campion's first bastard."

She thought of the irony of her and Buck, two people who had been dealt with so unfairly by Campion, loving and raising a child that was neither of theirs, but his. She thought of the changes that had come over Buck since their days of combat years ago. He was still a man of few words. She knew he always would be. But he'd become the man she knew was hidden somewhere deep inside, where he wouldn't let anyone enter. Until now.

She felt a sense of fatigue, but also a wonderful, fulfilling sense of peace. "I love you, Buck Randall."

He stroked her buttocks, pressing her against his full groin. She felt her answering response, but now knew there was no hurry.

"And I love you," he answered passionately.

Her heart leaped with joy. "You're not afraid to marry me?"

He chuckled, the sound rumbling in his chest. "I'm afraid *not* to."

🌿 Epilogue 🌿

Spring 1891

A warm May breeze ruffled the tops of the black walnut trees that edged the Randall ranch. Molly Randall stepped out onto the porch, shading her eyes against the bright morning sun as she watched her men work with the latest foal at the corral.

Her gaze roamed languidly over her husband. If it was possible, he'd only gotten more handsome. A familiar fluttering stirred her pelvis. He looked up just then, caught her gaze, and even from that distance, she thrilled at his private, searing, loving perusal. Her pulse quickened and she waved, one which he returned.

The boys, Dusty and Tomas, one firmly entrenched in manhood and the other still in the seedling of his youth, hollered at her from inside the stockade. She laughed at their animated behavior and waved enthusiastically.

She sat down at the small table on the porch and opened the newspaper, scanning the items. The door opened, and her mother, June, stepped out onto the porch.

"We're ready for school, Molly."

She turned, giving her mother and her daughter a warm smile. "Is the baby asleep?"

"Gemma threw up on Granny," Dinah announced.

"But she's all right now, Molly," her mother assured her. "She went right to sleep. Must've had a cramp on her tummy."

Molly grinned down at her four-year-old daughter. "You be a good girl, Dinah," she said, holding out her arms for a hug.

The child ran to her mother and crawled up into her lap. Gazing up at Molly with her enormous gold-rimmed brown eyes and her mop of golden curls, she lisped, "I can read, Mama. Granny and Auntie Anna teached me."

Molly hugged the child close. "I know they *teached* you, darling. And Papa and I are very proud of you."

Dinah played with one of Molly's buttons. "You gonna teach music today, Mama?"

"No, sweetheart. Not today. We're having company, remember? When you and the boys get back from school, there will be a very pretty lady here to visit with us."

Dinah touched her mother's cheek. "Not prettier'n you, Mama."

Molly planted a wet kiss on her daughter's forehead. "Thank you, sweetheart. Now," she added, inspecting her daughter's clothing, "here come Dusty and Tomas with the wagon. You mind your granny, and I'll see you later."

As the wagon clattered out of the yard, Buck sauntered toward her from the corral. Her heart fluttered. She'd loved him forever, yet, if it was possible, her love had grown each day.

He joined her on the porch and took her in his arms. "Ummm," he murmured, kissing her deeply. "My favorite part of the day."

She savored the taste of him, trapping it on her tongue, remembering the countless mornings they had made love after everyone had gone. "Unfortunately, not this day, darling."

Nuzzling her hair, he said, "You mean I'm going to miss my fix?"

"Can you manage?" she asked saucily, looking up into his handsome, weather-toughened face.

"For Nicolette, I'll manage."

"Oh, Buck. I'm so anxious to see her." Nicolette was on

the final lap of her first national solo piano tour. Molly and Buck hadn't been able to get away from the ranch to hear her play, but she'd apparently brought the house down in San Francisco. Not only was she a gifted musician, she was beautiful and so personable, that everyone loved her.

Over the years, they had received many letters from Nicolette in which she kept them current on the status of her son, Daniel, who was still being cared for by friends in Texas. Molly had to wonder if the young woman who had wanted it all, and apparently had it, was happy with it.

"I wonder if she's really happy," Buck mused.

Molly gave her husband a peck on the chin. "I was just wondering the same thing."

He pulled away briefly, bringing her slightly deformed wrist to his lips. "If it hadn't been for this, you could have done what she's doing."

His love and concern tunneled deep into her heart. "No," she answered. "I never wanted that to the exclusion of everything else, darling." She studied his renegade-handsome features. "Now, *you* I did want at the exclusion of everything else."

His familiar, heated gaze warmed her. "I love you, woman."

She kissed him again. "And I, you."

They stood together on the porch, looking out over their land. Each knew what the other was thinking, and both recognized that nothing in the world could be better than this.

Dear Readers:

Buck's story, *Forbidden Moon*, is the third and final story of the "Moon" trilogy. I've created many characters in these books that may warrant stories of their own, but for now, they will just continue to live in my imagination while I go on to other settings.

My goal is to entertain, although it's still necessary to create historically accurate settings. I met a young Micmac Indian woman from Nova Scotia on an airplane recently who appreciated romantic fantasy, but who also told me that in order for me to truly understand her way of life, I would have to live with her and her family for ten years. I believe this, and it would be *my* fantasy if I could actually do it.

Until then, I'll continue to read, study, write, and hopefully entertain.

Jane Bonander
Box 3134
San Ramon, CA 94583-6834